Lars Kepler

THE NIGHTMARE

Lars Kepler is the pseudonym of the critically acclaimed husband-and-wife team Alexandra Coelho Ahndoril and Alexander Ahndoril. Their number one internationally bestselling Joona Linna series has sold more than twelve million copies in forty languages. The Ahndorils were both established writers before they adopted the pen name Lars Kepler and have each published several acclaimed novels. They live in Stockholm, Sweden.

ALSO BY LARS KEPLER

The Joona Linna Series

The Hypnotist
The Fire Witness
The Sandman

THE NIGHTMARE

THE NIGHTMARE

A Joona Linna Novel

LARS KEPLER

Translated from the Swedish by

NEIL SMITH

Vintage Crime/Black Lizard
Vintage Books
A Division of Penguin Random House LLC
New York

A VINTAGE CRIME/BLACK LIZARD ORIGINAL, SEPTEMBER 2018

Library of Congress Cataloging-in-Publication Data
Names: Kepler, Lars, author. | Smith, Neil (Neil Andrew), translator.
Title: The nightmare / Lars Kepler ; translated from the Swedish
    by Neil Smith.
Other titles: Paganinikontraktet. Swedish
Description: New York : Vintage Books, a Division of Penguin Random
    House LLC, 2018. | Series: A Joona Linna novel ; 2 |
    Identifiers: LCCN 2018012008 (print) | LCCN 2018012751 (ebook)
Subjects: LCSH: Murder—Investigation—Fiction. | Terrorism—
    Prevention—Fiction. | GSAFD: Suspense fiction. | Mystery fiction.
Classification: LCC PT9877.21.E65 (ebook) | LCC PT9877.21.E65 P3413
    2018 (print) | DDC 839.73/8—dc23
LC record available at https://lccn.loc.gov/2018012008

Vintage Crime/Black Lizard Trade Paperback ISBN: 978-0-525-43310-1
eBook ISBN: 978-0-525-43311-8

www.blacklizardcrime.com

Printed in the United States of America
10 9 8 7 6 5 4 3 2 1

THE NIGHTMARE

THE YACHT is found drifting in the southern part of the Stockholm archipelago on a bright evening with no wind. The bluish-gray water is moving as gently as fog.

The old man calls out a couple of times from his rowboat, even though he has a feeling he's not going to get an answer. He's been watching the yacht from the shore for almost an hour as it drifts slowly backward on the offshore current.

The man angles his boat so that its side butts up against the yacht. He pulls the oars in, ties the rowboat to the swim platform, and climbs up the metal stairs and over the railing. In the middle of the aft deck is a pink deck chair. When he doesn't hear anything, he opens the glass door and goes down a few stairs into the salon. The large windows cast a gray light across the polished teak interior and the sofa's dark-blue upholstery. He walks down the steep wooden stairs, past the dark galley and head, and into the large cabin. Pale light is filtering through the narrow windows up by the ceiling, illuminating the arrow-shaped double bed. Toward the top of the bed, a young woman in a denim jacket is sitting against the wall in a limp, slumped posture. Her legs are wide apart, and one hand is resting on a pink cushion. She's looking the old man straight in the eye with a bemused expression on her face.

It takes a moment for the man to realize that the woman is dead.

There's a clip in her long, dark hair that's shaped like a dove, a peace dove.

When the old man goes over and touches her cheek, her head falls forward, and a thin stream of water trickles out of her mouth and down her chin.

THE WORD *"music"* comes from the Greek myth of the nine Muses, the daughters of the god Zeus and the titan Mnemosyne, goddess of memory. The Muse of music is Euterpe, whose name means *"bringer of joy."* She is usually depicted with a double flute between her lips.

"Musicality" has no generally accepted definition, but there are people who are born with an extensive musical memory and the sort of perfectly attuned hearing that enables them to identify any given note without a point of reference.

Through the ages, a number of exceptionally talented musical geniuses have emerged, some of whom became famous, such as Wolfgang Amadeus Mozart, who toured the courts of Europe from the age of six, and Ludwig van Beethoven, who composed many of his greatest works after going completely deaf.

The legendary Niccolò Paganini was born in 1782 in the Italian city of Genoa. He was a self-taught violinist and composer. To this day, very few violinists have been capable of playing Paganini's fast, complicated compositions. Right up until his death, Paganini was pursued by rumors that he had only acquired his unique talent by signing a contract with the devil.

1

A SHIVER runs down Penelope Fernandez's spine. Her heart starts to beat faster, and she glances quickly over her shoulder. It's as though she has a premonition of what is going to happen to her later that day.

In spite of the heat in the studio, Penelope's face feels cool. It's a lingering aftereffect from the makeup room, where the cool sponge was pressed to her skin. Then they removed the dove clip from her hair, so they could rub mousse in and gather her hair into twining locks.

Penelope is chairperson of the Swedish Peace and Arbitration Society. She is now being ushered silently into the news studio, and sits down in the spotlight opposite Pontus Salman, the managing director of Silencia Defense Ltd., an arms manufacturer.

The news anchor, Stefanie von Sydow, looks into the camera and starts to talk about the layoffs following British defense manufacturer BAE Systems Ltd.'s purchase of the Swedish company Bofors. She turns to Penelope:

"Penelope Fernandez, in a number of debates now, you have been highly critical of Swedish arms exports. Recently, you drew a comparison with the Angolagate scandal in France, in which senior politicians and businessmen were accused of bribery and weapons smuggling and given long prison sentences. We haven't seen anything like that in Sweden, though, surely?"

"There are two ways of looking at that," Penelope replies. "Either our politicians work differently, or our judicial system does."

"As you're well aware," Salman says, "we have a long tradition of—"

"According to Swedish law," Penelope interrupts, "all manufacture and export of military equipment is illegal."

"You're wrong," Salman says.

"Paragraphs three and six in the Military Equipment Act, 1992," Penelope specifies.

"But Silencia Defense has had all these contracts preapproved." He smiles.

"Yes, because otherwise we'd be talking about large-scale weapons offenses, and—"

"Like I said, we have a permit," he interrupts.

"Don't forget what military equipment is—"

"Hold on a moment, Penelope," Stefanie von Sydow says, nodding to Salman, who has raised his hand to indicate that he wasn't finished.

"Naturally, every deal is vetted beforehand," he explains. "Either directly by the government, or by the Inspectorate of Strategic Products, if you're familiar?"

"France has an equivalent body," Penelope replies. "Even so, military equipment worth eight billion kronor was approved for shipment to Angola in spite of the UN arms embargo, and in spite of an absolute ban on—"

"We're talking about Sweden now."

"I understand that people don't want to lose their jobs, but I'd still be interested in hearing how you can justify the export of huge quantities of ammunition to Kenya. A country that—"

"You don't have anything," he interrupts. "Nothing, not a single instance of wrongdoing, do you?"

"Unfortunately, I'm not in a position to—"

"Do you have any concrete evidence?" Stefanie von Sydow interrupts.

"No," Penelope Fernandez replies, and lowers her gaze. "But I—"

"In which case I think an apology is in order," Salman says.

Penelope looks him in the eye. She feels anger and frustration bubbling up inside her but forces herself to stay quiet. Salman gives her a disappointed smile and begins to talk about their factory in Trollhättan. Two hundred jobs were created when Silencia Defense was given permission to start manufacturing. He explains what preapproval entails and how far they've gotten with production. He expands on his point so much that there's no time left for his co-interviewee.

Penelope listens and tries to suppress her wounded pride. Instead, she thinks about the fact that she and Björn will soon be setting off on his boat. They'll make up the arrow-shaped bed and fill the fridge and little freezer. In her mind's eye, she sees the sparkle of frosted glasses full of vodka as they eat pickled herring, potatoes, boiled eggs, and crackers. They'll set the table on the aft deck, drop anchor by a small island in the archipelago, and sit and eat in the evening sun.

PENELOPE LEAVES Swedish Television's studios and starts to walk toward Valhalla Boulevard. She had spent almost two hours waiting for a follow-up interview on a different program before they dropped her to leave room for a segment on five easy tips for a flat stomach this summer.

Over on the grassy expanse of Gärdet, she can see the colorful tents of the Cirkus Maximum. Two of the performers are washing two elephants with a hose. One of them reaches into the air with its trunk to catch the water in its mouth.

Penelope is only twenty-four. She has curly dark hair that reaches just past her shoulders and always wears a short silver chain around her neck with a small crucifix from when she was confirmed. Her skin is golden, like honey. Her eyes are large and serious. She has been told more than once that she bears a striking resemblance to Sophia Loren.

Penelope takes out her phone and calls Björn to say she's on her way and is about to catch the subway from Karla Plaza.

"Penny? Did something happen?" he asks, sounding stressed.

"No—why?"

"Everything's ready. I left you a message. You're the only thing missing."

"There's no rush, is there?"

As Penelope takes the escalator down to the subway platform, her heart starts to beat faster with vague unease, and she closes her eyes. The escalator grows steeper and narrower, the air colder and colder.

Penelope comes from La Libertad, one of El Salvador's largest regions. Penelope's mother, Claudia, was imprisoned during the civil war, and Penelope was born and raised in a cell where fifteen other interred women did their best to help. Claudia was a doctor and had been active in a campaign to educate the population. She ended up in one of the regime's notorious prisons because she continued to campaign for indigenous people's right to form unions.

Penelope hates war and violence, a burning conviction that led her to study for a master's degree in peace-and-conflict studies at Uppsala University. She has worked for the French aid organization Action Contre la Faim in Darfur, and she wrote an acclaimed article for *Dagens Nyheter* about the attempts of women in the refugee camps to re-create some semblance of normal life. Two years ago, she succeeded Frida Blom as chair of the Swedish Peace and Arbitration Society.

Penelope doesn't open her eyes until she reaches the bottom of the escalator. The claustrophobic feeling vanishes, and she's completely calm by the time she gets on the subway. She thinks about Björn again, waiting at the marina on Långholmen. She loves swimming naked from his boat, diving into the water and not being able to see anything but sea and sky.

The train shakes as it rushes through the tunnel; then sunlight streams through the windows when it reaches the Old Town station.

Penelope gets off at Hornstull and emerges into the sunshine. She feels inexplicably anxious, so she hurries across the bridge to Långholmen and follows the road around, toward the marina.

Björn's boat is moored in the shadow of the Western Bridge; the movements of the water form a mesh of light that is reflected onto the gray steel beams high above.

She sees him at the stern of the boat, wearing a cowboy hat. He's standing still, with his arms wrapped around himself, his shoulders hunched.

Penelope puts two fingers in her mouth and wolf-whistles. Björn startles, and he seems suddenly afraid. He looks over toward the road and catches sight of her, but he still has a worried look in his eyes.

"What is it?" she asks, walking down the steps to the pier.

"Nothing," Björn replies, then adjusts his hat and tries to smile.

They hug. His hands are ice-cold, and his shirt is soaked through.

"You're covered with sweat," she says.

Björn looks away evasively. "I'm just eager to get going."

"Did you bring my bag?"

He nods and gestures toward the cabin. The boat is rocking gently beneath her feet, and she can smell sun-warmed plastic and polished wood.

"Hello?" she says breezily. "Where are you right now?"

His straw-colored hair is sticking out in every direction in small, matted dreads. His bright-blue eyes are childlike, smiling.

"I'm here," he replies, lowering his eyes.

"What's on your mind?"

"I just want us to be together," he says, putting his arms around her waist. "And have sex out in the open air."

He nuzzles her hair with his lips.

"Is that what you're hoping?" she whispers.

"Yes," he replies.

She laughs at him for being so up front.

"Most people—well, most women, anyway—probably find that overrated," she says. "Lying on the ground with lots of ants and stones and . . ."

"It's like swimming naked," he maintains.

"You're just going to have to convince me," she says flirtatiously.

"I'll do my best."

"How?" she says, laughing, as her phone starts to ring in her canvas bag.

Björn's smile seems to stiffen at the sound of the ringtone. The color drains from his cheeks. She looks at the screen.

"It's Viola," she says quickly to Björn before she answers: "*Hola*, little sister."

A car honks its horn, and her sister shouts something away from the phone. "Fucking lunatic," she mutters.

"What's going on?"

"It's over," her sister says. "I've dumped Sergey."

"Again," Penelope adds.

"Yes," Viola says quietly.

"Sorry," Penelope says. "You must be upset."

"I'll be all right, but . . . Mom said you were going out on the boat, and I was wondering . . . I'd love to come along, if that's okay?"

Neither of them speaks for a moment.

"Sure, come along," Penelope repeats, hearing the lack of enthusiasm in her own voice.

2

PENELOPE IS STANDING at the helm, wearing a light-blue sarong around her hips and a white bikini top with a peace sign over the right breast. She is bathed in the summer light coming through the windshield. She carefully steers around Kungshamn Lighthouse, then guides the yacht into the narrow strait.

Her sister, Viola, gets up from the pink deck chair on the aft deck. She's spent the past hour lying there wearing Björn's cowboy hat and an enormous pair of mirror sunglasses, sleepily smoking a couple of joints.

Viola makes five halfhearted attempts to pick up a box of matches with her toes before giving up. Penelope can't help smiling. Viola walks into the salon through the glass door and asks if Penelope would like her to take over.

"If not, I'll go and make a margarita," she says, going below.

Björn is lying out on the foredeck on a towel, using a paperback book as a pillow.

Penelope notices that the base of the railing by his feet has started to rust. Björn's father gave him the boat when he turned twenty, but he can't afford to maintain it properly. The yacht is the only gift his father ever gave him, other than a vacation. When his dad turned fifty, he invited Björn and Penelope to one of his finest luxury hotels, the Kamaya

Resort on the east coast of Kenya. Penelope only managed to put up with the hotel for two days before traveling to the refugee camp in Darfur, Sudan, where Action Contre la Faim was based.

Penelope decreases their cruising speed as they approach the Skurusund bridge. The heavy traffic above can't be heard at all on the water. Just as they're gliding into the shadow of the bridge, she spots a black inflatable boat by one of the concrete foundations. It's the same kind the naval special forces use: a RIB with a fiberglass hull and powerful motors.

Penelope has almost passed the bridge when she realizes that there's someone sitting in the boat—a man crouching in the gloom with his back to her. She doesn't know why her pulse quickens at the sight of him. There's something about the back of his head and his dark clothes that makes her feel she's being watched, even though he's facing the other way.

When she emerges into the sunshine again, she shivers and sees goose bumps on her arms.

She increases their speed once she's past Duvnäs. The two onboard motors rumble, the water foams behind them, and the boat takes off across the smooth sea.

Penelope's phone rings. She sees her mother's name on the screen and wonders for a second if her mom is calling to say she saw Penelope on television and to tell her she did well, but she knows that's just a fantasy.

"Hi, Mom," Penelope says.

"Ow," her mother whispers.

"What happened?"

"My back ... I need to get to the chiropractor," Claudia says. It sounds like she's filling a glass with water. "I just wanted to find out if Viola's spoken to you?"

"She's here on the boat with us," Penelope replies as she listens to her mother drink.

"Oh, great. I thought it would do her good."

"I'm sure it will," Penelope says quietly.

"What food do you have?"

"Tonight we're having pickled herring, potatoes, eggs. . . ."

"She doesn't like herring."

"Mom, Viola called me just as—"

"I know you weren't expecting her to come with you," Claudia interrupts. "That's why I'm calling."

"I've made some meatballs," Penelope says patiently.

"Enough for everyone?" her mother asks.

"Everyone? That depends on . . ."

She trails off and stares out across the sparkling water.

"I don't have to have any," Penelope says in a measured tone.

"If there aren't enough," her mother says. "That's all I meant."

"I get it," she says quietly.

"So it's poor you now, is it?" her mother asks with barely concealed irritation.

"It's just that . . . Viola's an adult, and . . ."

"I'm disappointed in you."

"Sorry."

"You always manage to eat my meatballs at Christmas and Midsummer and . . ."

"Maybe I shouldn't," Penelope snaps.

"Fine," her mother says abruptly. "Well, that's that."

"I just mean—"

"Don't bother coming for Midsummer," her mother interrupts angrily.

"Oh, Mom, why do you always have to—"

There's a click as her mother hangs up. Penelope feels frustration bubbling inside of her as she stares at the phone, then tosses it aside.

The stairs from the galley creak, and Viola wobbles into view with a margarita glass in her hand.

"Was that Mom?"

"Yes."

"Is she worried I'm not going to get anything to eat?" Viola asks with a smile.

"There's food," Penelope replies.

"Mom doesn't think I can take care of myself."

"She's just worried," Penelope replies.

"She never worries about you," Viola says.

"I'm fine."

Viola sips her drink and looks out the windshield.

"I saw the debate on television," she says.

"This morning? With Pontus Salman?"

"No, this was . . . last week," she says. "You were talking to an arrogant man who . . . He had a fancy name, and . . ."

"Palmcrona," Penelope says.

"That was it, Palmcrona. . . ."

"I got angry. My cheeks turned red, and I could feel tears in my eyes. I felt like reciting Bob Dylan's 'Masters of War' and running out, slamming the door behind me."

Viola watches as Penelope stretches up and opens the roof hatch.

"I didn't think you shaved your armpits," Viola says breezily.

"No, but I've been in the media so much that . . ."

"Vanity got the better of you," Viola jokes.

"I didn't want to get written off as a troublemaker just because I had hair under my arms."

"How's your bikini line, then?"

"Well . . ."

Penelope lifts her sarong, and Viola bursts out laughing.

"Björn likes it." Penelope smiles.

"He's one to talk, with his dreadlocks."

"But you shave everywhere, just like you're supposed to," Penelope says, a sharp note in her voice. "For your married men and muscle-bound idiots and—"

"So I have bad taste in men," Viola interrupts.

"You don't have bad taste in anything else."

"I've never really done anything, though."

"You just have to improve your grades, then . . ."

Viola shrugs her shoulders: "I just finished my exams."

They're plowing gently through the transparent water, followed by some gulls.

"How did it go?" Penelope eventually asks.

"I thought it was easy," Viola says, licking salt from the rim of the glass.

"So it went well?" Penelope smiles.

Viola nods and puts her glass down.

"How well?" Penelope asks, nudging her in the side.

"All A's," Viola says, looking down.

Penelope lets out a shriek of joy and hugs her sister hard.

"You know what this means, don't you?" Penelope says excitedly. "You can have your pick of colleges. You can study whatever you want—business studies, medicine, journalism."

Her sister blushes and laughs, and Penelope hugs her again, knocking her hat off. She strokes Viola's head, then arranges her hair just as she always did when they were little. She takes the clip with the dove from her own hair and uses it to fasten her sister's, then looks at her and smiles happily.

3

THE BOW CUTS the smooth surface of the water like a knife. They're going very fast. Large waves hit the shore in their wake. They turn sharply and bounce across breaking waves, spraying water around them. Penelope heads out into the open water with the engines roaring. The fore lifts up, and plumes of foaming white water spread out behind them.

"You're crazy!" Viola shouts.

Björn wakes up when they stop at Gåsö. They buy ice cream and coffee. Then Viola wants to play mini-golf, so it's late in the afternoon by the time they get going again.

The sea opens up on their port side.

The plan is to reach Kastskär, an uninhabited, long, thin island. There's a lush bay on the south side where they plan to drop anchor, swim, have a barbecue, and spend the night.

"I think I'll go down and take a rest," Viola says with a yawn.

"Go ahead," Penelope says, smiling.

Viola goes below, and Penelope looks ahead of them. She lowers their speed and keeps an eye on the electronic depth-sounder that warns them of reefs as they approach Kastskär. The water gets shallow very quickly, going from forty meters to just five.

Björn comes into the cabin and kisses Penelope on the back of her neck.

"Should I start making dinner?" he asks.

"Viola should probably sleep for an hour."

"You sound like your mother," he says gently. "Has she called yet?"

"Yes."

"To see if we let Viola come with us?"

"Yes."

"Did you have an argument?"

She shakes her head.

"What is it?" he asks. "Are you upset?"

"No, it's just that Mom . . ."

"What?"

Penelope smiles as she wipes the tears from her cheeks. "She doesn't want me there for Midsummer," she says.

Björn hugs her. "Just ignore her."

"I do," she replies.

Very slowly, Penelope maneuvers the boat as far into the bay as she can. The engines rumble softly. They're so close to the shore now that she can smell the plants.

They drop anchor, and the boat swings closer to the rocks. Björn jumps onto the steep slope and ties the rope around a tree.

The ground is covered with moss. He stops and looks at Penelope. Some birds move in the treetops.

Penelope pulls on a pair of sweatpants and her white sneakers, jumps ashore, and takes his hand. He wraps his arms around her.

"Shall we take a look at the island?"

"Wasn't there something you were going to try to convince me of?" she teases.

"The advantages of the Swedish 'right to roam,'" he says.

She nods and smiles, and he brushes her hair back and runs a finger across her prominent cheekbones and thick black eyebrows.

"How can you be so beautiful?"

He kisses her softly on the lips, then starts to walk toward the low-growing woods.

In the middle of the island is a small glade with dense clumps of tall meadow grass. Butterflies and small bumble-bees are drifting above the flowers. It's hot in the sun, and the water sparkles between the trees to the north. They stand still, hesitant, smiling as they look at each other, then turn serious.

"What if someone comes?" she says.

"We're the only people on the island."

"Are you sure about that?"

"How many islands are there in the Stockholm archipelago? Thirty thousand? More, probably," he says.

Penelope kicks her shoes off and takes off her bikini. She's standing on the grass completely naked. Her initial embarrassment is replaced almost at once with sheer delight. She finds the sea air on her skin and the heat radiating up from the ground intensely exciting.

Björn is muttering that he just wants to look at her. She's tall and curvy, with lean arms, a narrow waist, and strong legs.

Björn can feel his hands shaking as he pulls off his T-shirt and flowery knee-length shorts. He's younger than she is, and his body is boyish, almost hairless. His shoulders are already sunburned.

"Now I want to look at you," she says.

He blushes and walks over to her, smiling broadly.

"Can't I?"

He shakes his head and hides his face against her neck and hair.

They start to kiss, very gently. When Penelope feels his warm tongue in her mouth, a feeling of dizzy happiness courses through her. She forces herself to stop smiling so she can carry on kissing. They start to breathe faster, and she can feel Björn's erection growing as his heartbeat quickens. They lie down in the grass, finding a flat spot between the tussocks. His mouth traces its way down to her breasts; then he kisses her stomach and parts her thighs. When he looks at her, it seems to him that their bodies are glowing in the evening sun. Suddenly everything is intensely intimate. She's already wet and swollen when he starts to lick her, very softly and slowly, and she has to push his head away after a while. She presses her thighs together, smiles, and blushes. She whispers to him to come closer, guides him with her hand, and lets him slide into her. He breathes heavily in her ear, and she looks up at the pink sky.

Afterward, she stands naked in the warm grass, stretches, walks a few steps, and stares off into the trees.

"What is it?" Björn asks languidly.

She looks at him. He's sitting on the ground, still naked, smiling up at her.

"Your shoulders are burned."

"Every summer."

He gently touches the red skin.

"Let's go back—I'm hungry," she says.

"I just want to go for a quick swim."

She pulls her bikini bottoms and sweatpants back on, puts on her shoes, and stands there with her bikini top in her hand. She lets her eyes roam across his hairless chest, muscular arms, the tattoo on his sunburned shoulders, and his bright, playful eyes.

"Next time you get to lie underneath." She smiles.

"Next time," he repeats cheerfully. "You're already a convert. I knew it."

She laughs and waves at him dismissively. He lies back and stares up at the sky. She hears him whistling to himself as she walks through the trees toward the steep little beach where the boat is moored.

She stops to put her bikini top on before she goes down to the boat.

When Penelope gets on board, she wonders if Viola is still asleep. She decides to put a pan of potatoes on to boil with some dill, then take a shower and get changed. The aft deck is strangely wet, as if it had been raining. Viola must have swabbed it down for some reason. The boat feels different. Penelope can't put her finger on what it is, but her skin breaks out in goose bumps. It's almost completely silent. Even the birds have stopped singing. There's just the gentle lapping sound as the water hits the hull, and the faint creak of the rope around the tree. Penelope becomes very conscious of her own movements. She goes below and sees that the door to the guest cabin is open. The light is on, but Viola isn't there. Penelope notices that her hand is shaking when she knocks on the door of the head. She opens it and looks inside, then goes back up on deck. Farther along the bay, she sees Björn on his way down to the water. She waves to him, but he doesn't see her.

Penelope opens the glass door to the salon and walks past the blue sofas and teak table.

"Viola?" she calls quietly.

She goes down to the galley and takes out a saucepan, but puts it down immediately. She looks in the larger head, then goes into the forecabin, where she and Björn sleep. She opens the door and looks around in the gloom. At first she thinks she's looking at herself in the mirror.

Viola is sitting perfectly still at the top of the bed, her hand resting on a pink cushion.

"What are you doing in here?"

Penelope realizes that something isn't right. Viola's face is oddly pale and wet, and her hair is hanging in damp clumps.

Penelope goes over and takes her sister's face in her hands, lets out a moan, then screams, right in her face.

"Viola? What is it? Viola?"

But she already knows what's wrong—her sister isn't breathing. There's no warmth in her skin; there's nothing left in her. The cramped cabin gets darker, closing in around Penelope. She hears herself whimpering and stumbles backward, pulling clothes onto the floor, then hits her shoulder hard on the door when she turns and runs up the stairs.

When she emerges onto the aft deck, she gasps for breath as if she were suffocating. She coughs and looks around, a feeling of ice-cold terror in her body. A hundred meters away, on the shore, she can see a stranger dressed in black. Somehow Penelope realizes how it all fits together. She knows it's the same man who was sitting in the military inflatable.

The man is standing on the shore, waving to Björn, who is swimming twenty meters out. He's shouting, holding his arm up. Björn hears him and stops, treading water, then turns to look back toward land.

Time stands still. Penelope rushes to the helm and digs around in the toolbox, finds a knife, and runs back to the aft deck.

She sees Björn's slow strokes, the rings spreading out across the water around him. He's looking curiously at the man. The man beckons him. Björn smiles uncertainly and starts to swim back to shore.

"Björn!" Penelope screams as loudly as she can. "Swim away from shore!"

The man on the shore turns toward her, then starts running toward the boat. Penelope cuts through the rope, slipping on the wet wooden deck. She gets to her feet, hurries to the helm, and starts the engines. Without looking, she raises the anchor and puts the boat in reverse.

Björn must have heard her, because he's turned away from the shore and has started to swim toward the boat instead. Penelope steers toward him as she sees the man in black change direction and start running up the slope toward the other side of the island. Without really thinking about it, she realizes that the man must have left his black inflatable in the bay to the north.

She knows there's no way they can outrun him.

She steers toward Björn. She yells at him as she gets closer, then slows down and holds a boathook out to him. The water's cold, and he looks scared and exhausted. His head keeps disappearing below the surface. She hits him with the point of the boathook by mistake, cutting his forehead and making it bleed.

"You have to hold on!" she shouts.

The black inflatable is already coming into view at the end of the island. She can hear its engine. Björn is grimacing with pain. After several attempts, he finally manages to wrap his arm around the boathook. She pulls him toward the swimming platform as fast as she can.

"Viola's dead!" she screams, hearing the mixture of despair and panic in her voice.

As soon as Björn has climbed up, she runs back to the wheel and accelerates as hard as she can.

Björn clambers over the railing, and she hears him yell at her to steer straight for Ornö fjord.

The inflatable is rapidly approaching from behind.

She swings the boat around in a tight curve, and the hull rumbles beneath them.

"He killed Viola," Penelope whimpers.

"Watch the rocks," Björn warns, his teeth chattering.

The inflatable has rounded Stora Kastskär and is speeding across the flat, open water.

Blood is running down Björn's face from the cut on his forehead.

They're rapidly approaching the large island. Björn turns to see the inflatable some three hundred meters behind them.

"Aim for the pier!"

She turns and puts the engines in reverse, then switches them off when the fore hits the pier with a creak. The whole side of the boat scrapes some protruding wooden steps. The boat rocks sideways, and the wooden steps shatter as water washes over the railings. They leap off the boat and race for land as the black inflatable roars toward them. Penelope clambers up the steep rocks toward the trees, gasping for breath. The inflatable's engine goes quiet below them, and Penelope realizes they barely have a head start.

4

PARAGRAPH 21 of the Swedish Police Law allows a police officer to enter a house, room, or other location if there is reason to believe that someone may have died, be unconscious, or be otherwise incapable of calling for help.

It's a Saturday afternoon in June, and Police Officer John Bengtsson has been instructed to investigate the penthouse at 2 Grev Street because the director general of the Inspectorate for Strategic Products, Carl Palmcrona, has been absent from work with no explanation and missed a scheduled meeting with the foreign minister.

It's not the first time that John has had to break into someone's home to see if anyone is dead or injured. Mostly it happens when relatives suspect suicide. He's seen silent, frightened parents forced to wait in the stairwell while he goes in to check the rooms. Sometimes he finds young men with barely discernible pulses after a heroin overdose, and occasionally he has discovered a crime scene. A woman, beaten to death, lying in the glow from the television in the living room.

John is carrying his lock pick and an electric pick gun as he walks in through the imposing front entrance. He takes the elevator up to the fifth floor and rings the doorbell. He waits awhile, then puts his heavy bag down on the floor and inspects the lock. Suddenly he hears a shuffling sound in the stairwell, coming from the floor below. It sounds as if someone is trying to creep silently down the stairs. John listens for a while, then reaches out and tries the handle. The door isn't locked and glides open softly on its four hinges.

"Is anyone home?" he calls.

He waits a few seconds, then pulls his bag into the entryway and closes the door.

He hears gentle music from the neighboring room. He goes over, knocks, and walks in. It's a spacious reception room, sparsely furnished with three sofas, a low glass table, and a small painting of a ship in a storm. An ice-blue glow is coming from a transparent stereo system. Melancholic violin music is playing from its speakers.

John walks over to the double door and opens it. He finds himself looking into a living room with tall Art Nouveau windows. The summer light outside is refracted through the tiny panes of glass in the top sections of the windows.

A man is floating in midair in the center of the white room.

It looks supernatural.

John stares at the dead man. It feels like an eternity before he spots the clothesline tied to the lamp hook.

The well-dressed man is perfectly still, as if he's frozen mid-jump, with his ankles stretched and his toes pointing down at the floor.

He's hanging—but there's something else, something that doesn't make sense, something wrong.

John knows he can't enter the room: the scene needs to be left intact. His heart is beating quickly, and he can feel the heavy rhythm of his pulse. He swallows hard, but he can't tear his eyes away from the man.

A name has started to echo inside his head, starting out as a whisper: *Joona. I need to speak to Joona Linna.*

There's no furniture in the room, just the man, who in all likelihood is Carl Palmcrona.

The cord was tied to the lamp hook in the middle of the ceiling.

There was nothing for him to climb on, John thinks.

John tries to calm down, gather his thoughts, and register everything he can see. The hanged man's face is pale, and he can see no more than a few spots of blood in his blank eyes. He's wearing a thin overcoat on top of a pale-gray suit and a pair of low-heeled shoes. A black briefcase and a cell phone are lying on the floor a little way from the pool of urine that has formed immediately beneath the body.

The hanged man suddenly trembles.

John holds his breath.

There's a heavy thud from the ceiling and what sounds like hammer blows from the attic—someone is walking across the floor above. Another thud, and Palmcrona's body trembles again. Then he hears the sound of a drill, which stops abruptly. A man shouts something about needing more cable. "Get the extension," he calls.

John notices his pulse settle down as he walks back through the living room. In the entryway, the front door is open. He stops. He's sure that he closed it, but maybe he was mistaken. He leaves the apartment and, before he reports back to the station, takes out his cell phone and calls Joona Linna of the National Crime Unit.

5

IT'S SUMMER. In Stockholm, people have been waking up too early in the morning for weeks. The sun rises at half past three, and there's some light in the sky for almost the entire night. It's also been unusually warm for the time of year. The cherry trees were in blossom at the same time as the lilac, and heavy clusters of flowers spread their scent all the way from Kronoberg Park to the entrance to police headquarters.

The head of the National Crime Unit, Carlos Eliasson, is standing at his low window on the eighth floor, looking out at the steep slopes of Kronoberg Park. He's holding his phone and dials Joona Linna's number, but once again his call goes straight to voice mail. He puts the phone down on his desk and looks at his watch.

Petter Näslund comes into Carlos's office and clears his throat quietly, then leans against a poster that reads "We Watch, Scrutinize, and Irritate."

"Pollock and his team will be here soon," Petter says.

"I know how to tell the time," Carlos replies gently.

"The sandwiches are ready," Petter says.

Carlos suppresses a smile and asks, "Did you hear that they're recruiting?"

Petter's cheeks flush, and he lowers his eyes, then composes himself and looks up again.

"I'd ... Can you think of anyone who's better suited for the National Homicide Commission?" he asks.

The commission consists of six experts who assist with murder cases throughout Sweden. The workload is extreme. Its members are in such high demand that they rarely have time to meet at police headquarters.

When Petter leaves the room, Carlos sits down behind his desk and looks over at his aquarium and his paradise fish. Just as he is reaching for the jar of fish food, his phone rings.

"Yes?" he says.

"They're on their way up," the receptionist says.

"Thanks."

Carlos makes one last attempt to call Joona before leaving the room. As he reaches the hallway, the elevator dings and its doors slide open. The members of the Homicide Commission remind him of the Rolling Stones, whom he'd seen in concert a few years ago. The Stones were all wearing dark suits and ties and reminded him of laid-back businessmen.

Nathan Pollock is in front, his gray hair tied back in a ponytail, followed by Erik Eriksson, who is wearing his trademark diamond-studded glasses, which earned him his nickname: Elton. Behind him comes Niklas Dent, alongside P. G. Bondesson, and bringing up the rear is the forensics expert Tommy Kofoed, who is hunchbacked, staring morosely at the floor.

Carlos shows them into the conference room. Their operational boss, Benny Rubin, is already seated at the round table with a cup of black coffee, waiting for them. Kofoed takes an apple from the fruit bowl and starts to eat it noisily. Pollock looks at him with a smile and shakes his head, and Kofoed stops mid-bite and looks back quizzically.

"Welcome," Carlos says. "I'm glad you were all able to come, because we have a number of important issues on today's agenda."

"Isn't Joona supposed to be here?" Kofoed asks.

"Yes," Carlos replies hesitantly.

"That guy operates on his own schedule," Pollock adds quietly.

"Well, give him his due, though. Joona cleared up the Tumba murders a year or so back," Kofoed says. "I keep thinking about it, the way he was so sure ... he knew who was killed first. He saw things no one else saw."

"Against all logic," Elton says, smiling.

"There's not much about forensic science that I don't know," Kofoed continues, "but Joona just went in and looked at the footprints in the blood, I don't understand how ..."

Carlos clears his throat and looks down at the informal agenda.

"The marine police have contacted us this morning," he says. "Apparently, a fisherman has found a dead woman."

"In his net?"

"No, he saw a yacht drifting off Dalarö, rowed out and went on board, and found her sitting on the bed in the front cabin."

"That's hardly something for the commission," Petter says with a smile.

"Was she murdered?" Pollock asks.

"Probably suicide," Petter replies quickly.

"Nothing urgent," Carlos says, helping himself to a slice of cake. "I just thought I'd mention it."

"Anything else?" Kofoed says cheerfully.

"We received a request from the police in West Götaland," Carlos says. "There's a summary on the table."

"I won't be able to take it," Pollock says.

"I know you've all got your hands full," Carlos says, slowly brushing some crumbs from the table. "Maybe we should start by talking about recruitment."

Benny explains that the higher-ups are aware of the heavy workload and have agreed, as a first step, to authorize the expansion of the commission by adding one permanent post.

"Thoughts, anyone?" Carlos says.

"Wouldn't it be helpful if Joona was here for this discussion?" Kofoed asks, leaning across the table and digging through the wrapped sandwiches.

"I'm not sure he'll make it," Carlos says.

"Maybe we could break for coffee first," Eriksson says, adjusting his sparkling glasses.

Kofoed removes the wrapper from a salmon sandwich, pulls out the sprig of dill, squeezes some lemon juice onto it, and unwraps some silverware.

The door to the conference room opens, and Joona walks in, his blond hair sticking up.

"*Syö tilli, pojat,*" he says in Finnish with a grin.

"Exactly," Pollock says, chuckling. "Eat your dill, boys."

Pollock and Joona smile as their eyes meet. Kofoed's cheeks turn red, and he shakes his head with a smile.

"*Tilli,*" Pollock repeats, and bursts out laughing as Joona walks over and puts the sprig of dill back on Kofoed's sandwich.

"Can we continue the meeting?" Petter says.

Joona shakes Pollock's hand, then walks over to a spare chair, hangs his dark jacket on the back of it, and sits down.

"Sorry," he says quietly.

"Good to have you here," Carlos says.

"Thanks."

"We were just about to discuss the issue of recruitment," Carlos explains.

He pinches his bottom lip, and Petter begins to squirm on his chair.

"I think . . . I think I'll let Nathan speak first," Carlos goes on.

"By all means," Pollock says. "I'm not just speaking for myself, here; we all agree on this. . . . We're hoping you might want to join us, Joona."

The room goes quiet. Dent and Elton nod. Petter is sharply silhouetted in the light from the window.

"We'd like that very much," Kofoed says.

"I appreciate the offer," Joona says, running his fingers through his thick hair. "You're a very smart team, you've proved that, and I respect your work. . . ."

They smile.

"But . . . I'm afraid I can't work within such a specific framework," he explains.

"We appreciate that," Kofoed says quickly. "It's a little restrictive, but it can actually be helpful. It's been proven to . . ."

He trails off.

"Well, we just wanted to extend the invitation," Nathan Pollock says.

"I don't think it would work out," Joona replies.

They look down, someone nods, and Joona apologizes when his phone rings. He gets up from the table and leaves the room. A minute or so later, he comes back in and takes his jacket from the chair.

"I'm sorry," he says. "I'd like to stay for the meeting, but . . ."

"Has something serious happened?" Carlos asks.

"That call was from John Bengtsson, one of our uniforms," Joona says. "He's just found Carl Palmcrona."

"Found?" Carlos says.

"Hanged," Joona replies. His symmetrical face becomes serious, and his eyes shimmer like gray glass.

"Who's Palmcrona?" Pollock asks. "I can't place the name."

"Director general of the Inspectorate for Strategic Products," Kofoed answers quickly. "He makes decisions about Swedish arms exports."

"Isn't the identity of everyone who works for the ISP confidential?" Carlos asks.

"It is," Kofoed replies.

"So presumably the Security Police will be dealing with this?"

"I've already promised John that I'd take a look," Joona replies. "Apparently, something didn't make sense."

"What?" Carlos asks.

"It was . . . No, I should probably take a look first."

"Sounds exciting," Kofoed says. "Can I tag along?"

"Sure," Joona replies.

"I'll come, too, then," Pollock says quickly.

Carlos tries to say something about the meeting but realizes it's pointless.

6

TWENTY MINUTES LATER, Joona parks his black Volvo on Strand Street. A silver Lincoln Town Car pulls up behind him. Joona gets out of the car and waits for his two colleagues from the National Homicide Commission. They walk around the corner and in through the door of 2 Grev Street.

In the creaking old elevator, Kofoed asks, in a sullen voice, what Joona has been told so far.

"The ISP reported Palmcrona missing," Joona says. "He doesn't have any family, and none of his colleagues know him privately. But when he didn't show up for work, one of our patrols was asked to take a look. John went to the apartment and found Palmcrona had hanged himself, and called me. He said he suspected criminal activity and wanted me to come over at once."

Nathan Pollock frowns. "What made him suspect criminal activity?"

The elevator stops, and Joona opens the grille. John Bengtsson is standing outside the door to Palmcrona's apartment. He tucks his notepad into his pocket and shakes Joona's hand.

"Tommy Kofoed and Nathan Pollock from the National Homicide Commission," Joona says.

They shake hands briefly.

"The door was unlocked when I arrived," John says. "I could hear music. I found Palmcrona hanging in a large room. Over the years, I've cut down a fair number of men, but this time ... I don't think it's suicide, and given Palmcrona's standing in society...."

"It's good that you called," Joona says.

"Have you examined the body?" Kofoed asks.

"I haven't even set foot inside the room," John replies.

"Very good," Kofoed mutters, and, with John, starts to lay down protective mats.

Shortly afterward, Joona and Pollock are able to enter. John is waiting next to a blue sofa. He points toward the double doors leading to a brightly lit room. Joona walks over on the mats and pushes the doors wide open.

Carl Palmcrona is hanging in the middle of the spacious room. He's wearing a pale suit, a light summer coat, and low-heeled shoes. There are flies crawling around his eyes and the corners of his mouth, and buzzing around the pool of urine and briefcase on the floor. The thin clothesline has cut deep into Palmcrona's neck. The groove is dark red, and blood has seeped out and run beneath his shirt.

"Execution," Kofoed declares, pulling on a pair of protective gloves.

Every trace of moroseness suddenly vanishes from his face and voice. With a smile, he gets down on his knees and starts to take photographs of the hanging body.

"I'd say we're going to find injuries to his cervical spine," Pollock says, pointing.

Joona looks up at the ceiling, then down at the floor.

"He's been put on show," Kofoed says eagerly as he photographs the dead man. "I mean, the murderer isn't exactly trying to hide the crime. He wants to say something, wants to send a message."

"Yes, that's what I was thinking," John says eagerly. "The room's empty. There's no chair, no stepladder to climb on."

"So what's the message?" Kofoed asks, lowering the camera and squinting at the body. "Hanging is often associated with treachery, Judas Iscariot and—"

"Just hold on," Joona interrupts gently.

He gestures vaguely toward the floor.

"What is it?" Pollock asks.

"I think it was suicide," Joona says.

"Typical suicide," Kofoed says, and laughs a little too loudly. "He flapped his wings and flew up . . ."

"The briefcase," Joona says. "If he stood the briefcase on its side, he could have reached."

"But not the ceiling," Pollock points out.

"He could have attached the rope earlier."

"I suppose, but I think you're wrong."

Joona shrugs his shoulders and mutters, "Given the music and the knots, then . . ."

"Can we take a look at the briefcase?" Pollock asks tersely.

"I just need to secure the evidence first," Kofoed says.

They look on in silence as Kofoed crawls across the floor, unrolling black plastic wrap covered with a thin layer of gelatin on the floor. Then he carefully presses it down, using a rubber roller.

"Can you take out a couple of bio-packs and a wrapper?" he asks, pointing at his bag.

"Cardboard?" Pollock asks.

"Yes, please," Kofoed replies, catching the bio-packs that Pollock throws him.

He secures the biological evidence from the floor, then beckons Pollock into the room.

"You'll find shoeprints on the far edge of the briefcase," Joona says. "It fell backward, and the body swung diagonally."

Pollock says nothing, just goes over to the leather briefcase and kneels down. His silver ponytail falls over his shoulder as he leans forward to lift the case onto one end. Clear pale-gray shoeprints are visible on the black leather.

"What did I tell you?" Joona asks.

"Damn," Kofoed says, impressed, the whole of his tired face smiling at Joona.

"Suicide," Pollock mutters.

"From a purely technical perspective, anyway," Joona says.

They stand and look at the body.

"So what do we have here?" Kofoed asks, still smiling. "A man who makes decisions about arms exportation has committed suicide."

"Nothing for us." Pollock sighs.

Kofoed takes his gloves off and gestures toward the hanging man.

"Joona? What did you mean about the music and the knots?" he asks.

"It's a double sheet bend," Joona says, pointing to the knot around the lamp hook. "Which I assumed was linked to Palmcrona's long career in the navy."

"And the music?"

Joona stops and looks thoughtfully at him. "What do you make of the music?" he asks.

"I don't know. It's a sonata, for the violin," Kofoed says. "Early-nineteenth-century or . . ."

He falls silent when the doorbell rings. The four men look at one another. Joona starts to walk toward the entryway, and the others follow him but stop in the living room, out of sight of the front door.

Joona contemplates using the peephole but decides not to. He can feel the air blowing through the keyhole as he reaches out and pushes the handle down. The heavy door glides open, onto the dark landing. The timed lamps have gone out, and the light from the stairwell is weak. Joona hears slow, labored breathing very close to him, coming from someone he can't see. His hand goes to his pistol as he looks cautiously from behind the open door. In the thin strip of light between the hinges, he sees a tall woman with large hands. She looks as if she's in her mid-sixties. She's standing perfectly still. There's a large Band-Aid on her cheek, and her gray hair is cut short in a girlish bob. She looks Joona straight in the eyes without a trace of a smile.

"Did you take him down?" she asks.

"Take him down?" Joona repeats, staring at the woman.

"Mr. Palmcrona," she says matter-of-factly.

"What do you mean, 'take him down'?"

"I'm sorry. I'm only the housekeeper. I thought . . ."

The situation clearly troubles her, and she starts to walk down the stairs but stops abruptly when Joona replies to her initial question: "He's still hanging there."

"Yes," she says, turning to him with a completely neutral expression on her face.

"Did you see him hanging there earlier today?"

"No," she replies.

"What made you ask if we took him down? Did something happen? Did you notice anything unusual?"

"A noose hanging from the lamp hook in the living room," she replied.

"You saw the noose?"

"Of course."

"But you weren't worried?" Joona asks.

"Dying isn't such a nightmare," she says with a restrained smile.

"What did you say?"

But the woman merely shakes her head. "I don't know. . . . Maybe he needed help," she says cryptically.

"What do you mean by help?"

Her eyes roll back, and Joona thinks she's going to faint. She reaches out for the wall with one hand and meets his gaze again.

"There are helpful people everywhere," she says weakly.

7

JOONA THOUGHT he would be on time for the one o'clock meeting with the National Homicide Commission.

He was just going to have lunch with Disa at Rosendal Garden. Joona arrived early and stood in the sunshine for a while, watching the mist that lay over the little vineyard. Then he saw Disa walking toward him, her bag swinging over her shoulder. Her thin face with its intelligent features was covered with early-summer freckles, and her hair, which was usually gathered in two uneven braids, was hanging loose over her shoulders. She had dressed up and was wearing a floral-patterned dress and a pair of summery sandals with a stacked heel.

They hugged tenderly.

"Hello," Joona said. "You look lovely."

"So do you," Disa said.

They got food and sat at one of the outdoor tables. Joona noticed she was wearing nail polish. As a senior archaeologist, Disa usually had short and dirty fingernails. He looked away from her hands, across the fruit garden.

Disa started to eat and said with a full mouth, "Queen Christina was given a leopard by the duke of Courland. She kept it out here."

"I didn't know that," Joona said.

"I read in the palace accounts that the Treasury paid forty silver riksdalers to help cover the funeral costs of a maid who was killed by the leopard."

She leaned back and picked up her glass. "Joona Linna, stop talking so much," she said sarcastically.

"Sorry," Joona said. "I . . ."

He trailed off and suddenly felt as if all the energy were draining from his body.

"What?"

"Please, keep talking about the leopard."

"You look sad. . . ."

"I was thinking about Mom. . . . It was exactly a year ago yesterday that she died. I went and left a white iris on her grave."

"I miss Ritva very much," Disa said.

She put her knife and fork down and sat quietly for a while.

"Do you know what she said the last time I saw her? She took my hand," Disa said, "and she said I should seduce you and make sure I got pregnant."

"That sounds like her," Joona said, laughing.

The sun sparkled in their glasses and reflected off Disa's dark eyes.

"I said I didn't think that would work, and then she told me to leave you and never look back."

He nodded but didn't know what to say.

"But then you'd be all alone," Disa went on. "A big, lonely Finn."

He stroked her fingers. "I don't want that."

"What?"

"To be a big, lonely Finn," he said softly. "I want to be with you."

"And I want to bite you, hard. Can you explain that?

My teeth always start to tingle when I see you," Disa said, smiling.

Joona reached out his hand to touch her. He knew he was already late for the meeting but stayed seated, talking to Disa and simultaneously thinking that he should go to the National Museum to look at the Sami bridal crown.

8

THE SWIMMING POOL at police headquarters is silent and almost perfectly still. The water is illuminated from below, and the glow undulates gently across the walls and ceiling. Joona swims length after length.

As he swims, he thinks about Disa's face when she told him her teeth tingled when she looked at him.

Joona reaches the edge of the pool, turns beneath the water, and kicks off. He doesn't notice that he's swimming faster now that his thoughts are focused on Carl Palmcrona's apartment. In his mind's eye, he looks at the hanging body, the pool of urine, the flies on the dead man's face. He had been wearing his coat and shoes but had still taken the time to put some music on.

The whole thing had struck Joona as both planned and impulsive, though that's fairly typical with suicides.

He turns and swims faster and remembers opening Palmcrona's door when the bell rang. He sees the tall woman standing concealed behind the door, in the darkness of the stairwell.

Joona stops, breathing hard, and rests his arms on the edge of the pool.

Dying isn't such a nightmare, the tall woman had said with a smile.

Joona climbs out of the pool, feeling oddly uneasy. He doesn't know what it is, but Carl Palmcrona's death won't leave him alone. For some reason, he keeps seeing the bright, empty room, hearing the gentle violin music along with the dull buzzing of the flies.

Joona knows they're dealing with a suicide and tries to tell himself that there's no case. But he still feels like examining the apartment more thoroughly, searching every room, just to see if he missed anything.

During his conversation with the housekeeper, he assumed that she was confused. But now he tries to look at it from a different perspective. Maybe she wasn't shocked or confused and had answered his questions as accurately as she could. In which case the housekeeper, Edith Schwartz, was claiming that Palmcrona asked for help with the noose, and there were helping hands, helpful people. She was saying that his death wasn't entirely a self-imposed act and that he hadn't been alone when he died.

There's something that doesn't make sense.

Joona goes into the men's locker room, takes out his phone, and calls the chief pathologist, Nils "The Needle" Åhlén.

"I'm not finished," The Needle says when he answers.

"It's about Palmcrona. What are your first impressions, even if—"

"I'm not finished," Nils repeats.

"Even if you're not finished," Joona finishes.

"Come in on Monday."

"I'm coming now," Joona says.

"At five o'clock, I'm going to look at a sofa with my wife."

"I'll be with you in twenty-five minutes," Joona says, and ends the call before The Needle can protest further.

As Joona showers and gets dressed, he hears the sound of

children laughing and talking and realizes that a swimming lesson is about to start.

He ponders the significance of the fact that the director general of the Inspectorate for Strategic Products has been found hanged. The person who makes all the final decisions about the manufacture and export of Swedish arms is dead.

What if I'm wrong? What if he was murdered after all? Joona asks himself. I need to talk to Pollock before I go and see The Needle, because he and Kofoed may have gone over the material from the crime-scene investigation.

Joona strides along the hallway, runs down a flight of stairs, and calls his assistant, Anja Larsson, to find out if Nathan Pollock is still in police headquarters.

9

JOONA'S HAIR is still soaking wet when he opens the door to the classroom where Pollock is giving a lecture on how to handle hostage situations and rescues.

On the wall behind Pollock is a projection of an anatomical drawing of the human body. Several different types of handguns are laid out on a table, from a small silver Sig Sauer P238 to a matte-black assault rifle from Heckler & Koch with a forty-millimeter grenade-launcher attachment.

One of the young officers is standing in front of Pollock, who pulls a knife, holds it concealed against his body, then rushes forward and pretends to cut the officer's throat. Then he turns to the group. "The disadvantages of this kind of attack are that the enemy may have time to scream, that the enemy's body movement can't be controlled, and that it takes a while for them to bleed out, because you've only opened one artery," Pollock explains.

He goes over to the young officer again and wraps his arm around his face, so that the crook of his arm is covering his mouth. "But if I do it this way instead, I can muffle any scream, maneuver his head, and sever both arteries with a single cut."

Pollock lets go of the young officer and notices that Joona is standing just inside the door. The young police officer wipes his mouth and sits back down in his chair. Pollock smiles broadly and waves at Joona, beckoning him forward, but Joona shakes his head.

"I'd like a few words, Nathan," he says quietly.

Some of the officers turn to look. Pollock walks over to him, and they shake hands.

"Tommy pulled shoeprints from Palmcrona's home," Joona says. "I need to know if he found anything unexpected."

"I didn't think there was any urgency." Nathan replies in a muted voice. "Obviously, we photographed all the impressions, but we haven't had time to analyze the results. I can't give you an overview right now—"

"But you did see something," Joona says.

"When I put the images into the computer . . . it could be a pattern, but it's too early to—"

"Just tell me—I have to go."

"It looks like there were prints from two different sets of shoes moving in two circles around the body," Nathan says.

"Come with me to see Nils Åhlén," Joona says.

"Now?"

"I'm supposed to be there in twenty minutes."

"Damn, I can't," Nathan replies, gesturing toward the room. "But I'll have my phone on in case you need anything."

"Thanks," Joona says, and turns to leave.

"You . . . you don't want to say hello to the group?" Nathan asks.

The students have all turned around now, and Joona gives them a brief wave.

"So—this is Joona Linna. I've told you about him," Nathan Pollock says, raising his voice. "I'm trying to persuade him to give us a lecture on close combat."

The room is quiet as they all look at Joona.

"Most of you probably know more about martial arts

than I do," Joona says with a slight smile. "The only thing I've learned is ... when it's real, there are completely different rules. No art, just fighting."

"Pay attention to this," Pollock says.

"You only survive if you have the ability to adapt and take advantage of anything and everything that comes your way," Joona goes on calmly. "Practice making the most of the circumstances you're given.... You might be in a car or on a balcony. The room might be full of tear gas. Maybe the floor is covered with broken glass. There may be weapons, or things you could use as weapons. You don't know if you're at the beginning or the end of a fight, so you need to save your energy. You need to make sure you can keep working, get through a whole night if necessary ... so flying kicks and cool roundhouses are out of the question."

A few of them laugh.

"In unarmed close combat," Joona continues, "it's often a matter of accepting some pain in order to quickly neutralize the situation...."

Joona walks out of the lecture room. Two of the officers clap. Pollock smiles to himself as he walks back to the table.

"I was actually planning to save this for a later lesson," he says, clicking something on the computer. "This recording is already a classic. It's from the hostage drama at the Nordea Bank on Hamn Street nine years ago. Two robbers. Joona has already gotten the hostages out and has incapacitated one of the men, who was armed with an Uzi. It was a vicious firefight. The other guy is hiding, armed only with a knife. They'd sprayed all the security cameras but missed this one.... We'll watch it in slow motion, because it only lasts a matter of seconds."

The film starts to play slowly. A grainy shot of a bank filmed from above comes into view. The seconds tick by on the bottom of the screen. There's furniture everywhere, and the floor is littered with paper. Joona is moving smoothly sideways, his pistol raised, arm straight. The bank robber is hiding behind the open vault door with a knife in his hand. Suddenly he darts forward with long, fluid strides. Joona turns the pistol on him, aims straight at his chest, and fires.

"The pistol clicks," Pollock says. "Faulty bullet stuck in the chamber."

The grainy footage flickers. Joona moves backward as the man with the knife rushes at him. The whole thing is eerily silent. Joona ejects the cartridge but realizes that he's not going to have time to reload. Instead, he turns the now useless pistol around, so that the barrel runs parallel to the bone in his lower arm.

"I don't get it," one woman says.

"He turns the pistol into a tonfa," Pollock explains.

"A what?"

"It's a sort of club . . . like the ones American police officers use. It extends your reach and increases the power of any blow, because it shrinks the area of impact."

The man with the knife has reached Joona and takes a long, hesitant step. The knife blade glints in a semicircle, aimed at Joona's torso. The man's other hand is raised and follows the rotation of his body. Joona isn't even looking at the knife. He moves forward instead, striking hard. He hits the man on the neck, just below his Adam's apple, with the barrel of the pistol.

The knife spins as it falls toward the floor, and the man sinks to his knees. He opens his mouth wide, clutches his neck, and then collapses to the floor.

10

JOONA is on his way to Karolinska University Hospital, thinking about Palmcrona's hanging body: the tense clothesline, the briefcase on the floor.

Joona adds the two circles of shoeprints around the dead man to the picture.

This case isn't over yet.

Joona drives along the side of the canal. The tree branches are hanging low, sinking into the smooth, mirrorlike surface of the water.

In his mind's eye, he sees the housekeeper, Edith Schwartz, again. He lingers over every detail, from the veins on her large hands, to the way she said that there are helpful people everywhere.

The Forensic Medicine Department is situated among the trees and neat lawns of the large, redbrick Karolinska Hospital campus.

Joona pulls into the empty visitors' lot. He notes that The Needle has parked his white Jaguar in the middle of the lawn next to the main entrance.

Joona waves to the woman in reception, who responds by giving him a thumbs-up, so he walks down the hallway, knocks on Nils's door, and goes in. As usual, the sparsely decorated office is pristine. The blinds are drawn, but sunlight filters in between the blades.

The Needle is wearing his white-framed aviator glasses and a white polo under his lab coat.

"I've just given a white Jaguar a parking ticket," Joona says.

"Good for you," Nils says.

Joona stops in the middle of the floor and becomes serious. His eyes turn silvery dark.

"So—how did he die?" he asks.

"Palmcrona?"

"Yes."

The phone rings, and Nils nudges the postmortem toward Joona.

"You didn't have to come all the way out here to get an answer to that," he says before answering the call.

Joona sits down across from him on a white leather chair and leafs through the postmortem, reading different passages at random.

74. Kidneys weigh a total of 290 grams. Smooth surface. Tissue gray-red. Consistency firm, elastic. Clear delineation.

75. Urinary ducts appear normal.

76. Bladder empty. Mucous membrane pale.

77. Prostate normal size. Tissue pale.

The Needle nudges his aviators up his narrow, bent nose, then ends the call and looks up.

"As you can see," he says, yawning, "there's nothing unexpected. Cause of death is asphyxia.... With a hanging, of course, it's not usually suffocation in the way we normally think of it. It's more of a blockage of the arteries."

"The brain suffocates because the supply of oxygenated blood stops."

Nils nods. "Arterial compression, bilateral constriction of the carotid arteries. It happens very fast. Most people are unconscious within a matter of seconds. . . ."

"But he was still alive before he was hanged?" Joona asks.

"Yes."

The Needle's thin face is clean-shaven and gloomy.

"Can you estimate the height of the drop?" Joona asks.

"There are no fractures in the cervical spine or the base of the skull—so I'd guess ten, twenty centimeters."

"Right . . ."

Joona thinks about the briefcase and the prints from Palmcrona's shoes. He opens the report again and flips to the external examination: the skin of the neck and the estimated angle of the rope.

"What are you thinking?" The Needle asks.

"I'm wondering if there's any chance he was strangled with the same cord, and then strung up from the ceiling."

"No," Nils replies.

"Why not?" Joona asks.

"There was only one groove, and it was in perfect condition," Nils begins to explain. "When a person is hanged, the rope or cord cuts into the throat, and—"

"But a killer could also know that," Joona interrupts.

"It's practically impossible to reconstruct, though. When someone is hanged, the groove around the neck is shaped like an arrowhead, with the point at the top, by the knot. . . ."

"Because the weight of the body tightens the noose."

"Exactly . . . and that also means the deepest part of the groove should be exactly opposite the point."

"So he died from a hanging," Joona concludes.

"No question."

The tall, thin pathologist bites his bottom lip gently.

"But could he have been forced to commit suicide?" Joona asks.

"There's no sign of that."

Joona closes the report and drums on it with his hands. The housekeeper's comment that other people were involved in Palmcrona's death must have just been confused talk. But he can't get past the two different shoeprints Kofoed found.

"So you're certain of the cause of death?" Joona says, looking Nils in the eye.

"What were you expecting?"

"This," Joona says, putting his finger in the postmortem report. "This is exactly what I was expecting, but there's still something bugging me."

The Needle gives him a wry smile. "Take the report home with you. Bedtime reading."

"Okay," Joona says.

"But I think you can probably let go of Palmcrona. . . . It's a simple suicide."

The Needle's smile fades, and he lowers his gaze, but Joona's eyes are still sharp, focused.

"I daresay you're right," he says.

"I'm happy to speculate, if you'd like," Nils replies. "Carl Palmcrona was probably depressed, because his fingernails were ragged and dirty, his teeth hadn't been brushed for a few days, and he hadn't shaved."

"I see." Joona nods.

"You're welcome to take a look at him."

"No need," he replies, getting heavily to his feet.

Nils leans forward with alacrity, as if he's been looking forward to this moment. "But this morning I got something considerably more interesting. Do you have a few minutes?"

He gets up from his chair and gestures for Joona to follow him into the hallway. A pale-blue butterfly has somehow gotten into the building and is fluttering in the air ahead of them.

"Did that young guy leave?" Joona asks.

"Who?"

"The one who was here before, with the ponytail and . . ."

"Frippe? God, no. He's not allowed to leave. He has the day off. Megadeth are playing the Globe, with Entombed opening."

They walk through a dimly lit room with a postmortem table that smells like disinfectant, then walk into a cooler room, where bodies are kept in refrigerated drawers.

The Needle opens another door and turns the light on. The flickering fluorescent tubes illuminate a white-tiled room with a long, plastic-covered examination table that has a double rim and drainage channels.

On the table is an extremely beautiful young woman.

She's tan, and her long, glossy dark hair lies in curls across her forehead and shoulders. It looks as if she's gazing up at the room in surprise.

There's something almost playful about the set of her mouth. She looks like someone who laughed and smiled a lot.

But there's no sparkle in her big, dark eyes. Tiny dark-brown spots have already begun to appear.

Joona stops and looks at the woman. He guesses she's nineteen, twenty at most. Not long ago, she was a young child sleeping with her parents. Now she's dead.

Across the woman's chest, on the skin above her breastbone, is a faint curved line, like a smile, some thirty centimeters long.

"What's that line?" Joona asks, pointing.

"No idea. An impression from a necklace, maybe, or her shirt. I'll take a closer look later."

Joona looks at the lifeless body, takes a deep breath, and—as always when confronted by the absolute implacability of death—feels a gloom settle on him, a colorless loneliness.

Life is so fragile. It's terrifying.

Her finger- and toenails are painted a pinkish-beige color.

"What's so special about her?" he asks.

Nils looks at him gravely, and his glasses glint as he turns back toward the body again.

"The marine police brought her in," he says. "She was found sitting on the bed in the front cabin of a yacht drifting in the archipelago."

"Dead?"

Nils meets his gaze and says, with a new lilt in his voice, "She drowned, Joona."

"Drowned?"

The Needle nods and smiles brightly.

"She drowned on board a boat that was still afloat," he says.

"So someone found her in the water and brought her on board."

"Well, if that had happened I wouldn't be taking up your valuable time," Nils says.

"So what's this all about?"

"There's no trace of water on the rest of the body. I've sent her clothes for analysis, but the lab won't find anything, either."

The Needle falls silent, flips through the preliminary report, then glances at Joona to see if he's managed to pique his curiosity. Joona is standing stock-still, and his face looks completely different now. He's looking at the dead body with an expression of intense concentration. Suddenly he takes a pair of latex gloves from the box and pulls them on. Nils smiles happily as Joona leans over the girl, carefully lifting her arms and studying them.

"You won't find any signs of violence," Nils says, almost inaudible. "It's incomprehensible."

11

THE YACHT is moored at the police marina on Dalarö, anchored between two police boats.

The marina's tall metal gates are open. Joona drives slowly in along the gravel road, parks, and walks toward the water.

A boat has been found abandoned, drifting in the archipelago, thinks Joona. On the bed in the front cabin sits a girl who has drowned. The boat is afloat, but the girl's lungs are full of seawater.

Joona stops and looks at the boat from a distance. The front of the hull has been wrecked. Long scratches from a violent collision run along the side. The paint and the fiberglass underneath are both damaged.

He calls the marine police.

"Lennart," a voice answers brightly.

"Lennart Johansson?" Joona asks.

"Yes, that's me."

"My name is Joona Linna, National Crime."

The line is quiet, and Joona can hear what sounds like waves lapping.

"The yacht you brought in," Joona says. "I was wondering if it's taken on any water?"

"Water?"

"The hull is damaged."

Joona takes a few steps closer to the boat as Lennart explains in a tone of heavy resignation, "Dear Lord, if I had a penny for every drunk who crashed—"

"I need to look at the boat," Joona interrupts.

"Look, here's what happened," Lennart says. "Some kids— from . . . I don't know, let's say Södertälje—steal a boat, pick up some girls, cruise around, listen to music, party, drink a lot. In the middle of it all, they hit something. It's a pretty hard collision, and the girl falls overboard. The guys stop the boat, drive back and find her, get her up on deck. When they realize she's dead, they panic and just take off."

Lennart stops and waits for a response.

"Not a bad theory," Joona says slowly.

"It's not, is it?" Lennart says cheerfully. "It's all yours. Might save you a trip to Dalarö."

"Too late," Joona says, as he heads for a police boat.

It's moored behind the motor cruiser. A tan, bare-chested man in his mid-twenties is standing on deck, holding a phone to his ear.

"Suit yourself," he says. "Feel free to book a tour."

"I'm here already—and I think I'm looking right at you, if you're standing on one of your shallow . . ."

"Do I look like a surfer?"

The tan man looks up with a smile and scratches his chest.

"Pretty much," Joona says.

They hang up and walk toward each other. Lennart pulls on a short-sleeved uniform shirt and buttons it as he crosses the gangplank.

Joona holds up his thumb and little finger in a hang-ten gesture. Lennart's white teeth flash.

"I go surfing whenever there's enough swell—that's why they call me Lance, like from *Apocalypse Now*."

"I can see why," Joona jokes dryly.

"Right?" Lennart laughs.

They walk over to the boat.

"A Storebro 36, Royal Cruiser," Lennart says. "Good boat, but it's seen better days. Registered to a Björn Almskog."

"Have you contacted him?"

"Haven't had time."

They take a closer look at the damage to the boat's hull. It looks recent: there's no algae in the glass fibers.

"I've asked a forensics specialist to come out—he should be here soon," Joona says.

"She's taken a serious knock," Lennart says.

"Who's been on board since the boat was found?"

"No one," he replies quickly.

Joona smiles and waits, a patient expression on his face.

"Well, me, of course," Lennart says hesitantly. "And Sonny, my colleague. And the paramedics who removed the body. And our forensics guy, but he used floor mats and protective clothing."

"Is that all?"

"Apart from the old guy who found the boat."

Joona doesn't answer, just looks down at the sparkling water and thinks about the girl on The Needle's table. "Do you know if your forensics guy secured all the surface evidence?" he asks after a while.

"He's done with the floor, and he filmed the scene."

"I'm going on board."

A narrow, worn gangplank leads from the pier to the boat. Joona climbs aboard and then stands on the aft deck. He looks around slowly, scanning everything carefully. This is his only chance to get an unbiased first impression of the crime scene. Every detail he registers now could be vital: shoes, an overturned deck chair, a large towel, a paperback that's turned yellow in the sun, a knife with a red plastic handle, a bucket on a rope, beer cans, a bag of charcoal, a tub with a wetsuit in it, bottles of sunscreen and lotion.

He looks through the large window at the wooden furnishings in the salon. From a certain angle, he can see fingerprints on the glass door standing out in the sunlight, impressions of hands that have pushed the door open and closed again, or reached for it when the boat rocked.

Joona enters the small salon. The afternoon sun is glinting off the veneers and the chrome. There's a cowboy hat and a pair of sunglasses on the navy-blue cushions on one of the sofas.

The water outside is lapping against the hull.

Joona's eyes roam across the worn floor of the salon and down the narrow stairs to the boat's cabins. It's as dark as a deep well down there. He can't see anything until he turns his flashlight on; the cool, tightly focused beam illuminates the steep passageway. The bloodred wood shimmers. Joona goes down the creaking stairs, thinking about the girl, toying with a theory: She was alone on the boat, dived from the foredeck, and hit her head on a rock. She breathed water into her lungs but somehow managed to get back on board and change out of her wet bikini into dry clothes. Maybe she felt tired and went down into the cabin, not realizing how badly hurt she was, not realizing that she had a serious concussion.

But if that were the case, Nils would have found traces of brackish water all over her body.

It doesn't make sense.

Joona goes below, past the galley and head, into the main cabin.

He can still feel her on the boat; her death lingers even though her body has been moved to Karolinska. It's the same feeling every time.

The boat seems to creak in a different way as it leans to one side. Joona waits and listens, then makes his way into the cabin.

Summer light is streaming through the narrow windows by the ceiling onto a double bed, shaped to fit the bow of the boat. This is where they found her, sitting on the bed. There's an open gym bag on the floor and a polka-dot nightdress that someone unpacked. A pair of jeans and a thin cardigan have been flung over the back of the door, and a shoulder bag is hanging from a hook.

The boat sways again, and a glass bottle rolls across the deck above his head.

Joona photographs the bag from various angles with his cell phone. The flash makes the little room shrink, as if the walls, floor, and ceiling all moved closer for an instant.

He carefully takes the bag off the hook and carries it up on deck. The stairs creak under his weight. He can hear a metallic clicking sound from outside. When he reaches the salon, an unexpected shadow crosses the glass door, and Joona reacts instinctively, taking a step back into the gloom of the stairwell.

12

Joona stands completely still, near the top of the yacht's dark flight of stairs. He can see the bottom of the glass doors and some of the aft deck. A shadow crosses the dusty glass, and then a hand comes into view. Someone is creeping across the deck. He recognizes Erixon's face. Drops of sweat are running down the forensics officer's cheeks as he rolls his gelatin foil out around the door.

Joona takes the bag from the cabin up into the salon with him. He carefully dumps it out on the little hardwood table. He sees a red wallet and pokes it open with his pen. There's a driver's license in the worn plastic pocket. He looks more closely and sees that the photograph is of a woman with a beautiful, serious face. She's leaning back slightly, as if she were looking up. Her hair is dark and curly. She looks like the woman he saw in the pathology lab.

"Penelope Fernandez," he reads on the driver's license, thinking that he's heard that name before.

In his mind, he goes back to the pathology lab. He can see the naked body on the table with its slack-featured face.

Outside, in the sunshine, Erixon's bulky frame is very slowly securing fingerprints from the railing by brushing them with magnetic powder and using tape to lift them.

Joona can hear him sighing deeply the whole time, as if

each movement requires painful effort and he's just expended the last of his energy.

Joona looks out at the deck and sees a bucket on a rope next to a sneaker. He catches a faint smell of potatoes coming from the galley.

He turns back to the driver's license with its little photograph and looks at the young woman's mouth, the slightly parted lips; suddenly he realizes that something is missing.

He feels he's seen something important but forgotten it.

He startles when his phone vibrates in his pocket. He sees that it's The Needle and answers. "Joona."

"My name is Nils Åhlén, and I'm the chief pathologist at the Department of Forensic Medicine in Stockholm."

Joona smiles; they've known each other for twenty years, and he'd recognize Nils's voice anywhere.

"Did she hit her head?" Joona asks.

"No," Nils replies, surprised.

"I thought maybe she hit a rock while she was diving."

"No, nothing like that. She drowned; that was the cause of death."

"You're sure?" Joona persists.

"I've found fungus inside her nostrils and perforations in the mucous membrane in her throat, probably the result of a severe vomit reflex. There are bronchial secretions in both her trachea and bronchi. Her lungs look typical for a drowning: full of water, increased weight. . . ."

The line is quiet. Joona can hear a scraping sound, as if someone were pushing a metal cart.

"You had a reason for calling," Joona says.

"Yes."

"Do you feel like telling me?"

"She had a high concentration of tetrahydrocannabinol in her urine."

"Marijuana?"

"Yes."

"But she didn't die from it," Joona says.

"Hardly," Nils says, sounding amused. "I just assumed that you would reconstruct the sequence of events on the boat and that this was one little detail of the puzzle that you may not have known about."

"Her name is Penelope Fernandez," Joona says.

"Good to know," Nils mutters.

"Is there anything else?"

"No."

Nils breathes down the phone.

"Say it," Joona says.

"It's just that this isn't an ordinary death."

He stops speaking.

"What have you spotted?"

"Nothing. It's just a feeling. . . ."

"Great," Joona says. "Now you're starting to sound like me."

"I know, but . . . Obviously, it could be a case of *mors subita naturalis*, a swift but entirely natural death. . . . There's no evidence to contradict that. But if this is a natural death, it's a very unusual natural death."

They end the call, but The Needle's words are echoing through Joona's head: *mors subita naturalis*. There's something mysterious about Penelope Fernandez's death. Her body wasn't just found in the water and brought on board. If that were the case, she would have been lying on the deck. Whoever found her may have wanted to show the dead woman some respect. But in that case, they would have carried her into the salon and laid her on the sofa.

Another possibility, Joona thinks, *is that she was found and taken care of by someone who loved her, who wanted to put her to bed in her own room, in her own bed.*

But she was sitting on the bed. Sitting.

Maybe The Needle is wrong. Maybe she was still alive when she was helped back on board and taken to her room. Her lungs could have been badly damaged, beyond saving, without her knowing. Maybe she felt sick and wanted to lie down.

But why was there no water on her clothes or the rest of her body?

There's a freshwater shower on board, Joona thinks. He tells himself that he's going to have to search the rest of the boat: check the aft cabin, as well as the head and the galley. There's a lot left to look at before the whole picture starts to emerge.

Erixon gets to his feet and takes a couple of steps, and the whole boat rocks.

Once more Joona looks out the glass doors, and for a second time he finds himself staring at the bucket on a rope. It's next to a zinc tub with a wetsuit in it. There are water skis by the railing. Joona looks at the bucket again. He looks at the rope tied to its handle. The curved zinc tub shimmers in the sun, shining like a new moon.

Suddenly it hits him, and Joona can see the sequence of events with icy clarity. He waits, letting his heart settle down, and thinks through what happened once more, until he is absolutely certain that he's right.

The woman now identified as Penelope Fernandez was drowned in the tub.

Joona thinks back to the curved mark on her chest.

She was murdered, then placed on the bed in her cabin.

His thoughts start to come faster now, as adrenaline pumps through his body. She was drowned in brackish seawater and then placed on her bed.

This isn't an ordinary death, and this isn't an ordinary murderer.

A tentative voice starts to echo inside him, getting louder and more insistent. It keeps repeating the same five words: *Get off the boat now, get off the boat now.*

Joona looks at Erixon through the glass as he drops a swab into a small paper bag.

"Peekaboo." Erixon smiles.

"We're going ashore," Joona says calmly.

"I don't like boats, either—they never stop moving—but I've only just gotten—"

"Take a break," Joona says sharply.

"What's gotten into you?"

"Just follow me, and don't touch your phone."

They go ashore, and Joona leads Erixon a short way from the boat before he stops. He can feel his cheeks flush as he tries to calm down.

"There could be a bomb on board," he says quietly.

Erixon sits down on the edge of a concrete plinth. Sweat is dripping from his forehead.

"What are you talking about?"

"This is no ordinary murder," Joona says. "There's a risk that—"

"Murder? Who said anything about—"

"Hold on," Joona interrupts. "I'm sure Penelope Fernandez was drowned in the tub on deck."

"Drowned? What the hell are you saying?"

"She drowned in seawater in the tub, then was moved to the bed," Joona goes on. "And I think the plan was for the boat to sink."

13

AT SEVEN O'CLOCK THAT EVENING, five very serious men meet in Room 13 of the Forensic Medicine Department at Karolinska. Joona wants to take over the case of the woman found drowned on the abandoned boat. Even though it's Saturday, he has summoned his boss, Petter Näslund, and Senior Prosecutor Jens Svanehjälm to a reconstruction in order to convince them that they're dealing with a murder.

One of the fluorescent tubes in the ceiling keeps flickering.

"We need to change the bulb," The Needle murmurs.

"Yes," Frippe agrees.

Petter mutters something under his breath. His wide, strong face looks as if it's shaking in the flickering light. Beside him, Jens Svanehjälm has an annoyed expression on his face. He seems to be considering the risks of putting his leather briefcase down on the floor.

The room smells like disinfectant. Large adjustable lamps hang from the ceiling above a freestanding stainless-steel autopsy table. A zinc tub like the one on the boat is already half full of water. Joona continues pouring more water from a bucket into the tub.

"Just because someone is found drowned on a boat doesn't necessarily mean a crime has been committed," Svanehjälm says impatiently.

"Exactly," Petter says.

"This could just be an accidental drowning that hasn't been reported yet," Svanehjälm says.

"The water in her lungs is the same water the boat was floating in, but there's almost no trace of that water on her clothes or the rest of her body," The Needle says.

"Well, that is strange," Svanehjälm says.

"There has to be a rational explanation," Petter says with a smile.

Joona empties one last bucket into the tub, then thanks everyone for coming. "I know it's the weekend and we'd all rather be at home," he says. "But I think I've noticed something important."

"Of course we're going to come if you tell us it's important," Svanehjälm says amiably, finally putting his briefcase down between his feet.

"The killer made his way onto the yacht," Joona says seriously. "He went below to the front cabin and saw Penelope Fernandez asleep, then went back up to the aft deck, dropped the bucket into the water, and started to fill the tub on deck."

"Five, six buckets," Petter says.

"Then, when the tub was full, he went down to the cabin and woke Penelope. He took her out onto the deck, where he drowned her in the tub."

"Who would do something like that?" Svanehjälm asks.

"I don't know yet. Maybe it was some sort of torture, like waterboarding. . . ."

"Revenge? Jealousy?"

Joona tilts his head and says thoughtfully, "This isn't an ordinary murder. Maybe the killer wanted information from her and was trying to get her to say or admit to something."

"What does our pathologist say?" Svanehjälm asks.

The Needle shakes his head. "If she was forcibly drowned,"

he says, "then I would expect to find signs of violence on her body, bruises and—"

"Can we hold the objections until later?" Joona interrupts. "I'd like to start by showing what I think happened, the way it looks in my head. And then, once I'm done, I'd like us all to go and look at the body and see if there's any basis for my theory."

"Why can't you ever do anything the easy way?" Petter asks.

"I need to go home soon," the prosecutor warns.

Joona looks at him with a glint in his pale eyes. "Penelope Fernandez," he begins, "had been sitting on deck just before, smoking a joint. It was a warm day, and she felt tired, so she went down to rest for a while, and fell asleep wearing her jean jacket."

He gestures toward Nils's young assistant, who is waiting in the doorway.

"Frippe has agreed to help with the reconstruction."

Frippe smiles and takes a step forward. His dyed black hair is hanging in clumps down his back, and his worn leather pants are studded with rivets. He carefully zips his leather jacket over his black T-shirt.

"Look," Joona says quietly, and demonstrates how with one hand he can firmly grip both jacket sleeves to lock Frippe's arms behind his back, allowing him to grab hold of Frippe's long hair with his other hand.

"I have complete control of Frippe now, and yet there won't be a single bruise on him."

Joona raises the young man's arms behind his back. Frippe whimpers and leans forward.

"Take it easy," he says, laughing.

"Obviously, you're much bigger than the victim, but I still think I could push your head down into the tub."

"Be careful with him," The Needle says.

"I'm just going to mess up his hair."

"Forget it," Frippe says with a smile.

It's a silent tussle. Nils looks worried, Svanehjälm uncomfortable. Petter swears. Without much difficulty, Joona manages to push Frippe's head down into the water and hold him there for a few seconds before letting go and backing away. Frippe wobbles as he straightens up, and Nils hurries forward with a towel.

"Couldn't you have just described it?" he says irritably.

Once Frippe has finished drying himself off, they all go into the next room, where the cool air is heavy with the stench of decay. One wall is covered with three layers of stainless steel fridge doors. Nils opens Compartment 16 and pulls out the tray. The young woman is lying on the narrow bunk, naked and pale, with brown, spidery veins around her neck. Joona points at the thin curved line over her chest.

"Take your clothes off," he says to Frippe.

Frippe unbuttons his jacket and pulls off his black T-shirt. Across his chest is a faint pink mark from the edge of the tub—a curved line, like a smiling mouth.

"Oh shit," Petter says.

The Needle inspects the roots of the dead woman's hair. He takes out a small flashlight and points it at the pale skin under her hair. "I don't even need a microscope for this. Someone's held her very tightly by her hair."

He turns the flashlight off and puts it back into the pocket of his white coat.

"In other words . . . ," Joona says.

"In other words, you're right, of course," Nils says.

"Murder." Svanehjälm sighs.

"Impressive," Frippe says, wiping off some eyeliner that has smeared across one cheek.

"Thanks," Joona says distantly.

Nils looks at him quizzically. "What is it, Joona? What do you see?"

"It's not her," he says.

"What?"

Joona meets Nils's gaze, then points at the body in front of them.

"This isn't Penelope Fernandez," he says, and meets the eyes of the prosecutor. "She looks a lot like her, but I've seen Penelope's driver's license, and I'm sure this isn't her."

"But what—"

"Maybe Penelope is dead, too," Joona says. "But if so, we haven't found her yet."

14

PENELOPE'S HEART is still beating horribly fast—she's trying to breathe quietly, but the air is caught in her throat. She and Björn have been running in a blind panic, not looking back. They've stumbled and fallen and gotten back up. They've clambered over fallen trees, scraping their legs, knees, and hands, but they keep pushing on.

Penelope no longer has any sense of how close their pursuer is. Maybe he's already caught sight of them again, or maybe he's given up and decided to wait.

She can't understand why they're being hunted.

Maybe it's all a mistake, she thinks. A terrible mistake.

Her racing pulse starts to slow down.

She feels sick, and almost throws up, but swallows hard instead.

"Oh God, oh God," she whispers to herself. "This is impossible. We have to get help. Someone needs to find the boat soon and start looking for us—"

"Shhh," Björn hisses, fear in his eyes.

Her hands are shaking. A series of rapid-fire images plays in her mind. She tries to blink them away by looking at her white sneakers, at the brown fir needles on the ground, at Björn's dirty, bloody knees, but the images keep forcing their way through: Viola, dead, sitting on the bed with her eyes wide open, the look in them unreadable, her face blotchy and white and wet, her hair lank and dripping.

Somehow Penelope had known that the man standing on the shore beckoning Björn back to land was the person who had killed her sister. She could feel it. She put the few pieces she had together and interpreted the image in an instant. If she hadn't, they would both be dead.

Something happens to your mind when you're seized by panic. The panic isn't constant—every so often, it is replaced by rational thought. It's like switching a loud noise off and finding yourself surrounded by silence and an unexpected, clear overview of the situation. Then the fear comes back, and your thoughts are one-track again, and all you want to do is run, get away from whoever is chasing you.

Penelope keeps thinking that they need to find other people—there must be hundreds of them on Ornö that evening. They need to find the inhabited parts of the island, farther south, and then get help, get a phone and call the police.

As she runs, Penelope feels their pursuer's presence again and thinks she hears his long, quick steps. She knows he hasn't stopped running. He'll catch up if they don't get help soon.

A wave of hysteria runs through her. She wants just to stand still and scream for help, but she forces herself to keep going, to keep climbing.

Björn coughs behind her, gasping for breath.

What if Viola isn't dead? What if she just needs help? Penelope knows that she's thinking impossible things because the reality is so much worse. She knows Viola is dead, but it's incomprehensible. She doesn't want to understand, doesn't even want to try.

They scramble up another steep cliff, past pine trees, rocks, and lingonberry bushes. On the other side of the ridge, the forest slopes toward the western shore of the island, and between the dark trees they see the pale surface of the water close by. They run down the slope. She hears music, followed by loud voices and laughter.

Björn appears beside her and pulls her along, pointing: there's a party somewhere up ahead of them. Taking each other's hands, they start to run. Between the dark trees they see colored garlands of lights wound through the railings of a wooden porch overlooking the water.

They walk on warily.

A group of people is sitting around a table in front of a beautiful red summerhouse. Penelope realizes it must be the middle of the night, but the sky is still bright. The meal is long over. The table is strewn with glasses and coffee cups, napkins, and empty snack bowls.

Some of the people at the table are singing; others are talking and topping up wineglasses. The grill is still radiating heat. To Björn and Penelope, they all look as if they're from a completely different world. Their faces are bright and calm.

Only one person is outside the circle. He's standing off to one side with his face toward the forest, as if he were expecting visitors. Penelope stops abruptly and clutches Björn's hand. They sink to the ground, creeping behind a tree. Björn looks frightened—he doesn't understand—but she's sure of what she's seen. Their pursuer figured out which way they were heading and got to the house ahead of them. He realized how irresistible the lights and sounds of the party would be to them. So he's waiting, watching for them among the dark trees, eager to head them off at the edge of the forest.

And then he's gone.

She's just starting to think that their flight might finally be over, that she and Björn can go down to the party and alert the police, when she catches sight of him again.

He's standing beside a tree trunk, not far away at all.

With measured movements, their pursuer raises a pair of binoculars with pale-green lenses.

15

IT SOUNDS as if someone is repeatedly throwing a ball at the wall below The Needle's window. He and Joona are waiting for Claudia Fernandez in silence. She's been asked to come to the Forensic Medicine Department early this Sunday morning to help identify the dead woman.

When Joona called her to say that they feared her daughter Viola had died, Claudia's voice had sounded strangely calm.

"No, Viola's out in the archipelago with her sister," she said.

"On Björn Almskog's boat?" Joona asked.

"Yes. I was the one who suggested she call Penelope and ask if she could go with them. I thought it would do her good to get away for a while."

"Was anyone else going with them?"

"Well, Björn, obviously."

Joona let several seconds pass. Then he cleared his throat and said very gently, "Claudia, I'd like you to come to the Forensic Medicine Department in Solna."

"What for?" she asked.

Now Joona is sitting in an uncomfortable chair in The Needle's office. Nils has slipped a small picture of Frippe into the bottom of his framed wedding photograph. They can still hear the sound of the ball thudding against the wall, a hollow, lonely sound. Joona thinks back to how Claudia's breathing changed when she finally realized they may actually have found her daughter.

He called a taxi to pick Claudia up from her row house in Gustavsberg. She should be with them in a few minutes.

Nils makes a halfhearted attempt at small talk, but he gives up when he realizes Joona isn't going to respond.

They both just want this to be over.

They can hear footsteps in the hallway and get to their feet at the same time.

Seeing the dead body of a family member is an important, necessary part of the grieving process, Joona tells himself. He has read that identification constitutes a form of liberation, because there's no longer any opportunity for wild fantasies about the loved one's being alive.

Still, Joona can't help thinking that's just hollow nonsense. Death is never anything but terrible.

Claudia, a frightened-looking woman in her sixties, is standing in the doorway. Her face bears traces of tears and anxiety, and her body looks frozen and hunched.

"Hello, my name is Joona Linna. I'm a detective. We spoke on the phone," Joona says gently.

Nils introduces himself very quietly, then immediately turns his back to her, pretending to sort through some files. He may appear brusque and dismissive, but Joona knows that he's very upset.

"I've tried calling, but I can't get hold of either of my girls," Claudia whispers. "They should—"

"Shall we go?" Nils interrupts, as if he hasn't heard her.

They move silently through the familiar hallways. With each step, Joona can't help thinking that the air is getting thinner. Claudia is in no hurry to get to what lies ahead, and she walks slowly, several meters behind Nils, whose tall, sharply defined figure hurries off ahead of them. Joona turns and tries to smile at Claudia, but he has to steel himself against the panicking, pleading look in her eyes.

They're taking her into the cold room where the bodies are kept.

Nils bends over, unlocks one of the stainless steel doors, and pulls out the drawer.

The young woman comes into view. Her body is covered with a white sheet. Her eyes are dull and half closed; her cheeks are sunken.

Her hair lies like a black wreath around her beautiful head.

A small, pale hand is visible beside her hip.

Claudia is breathing fast. She reaches out and cautiously touches the hand, then lets out a moan. It comes from deep within her, as if she is breaking apart, as if her soul is shattering.

Claudia's body starts to shake, and she sinks to her knees, pressing her daughter's lifeless hand to her lips.

"No, no," she sobs. "Oh God, dear God, not Viola. Not Viola . . ."

Joona is standing a few steps behind Claudia, and sees her back shake with weeping, hears her desperate sobbing get louder, then slowly die away.

She wipes the tears from her face, but she is still breathing fitfully when she gets up from the floor.

"Can you confirm that this is Viola Fernandez, your . . ."

The Needle's voice trails off, and he clears his throat quickly and angrily.

Claudia shakes her head and gently strokes her daughter's cheek with her fingertips. "Viola, Violita . . ."

Very shakily, she pulls her hand back, and Joona says gently, "I'm so very, very sorry."

Claudia almost falls, but she reaches out for the wall for

support, turns away, and whispers to herself, "We were going to the circus on Saturday; it was a surprise for Viola. . . ."

They look at the dead woman, her pale lips, the veins on her neck.

"I've forgotten your name," Claudia says helplessly, looking at Joona.

"Joona Linna," he says.

"Joona Linna," the woman repeats in a thick voice. "I'll tell you about Viola. She's my little girl, my youngest, my happy little . . ."

Claudia glances over at Viola's white face and sways sideways. Nils pulls up a chair, but she just shakes her head.

"Sorry," she says. "It's just that . . . my older daughter, Penelope, she went through so many terrible things in El Salvador. When I think about what they did to me in that prison, when I remember how frightened Penelope was . . . She cried and called out for me, hour after hour, but I couldn't go to her. I couldn't protect her. . . ."

Claudia looks Joona in the eye and takes a step toward him, and he gently puts his arm around her. She leans heavily against his chest, catches her breath, then pulls away and fumbles for the back of the chair; she sits down without looking at her dead daughter.

"My proudest achievement . . . was making sure that little Viola was born here in Sweden. She had a beautiful room, with a pink lampshade and lots of toys and dolls; she went to school, watched *Pippi Longstocking*. . . . I don't suppose you understand, but I was so proud that she never had to be hungry or afraid. Not like us . . . like Penelope and me. We still wake up in the middle of the night, ready for someone to break in and do terrible things. . . ."

She stops speaking, then whispers, "Viola has known nothing but happiness and . . ."

Claudia leans forward and hides her face in her hands, weeping softly. Joona very gently puts his hand on her back.

"I'll go now," she says, still crying.

"There's no hurry."

She calms down, but then her face contorts into another fit of tears. "Have you spoken to Penelope?" she asks.

"We haven't been able to get in touch with her," Joona says quietly.

"Tell her I want her to call me, because . . ."

She stops herself; the color drains from her face again, and then she looks up.

"I just thought maybe she wasn't answering because I was the one calling, because I . . . I was . . . I said a terrible thing, but I didn't mean it, I didn't mean . . ."

"We've started to look for Penelope and Björn Almskog with a helicopter, but . . ."

"Please, tell me she's alive," she whispers to Joona. "Tell me that much, Joona Linna."

Joona's jaw muscles tense as he strokes Claudia's back. Then he says, "I'm going to do everything I can to—"

"She's alive. Say it!" Claudia interrupts. "She has to be alive."

"I'm going to find her," Joona says. "I know I'm going to find her."

"Say that Penelope's alive."

Joona hesitates. Thoughts flash through his head, and suddenly he hears himself say:

"She's alive."

16

JOONA HELPS CLAUDIA into a taxi, then waits until the car is out of sight before he starts to search his pockets for his phone. When he realizes he must have left it somewhere, he hurries back into The Needle's office, picks up Nils's phone, and dials Erixon's number.

"Let me sleep," Erixon says when he answers. "It's Sunday."

"You're on the boat."

"I'm on the boat," Erixon admits.

"So there weren't any explosives?" Joona says.

"Not exactly—but you were still right. It could have exploded at any moment."

"What do you mean?"

"The insulation on the cables is seriously damaged in one place. It looks like they've been pinched. . . . The metal's not touching, because that would trip the circuit, but it's exposed . . . and when you start the boat, you could easily get an electrical surge . . . and arcing."

"What?"

"This arcing has a temperature of over three thousand degrees and could easily set fire to an old cushion someone squeezed in there," Erixon goes on. "And then the fire could find its way along the tube from the fuel tank and . . ."

"So it would be fast?"

"Well ... the arcing might take ten minutes or so, maybe more ... but after that it would be pretty quick—fire, more fire, explosion. The boat would fill with water almost instantly and sink."

"So if the engine had been left running there would have been a fire and an explosion?"

"Yes, but it hasn't necessarily been done on purpose," Erixon says.

"The cables could have been damaged by accident? And the cushion could have just ended up there by chance?"

"Absolutely," he replies.

"But you don't believe that?" Joona asks.

"No."

Joona thinks about the fact that the boat was found drifting, then clears his throat and says thoughtfully, "If the murderer did this ..."

"Then he's no ordinary killer," Erixon concludes.

Joona repeats the thought to himself: they're not dealing with an ordinary murderer. Run-of-the-mill killers tend to react emotionally, even if they've planned the murder beforehand. There are always a lot of heightened emotions at play, and murders often have an element of hysteria about them. If there is a concrete plan, it usually doesn't emerge until afterward, in an effort to conceal the act and construct an alibi. But here the killer seems to have followed a very specific plan from the outset.

But something still went wrong.

Joona stares into space for a while, then writes Viola Fernandez's name on the top page of The Needle's notepad. He circles it, then adds Penelope Fernandez's and Björn Almskog's names underneath. The two women are sisters. Penelope and Björn are in a long-term relationship. Björn owns the boat. Viola asked if she could go with them at the last minute.

Identifying the motive behind a murder is a long and winding road.

If he were to follow the National Homicide Commission's template, his suspicions would be directed at Viola's boyfriend—and maybe Penelope and Björn, seeing as they were on the boat. Alcohol or drugs may have been involved. Maybe there was jealousy between them, or they had a disagreement.

Joona tries to understand why the killer would want to make the fuel tank explode. Viola was drowned in the zinc tub on deck, and then the killer carried her down to the cabin and left her on the bed.

Joona knows he's thinking about too many things at the same time. He needs to stop and begin to structure things based on what he actually knows and the questions that still need to be answered.

He draws another circle around Viola's name and starts again.

He knows that Viola was drowned in a tub and then placed on the bed in the front cabin, and that Penelope Fernandez and Björn Almskog haven't been found yet.

But that's not all, he tells himself, turning a new page.

Details.

He writes the word "calm" on the pad.

The boat was found drifting near Dalarö, on calm seas with no wind.

The front of the boat is damaged, from a forceful collision.

Joona throws Nils's notepad at the wall hard and closes his eyes.

"*Perkele*," he whispers.

Something has slipped out of his grasp again. He had it. He was on the brink of making a breakthrough, but then he lost it again.

Viola, Joona thinks. You died on the aft deck of the boat. So why were you moved after you died? Who moved you? The murderer, or someone else?

If you find someone on deck, lifeless, you probably try to resuscitate her. You call 112, that's what you do. And if you realize that she's dead, that it's already too late, maybe you don't just want to leave her lying there; you want to take her inside, cover her with a sheet. But a dead body is heavy and awkward to move, even if there are two of you. It wouldn't have been too difficult to move her into the salon. It's only five meters, through just a pair of wide glass doors and down a step.

That's possible, even without any specific intention.

But you don't drag her down a steep set of stairs and through a narrow passageway just to put her on the bed in the cabin.

You only do that if you want her to be found drowned in her room on a submerged boat.

"Exactly," he mutters, standing up.

He looks out the window at a woman riding a bicycle disappearing between the trees, and suddenly he realizes what the missing component is.

Joona sits down again and drums his fingers on the desk.

It wasn't Penelope who was found dead on the boat; it was her sister, Viola. But Viola wasn't found on her own bed, in her own cabin on the boat. She was in the front cabin, on Penelope's bed.

The murderer could have made the same mistake I did, Joona thinks, as a shiver runs down his spine.

He thought he killed Penelope Fernandez.

That's why he put her on the bed in the front cabin.

That's the only explanation.

And that means that Penelope and Björn aren't responsible for Viola's death, because they wouldn't have placed her on the wrong bed.

Joona startles as The Needle shoves the door open with his back, then comes in carrying a large oblong box covered with red flames and the words "Guitar Hero" on the front.

"Frippe and I are going to start—"

"Quiet," Joona snaps.

"What happened?" Nils asks.

"Nothing, I just need to think," he replies quickly.

Joona gets up and leaves the room without another word. He walks out of the building into the early sunshine and stops on the grass by the parking lot.

A fourth person, someone who doesn't know the two women, killed Viola, Joona thinks. He killed Viola, but he thought he killed Penelope. That means that Penelope was still alive when Viola was killed, because otherwise he wouldn't have made that mistake.

Maybe she is still alive, Joona thinks. It's possible that she's lying dead somewhere out in the archipelago, but there's every reason to hope that she's still alive and, if she is alive, that she'll be found before too much longer.

Joona strides off purposefully toward his car and sees his phone on its roof. He must have left it there when he locked the car. He calls Anja, but there's no answer. He sits in the car, trying to find a flaw in his reasoning.

The air is stuffy, but the heavy scent of the lilac bushes eventually drives the yeasty smell of the mortuary from his nostrils.

His phone rings in his hand, and he looks at the screen before answering.

"I've just been talking to your doctor," Anja says.

"Why were you talking to him?" Joona asks in surprise.

"Janush says you never show up," she chides.

"I haven't had time."

"But you're taking the medication?"

"It's disgusting," Joona jokes.

"Seriously, though . . . he called because he's worried about you," she says.

"I'll talk to him."

"When you've solved this case, you mean?"

"Do you have a pen and paper handy?" Joona asks, changing the subject.

Anja sighs. "Yes."

"The woman who was found on the boat isn't Penelope Fernandez."

"No, it was Viola. I know," she says. "Petter told me."

"Good."

"You were wrong, Joona."

"Yes, I know. . . ."

"Say it," she jokes.

"I'm always wrong," he says quietly.

Neither of them speaks for a moment.

"So we're not allowed to joke about that?" she asks tentatively.

"Have you managed to find out anything about the boat or Viola Fernandez?"

"Viola and Penelope are sisters," she says. "Penelope and Björn have been in a relationship for the past four years."

"Yes, that's pretty much what I thought."

"Okay. Do you want me to go on, or do you know everything?"

Joona doesn't answer, just leans his head back.

"Viola wasn't supposed to be on the boat with them,"

Anja goes on. "She had a fight with her boyfriend, Sergey Jarushenko, that morning, and called her mother in tears. It was her mother's idea to have her ask Penelope if she could go with them."

"What do you know about Penelope?"

"I've been prioritizing the victim, Viola, seeing as—"

"But the murderer thought he'd killed Penelope."

"Hang on, what did you just say, Joona?"

"He made a mistake. He was planning to cover the murder up, make it look like an accident, but he put Viola on her sister's bed."

"Because he thought Viola was Penelope."

"I need to know everything about Penelope Fernandez and her—"

"She's one of my biggest idols," Anja says, cutting him off. "She's a peace campaigner who lives at 3 Sankt Pauls Street."

"We have an alert out for her and Björn Almskog," Joona says. "And the coast guard has two helicopters searching the area around Dalarö, but they'll need to organize a full search of the island with the marine police."

"I'll find out what's going on," she says.

"And someone needs to talk to Viola's boyfriend, and Bill Persson, the fisherman who found her. We need a comprehensive forensics report on the boat, and we need to expedite the results from the lab."

"Do you want me to call Linköping?"

"I'll talk to Erixon; he knows them. I'll be seeing him shortly to take a look at Penelope's apartment."

"Sounds like you're in charge of the investigation."

17

THE SUMMER SKY is still clear, but the air is getting humid, as if a storm is brewing.

Joona and Erixon park outside an old bait-and-tackle store that always has pictures of people holding up salmon.

Joona's phone rings, and he sees that it's Claudia Fernandez. He walks over to the wall before answering.

"You said I could call you," she says in a weak voice.

"Of course."

"I realize that you probably say the same thing to everyone, but I was thinking. . . . My daughter, Penelope. I mean . . . I need to know if you find anything, even if . . ."

Claudia's voice fades away.

"Hello? Claudia?"

"Yes, sorry," she whispers.

"I'm a detective. . . . I look into criminal activity. The coast guard is looking for Penelope," Joona explains.

"When are they going to find her?"

"They usually start by searching the area with helicopters. They also organize a ground search of the islands, but that takes longer, so they start with helicopters."

Joona can hear Claudia trying to muffle her tears.

"I don't know what to do, I . . . I need to know if there's anything I can do. Should I keep talking to her friends?"

"The best thing to do is stay at home," Joona says. "Because Penelope might try to contact you, and then—"

"She won't call me," she interrupts.

"I think she—"

"I've always been too hard on Penelope. I get angry with her, I don't know why. I . . . I don't want to lose her. I can't lose Penelope, I . . ."

Claudia cries into the phone, tries to stop herself, apologizes, and hangs up.

The tackle shop is across from 3 Sankt Pauls Street, where Penelope lives. Joona walks over to Erixon, who is waiting for him in front of a store window full of manga pictures. The shelves are full of bobblehead dolls. The entire shop is a garish contrast to the dirty brown façade of the building.

"Big head," Erixon says, pointing at one of the bobbleheads.

"Cute," Joona mumbles.

"I got that backward. I'm stuck with a big body," Erixon jokes.

Joona smiles as he opens the wide door for him. The stairwell smells like sun, dust, and detergent. Erixon grabs the handrail, worn smooth with use, and it creaks as he heaves himself up behind Joona. They look at each other when they reach the third floor. Erixon is shaking from the exertion. He nods and wipes the sweat from his brow as he whispers an apology to Joona.

"It's hot today," Joona says.

There are several stickers by the doorbell: a peace symbol, the fair-trade logo, and an anti-nuclear-power design. Joona glances at Erixon, and his gray eyes narrow when he puts his ear to the door and listens.

"What is it?" Erixon whispers.

Still listening, Joona rings the doorbell. He waits a few seconds, then pulls a small case from his inside pocket.

"Probably nothing," he says, as he carefully picks the lock.

Joona opens the door, then seems to change his mind and closes it again. He gestures to Erixon to remain where he is, without really knowing why. They hear an ice-cream truck outside. Erixon looks worried and rubs his chin. A shiver runs through Joona's arms, but he opens the door calmly and walks in. There are newspapers, ad brochures, and a letter from the Left Party on the welcome mat. The air is still, stale. A velvet curtain has been pulled across the closet.

Joona doesn't know why, but his hand moves to his holstered pistol, which he nudges with his fingertips but doesn't draw. He looks at the curtain, then the kitchen door. He is breathing quietly, trying to see through the textured pane of glass in the door to the living room.

Joona takes a step forward, even though he really wants to get out of the apartment; instinct tells him to call for backup. Something dark moves behind the textured glass. A wind chime with dangling brass weights is swaying but makes no noise. Joona sees the motes of dust in the air change direction, following a new air current.

He's not alone in Penelope's apartment.

Joona's heart starts to beat faster. Someone is moving through the rooms; he can sense it. He turns to look at the kitchen door, and then everything happens very fast. The wooden floor creaks, and he hears a rhythmic sound, like little clicks. The door to the kitchen is half open, and Joona catches sight of movement in the crack between the hinges. He presses himself against the wall. Someone moves quickly through the darkness of the long hallway. He can just see the person's back, a shoulder, an arm. The figure approaches rapidly, then spins around. Joona catches just a glimpse of the knife, like a white tongue. It shoots up from below like a projectile. The angle is so unexpected that he doesn't have time to parry the blow, and the sharp blade cuts through his clothes; its tip hits his pistol. Joona strikes out at the figure but misses. He hears the knife slash the air a second time and throws himself back. This time the blade comes from above. Joona hits his head on the bathroom door. He sees a long splinter of wood peel off as the knife cuts into the door frame. Joona falls to the floor, rolls over, and kicks out low, in an arc. He hits something, possibly one of his attacker's ankles. He rolls away, draws his pistol, and removes the safety in the same fluid movement. The front door is open now, and he hears rapid footsteps going down the stairs. Joona gets to his feet and is about to set off after the man when he hears a rumbling sound behind him. He instantly knows what the noise is and rushes into the kitchen. The microwave is on. It's crackling, and black sparks are visible through the glass door. The valves of the four burners on top of the gas stove are open, and gas is streaming into the room. Joona throws himself at the microwave. The crackling noise is getting louder, and Joona sees a can of insect spray revolving on the glass plate inside. He pulls the plug from the wall, and the noise stops. Now the only sound is the monotonous hiss of the open burners. Joona turns off the gas. The chemical smell makes his stomach heave. He opens the kitchen window and then looks at the aerosol in the microwave, which is badly swollen; it could explode at the slightest touch.

Joona leaves the kitchen and quickly searches the rest of the apartment. The rooms are empty, untouched. The air is still thick with gas. On the landing outside the door, Erixon is lying on the floor with a cigarette in his mouth.

"Don't light it!" Joona shouts.

Erixon smiles and waves his hand.

"Chocolate cigarettes," he whispers.

He coughs weakly, and Joona suddenly sees the pool of blood beneath him.

"You're bleeding."

"Nothing too serious," he says. "I don't know how he did it, but he cut my Achilles tendon."

Joona calls for an ambulance, then sits down beside him. Erixon is pale, and his cheeks are wet with sweat. He looks distinctly ill.

"He cut me without even stopping. It was . . . it was like being attacked by a ninja."

They fall silent, and Joona thinks about the lightning-fast movements behind the door and the way the knife moved with a speed and a purposefulness unlike anything he's ever experienced.

"Is she in there?" Erixon pants.

"No."

Erixon smiles with relief.

"But he was still planning to blow the place up?" he asks.

"Presumably, to get rid of evidence," Joona says.

Erixon tries to peel the paper from the chocolate cigarette but drops it and closes his eyes. His cheeks are grayish white now.

"I take it you didn't see his face, either," Joona says.

"No," Erixon says weakly.

"But we saw something. People always see something. . . ."

18

THE PARAMEDICS repeatedly reassure Erixon that they're not going to drop him.

"I can walk," Erixon says, shutting his eyes.

His chin trembles with every step they take.

Joona returns to Penelope's apartment. He opens the rest of the windows, airing out the gas, and sits down on the comfortable apricot-colored sofa.

If the apartment had exploded, it would probably have been written off as an accident caused by a gas leak.

Joona reminds himself that memories never disappear, and nothing you see is ever lost. You just need to let it drift up from the depths like flotsam.

So what did I see, then?

He didn't see anything, just rapid movement and a white knife blade.

That was what I saw, Joona suddenly thinks. Nothing.

He tells himself that the very absence of observation supports the idea that they're not dealing with a typical murderer.

They're dealing with a professional hit man, a problem solver, a fixer. And that means someone else, someone very powerful, is behind this.

He already had his suspicions, but after this encounter he's convinced.

He's sure that the person he met in the hallway is the same person who murdered Viola. His intention had been to kill Penelope, sink the yacht, and make the whole thing look like an accident. It was the same pattern here, before he was disturbed. He wants to remain invisible, to get on with his business but hide it from the police.

Joona looks around slowly, trying to gather his scattered observations into a coherent whole.

It sounds as if children are rolling balls across the floor in the apartment upstairs. They would have been trapped in an inferno of fire if Joona hadn't pulled the microwave's plug in time.

He's never been subjected to such a deliberate, dangerous attack before. He's convinced that the person who was inside the peace campaigner Penelope Fernandez's home isn't a member of a fascist hate group. Those groups may sometimes carefully plan acts of violence, but this individual is a trained professional in a league above any of the extreme right-wing groups in Sweden.

So what were you doing here? Joona asks himself. *What is a fixer doing with Penelope? What has she gotten herself caught up in?*

He thinks about the man's unpredictable movements. The knife technique he used was designed to get past any standard defensive maneuvers, including techniques taught by the police and military.

He shivers when he realizes that the first blow would have hit his liver if his pistol hadn't been hanging below his right arm, and the second would have hit his head if he hadn't thrown himself backward.

Joona goes into the bedroom, where he looks at the neatly made bed and the crucifix hanging above it.

A hit man thought he had murdered Penelope, and his intention was to make it look like an accident. . . .

But the boat didn't sink.

Either the murderer was interrupted, or he left the scene of the crime intending to return later and finish the job. But he certainly couldn't have meant for the boat to be found drifting by with a drowned girl on board. Something went wrong along the way, or else his plans changed suddenly. Maybe he received new orders, but, for whatever reason, a day and half after Viola's murder, he was in Penelope's apartment.

You must have had very strong reasons for breaking into her apartment. What would motivate you to take a risk like that? Was there something there that connects you or whoever sent you to Penelope?

You did something here: removed fingerprints, erased a computer file or a message on an answering machine, or collected something, Joona thinks.

That was what you were planning, anyway, but maybe you were interrupted when I arrived.

Maybe you were planning to use the fire to get rid of the evidence?

It's a possibility.

Joona could use Erixon right now. He can't conduct a crime-scene investigation without a forensics expert. He doesn't have the right equipment, and he could ruin evidence if he were to search the apartment on his own. He might contaminate DNA and miss invisible clues.

Joona goes over to the window and looks down at the street.

He realizes he's going to have to go to police headquarters and talk to his boss, Carlos, and ask to be put in charge of the investigation. That's the only way to get access to another forensics expert who can help while Erixon is injured.

Joona's phone rings just as he makes up his mind to go talk to Carlos and Svanehjälm and put together a small investigative team.

"Hi, Anja," he says.

"I'd like to have a sauna with you."

"A sauna?"

"Yes, can't the two of us have a sauna together? You could show me what a proper Finnish sauna is like."

"Anja," he says slowly, "I've lived almost my entire life here in Stockholm."

He goes out into the hallway, then heads for the front door.

"You're a Swedish Finn, I know," Anja goes on. "Could there be anything more boring? Why can't you be from El Salvador? Have you read any of Penelope Fernandez's articles? And you should've seen her the other day, when she went on the attack against Swedish arms exports on television."

As Joona leaves Penelope's apartment, he sees the paramedics' bloody footprints on the stairs and feels his scalp prickle at the thought of his colleague lying in the hall with his legs wide apart, his face getting paler and paler.

Joona thinks again about the fact that the fixer thought he had killed Penelope Fernandez, and so that part of his job was done. The second part involved breaking into her apartment, for some reason. If she's still alive, finding her has to be a priority, because it won't be long before the fixer realizes his mistake and goes after her.

"Björn and Penelope don't live together," Anja says.

"Yes, I gathered that," he replies.

"People can still love each other even if they live apart—just like you and me."

"Yes."

Joona emerges into the strong sunshine. The air is heavy, and it's even more humid than it was earlier. "Can you give me Björn's address?"

Anja's fingers fly over her keyboard with tiny clicking sounds.

"Almskog, 47 Pontonjär Street, second floor . . ."

"I'll head over there before—"

"Hang on," Anja says abruptly. "Not possible . . . Listen to this: I've just double-checked the address. There was a fire in the building on Friday."

"And Björn's apartment?"

"That entire floor was destroyed," she replies.

19

JOONA GOES UP THE STAIRS, then stands absolutely still as he gazes into a black room. The floor, walls, and ceiling are badly burned, and there's still a strong acrid smell. Practically nothing is left of the internal walls. Black stalactites hang from the ceiling, and charred stumps rise up from within an undulating landscape of ash where posts used to be. In some places, you can see through the beams to the rooms below. It's no longer possible to tell where Björn's apartment was.

Gray plastic has been hung over the empty windows, blocking out the summer day.

The only reason no one was injured in the fire at 47 Pontonjär Street is that most people were at work when it broke out.

Emergency services got the first call at five after eleven. Even though the Kungsholmen fire station is very close to the building, the fire spread so rapidly that four apartments were completely destroyed.

Joona thinks about his conversation with Fire Investigator Hassan Sükür. He categorized the fire as being at the second-highest level on the official scale and explained that their findings indicated that the fire had started in the home of Björn's eighty-year-old neighbor, Lisbet Wirén. She had gone down to the shop on the corner to cash a small win on a lottery scratch card and exchange it for two new cards, and she couldn't remember if she'd left the iron on. The fire department found the remains of an iron and an ironing board in Wirén's living room.

Joona looks around at the charred remains of the apartments on that floor. All that is left of the furniture is a few twisted metal shapes, part of a fridge, a mattress frame, and a sooty bathtub.

When Joona goes back downstairs, he sees that the walls and ceiling of the stairwell have smoke damage. He stops at the police cordon and looks up toward the blackness again.

As he bends down to pass under the tape, he sees that the fire investigators dropped on the floor a few ziplock bags, used to secure fluids. Joona walks through the green marble hall and out onto the street, toward police headquarters, taking his phone out to call Hassan Sükür again. Hassan answers immediately, lowering the volume on a radio.

"Have you found any trace of flammable liquids?" Joona asks. "You dropped some ziplock bags in the stairwell, and I was wondering . . ."

"Look, if someone uses any sort of flammable liquid to start a fire, then, obviously, that burns first. . . ."

"I know, but . . ."

"But I can usually find evidence of it anyway," he goes on. "Because often it runs between cracks in the floorboards, or it ends up in the insulation or trapped between floors."

"But not this time?" Joona asks as he walks down Hantverkar Street.

"Nothing," Hassan says.

"But if someone knew where traces of flammable liquids are often found, it would be possible to avoid detection."

"Of course . . . I'd never make a mistake like that if I was a pyromaniac," Hassan replies brightly.

"You're still convinced that the iron was the cause of this particular fire?"

"Yes, it was an accident."

"So you've dropped the investigation?" Joona asks.

20

Terror seizes Penelope again. She wipes the tears from her cheeks and tries to stand up. Cold sweat runs down her sides and between her breasts. Her body aches, and blood is seeping through the dirt on her hands.

It's still dark in the forest, but night is slowly turning to morning. Together they walk quickly down toward the shore again, far to the south of the house with the party.

The forest opens up gradually as they approach the water, and they start running again. Between the trees, they see another house, half a kilometer away, maybe less.

Björn seems dazed, and whenever Penelope sees him lean on the ground or against a tree, she worries that he won't be able to run anymore.

A branch creaks somewhere behind them, as if it's been snapped by someone standing on it.

Penelope starts to run through the forest as fast as she can.

The trees are thinning out, and she can see the house again, just a hundred meters away. The lights in the window are reflecting off the red paint of a Ford parked outside.

Panting and wary, they emerge onto the gravel driveway.

They walk up the front steps, open the door to the porch, and go inside.

"Hello? We need help!" Penelope calls.

The house is warm from the sun. Björn is limping, and his bare feet leave bloody prints on the floor.

The house is empty. They've probably slept over at their neighbors' after the party, she thinks, standing at the window and looking out. She waits for a while but can't detect any movement in the forest, on the lawn, or on the driveway. Maybe their pursuer has finally lost track of them, or maybe he's still waiting at the other house. She goes back to the entryway, where Björn is sitting on the floor, looking at the wounds on his feet.

"We need to find you a pair of shoes," she says.

He looks up at her with a blank expression, as though she is speaking a foreign language.

"This isn't over," she says. "You need to put something on your feet."

Björn starts to hunt through the closet in the entryway, pulling out flip-flops and Wellington boots.

Penelope hunts as quickly as she can for a phone, avoiding all the windows. She checks the table in the entryway, the briefcase on the sofa, the bowl on the coffee table, and searches through the keys and paperwork on the kitchen counter.

There's a sound outside, and she stops to listen.

Maybe it was nothing.

Crouching, she hurries into the main bedroom and pulls out the drawers in an old chest. The drawers are empty. Penelope opens the closet, pulls the few items of clothing from their hangers, and takes a knit sweater and a hoodie that looks like something a fifteen-year-old would wear.

She hears a faucet running in the kitchen and hurries in. Björn is leaning over the sink, drinking water. He has a pair of old sneakers on his feet, a couple of sizes too big.

We have to find someone who can help us, she thinks. *This is getting ridiculous. There must be people here.*

Penelope goes over to Björn and hands him the sweater. Suddenly there's a knock at the door. Björn smiles in surprise, pulls the sweater on, and mutters something about finally having a bit of luck. Penelope walks toward the entryway, brushing her hair from her face. She's almost there when she sees the silhouette through the frosted glass.

She stops abruptly, looking at the shadow through the glass. She can't bring herself to reach out her hand and open the door. She recognizes his posture, the shape of his head and shoulders.

Slowly, she backs away into the kitchen. Her body is twitching. She wants to run; her whole body wants to run. She stares at the glass window, at the indistinct face, the narrow chin. She feels dizzy as she moves backward, trampling over bags and boots. She reaches out to the wall for support and runs her fingers across the wallpaper, knocking a mirror askew.

Björn stops beside her. He's clutching a broad-bladed kitchen knife in his hand. His cheeks are white, and his mouth is half open. He's staring at the window in the door.

Penelope backs into a table as she sees the door handle slowly being pushed down. She goes into the bathroom quickly and turns the faucet on, then calls out in a loud voice, "Come in! The door's open!"

Björn startles. He's holding the knife in front of him, ready to defend himself, to attack, as he sees their pursuer slowly let go of the door handle. The silhouette disappears from the window, and a few seconds later he hears footsteps on the gravel path beside the house. Björn glances to his right. Penelope comes out of the bathroom. He points to the window in the television room, and they move into the kitchen as they hear the man walk across the wooden deck. Penelope tries to figure out what their pursuer can see, wondering if the angles and light will reveal the shoes scattered across the entryway, Björn's bloody footprints on the floor. The deck creaks again. He's making his way around the house, toward the kitchen window. Björn and Penelope huddle together on the floor, pressing against the wall beneath the window. They try to lie still and breathe quietly. They hear him at the window. His hands slide across the sill, and they realize he's looking into the kitchen.

Penelope can see their pursuer reflected in the glass door of the oven. He's looking around the room. It occurs to her that he'd be looking her right in the eye if he happened to look at the oven door. It won't be long before he realizes that they're hiding in there.

The face in the window disappears. They hear footsteps across the deck again, then along the gravel path leading to the front of the house. When the front door opens, Björn walks quickly over to the kitchen door, puts the knife down, turns the key that's sitting in the lock, pushes the door open, and rushes out.

Penelope follows him, remembering something she read once. There was a woman in Rwanda who survived the Hutus' genocide of the Tutsis by hiding in marshes and running every day. She ran as long as the genocide lasted. Her former neighbors and friends came after her with machetes. *We imitated the antelope*, the woman explained. *Those of us who survived in the jungle imitated the antelope's flight from its predators. We ran, we chose unexpected paths, we split up and changed direction to confuse our pursuers.*

Penelope knows that the way she and Björn are running is completely wrong. There's no guile to it. And their pursuer understands that they're trying to find help.

21

THE MAIN OFFICES of the Security Police are on the third floor of police headquarters. The sound of a whistle can be heard from the top floor, which houses the exercise yard of the prison.

Verner Zandén is the head of the Security Police. He is a tall man with a pointed nose, jet-black eyes, and a very deep voice. He's sitting on the chair behind his desk, holding up a calming hand. Weak light is coming in through the little window facing the inner courtyard. The room smells like dust and hot lightbulbs. In this drab room stands a young woman named Saga Bauer. She is a twenty-five-year-old detective who specializes in counterterrorism. She has green, yellow, and red ribbons threaded through her long blond hair, and looks like an illustration of a wood nymph, except that she is wearing a large-caliber pistol in a shoulder holster beneath a hoodie with the Narva Boxing Club logo on it.

"I've led the operation for more than a year," she pleads. "I've done the surveillance, I've spent nights and weekends—"

"But this is different," her boss interrupts with a smile.

"Please . . . You can't just ignore me again."

"Ignore you? A forensics expert from National Crime has been seriously injured, a detective has been attacked, the apartment could have exploded, and—"

"I know all that. I'm on my way there now. . . ."

"I've already sent Göran Stone."

"Göran Stone? I've worked here for three years, and I haven't been allowed to finish a single case. This is my area of expertise. Göran doesn't know anything about—"

"He did well in the tunnels."

Saga swallows hard before replying: "That was my case, too. I found the link between—"

Verner says seriously, "But it got dangerous, and I still think I made the right decision."

She composes herself, and then says calmly: "I can do this. It's what I've been trained to . . ."

"Yes, but I've already made my decision."

He rubs his nose, sighs, then puts his feet up on the wastebasket under the desk.

"You know I'm not here because of some equal-opportunity program," Saga says slowly. "I'm not part of any quota. I got top grades on all the tests. I'm the best sniper the department's ever had. I've investigated two hundred and ten different—"

"I'm just worried about you," he says.

"I'm not a doll."

"But you're so . . . so . . ."

Verner turns bright red, and then he holds his hands up helplessly.

"Okay, what the hell, you can be in charge of the investigation, but Göran is part of the team, so he can keep an eye on you."

"Thanks," she says with a relieved smile.

"This isn't a game, remember that," he says in his deep voice. "Penelope Fernandez's sister is dead, executed, and Penelope is missing. . . ."

"And I've noticed an increase in activity among a number of extremist left-wing groups," Saga says. "We're investigating whether the Revolutionary Front are behind the theft of explosives in Vaxholm."

"Obviously, the most important thing is to find out if there's any immediate threat," Verner explains.

"Right now, there's a lot of radicalization going on," she says, a little too eagerly. "I've just been in touch with Dante Larsson at the Military Intelligence and Security Service, and he says they're expecting several acts of sabotage during the summer."

"But for the time being we're concentrating on Penelope Fernandez," Verner says, smiling.

"Of course," Saga says quickly. "Of course."

"The forensics examination is a collaboration with National Crime, but, other than that, they're to be kept out of it."

Saga Bauer nods and waits a few moments before asking: "Am I going to be allowed to conclude this investigation? It's very important to me, so that—"

"As long as you're still sitting in the saddle," he interrupts. "But we have no idea where this is going to end. We don't even know where it starts."

22

On Rekyl Street in Västerås there's a very long white housing complex. The people who live there have easy access to Lillhags School, the soccer field, and tennis courts.

A sixteen-year-old boy carrying a motorcycle helmet in one hand comes out of the door to number 11. His name is Stefan Bergkvist, and he attends the technical college and lives with his mom and her partner. He has long fair hair, and he's wearing a black T-shirt and baggy jeans.

He ambles down to the parking lot, hangs the helmet on the handlebars of his motocross bike, rides slowly onto the path around the building, and then heads under the viaduct, into the industrial complex; here he stops next to a wooden shack covered with blue-and-silver graffiti.

Stefan and his friends usually meet here to race on the circuit they've made along the railway embankment, riding up and down the various tracks before returning to Terminal Street.

They started coming here four years ago, when they found the keys to the abandoned shack hidden on a nail at the back.

Stefan gets off his bike, unlocks the padlock, and goes inside the shack. When he checks the time on his phone, he sees that his mom's called.

He doesn't notice that he's being watched by an over-weight man of about sixty wearing a gray suede jacket and light-brown shoes. His clothes are clearly well made, but worn and rumpled. The man is standing behind a dumpster by the building on the other side of the railroad tracks.

Stefan goes over to the little kitchen, picks up a bag of chips from the sink, and eats the last few crumbs.

The light inside the shack comes from two dirty windows with bars across them.

Stefan waits for his friends, leafing through one of the old magazines that were left on top of the map cabinet, a copy of a soft-porn magazine.

The man in the suede jacket calmly leaves his hiding place and crosses the brown embankment. He goes over to Stefan's motorcycle and wheels it over to the door of the shack.

The man looks around, then leans the motorcycle on the ground and pushes it with his foot so that it's wedged tightly against the door. He opens the fuel tank and lets the gas run out beneath the shack.

Stefan flips through the old magazine, looking at faded photographs of women in a prison setting. One blonde woman is sitting in a cell with her legs wide apart, showing her genitals to a prison guard. Stefan stares at the picture, then jumps when he hears a rustling sound from outside. He listens, thinks he can hear footsteps, and quickly closes the magazine.

The man in the suede jacket has pulled out the red gas-can the boys hide among the bushes and is emptying it around the shack. Only when he reaches the back wall does he hear the shouts from inside. The boy is banging on the door, trying to push it open. His footsteps thud across the floor, and his worried face appears at one of the dirty windows.

"Open the door. This isn't funny!" he shouts loudly.

The man in the suede jacket walks around the shack, empties the last of the gas, then puts the can down.

"What are you doing?" the boy cries.

He throws himself at the door, trying to kick it open, but it won't budge. He calls his mom, but her phone is switched off. His heart is beating hard as he tries to look through the gray-streaked windows, moving from one to the other.

"Are you crazy?"

When he notices the acrid smell of gas, fear rises up inside him, and his stomach clenches.

"Hello?" he shouts in a frightened voice. "I know you're still there!"

The man pulls a box of matches from his pocket.

"What do you want? Please, just tell me what you want. . . ."

"Sometimes nightmares come true," the man says without raising his voice. He lights a match.

"Let me out!" the boy screams.

The man drops the match in the wet grass. There's a sucking sound, like a big sail suddenly filling with air. Pale-blue flames shoot up with such ferocity that the man is forced to take several steps back. The boy cries for help. The flames surround the shack. The man keeps backing away as he feels the heat on his face and hears the terrified screams.

The shack is ablaze in a matter of seconds, and the glass shatters in the heat.

The boy shrieks when the flames set his hair on fire.

The man walks across the railroad tracks, stands beside the industrial building, and watches the old shack burn.

A few minutes later, a freight train approaches from the north. It comes rolling slowly down the track, and with a scraping, rattling sound the row of brown wagons passes the dancing flames as the man in the suede jacket vanishes along Stenby Street.

23

EVEN THOUGH it's the weekend, Carlos is in his office. The door is closed and, as usual, to avoid visitors, he has switched on the "engaged" light he had specially installed. Joona knocks and opens the door in a single movement.

"I need to know if the marine police find anything," he says.

Carlos puts his book down on the desk and calmly replies: "You and Erixon were attacked. That's a traumatic experience, and you need to take care of yourselves."

"We will," Joona says.

"The helicopter search is over."

Joona stiffens. "Over? How large of an area did—"

"I don't know," Carlos interrupts.

"Who's in charge of the operation?"

"It's out of our hands," Carlos explains. "The marine police are—"

"But it would be useful to know if we're investigating one or three murders," Joona says sharply.

"Joona, right now you're not investigating anything. I've discussed the matter with Jens Svanehjälm. We're putting together a joint team with the Security Police. Petter will represent National Crime, Tommy Kofoed the National Homicide Commission, and—"

"What's my role?"

"Take a week off."

"No."

"Then go out to the Police Academy and give some lectures."

"No."

"Don't be stubborn," Carlos says. "That obstinacy of yours isn't as charming as—"

"I don't give a damn what you think," Joona says. "Penelope—"

"You don't give a damn about me?" Carlos says in astonishment. "I'm head of—"

"Penelope Fernandez and Björn Almskog could still be alive," Joona continues in a hard voice. "His apartment has been burned down, and hers would have been if I hadn't gotten there in time. I think the murderer is looking for something that they have. I think he tried to get Viola to talk before he drowned her—"

"Thank you very much," Carlos interrupts, raising his voice. "Thank you for your interesting ideas, but we've— No, let me finish. I know you have trouble accepting this, Joona, but you're not the only police officer in the country. And most of the others are very good, you know."

"Agreed," Joona says slowly. "And you should take care of them, Carlos."

Joona looks at the brown stains on his cuffs from Erixon's blood.

"What do you mean?"

"I met the killer, and I think we need to be prepared for police fatalities in this case."

"You were taken by surprise. I understand it was unpleasant. . . ."

"Okay," Joona says harshly.

"Tommy Kofoed is in charge of the crime-scene investigation, and I'll call Britta at the Police Academy and tell her you'll be a guest lecturer next week," Carlos says.

THE SUMMER HEAT hits Joona when he emerges from police headquarters. As he takes his jacket off, he realizes that someone is approaching him from behind, stepping out between the parked cars. He turns around and sees that it's Penelope's mother, Claudia.

"Joona Linna," she says in a tense voice.

"Claudia, how are you?" he asks gravely.

She just shakes her head. Her eyes are bloodshot, and her face looks anguished.

"Find her. You have to find my little girl," she says, handing him a thick envelope.

Joona opens the envelope and sees that it's full of banknotes. He tries to give it back, but she won't take it.

"Please, take the money. It's all I have," she says, "but I can get more—I'll sell the house—as long as you find her."

"Claudia, I can't take your money," he says.

Her tormented face crumples. "Please . . ."

"We're doing everything we can."

Joona gives the envelope back to Claudia, and she holds it stiffly in her hand, then mumbles that she'll go home and wait by the phone. She stops him and tries to explain: "I told her not to come to my place anymore. . . . She's never going to call me."

"You had an argument, Claudia, but that's not the end of the world."

"But how could I say that? Can you imagine?" she asks, rapping her knuckles against her forehead. "Who says a thing like that to their own child?"

"It's easy to just . . ."

Joona's voice trails off. He feels his back sweating and forces himself to suppress his memories.

"I can't bear it," Claudia says quietly.

Joona takes Claudia's hands and tells her he's doing all he can.

"You have to get my daughter back," she whispers.

He nods, and they go their separate ways. Joona hurries down Berg Street and peers up at the sky as he walks to his car. It's sunny but a little hazy, and still very humid. Last summer, he was sitting in the hospital, holding his mother's hand. As usual, they spoke Finnish to each other. He told her they'd go to Karelia together as soon as she felt better. She was born there, in a little village.

Joona buys a bottle of Pellegrino from Il Caffè and drinks it before getting into the warm car. The steering wheel is hot, and the seat burns his back. Instead of driving to the Police Academy, he drives back to Penelope's apartment. He thinks about the man he encountered there. His movements had a remarkable speed and precision to them, as if the knife itself had been alive.

Blue-and-white tape has been strung up across the door, with the words "Police" and "No Entry" on it.

Joona shows his ID to the uniformed officer on guard and shakes his hand. They've met before but never worked together.

"Hot today," Joona says.

"Just a bit," the police officer says.

"How many forensics people do we have?" he asks, nodding toward the stairwell.

"One of ours and three from the Security Police," the officer says brightly. "They want to get DNA as quickly as possible."

"They won't find any," Joona says, almost to himself, as he starts to walk toward the stairs.

An older police officer, Melker Janos, is standing outside the door to the third-floor apartment. Joona remembers him from training as an unpleasant senior officer. Back then, Melker's career was on the rise, but an acrimonious divorce and sporadic alcohol abuse gradually got him demoted to a beat officer again. When he sees Joona, he greets him curtly and irritably, then opens the door for him with a sarcastic servile gesture.

"Thanks," Joona says.

Inside, he finds Kofoed scuttling about sullenly. Kofoed only comes up to Joona's chest. When their eyes meet, he opens his mouth in an almost childishly happy grin.

"Joona, great to see you. I thought you were going to the Police Academy."

"I got the directions wrong."

"Good."

"Did you find anything?" Joona asks.

"We've got all the shoeprints from the hall," he says.

"They probably match my shoes," Joona says as he shakes Kofoed's hand.

"And the attacker's," Kofoed says with an even broader smile. "We've got four prints. He moved in a weird way, didn't he?"

"Yes," Joona replies curtly.

Protective mats are laid out in the entryway. The forensics team has looked for invisible shoeprints by shining light almost parallel to the floor. Then they've taken the prints electrostatically and identified the killer's steps through the hall from the kitchen.

Joona can't help thinking that their precision is a waste of effort. The attacker's shoes, gloves, and clothes have almost certainly already been destroyed.

"How exactly did he run through here?" Kofoed asks, pointing at the marks. "There, there . . . and then across to there; then there's nothing until here and here."

"You missed one," Joona says, smiling.

"Like hell we have."

"There." Joona points.

"Where?"

"On the wall."

"Holy shit."

Some seventy centimeters above the floor, there's a faint shoeprint on the pale-gray wallpaper. Kofoed calls one of his colleagues and asks him to take a gelatin print.

"Is it okay to walk on the floor now?" Joona asks.

"As long as you don't walk on the walls," Kofoed grunts.

24

A MAN IN JEANS and a light-brown blazer with leather elbow patches is standing in the kitchen. He strokes his blond mustache as he talks loudly and points at the microwave. Joona walks in and watches as an officer in a protective mask and gloves packs the buckled aerosol can into a paper bag.

"You're Joona Linna, aren't you?" the man with the blond mustache says. "If you're as good as everyone says, you should come over to us."

They shake hands.

"Göran Stone, Security Police," the man says proudly.

"Are you in charge of the investigation?"

"Yes, I am . . . Well, formally, Saga Bauer is—for the sake of statistics." He grins.

"I've met Saga," Joona says. "She seems capable of . . ."

"Doesn't she, just?" Göran says, then bursts out laughing.

Joona looks out the window and thinks about the boat that was found adrift. He knows it's far too early in the investigation to draw any conclusions, but it's always useful to consider different hypotheses. The only person the killer was almost certainly after was Penelope, Joona thinks. And the only person he probably didn't mean to kill was Viola, because he couldn't have known that she was going to be on the boat, Joona tells himself as he walks to the bedroom.

The bed is neatly made, the cream-colored bedspread smooth. Saga Bauer is standing in front of a laptop that she's placed on the windowsill as she talks on her phone. Joona remembers her from a counterterrorism seminar.

Joona sits down on the bed and tries to gather his thoughts. He imagines Viola and Penelope standing in front of him, then puts Penelope's boyfriend, Björn, next to them. They can't all have been on the boat when Viola was murdered, he tells himself, or the killer wouldn't have made his mistake. If he got on board when they were out at sea, he would have murdered all three, put them on the right beds, and sunk the boat. So Penelope can't have been on the boat. Which means they must have been docked somewhere.

Joona walks into the living room. He looks at the wall-mounted television, the red sofa, the coffee table with its piles of magazines and newspapers, then walks over to the floor-to-ceiling bookcase on one wall, stops, and thinks about the pinched cables that could have blown the ship up. But the boat didn't sink. The engine can't have been running for long enough.

There's no such thing as coincidence here.

Björn's apartment was destroyed, Viola was murdered the same day, and if the boat hadn't been abandoned, the fuel tank would have exploded.

Then the murderer attempted to set off a gas explosion in Penelope's apartment.

Björn's apartment, the boat, Penelope's apartment.

He wants something that Björn and Penelope have. He started by searching through Björn's apartment, and when he didn't find what he was looking for, he burned it. Then, when he didn't find anything on the boat, he tried to force Viola to talk, and when she couldn't give him any answers, he went to Penelope's apartment.

Joona helps himself to a pair of protective gloves, then goes back to the bookcase and looks at the thin layer of dust in front of the books. He notes that there's no dust in front of some of the spines, suggesting that someone has looked at those books in the past few weeks.

"I don't want you here," Saga says behind him. "This is my investigation."

"I'll go in a minute. I just need to find something first," Joona replies quietly.

"Five minutes," she says.

He turns around. "Can you photograph the books?"

"Already done," she says curtly.

"From a certain angle you can see the dust," he goes on, unconcerned.

She realizes what he means, but her expression doesn't change; she just borrows a camera from one of the officers, photographs all the shelves she can reach, then tells him he can look at the books on the bottom five shelves.

Joona pulls out Karl Marx's *Capital*, leafs through it, and notices that it's full of underlined passages and notes in the margins. He peers into the gap between the books but can't see anything. He moves on to a biography of Ulrike Meinhof, a worn anthology entitled *Key Texts of Political Feminism*, and the collected works of Bertolt Brecht.

On the second shelf up, he spots three books that have evidently been pulled out from the bookcase recently: *The Strategy of Antelopes*, a book about the genocide in Rwanda; *Cien sonetos de amor*, a collection of Pablo Neruda's poetry; and *The Intellectual Roots of Swedish Eugenics*.

Joona flips through them one at a time, and when he reaches the last one, a photograph falls out. It's a black-and-white photograph of a serious-looking girl with tightly braided hair. He recognizes Claudia Fernandez at once. She can't be more than fifteen in the photograph, and she looks strikingly similar to her daughters.

But who would put a photograph of her mother in a book about eugenics? he asks himself, turning the picture over.

On the back of the photograph, someone has written, "*No estés lejos de mí un solo día,*" in pencil.

It's clearly a line from a poem: "Don't go far off, not even for a day."

Joona pulls out the volume of Neruda's poetry again, leafs through it, and soon finds the whole first verse.

This is where the photograph should have been.

But if the murderer was searching the books for something, the picture could have fallen out.

He stood here, Joona thinks, and looked at the dust on the shelves, just like me, and quickly leafed through the books that had been pulled out recently. Then he must have noticed that a photograph fell out onto the floor and put it back, but in the wrong book.

Joona closes his eyes.

The fixer searched these books.

If he knew what he was looking for, that means the object can fit between the pages of a book.

So what could it be?

25

JOONA LEAVES the living room and looks into the bathroom, which is in the process of being photographed in detail. He walks out through the open front door to the landing and stops in front of the mesh covering the elevator shaft.

The name Nilsson is on the door next to the elevator. He raises his hand and knocks, then waits. After a while, he hears footsteps inside. A rotund woman in her sixties opens the door and peers out.

"Yes?"

"Hello, my name is Joona Linna. I'm a detective, and I—"

"I already told you, I didn't see his face," she interrupts.

"Did the police already speak to you? I didn't know that."

"He was wearing a Dracula mask," the woman says impatiently, as if she's already explained this numerous times.

"Who?"

"Who," she mutters, walking into the apartment.

She returns shortly afterward with a yellowing newspaper clipping. Joona glances at the article, which is twenty years old, about a flasher who dressed up as Dracula when he exposed himself to women on Södermalm.

"He didn't have anything on down below. . . ."

"I was actually—"

"Not that I looked," she goes on. "But I already told your people all about it."

Joona looks at her and smiles.

"I was actually thinking about something completely different."

The woman opens her eyes wide. "Then why didn't you say so?"

"I was wondering if you know Penelope Fernandez, your neighbor, who—"

"She's like a granddaughter to me," the woman interrupts. "Such a sweet girl. So kind and pretty and—"

She stops abruptly, then asks quietly: "Is she dead?"

"Why do you ask?"

"Because the police have been here, asking horrible questions," she says.

"I was just wondering if she had any unusual visitors in the past few days."

"Just because I'm old doesn't mean I poke my nose into other people's business and keep tabs on what they do."

"Of course not. I was just thinking that you might have happened to notice something."

"Well, I haven't."

"Has anything else out of the ordinary happened?"

"Definitely not. She's a very smart, well-behaved girl."

Joona thanks her for her time and says that he may come back if he has more questions, then stands aside so the woman can close the door.

There are no other apartments on the third floor. He starts to walk up the stairs, but halfway up he sees a child sitting on one of the steps. It looks like an eight-year-old boy: short hair, jeans, and a washed-out T-shirt, clutching a plastic bag with a water bottle, its label almost rubbed off, and half a loaf of bread.

Joona stops in front of the child, who looks up at him warily.

"Hello," he says. "What's your name?"

"Mia."

"Mine's Joona."

He notices the dirt on the girl's thin neck.

"Do you have a gun?" she asks.

"Why do you ask?"

"You told Ella that you're a policeman."

"That's right—I'm a detective."

"Do you have a gun?"

"Yes, I do," Joona says in a neutral voice. "Do you want to practice shooting it?"

The child looks at him in astonishment. "You're kidding?"

"Yeah," Joona says with a smile.

The child laughs.

"Why are you sitting on the stairs?" he asks.

"I like it. You get to hear stuff."

Joona sits down beside her.

"What kind of stuff have you heard?" he asks calmly.

"I just heard that you're a policeman, and I heard Ella lie to you."

"What did she lie to me about?"

"When she said she likes Penelope," Mia says.

"Doesn't she?"

"She puts cat poo through her mail slot."

"Why does she do that?"

The girl shrugs and fiddles with the plastic bag. "I don't know."

"What do you think of Penelope?"

"She usually says hello."

"But you don't really know her?"

"No."

Joona looks around.

"Do you live on the stairs?"

The girl tries not to smile.

"No, I live on the first floor, with my mom."

"But you hang out on the stairs."

Mia shrugs again. "Most of the time."

"Do you sleep here?"

The girl picks at the label on the bottle and says quickly, "Sometimes."

"On Friday," Joona says slowly, "very early in the morning, Penelope left her apartment. She took a taxi."

"She was really unlucky," the child says quickly. "She missed Björn by a few seconds. He arrived just after she left. I told him she'd just gone."

"What did he say?"

"That it didn't matter, because he was only going to pick something up."

"Pick something up?"

Mia nods.

"He usually lets me borrow his phone to play games, but he didn't have time that day; he just went into the apartment and came back out again right away; then he locked the door and ran down the stairs."

"Did you see what he picked up?"

"No."

"What happened after that?"

"Nothing. I went to school at eight-forty-five."

"What about after school, later that day? Did anything happen then?"

Mia shrugged again. "Mom was out, so I stayed at home. I had some macaroni and watched TV."

"How about yesterday?"

"She was gone yesterday, too, so I was home."

"So you didn't see anyone coming and going?"

"No."

Joona pulls out his card and writes a phone number on it. "Take this, Mia," he says. "These are two really good phone numbers. One of them's mine."

He points at the number printed on the card beside the police logo.

"Call me if you ever need help, if anyone's mean to you. And the other number, the one I've just written, 0200-230230, that's the number for Childline. You can call them anytime and talk about whatever you like."

"Okay," Mia says, taking the card.

"And don't throw it away as soon as I leave," Joona says. "Because even if you don't want to call now, you might want to later."

"Björn was holding his hand like this when he left," Mia says, holding her hand to her stomach.

"As if he had a tummyache?"

"Yes."

26

JOONA KNOCKS on the other doors in the building but doesn't learn anything else, beyond the fact that Penelope is a fairly quiet, almost shy neighbor who has taken part in annual cleaning days and residents' committee meetings but not much else. When he's finished, he walks slowly back down the stairs to the third floor.

Penelope's apartment door is open. One of the Security Police's forensics experts has just dismantled the lock and placed it in a plastic bag.

Joona goes in and stands in the background, watching. He's always liked seeing the experts at work—how systematically they photograph everything, the way they secure all the evidence and make careful notes about each part of the process. A crime-scene investigation destroys evidence as it proceeds—things get contaminated as the layers are stripped back—which means it's important to wreck the crime scene in the right order, so that no evidence or vital clues are lost.

Joona looks around at Penelope's neat apartment. What was Björn doing here? He showed up as soon as Penelope left, almost as if he'd been hiding outside the building, waiting for her to go.

It could just be a coincidence, but it's also possible that he didn't want to see her.

Björn hurried inside and bumped into the little girl on the stairs. He didn't have time to talk to her, but he explained that he was going to pick something up. He was only in the apartment for a few minutes.

Presumably, he did take something, as he told the child. Maybe he'd hidden the key to the boat there, or something else he could slip into his pocket.

But what if he just needed to look at something, check some information—maybe a phone number?

Joona goes into the kitchen and looks around. "Did you check the fridge?"

A young man with a full beard looks at him. "Hungry?" he asks in a broad Dalarna accent.

"It's a good place to hide things," Joona says dryly.

"We haven't gotten there yet," the man says.

Joona goes back into the living room and notes that Saga is talking into a voice recorder in one corner of the room.

Kofoed presses a strip of tape with fibers on it onto transparent film, then looks up, only his eyes visible above his breathing mask.

"Have you found anything unexpected?" Joona asks.

"Unexpected? Well, there was a shoeprint on the wall. . . ."

"Anything else?"

"We don't usually know much until we get the results from the lab."

"So we should have results within a week?" Joona asks.

"If we nag the hell out of them," he replies, shrugging his shoulders. "I'm just about to take a look at the door frame, where the knife went in, to make an impression of the blade."

"Don't bother," Joona mutters.

Kofoed interprets this as a joke and laughs, then turns serious. "Did you get a glimpse of the knife? Steel?"

"No, the blade was lighter, maybe tungsten carbide—some people prefer that. But none of it will get us anywhere."

"What?"

"This whole crime-scene investigation," Joona replies. "We won't find any DNA or fingerprints that will help identify the killer."

"So what should we be doing?"

"I think the killer came here to look for something, and I think he was interrupted before he had time to find it."

"You mean whatever he was looking for is still here?" Kofoed asks.

"It's possible," Joona replies.

"But you have no idea what it is?"

"It's something small enough to fit inside a book."

Joona's granite-gray eyes stare into Kofoed's brown ones for a moment. Göran is photographing both sides of the bathroom door, then sits down on the floor to photograph the white ceiling. Joona is about to open the glass door to the entryway to ask him to take some pictures of the journals on the coffee table when a camera flash goes off. The glare takes him by surprise, and he has to stop, as four white dots slide across his vision, then an oily pale-blue hand. Joona looks around. He can't understand where the hand came from.

"Göran," Joona calls loudly through the glass door. "Take another picture!"

Everyone in the apartment stops and looks at Joona with interest. Kofoed takes his breathing mask off and scratches his neck. Stone is still sitting on the floor, with a curious look on his face.

"Just like you did a few seconds ago," Joona says, pointing. "Take another picture of the bathroom ceiling."

Göran shrugs, raises his camera, and takes another photograph of the ceiling. The flash goes off, and Joona feels his pupils contract as his eyes start to water. He closes his eyes and once again sees a black square, which he realizes is the glass panel in the door. Because of the flash, he's seeing it in negative.

In the middle of the square are four white dots, and beside them a pale-blue hand.

He knew he'd seen it.

Joona blinks, his vision returns to normal, and he looks closer at the glass door. The remnants of four pieces of tape form an empty rectangle, and there's a handprint on the glass beside them.

Kofoed walks over to stand next to Joona.

"A handprint," he says.

"Can you get it?" Joona says.

"Göran," Kofoed says, "we need a picture of this."

Göran gets up from the floor with his camera and looks at the handprint, humming to himself.

"Yes, someone's been a little messy here," he says happily, and takes four pictures.

He moves out of the way and waits as Kofoed pulls the prints.

Göran waits a few seconds, then takes two more pictures.

"Now we've got you," Kofoed whispers to the print, as he carefully lifts it onto transparent plastic.

"Can you check it right away?" Joona asks.

Kofoed takes the print out into the kitchen, and Joona stays where he is, staring at the four pieces of tape on the pane of glass. Behind one of them is the torn-off corner of a sheet of paper. Whoever left the handprint didn't have time to remove the tape carefully, just tugged the paper from the door, leaving one corner behind.

Joona looks more closely at the torn-off corner. He sees

right away that it isn't ordinary paper. It's photographic printing paper, used for color photographs.

A photograph stuck on the glass door to be looked at and studied. And then something happens, and there's no time to remove the photograph carefully; instead, someone rushed up to the door, put their hand on the glass to steady it, and pulled it free.

"Björn," Joona says quietly.

He was holding his hand to his stomach not because it hurt but because he was hiding a photograph under his jacket.

Joona moves his head slightly so he can see the impression of the handprint in the light, the narrow lines of the palm.

A human being's papillary lines never change, never age. And, unlike DNA, fingerprints are unique to each individual, even identical twins.

Joona hears quick footsteps behind him and turns around.

"Okay, that's more than fucking enough!" Saga yells. "This is my investigation. Christ, you're not even supposed to be here!"

"I just wanted—"

"Shut up!" she snaps. "I've just spoken to Petter Näslund. You have nothing to do with this. You're not supposed to be here—you're not allowed to be here!"

"I know. I'm about to go," he says, looking back at the pane of glass.

"Fucking Joona Linna," she says. "You can't just show up here and pick at little bits of tape. . . ."

"There was a photograph stuck to the glass," he replies calmly. "Someone tore it off. They leaned over this chair, rested their hand on the glass, and pulled it off."

She looks at him reluctantly, and he notices a white scar running across her left eyebrow.

"I'm perfectly capable of running this investigation," she says firmly.

"The handprint is probably Björn Almskog's," Joona says, walking toward the kitchen.

"Wrong way, Joona."

He ignores her.

"This is my investigation!" she shouts.

The forensics team has set up a small workstation in the middle of the floor: two chairs and a table with a computer, scanner, and printer. Kofoed is standing behind Göran, who has connected his camera to the computer. They've imported the handprint and are running an initial test for a fingerprint match.

Saga follows Joona.

"What do you have?" Joona asks, without bothering about Saga.

"Don't talk to Joona," she says sharply.

Kofoed looks up. "Don't be ridiculous, Saga," he says, then turns to Joona. "No luck this time. The print's from Björn Almskog, Penelope's boyfriend."

"He's in the suspect database," Göran says.

"What was he suspected of?" Joona asks.

"Violent rioting and threatening a public servant," Göran replies.

"Those pacifists are the worst," Kofoed jokes. "He probably took part in a peace march."

"Funny," Göran says sourly. "Not everyone in the force is quite so entertained by the rioting and sabotage, and—"

"Speak for yourself," Kofoed interrupts.

"The rescue operation speaks for itself." Göran grins.

"What?" Joona asks. "What do you mean? I haven't had time to keep up with the operation—what happened?"

27

When Joona throws his door open, Carlos jumps, spilling fish food into the aquarium.

"Why is there no ground search?" he asks in a hard voice. "There are two lives at stake, and we can't get any boats."

"The marine police made the call, which you know already," Carlos replies. "They've searched the entire area by helicopter, and everyone agrees that either Penelope Fernandez and Björn Almskog are dead or they don't want to be found ... and neither option suggests that there needs to be an urgent ground search."

"They have something the killer wants, and I honestly believe—"

"There's no point guessing. . . . We don't know what happened, Joona. The Security Police seem to think they've gone underground. They may well be sitting on the train to Amsterdam by—"

"Stop that," Joona interrupts sharply. "You can't rely on the Security Police when it comes to—"

"This is their case."

"Why? Why is it their case? Because Björn Almskog was once suspected of taking part in a riot? That doesn't mean anything."

"I spoke to Verner Zandén, and he was quick to point out

that Penelope Fernandez has links with extremist left-wing groups."

"Maybe, but I'm convinced that this murder is about something else entirely," Joona says stubbornly.

"Of course you are! Of course you're convinced," Carlos shouts.

"I don't know what it is yet, but the person I encountered in Penelope's apartment was a professional killer, not just—"

"The Security Police seem to think that Penelope and Björn were planning an attack."

"Is Penelope Fernandez supposed to be a terrorist now?" Joona asks in astonishment. "Have you read any of her articles? She's a pacifist and always condemns—"

"Yesterday," Carlos says, cutting him off. "Yesterday someone from the Brigade was arrested by the Security Police, just as he was on his way into her apartment."

"I don't even know what the Brigade is."

"A militant left-wing organization . . . They're loosely connected to Anti-Fascist Action and the Revolutionary Front, but they're independent. They're close to the Red Army Faction ideologically, and they want to become as active as Mossad."

"That doesn't make sense," Joona says.

"You don't want it to make sense, which is a different matter," Carlos says. "There'll be a ground search in due time, and we'll check the currents and see how the boat drifted, so that we can start dragging and maybe send some divers down."

"Good," Joona says.

"Right now, we're trying to figure out why they were killed . . . or why and where they're hiding."

Joona opens the door to the hallway but stops and turns back toward Carlos again.

"What happened to the guy from the Brigade who tried to get into Penelope's apartment?"

"He was released," Carlos replies.

"Did they find out what he was doing there?" Joona asks.

"He was just visiting."

"Visiting." Joona sighs. "That's all the Security Police managed to get?"

"You're not to investigate the Brigade," Carlos says with sudden anxiety in his voice. "I hope that's understood?"

Joona leaves the room and takes his phone out as soon as he's in the hallway. He hears Carlos shout that he's given him an order and that Joona doesn't have permission to interfere with the Security Police investigation. As Joona walks away, he looks up Nathan Pollock's number and calls him.

"Pollock," Nathan says when he answers.

"What do you know about the Brigade?" Joona says as the elevator doors open.

"The Security Police have spent several years trying to infiltrate and map the militant left-wing groups in Stockholm, Gothenburg, and Malmö. I don't know if the Brigade is particularly dangerous, but the Security Police seem to believe that they have weapons and explosives. Several of the members were in youth-custody centers and have previous convictions for violent offenses."

The elevator glides downward.

"I understand that the Security Police arrested a Brigade member outside Penelope Fernandez's apartment."

"His name's Daniel Marklund. He's part of the inner circle," Nathan replies.

"What do you know about him?"

"Not much," Pollock says. "He has a suspended sentence for vandalism and unlawful hacking."

"What was he doing at Penelope's?" Joona asks.

The elevator stops and the doors open.

"He was unarmed," Nathan says. "Demanded legal representation at the start of the interview, refused to answer any questions, and was released the same day."

"So they don't know anything?"

"No."

"Where can I get hold of him?" Joona asks.

"He has no home address," Nathan explains. "According to the Security Police, he lives with the other key members of the group in the Brigade's premises at Zinkensdamm."

28

As Joona strides toward the parking lot beneath Rådhus Park, he finds himself thinking about Disa, and a sudden longing courses through him. He wishes he could touch her slender arms, smell her soft hair. It calms him down to hear her talk about her archaeological finds, fragments of bone with no connection to crime, the remains of people living their lives long ago.

Joona knows he needs to talk to Disa. He's been far too busy for far too long.

He is walking between the parked cars in the garage when he detects movement behind one of the concrete pillars. There's someone waiting next to his Volvo. He can see a figure, almost hidden by a van. There's no sound over the roar of the large ventilation units.

"That was quick," Joona calls.

"Teleport," Pollock replies.

Joona stops, closes his eyes, and presses his temple with one finger.

"Headache?" Pollock asks.

"I haven't been getting much sleep."

They get in the car, and an Astor Piazzolla tango starts to play from the speakers; it sounds like two violins circling each other. Pollock turns the volume up slightly.

"Obviously, you didn't hear any of this from me," he says.

"Of course," Joona replies.

"I just found out that the Security Police are planning to use Daniel Marklund's attempt to get into Penelope's apartment as a pretext for mounting a raid on the Brigade's premises."

"I have to talk to him before then."

"You'd better hurry," Pollock says.

"How much of a hurry?" Joona asks, turning right onto Kungsholm Street.

"I think they're on their way now."

"Show me where the entrance to the Brigade is and you can get back to police headquarters and pretend you don't know anything about this," Joona says.

"What's your plan?"

"Plan?" Joona asks playfully.

Pollock laughs.

"The plan is just to find out what Daniel Marklund intended to do in Penelope's apartment," Joona explains. "There's a chance he might know what's going on."

"But . . ."

"It's no coincidence that the Brigade tried to get into her apartment. At least, I really can't believe that it is. The Security Police seem convinced that the extreme left are planning some sort of attack, but . . ."

"They always think that. It's their job to think that." Pollock smiles.

"Well, I need to talk to Daniel Marklund before I let go of this case."

"Even if you do get there before the Security Police, there's no guarantee the Brigade is going to want to talk to you."

29

Saga inserts thirteen rounds into the magazine, then slides it into her pistol, a .45-caliber Glock 21.

She's sitting with three colleagues inside a minibus. They're all in plain clothes and are planning to head into a fast-food restaurant in fifteen minutes to wait for the SWAT team's arrival.

In recent months, the Security Police have reported an increase in left-wing extremist activity in Stockholm. The Security Police's best strategists believe that several militant groups have come together to plan a large act of sabotage. They have also linked the murder of Viola Fernandez and the attempt to blow up Penelope Fernandez's apartment to the impending attack. According to the strategists, Daniel Marklund could very well be the same person who attacked Joona and his colleague.

Göran smiles as he puts on his bulletproof vest. "Now we're going to get those cowardly bastards."

Anders Westlund laughs but doesn't manage to hide his nerves. "Fuck, I hope they fight back. I'd love to neutralize at least one commie."

Saga thinks about Marklund's capture outside Penelope's apartment. Verner decided that Göran should conduct the interview. He went in aggressively in order to provoke a reaction, which just made Marklund demand legal representation and refuse to talk.

The minibus door opens, and Roland Eriksson climbs in with a can of Coke and a bag of sour candy and sits down.

"I'm going to shoot if I so much as see a gun," Roland says, sounding stressed. "It all goes so damn fast, you just shoot. . . ."

"We do as we discussed," Göran Stone says. "But if there's a firefight, you don't have to aim for their legs. . . ."

"Right in their mouths!" Roland cries.

"Take it easy, now," Göran says.

"My brother's face is—"

"What the fuck, Roland? We know," Anders interrupts anxiously.

"A fucking firebomb in his face," Roland goes on. "After eleven operations he still—"

"Are you going to be able to keep it together?" Göran asks sharply.

"Yes," Roland replies quickly.

"Really?"

"No problem."

Roland looks out the window and scrapes the top of a tub of chewing tobacco with his thumb.

Saga opens the door to let some air into the minibus. She agrees that it's a good time to mount a raid—there's no reason to wait. But, at the same time, she'd like to understand the connection to Penelope better. She can't picture Penelope's role among the left-wing extremists or why her sister was murdered. Too many details are unclear. She would have liked to question Marklund before the raid—look him in the eye and ask him some direct questions. She's tried to explain this to her boss, pointing out that they might not be able to interview anyone after the raid.

This is still my investigation, Saga thinks as she gets out

of the minibus and stands on the sidewalk in the sweltering heat.

"The SWAT team goes in here, here, and here, and we wait here," Göran repeats, pointing at the map of the building. "We might have to enter via the theater. . . ."

"Where the hell is Saga Bauer?" Roland asks.

"Probably chickened out or got her period." Anders grins.

30

Joona and Pollock park on Horn Street and glance at a grainy photo of Daniel Marklund. They hurry across the busy road and in through the door of the Tribunal Theater, the Brigade's headquarters.

Joona and Pollock hurry down the broad staircase to the combined bar and ticket counter. A woman with straight, dyed black hair and a silver nose ring smiles at them. They both give her a friendly nod but walk past without a word.

"Are you looking for someone?" she calls as they start to head up the metal staircase.

"Yes," Pollock replies almost inaudibly.

They reach a messy office holding a photocopier, a desk, and a corkboard covered with newspaper clippings. A thin man with scruffy hair and an unlit cigarette in his mouth is sitting in front of a computer.

"Hello, Richard," Pollock says.

"Who are you?" the man asks distractedly, before he looks back at the screen.

They continue into the dressing rooms, full of neatly arranged costumes, makeup tables, and bathrooms.

Pollock looks around, then indicates where they should go. They hurry toward a steel door labeled "Electricity."

"Should be through here," Pollock says.

"In the electrical room inside a theater?"

Pollock doesn't answer, just deftly picks the lock. They find themselves looking into a cramped space full of electricity meters, fuse panels, and a lot of boxes. The light in the ceiling doesn't work, but Joona climbs in past the boxes, trampling on bags of old clothes, and discovers another switch, behind a bunch of extension cords. He opens the door and hurries through a narrow passageway that has bare concrete walls. Nathan Pollock follows him. The air is stale and smells like garbage and damp soil. They can hear distant music. On the floor, there's a poster of Che Guevara with a burning fuse sticking out of his head.

"The Brigade has been hiding out here for a couple of years," Pollock says quietly.

"I should have brought a housewarming present."

"Promise me you'll be careful."

"I'm just worried Marklund isn't going to be here."

"He will be. He seems to spend most of his time here."

"Thanks for your help, Nathan."

"Maybe it would be best if I came in with you?" Pollock says. "You'll only have a couple of minutes, and when the Security Police storm in, things could get dangerous."

Joona's gray eyes narrow, but his voice is calm when he says, "I'm just making a social call."

Nathan goes back to the theater and coughs as he pulls the doors closed behind him. Joona stands still for a moment, alone in the empty hallway, then draws his pistol, checks that the magazine is full, and slips it back into its holster. The steel door at the end of the hallway is locked, and he wastes valuable seconds picking it.

Someone has scratched "the brigade" into the blue paint on the door in very small letters.

Joona cautiously opens the door and is met by loud, dis-

cordant music that sounds like a digitally manipulated version of Jimi Hendrix's track "Machine Gun." The shrieking
guitars have a dreamlike, rolling rhythm that drowns out all
other sounds.

Joona jogs into a cluttered room. Piles of books and newspapers reach all the way to the ceiling.

It's almost completely dark, but Joona realizes that the
stacks form a system of hallways in the room, a labyrinth
that leads to more doors.

He walks quickly until he reaches a more brightly lit area
where the path divides. He turns right, then quickly spins
around.

He thought he saw something, a flash of movement.

A shadow that vanished out of the corner of his eye.

He's not sure.

Joona moves on. Through the music, he suddenly hears
a roar, someone screaming in another room. He stops and
retraces his steps, peering into a passageway where a stack of
magazines has toppled over.

Joona's head is starting to ache. It occurs to him that he
needs to eat something. He should have brought some food
with him, even just a few pieces of dark chocolate.

He clambers over the toppled magazines and reaches a
spiral staircase leading to the floor below. There's a sweet,
smoky smell in the air. Holding on to the handrail, he creeps
down as quickly as he can. On the bottom step, he stops in
front of a black velvet curtain and puts his hand on his pistol.

The music isn't as loud here.

Red light reaches through the gap in the curtains, along
with the heavy smell of cannabis and sweat. Joona tries to
see through the gap, but his field of vision is limited. In one
corner, there's a plastic clown with a red nose. Joona hesitates
for a couple of seconds, then steps through the black velvet

curtain. His pulse speeds up and his headache gets worse as he glances around the room. On the polished concrete floor he can see a double-barreled shotgun and an open box of slugs. A naked man is sitting on an office chair, smoking with his eyes closed. It isn't Daniel Marklund, Joona notes. A bare-breasted blonde woman is squatting on a mattress against the wall with a blanket over her hips. She meets Joona's gaze, blows him a kiss, then takes a swig from a can of beer.

He hears a scream echo from the only doorway.

Without taking his eyes off the pair, he picks up the shotgun, aims it at the floor, and stands on it to bend the barrel.

The woman puts the beer can down and absentmindedly scratches her armpit.

Joona puts the shotgun down, then walks past the woman on the mattress into a hallway with a low ceiling. Heavy smoke hangs in the air. A strong light is shining at him, and he tries to block it with his hand. The end of the hallway is covered by wide strips of industrial plastic. Joona is dazzled and can't really see what's going on. He can only vaguely discern movement and hear an echoing voice full of fear. Someone starts to scream loudly, very close to him. The scream, coming from deep in the person's throat, is followed by quick, gasped breathing. Joona creeps forward quickly, past the blinding light, and can suddenly see into the room behind the thick plastic.

It's veiled in smoke.

A short, muscular woman wearing a balaclava, black jeans, and a brown T-shirt is standing in front of a man in his socks and underwear. His head is shaved, and he has the words "White Power" tattooed on his forehead. He's bitten his tongue, and blood is running down his chin and neck.

"Please," he whispers, shaking his head.

Joona looks at the cigarette the woman is dangling in

her hand. She walks up to the man and presses the lit end against the tattoo on his forehead, making him scream out loud. He wets himself, and a dark stain spreads across his underwear as urine trickles down his bare legs.

Joona draws his pistol and moves closer to the gap in the thick plastic curtain, trying to figure out if there are other people in the room. He can't see anyone else and has opened his mouth to shout when he sees his pistol fall to the floor.

It clatters on the bare concrete and comes to rest by the plastic screen. He looks in confusion at his own hand, sees it shaking, and then feels the pain. Joona's vision fades, and he feels a heavy thumping behind his forehead. He can't hold back a groan and has to reach for the wall with one hand for support. He can feel that he's at the point of passing out as he hears the voices of the people on the other side of the plastic.

"Fuck it!" the woman with the cigarette shouts. "Just tell me what the fuck you did!"

"I don't remember," the neo-Nazi sobs.

"What did you do?"

"I was just giving a guy a hard time."

"In detail!"

"I burned him in the eye."

"With a cigarette," she says. "A ten-year-old boy . . ."

"Yes, but I—"

"Why? What did he do?"

"We followed him from the synagogue and down to . . ."

Joona doesn't notice himself pull a heavy fire extinguisher off the wall. He loses all sense of time. The whole room vanishes. All that exists is the pain inside his head and a loud ringing tone in his ears.

31

Joona leans against the wall, blinking to get his sight back, and realizes that someone's followed him and is standing in front of him. He feels a hand on his back and can make out a face through the dark veils of pain.

"What happened?" Saga says quietly. "Are you injured?"

He tries to shake his head, but he's in too much pain. It feels as if someone is dragging a hook through his skull.

Joona sinks to his knees.

"You have to get out of here," she says.

He feels Saga lift his face, but he can't see anything. His whole body is covered with sweat. He can feel it running down from his armpits.

Saga is patting his clothes. She assumes he's having an epileptic fit and is trying to find medication in his pockets. He realizes that she's taken his wallet and is looking for the symbol to show that he suffers from epilepsy.

After a while, the pain eases. Joona moistens his mouth with his tongue and looks up. His jaw muscles feel tight, and his whole body is aching from the migraine.

"You can't come in yet," he whispers. "I need to . . ."

"What the hell happened?"

"Nothing," Joona replies, picking his pistol up off the floor.

He stands and walks as quickly as he can past the hanging plastic strips and into the room. It's empty, but he sees an illuminated emergency-exit sign on the far wall. Saga follows him, shooting him a questioning glance. Joona opens the emergency exit and sees a steep flight of stairs leading up to a metal door facing the street.

"*Perkele,*" he mutters.

"Talk to me," Saga says angrily.

Joona always tries to keep the cause of his illness at arm's length. He refuses to think about what happened years ago—the reason his brain sometimes throbs with a pain that almost knocks him out completely for a couple of minutes. According to his doctor, it's an extreme form of migraine brought on by physical trauma.

The only thing that helps his headaches is the epilepsy medication topiramate. Joona is supposed to take it all the time, but when he has to think clearly he refuses to take it, because it makes him tired, because it makes his thoughts cloudy.

"They were torturing a guy, a neo-Nazi, I think, but . . ."

"Torturing?"

"Yes, with a cigarette," he replies as he starts to walk back along the passageway.

"What happened?"

"I couldn't—"

"Look," she interrupts calmly. "Maybe you shouldn't, I mean . . . be on duty, if you're sick."

She rubs her face.

"What a fucking mess," she whispers.

Joona walks back into the room with the plastic clown and hears Saga following him.

"What the hell are you doing here anyway?" she asks behind him. "The SWAT team is about to storm in. If they see that you're armed they'll shoot, you know that. It'll be dark, there'll be tear gas, and—"

"I have to talk to Daniel Marklund," Joona interrupts.

"You shouldn't even know about him," she says, following him up the spiral staircase. "Who told you?"

Joona starts walking down one of the hallways but stops when he sees Saga gesturing in a different direction. When he sees that she's started to run, he draws his pistol. He hears her shout.

Saga is standing in the doorway of a room containing five computers. In one corner stands a young man with a beard and dirty hair. It's Daniel Marklund. He's clutching a bayonet knife.

"We're police officers, and we're asking you to put the weapon down," she says calmly, holding up her ID.

The young man shakes his head, moving the blade through the air in front of him, rapidly changing the angle.

"We just want to talk to you," Joona says, putting his pistol back in its holster.

"So talk," Daniel says in a tense voice.

Joona walks toward him, ignoring the knife.

"Daniel, you're not very good at that," Joona says with a smile.

He can smell gun grease from the shiny blade. Marklund waves the knife faster, and there's a look of concentration in his eyes as he says, "Finns aren't the only ones who can—"

Joona darts forward and grabs the young man's hand, twisting the knife free with a fluid movement. He puts it down on the table.

The room is quiet. They look at each other, and then Marklund shrugs his shoulders.

"I mostly do IT," he says.

"We're going to be interrupted soon," Joona says. "Just tell me what you were doing at Penelope Fernandez's apartment."

"I was visiting."

"Daniel," Joona says darkly. "You'd get a guaranteed prison sentence for that business with the knife, but I've got more important things to do than haul you in, so I'm giving you a chance to save me some time."

"Is Penelope a member of the Brigade?" Saga asks quickly.

"Penelope Fernandez?" Daniel smiles. "Let's just say she doesn't like our methods."

"So what were you doing with her?" Joona wonders.

"What do you mean, she 'doesn't like your methods'?" Saga asks. "Is there some sort of power struggle . . . ?"

"Don't the Security Police know anything?" Daniel asks with a weary smile. "Penelope Fernandez is a total pacifist, a committed democrat. So she doesn't like us . . . but we like her."

He sits down on a chair in front of two computers.

"Like?"

"She has our respect," he says.

"Why?" Saga asks, surprised. "Why would . . . ?"

"You have no idea how much people hate her. . . . I mean, Google her name—the results are pretty brutal—and now it looks like someone's crossed the line."

"'Crossed the line'?"

Daniel looks at them carefully. "You must know she's missing, right?"

"Yes," Saga replies.

"Good," he says. "That's good, but for some reason I don't really believe the police are going to put out much effort to find her. That's why I went to her apartment. I needed to check her computer to see who was behind it. I mean, the Swedish Resistance Movement sent out an unofficial message to their members back in April, encouraging them to kidnap 'communist bitch Penelope Fernandez' and turn her into a sex slave for the organization. But check this out. . . ."

Daniel types something on one of the computers, then turns the screen to face Joona.

"This site has direct links to the Aryan Brotherhood," he says.

Joona scans the online chat room. It's full of horrifically vulgar threats about Aryan cocks and how they're going to kill Penelope.

"But these groups have nothing to do with Penelope's disappearance," Joona says.

"They don't? Who was it, then? The Nordic Association?" Daniel asks eagerly. "Come on! It's not too late!"

"What do you mean, 'it's not too late'?" Joona asks.

"I managed to intercept a message from her mom's voice mail. I mean, it seemed pretty fucking urgent, but still not too late, so I wanted to check her computer and—"

"'Managed to intercept'?" Joona interrupts.

"She tried to call her mother yesterday morning," the young man replies, scratching his messy hair nervously.

"Penelope?"

"Yes."

"What did she say?" Saga asks quickly.

"That she's being hunted," Daniel says tersely.

"What did she say, exactly?" Joona asks.

Daniel glances at Saga Bauer, then asks, "How long do we have before the rest of you storm the building?"

Saga looks at her watch. "Between three and four minutes," she replies.

"Then you have time to listen to this," Daniel says, typing a couple of quick commands on the other computer, then playing an audio file.

The speaker crackles; then there's a click as Claudia Fernandez's voice-mail greeting plays. They hear three short beeps, followed by a lot of hissing and crackling. Somewhere behind the static there's a faint voice. It's a woman, but her words are unintelligible. After just a few seconds, a male voice can be heard, saying, "Get a job!" And then there's a click.

"Sorry," Daniel mutters. "I need to run it through some filters."

"The clock's ticking," Saga murmurs.

He taps at the computer, adjusts the settings, then plays the recording again:

"You've reached Claudia—I can't answer right now, but if you leave a message I'll get back to you as soon as I can."

The three beeps sound different this time, and the crackling is more like gentle metallic tinkling.

Suddenly they hear Penelope Fernandez's voice clearly: "Mom, I need help, I'm being hunted by—"

"Why don't you get a job!" the man says. Then the line goes dead.

32

SAGA LOOKS at the time and says that they have to leave. Daniel Marklund mutters a joke about staying to mount the barricades, but there's a frightened look in his eyes.

"We're going to hit you hard. Put the knife down, don't resist, surrender immediately, no rapid movements," Saga says quickly before she and Joona leave the little office.

Marklund remains seated, watching them go; then he picks up the bayonet and tosses it in the garbage.

Joona and Saga leave the Brigade's labyrinthine premises and emerge onto Horn Street, where Saga goes back to Göran's group of plainclothes officers.

Two minutes later, fifteen heavily armed officers in full gear rush out of four black vans. The SWAT team breaks down all the entrances, and tear gas spreads through the rooms. Five young people, including Daniel Marklund, are found sitting on the floor with their hands on their heads. They're dragged out onto the street, coughing, their arms fastened behind their backs with zip ties.

The weapons seized by the Security Police really only demonstrate the Brigade's low-level militancy: an old Colt army pistol, a rifle, a shotgun with a bent barrel, a box of slugs, four knives, and two throwing stars.

———————

As he drives along Söder Mälarstrand, Joona takes out his phone and calls Carlos.

"How are you enjoying the Police Academy, Joona?" he asks.

"I'm not there."

"I know that, because—"

"Penelope Fernandez is alive," Joona interrupts. "She's being hunted; she's running for her life."

"Says who?"

"She left a message on her mother's voice mail."

The line goes quiet; then Carlos takes a deep breath.

"Okay, she's alive. . . . What else do we know? She's alive, but . . ."

"We know she was alive thirty hours ago, when she made the call," Joona says. "And that someone's after her."

"Who?"

"She didn't have time to say, but . . . if it's the same man I ran into, there's no time to lose," Joona says.

"You think we're dealing with a professional?"

"I'm sure that the person who attacked me and Erixon is a professional fixer, a *grob*."

"A *grob*?"

"The Serbian word for 'grave.' They're expensive, they work alone, but they do what they're paid for."

"That sounds extremely unlikely."

"I'm right," Joona says tersely.

"You always say that, but if we really are dealing with a professional killer, Penelope shouldn't have lasted this long. It's been almost two days," Carlos says.

"If she's alive, it means the fixer has other priorities."

"You still think he's looking for something?"

"Yes," Joona replies.

"What?"

"I'm not sure, but it could be a photograph."

"Why do you think that?"

"It's the best theory I've got right now."

"You think the killer was looking for a photograph that Björn already picked up?"

"My guess is that he began by searching Björn's apartment, and when he didn't find it, he doused the place with gasoline and turned the neighbor's iron on. The fire department got the call at five after eleven, and that whole floor was completely burned before they got the fire under control."

"And that same evening he kills Viola."

"He probably assumed that Björn had taken the photograph onto the boat with him, so he made his way on board, drowned Viola, searched the boat, and was planning to sink it when something made him change his mind and return to Stockholm, where he started searching Penelope's apartment. . . ."

"But you don't think he found the photograph?" Carlos asks.

"Either Björn has it with him, or he's hidden it with a friend or in a storage locker—it could be anywhere, really."

The line goes silent. Joona hears Carlos breathing heavily.

"But if we can find this photograph first," Carlos says thoughtfully, "then, presumably, this would all be over."

"Yes," Joona replies.

"I mean . . . if we've seen the photograph, if the police have seen it, it's not a secret anymore, so it's hardly the sort of thing worth killing for."

"I hope it's as simple as that."

"Joona, I . . . I can't take the investigation away from Petter, but I assume—"

"That I'm going to go out to the Police Academy and give some lectures," Joona interrupts.

"That's all I need to know." Carlos laughs.

On his way back to Kungsholmen, Joona listens to his voice mail, which includes a number of messages from Erixon. In the first, he explained that he could work perfectly well from the hospital. Thirteen minutes later, he demanded to be included in the work, and twenty-seven minutes after that, he was yelling that not having anything to do was driving him crazy. Joona calls him, and Erixon answers in a tired voice:

"Quack, quack . . ."

"Am I too late?" Joona asks. "Have you gone crazy already?"

Erixon merely hiccups in response.

"I don't know how much you can understand," Joona says. "But things are getting urgent. Yesterday morning, Penelope Fernandez left a voice mail for her mother."

"Yesterday?" Erixon repeats, suddenly alert.

"She said she was being hunted."

"Are you on your way here?"

Joona can hear Erixon's labored breathing as he explains that Penelope and Björn didn't spend Thursday night together. She was picked up by taxi at six-forty and driven to a television studio to take part in a debate. Just a minute or so after the taxi left Sankt Pauls Street, Björn arrived at the apartment. Joona tells him about the handprint on the door, the tape, and the torn corner and goes on to say that he is convinced that Björn had been waiting outside the building for Penelope to leave so he could pick up the photograph quickly without her knowledge.

"And I think the person who attacked us is a fixer, and that he was looking for the photograph when we caught him by surprise," Joona says.

"Maybe," Erixon whispers.

"He wanted to get away from the apartment and chose to prioritize that over killing us," Joona says.

"Because, if he hadn't, we'd be dead," Erixon replies.

The line crackles, and Erixon asks someone to leave him alone. Joona hears a woman repeat that it's time for physiotherapy.

"We know that the fixer hasn't found the photograph," Joona goes on. "Because if he'd found it on the boat, he wouldn't have been searching Penelope's apartment."

"And it wasn't in her apartment because Björn had already taken it."

"I think the attempt to set fire to the apartment shows that the fixer isn't really interested in getting the photograph; he just wants to destroy it."

"So why was it taped to Penelope's living room door if it was that damned important?" Erixon wonders.

"I can think of several reasons," Joona says. "The most likely is that Björn and Penelope took a photograph that proves something, but they didn't realize its significance."

"That could definitely be the case," Erixon says animatedly.

"To them, there's no reason to hide the photograph, and it's certainly not worth killing anyone for."

"But Björn changed his mind."

"Maybe he found something out; maybe he realized it was dangerous, and that's why he took it," Joona says. "There's a lot we don't know, and the only way we're going to get any answers is through good, honest police work."

"Exactly!" Erixon says, almost shouting.

"Can you track down all their phone calls in the past week, as well as text messages, bank withdrawals, et cetera? Receipts, bus tickets, meetings, work . . ."

"Of course I can."

"Actually, forget I asked."

"What do you mean, forget it?"

"Your physiotherapy," Joona says with a smile. "You have an appointment with the physiotherapist."

"Very funny," Erixon says, with suppressed anger. "Physiotherapist? What sort of a fucking job is that?"

"But you do need to rest," Joona teases. "There's another forensics expert. . . ."

"Just lying here doing nothing is driving me crazy."

"You've been on leave for six hours."

"I'm climbing the walls here," Erixon says with a moan.

33

Joona is driving east toward Gustavsberg. He thinks about phoning Disa, but instead he calls Anja.

"I need Claudia Fernandez's address."

"Number five Maria Street," she says instantly. "Not far from the old porcelain factory."

"Thanks," Joona replies.

Anja doesn't hang up.

"I'm waiting," she says in a singsong voice.

"What are you waiting for?" he asks softly.

"For you to say we're going to Turku, and that you've rented a little cottage with a wood-fired sauna beside the water."

"Sounds lovely," Joona says slowly.

The weather is that special type of summer gray, hazy and humid. He parks outside Claudia's house and gets out of the car, smelling the bitter scent of boxwood and blackberry bushes. He stands completely still for a moment, caught in a memory. The face that came to mind gradually fades as he rings the doorbell. The nameplate has "Fernandez" branded into it in childish lettering, clearly the product of a school woodworking class.

After a while, he hears slow footsteps.

Claudia opens the door with a worried look on her face.

When she sees Joona, she retreats backward, knocking a coat onto the floor.

"No," she whispers. "Not Penny . . ."

"Claudia, it's nothing bad," he says quickly.

She sinks to the floor, breathing like a frightened animal.

"What's happened?" she asks in a scared voice.

"We don't know much, but yesterday morning Penelope tried to call you."

"She's alive," Claudia says.

"Yes, she is," Joona replies.

"Oh, dear God, thank you," she whispers. "Thank God . . ."

"We picked up her message from your voice mail."

"From my . . . No," she says, getting to her feet.

"There was so much interference that it required special equipment to hear her voice," Joona explains.

"The only . . . There was just a man telling me to get a job."

"Yes, that's right," Joona says. "Penelope spoke before that, but she's very hard to hear."

"What does she say?"

"She says she needs help. The marine police are going to organize a ground search."

"What about tracing the phone, though? Surely . . ."

"Claudia," Joona says calmly, "I need to ask you a few questions."

"What kind of questions?"

"Shall we sit down?"

They go into the kitchen.

"Joona Linna, can I ask you something?"

"You can ask, but I might not know the answer."

Claudia gets cups out for them. Her hand is shaking. She sits down across from him and looks at him intently. "You have a family, don't you?" she asks.

The bright, yellow kitchen is very quiet.

"Do you remember the last time you were in Penelope's apartment?" Joona asks after a while.

"It was last week, on Tuesday. She helped me hem a pair of Viola's pants."

Joona nods and sees Claudia's mouth tremble with suppressed sobs.

"I want you to think carefully now, Claudia," he says, leaning forward. "Did you see a photograph stuck to the living room door?"

"Yes."

"What was it of?" Joona asks, trying to keep his voice calm.

"I don't know. I didn't look."

"But you do remember a photograph there—you're sure about that?"

"Yes." Claudia nods.

"Were there any people in the picture?"

"I don't know. I suppose I thought it was something for her work."

"Was it taken indoors or outside?"

"No idea."

"Try to see it in your mind's eye."

Claudia closes her eyes but then shakes her head. "I can't."

"Try. It's important."

She lowers her eyes and thinks, but shakes her head again. "All I can remember is that I thought it was odd that she'd stuck a picture on the door; it didn't look good at all."

"Why did you think it was something for her work?"

"I don't know," Claudia whispers.

Joona excuses himself when his phone rings in his jacket. He sees that it's Carlos and answers.

"Yes?"

"I just spoke to Lance, with the marine police out on Dalarö, and he says they're organizing a ground search tomorrow. Three hundred people, and almost fifty boats."

"Good," Joona says, as he watches Claudia walk into the entryway.

"And then I called Erixon to see how he was doing," Carlos says.

"He seems to be on the mend," Joona says in a neutral tone of voice.

"Joona, I don't want to know what you're doing . . . but Erixon warned me that I'm going to have to admit that you were right."

After the call, Joona goes out into the entryway and sees that Claudia has put on a jacket and a pair of Wellington boots.

"I heard what he said over the phone," she says. "And I can help look. I can look all night. . . ."

She opens the door.

"Claudia, you need to let the police do their job."

"My daughter called me, asking for help."

"I know it's terrible having to wait. . . ."

"Please, can't I come with you? I won't get in the way. I can make food and answer the phone so you don't have to think about it."

"Isn't there anyone who could stay here with you? A relative or a friend, or—"

"I don't want anyone here. I just want Penny," she interrupts.

34

In his lap, Erixon has a folder and a large envelope that have been couriered to his hospital room. He's holding a small, whirring fan in front of his face as Joona pushes him along the hospital hallway in a wheelchair.

His Achilles tendon has been repaired, and instead of a cast his foot is fixed to a special type of boot that keeps his toes pointing downward. He's been muttering that he's going to need a ballet slipper for the other foot if they want to see his *Swan Lake*.

"The same morning they set out in the boat, Björn bought an envelope and two stamps at the Central Station," Erixon says. "He had the receipt in his wallet on the boat, and I got the security company to e-mail me the footage from the surveillance cameras. It's definitely a photograph, just like you thought."

"So he sends the photograph to someone?" Joona asks.

"It's impossible to know what he wrote on the envelope."

"Maybe he sent it to himself."

"But his apartment burned down; there isn't even a door anymore," Erixon says.

"Call and check with the post office."

When they reach the elevator, Erixon starts to make weird swimming motions with his arms. Joona looks at him placidly without asking what he's doing.

"Jasmin says it's good for me," Erixon explains.

"Jasmin?"

"My physiotherapist. . . . She's a tiny little thing but wonderfully strict: 'Shut up, sit up straight, stop whining.' She even called me lard-ass," Erixon says with a shy smile. "Do you know how long they have to train?"

They get out of the elevator and go into a chapel adorned with a plain wooden cross on a stand and a simple altar. On the wall is a multicolored tapestry of Jesus.

Joona goes out into the hallway, opens a closet, and takes out an easel with a large pad of paper, and some markers. When he returns to the chapel, he sees Erixon nonchalantly pulling down the tapestry and draping it over the cross, which he's moved to the corner.

"What we know is that, to someone, this photograph is worth killing people for," Joona says.

"Yes, but why?"

Erixon pins the printout of Björn Almskog's bank statement to the wall, then adds the list of calls, copies of bus and subway tickets, receipts from Björn's and Penelope's wallets, and transcripts of their voice mails.

"The photograph must reveal something someone wants to keep secret. It must have important information, maybe confidential industrial material," Joona says, as he starts to construct a timeline on the pad of paper.

"Maybe," Erixon says.

"Let's find this photograph so we can put an end to this," Joona says.

He picks up one of the markers and writes:

06:40 Penelope picked up from her apartment by taxi.
06:45 Björn arrives at Penelope's apartment.
06:48 Björn leaves the apartment with the photograph.
07:07 Björn mails the photograph at Central Station.

Erixon looks at the times as he unwraps a bar of chocolate. "Penelope Fernandez leaves the studio after ten o'clock and calls Björn five minutes later," he says, pointing to the list of phone calls. "Her bus ticket was stamped at ten-thirty. She gets a call from her sister, Viola, at ten-forty-five. By then, Penelope is probably already with Björn at the marina."

"So what was Björn doing?"

"That's what we're going to figure out," Erixon says happily, wiping his fingers on a white handkerchief.

He moves along the wall and points to one of the subway tickets. "Björn leaves Penelope's apartment with the photograph. He gets straight on the subway, and at seven after seven he buys the envelope and two stamps at Central Station."

"And mails the envelope," Joona says.

Erixon clears his throat and continues: "The next fixed point is a transaction on his Visa, twenty kronor at the Dream Bow Internet Café on Vattu Street, at seven-thirty-five."

"Twenty-five to eight," Joona says, adding it to the timeline.

"Remind me, where the hell is Vattu Street?"

"It's pretty small," Joona replies. "Tucked away in the old Klara district."

Erixon nods and goes on: "I'm guessing Björn got the train to Fridhem Plaza before the stamp on his ticket expired. Because then we have a call made from the landline in his apartment to his father, but his dad doesn't answer."

"We'll have to talk to his father."

"Next is another stamp on his bus ticket, at nine. Looks

like he caught the number four bus from Fridhem Plaza to Högalid Street, then walked to the boat."

Joona adds everything to the timeline, then looks at their map of that morning. "Björn was in a hurry to get the photograph," he says. "But he didn't want to run into Penelope that morning, so he waited until she left in the taxi, then rushed in, took the photo off the door, left the apartment, and went to Central Station."

"I want to look at the security-camera footage."

"Then Björn goes to an Internet café nearby," Erixon goes on. "He spends about half an hour there, then goes . . ."

"That's it!" Joona says, heading for the door.

"What?"

"Penelope and Björn both have broadband at home."

"So why use an Internet café?" Erixon asks.

"I'll head over there," Joona says, leaving the room.

35

JOONA PARKS on Vattu Street and gets out of the car, then hurries through an anonymous-looking metal gate and walks down a sloping concrete path.

There's not much going on in the Dream Bow Internet Café. The floor has been freshly cleaned, and the room smells like lemon. Shiny plastic chairs are lined up at small computer tables. The only movement comes from the slow patterns of the screen savers.

An overweight man with a pointy black beard is leaning on a tall counter, sipping coffee from a mug with "Lennart Means Lion" on it. His jeans are baggy, and one of his shoes is untied.

"I need a computer," Joona says before he gets to the counter.

"Get to the back of the line," the man jokes, making a sweeping gesture toward all the empty desks.

"One computer in particular," Joona goes on with a glint in his eyes. "A friend of mine was here last Friday, and I'd like the same computer he used."

"I don't know if I can let . . ."

"It's important."

"I'll check Friday's list," the man says, as two red circles appear on his cheeks. "What's his name?"

"Björn Almskog," Joona replies.

"Number five, over in the corner," he says. "I just need to see some ID."

Joona hands the man his police ID; the man looks confused as he makes a note of Joona's name and date of birth in the register.

"Okay, all yours."

"Thanks," Joona says warmly, going over to the computer.

He takes out his mobile and calls Johan Jönson, a techie at National Crime.

"Hang on a second," a croaky voice says. "I've swallowed part of a tissue. I was blowing my nose, then breathed in before I sneezed. . . . Why am I trying to explain this? Who am I talking to, anyway?"

"Joona Linna, National Crime."

"Damn, Joona, hi!"

"You sound better already," Joona says.

"Yes, I got it out."

"I need to see what a guy was doing on a computer last Friday."

"Say no more!"

"I'm in a hurry. I'm sitting in an Internet café."

"And you have access to the computer?"

"It's right in front of me."

"That makes things easier. Try looking at the browser history. It's probably been deleted—they're supposed to reset the computers after each user—but things are usually still on the hard drive, you just have to . . . Actually, the easiest and most thorough way to do this is if you can bring it in so I can run a program I designed to—"

"Meet me in fifteen minutes in the chapel of Sankt Göran's Hospital," Joona says. He disconnects the computer, tucks it under his arm, and starts to walk toward the door.

The man holding the coffee mug looks at him in astonishment and tries to block his path.

"The computer's not allowed to leave—"

"It's been arrested," Joona says.

36

The parking lot in front of Sankt Göran's Hospital is hot, and the air is unpleasantly humid.

Erixon is maneuvering his wheelchair around the chapel, where he's set up a functional base station with three different phones, which are ringing nonstop.

Joona comes in with the computer in his arms and puts it on a chair. Johan Jönson is already sitting on a small sofa. He's twenty-five years old and dressed in an ill-fitting black tracksuit. He has a shaved head and thick eyebrows that meet over his nose. He stands up and glances at Joona bashfully, then shakes hands and puts his red computer-bag down.

"*Ei saa peittää,*" he says, taking out a thin laptop.

Erixon pours Fanta from a bottle into some small paper cups.

"I usually put the hard drive in the freezer for a few hours if it's playing up," Johan says. "And then just hook up an ATA/SATA connector. Everyone has a different system. I mean, I've got a friend at Ibas Computing who works with remote data recovery, and he doesn't even meet his clients—he just does the whole thing over an encrypted phone line. You can usually retrieve most things that way, but I don't want most of it, I want it all—that's my thing—and for that you need a program called Hangar 18. . . ."

He throws his head back and pretends to laugh like a mad scientist. "Mwah-ha-ha! I designed it myself," he goes on. "It works like a digital vacuum cleaner: it sucks up absolutely everything and reconstructs it in chronological order, down to the microsecond."

He sits down on the altar rail and connects the computers. He types commands at an astonishing speed, reads the screen, scrolling down quickly, and then types more commands.

"Will it take long?" Joona asks after a while.

"I don't know," Johan mutters. "No more than a month."

He swears quietly to himself, types another command, and looks at the digits flickering past.

"I'm kidding," he says.

"I realize," Joona replies patiently.

"I'll know how much can be retrieved within fifteen minutes," Johan says, looking at Joona's note of the day and time Björn Almskog visited the Internet café. "The browser history seems to have been deleted several different times, which is kind of a pain. . . ."

Fragments of old graphics flit across the screen. Johan inserts a portion of chewing tobacco under his lip, wipes his fingers on his pants, and waits, half an eye on the screen.

"They've done their housekeeping," he says languidly. "But you can't ever erase anything. There are no secrets. . . . Hangar 18 can find rooms that don't even exist."

His laptop starts to beep, and he types something, then reads a long list of numbers. He types some more, and the beeping stops abruptly.

"What's happening?" Joona asks.

"Not much," Johan says. "Firewalls, sandboxes, and fake virus protection just make it a little chewier, that's all. . . . It's a miracle that computers work these days, with all the barriers set up inside them."

He shakes his head and licks a piece of tobacco from his top lip. "I've never had a single virus program, and— Okay, shut up," he tells himself, breaking off mid-flow.

Joona comes closer and looks over his shoulder.

"What have we got here?" Johan whispers. "What have we got here?"

Johan leans back and rubs his neck, then types something with one hand, presses "enter," and smiles. "Here it comes," he says.

Joona and Erixon stare at the screen.

"Give me a second. . . . It's not that easy, it's coming in tiny little pieces. . . ."

He shades the screen with his hand and waits. Slowly, letters and fragments of graphics start to appear.

"Look, the door's slowly opening now. . . . Let's see what Björn was doing on this computer."

Erixon has put the brakes on his wheelchair and is leaning forward to see the screen.

"That's just a few random lines," he says.

"Look at the corner."

At the bottom right of the screen is a colorful little flag.

"He was using Windows," Erixon says. "How original . . ."

"Hotmail," Joona says.

"Logging in," Johan replies.

"Now things might get interesting," Erixon says.

"Can you see a name?" Joona asks.

"It doesn't work like that—we can only tell when the messages were sent, not who sent them or who they were sent to," Johan says, scrolling down.

"What was that?" Joona asks, pointing.

"We're inside his 'sent' folder," he replies.

"Did he send something?" Joona asks in a tense voice.

Fragments of ads for cheap flights to Milan, "New Y k,"

"Lo d n," and "P ris" appear on the screen. And at the bottom is a pale-gray number, a time: "07.44.42 AM."

"We've got something here," Johan says.

More fragments appear on the screen:

orge I   contact d y

"Personal ads." Erixon grins. "They don't work, I've—"

He cuts himself off abruptly. Johan scrolls carefully past incomprehensible shreds of graphics, then stops suddenly. He moves away from the laptop, smiling.

Joona takes his place, squints against the sunlight, and reads what it says in the middle of the screen:

Carl Palmcr
ent t e   graph.   orget I   contact d you

Joona feels the hairs on the back of his neck stand up, and a shiver runs down his arms and back. Palmcrona, he thinks as he writes down the fragments the way they appear on the screen; then he runs his fingers through his hair and goes over to the window. He tries to breathe calmly so he can think clearly. A tiny migraine threatens. Erixon is still staring at the screen, swearing to himself repeatedly.

"Are you sure Björn Almskog wrote this?" Joona asks.

"No doubt," Johan replies.

"Completely sure?"

"If he was sitting at this computer at that time, this is his e-mail."

"Then it's his e-mail," Joona concludes, his mind already elsewhere.

"Bloody hell," Erixon whispers.

Johan looks at the fragment in the address box, "crona

@isp.se," and drinks some Fanta straight from the bottle. Erixon leans back in his wheelchair and closes his eyes for a while.

"Palmcrona," Joona says intently, mostly to himself.

"This is crazy," Erixon says. "What's Carl Palmcrona got to do with this?"

Joona walks toward the door, immersed in thought. He says nothing as he leaves the hospital and his colleagues behind. He just strides across the parking lot in the bright sunlight toward his black car.

37

To Joona's surprise, the door to Carlos's office is wide open, and Carlos is looking out through the window. He sees Joona and sits back down at his desk.

"She's still there," he says.

"Who?"

"The girls' mother."

"Claudia?" Joona says, going over to the window.

"She's been standing there for the past hour."

Joona looks but can't see her. A father in a dark-blue suit with a crown on his head walks past with a little girl dressed in a princess costume.

Then, across from the main entrance to the National Police Authority, he sees a hunched woman next to a dirty Mazda pickup. Claudia Fernandez. She's standing perfectly still, staring intently at the entrance.

"I went out and asked if she was waiting for anyone in particular. I thought you might have forgotten that you were going to see her. . . ."

"No," Joona says quietly.

"She said she was waiting for her daughter Penelope."

"Carlos, we need to talk. . . ."

Before Joona gets a chance to tell him about Björn's e-mail, there's a knock on the door, and Verner Zandén, the head of the Security Police, comes in.

"Good to see you," the tall man says, shaking Carlos's hand.

"Welcome."

Verner shakes Joona's hand, then looks around the room and behind him.

"Where the hell is Saga?" he asks in his very deep voice.

She slowly walks in through the door.

"I didn't notice you'd fallen behind," he says, smiling.

Carlos turns to Saga but doesn't seem to know what to do or whether it's appropriate to shake hands with her. He chooses to take a step back and gesture invitingly toward the room.

"Come in, come in," he says in a shrill tone.

"Thanks," she says.

"You've already met Joona Linna."

Saga's eyes are hard; her jaw is clenched determinedly. The scar running through one of her eyebrows shimmers chalk-white.

"Make yourselves at home," Carlos says, managing to sound almost jolly.

Saga sits down stiffly on the sofa next to Joona. Carlos puts a shiny folder titled "Strategies for Collaboration" on the table.

Verner jokily raises his hand like a schoolboy before speaking: "From a formal perspective, the entire investigation comes under the Security Police's remit. But without National Crime and Joona, we wouldn't have made the breakthrough in the case."

Verner gestures toward the folder, and Saga's face turns bright red.

"Maybe we shouldn't call it a breakthrough," she murmurs.

"What?" Verner asks.

"Joona just managed to find a handprint and the remains of a photograph."

"And you—together with him—discovered that Penelope Fernandez is alive and being hunted. I'm not saying that's entirely his doing, but—"

"This is fucking ridiculous," Saga says. "How the hell can you sit here heaping praise on him when he wasn't even supposed to be there? He wasn't even supposed to know that Daniel Marklund was—"

"But he was, and he did," Verner interrupts.

"The whole damn thing's supposed to be confidential," she goes on loudly.

"Saga," Verner says sternly, "you weren't supposed to be there, either!"

"No, but if I hadn't been—"

She stops abruptly.

"Can we continue?" Verner asks.

She looks at her boss for a moment before turning to Carlos. "Sorry, I didn't mean to get angry."

Her forehead is still flushed with frustration. "I'm very sorry," she repeats.

Carlos clears his throat, then turns to her tentatively. "We're still hoping that Joona's contribution, or whatever you want to call it, will make you willing to let him join the investigation," he says.

"Seriously, though," Saga says to her boss, "I don't want to be negative, but I don't understand why we should let him into our investigation. We don't need him. You talk about a breakthrough, but I don't think . . ."

"I agree with Saga," Joona says slowly. "I'm sure you would have found that handprint and the corner of the photograph without my help."

"Maybe," Verner says.

"Can I go now?" Saga asks her boss in a composed voice, getting to her feet.

"But what you don't know," Joona goes on steadily, "is that Björn Almskog secretly contacted Carl Palmcrona the same day Viola was murdered."

Silence descends on the room. Saga slowly sits down again.

Verner leans forward, lets his thought settle, and then clears his throat. "Are you suggesting that Carl Palmcrona's and Viola Fernandez's deaths are connected?" he asks.

"Joona?" Carlos says.

"Yes, the two murders are linked," he confirms.

"This is bigger than we thought," Verner says, almost in a whisper.

"Good work," Carlos says.

Saga has folded her arms and is staring at the floor, her forehead flushed.

"Joona," Carlos says, clearing his throat, "I can't override Petter. He's still in charge of the investigation, but I would be prepared to second you to the Security Police."

"What do you say, Saga?" Joona asks.

"That would be perfect," Verner cuts in.

"I'm leading this investigation," Saga says, and walks out of the room.

Verner excuses himself and follows her.

Joona's gray eyes glint icily. Carlos, remaining seated, clears his throat and says: "She's young. You're going to have to try . . . I mean, be nice. Take care of her."

"I think she's more than capable of taking care of herself," Joona replies curtly.

38

SAGA IS THINKING about Carl Palmcrona and doesn't turn her head quickly enough. She sees the punch a little too late. It comes from the side. A low hook that passes over her left shoulder and hits her ear and cheek. She staggers. Her helmet is off-balance, and she can barely see, but she realizes a second blow is coming, so she lowers her chin and protects her face with both hands. It's a hard punch, followed up with another, to the top of her ribs. She stumbles backward into the ropes. The referee hurries over, but Saga has already slipped out of the trap. She moves sideways, toward the center of the ring, and takes stock of her opponent: Svetlana Krantz, a heavyset woman in her forties, with sloping shoulders and a Guns N' Roses tattoo on her neck. Svetlana is breathing through her mouth, following Saga with heavy footsteps, confident of winning by a knockout. Saga skips gently backward. *Boxing is easy*, she thinks, and feels a sudden joy fill her chest. She stops and smiles so broadly that she almost loses her mouth shield. She knows she's the better boxer, but she hadn't been planning to knock out Svetlana—she had decided to win on points. But when she heard Svetlana's boyfriend screaming about smashing the little blonde cunt's face in, she changed her mind.

Svetlana moves quickly across the ring. Her right hand is

eager, too eager. She's so intent on beating Saga that she's no longer following Saga's movements and has decided to finish things off with one or more heavy right hooks. She thinks that Saga is sufficiently shaken and that she'll be able to hammer the blows in, straight through her guard. But Saga isn't weakened, and she's extremely focused. She dances on the spot, waiting for her opponent to rush her, holding her hands up in front of her face as if she only wants to protect herself. Then, at precisely the right moment, she performs a surprising movement with her shoulders and feet, and with one forward step slips out of her opponent's line of attack. Saga ends up beside her but manages to put all her momentum into a body blow, right at the other woman's solar plexus.

She feels the edge of Svetlana's chest protection through her glove as her body folds forward. The next blow doesn't connect as well—she only hits the padding—but the third is almost perfect, a hard hit from below, right in the mouth.

Svetlana's head jolts backward. Sweat and snot fly from her face, and her dark-blue mouth guard falls out. Svetlana's knees buckle, and she thuds helplessly to the canvas, rolls over, and lies there for a moment before starting to move again.

After the match, Saga stands in the women's locker room feeling her body slowly relax. There's that familiar taste in her mouth, a mixture of blood and adhesive, because she uses her teeth to remove the tape covering the laces of her gloves. She looks in the mirror and quickly wipes away a few tears. Her nose is throbbing after that hard punch Svetlana landed. Her mind was elsewhere at the start of the match, on the conversation with her boss and Carlos, and their decision to make her work with Joona.

Saga's hands are shaking as she pulls off her clothes. Shivering, she walks into the tiled showers and stands in one of the cubicles. The water runs down her neck and back. She forces herself to stop thinking about Joona.

When she walks back into the locker room, she finds there are about twenty other women, who have just finished up a *ki* session. Saga doesn't notice the other women stop and almost glaze over at the sight of her. She is very beautiful. Perhaps it's the fact that she's related to fairy-tale artist John Bauer that makes people think of an elf or a fairy. Her face is neat and symmetrical, and her eyes are big and blue. She's petite and finely proportioned. Most people would probably guess she was a ballet dancer if they saw her, not a boxer and a Security Police officer.

John Bauer, a legendary figure in the fantasy-art world, had two brothers, Hjalmar and Ernst. Ernst, the younger brother, is Saga's great-grandfather. She can still remember her grandfather talking about his father, and his grief when his big brother John drowned with his wife, Ester, and their little son one November night.

Three generations later, it's as if John Bauer's paintings have found a remarkable reflection in reality. Saga looks like his illustration of Princess Tuvstarr standing in front of a big troll without any trace of fear.

Saga knows she's a good police officer, even though she's never been allowed to complete an investigation on her own. She's used to having her work taken away from her, being shut out after many weeks of dedicated effort. She's used to being overprotected and sidelined on operations.

She's used to it, but that doesn't mean she likes it.

She makes sure to keep her skills sharp and also gets a lot of physical exercise. She goes running every day, spars or boxes in matches at least twice a week, and practices shooting with her Glock and the police sniper rifle every week.

Saga lives with Stefan Johansson, who plays piano in a jazz group called the Red Bop Label. When Saga gets home from work or training, she usually lies on the sofa, eating candy and watching movies on mute, while Stefan plays his piano for hours at a time.

When Saga leaves the gym, she sees that her opponent is waiting for her by one of the concrete plinths. "I just wanted to say thanks and congratulate you," Svetlana says.

Saga stops. "Well, thank you."

Svetlana flushes slightly. "You're really good."

"So are you."

Svetlana looks down and smiles.

"Are you catching the train?" Saga asks.

"Yes, I should probably get going."

Svetlana picks up her bag, then stops. She seems to want to say something but hesitates. "Saga . . . I'm sorry about my boyfriend," she says eventually. "I don't know if you heard what he was shouting. It's the last time I'm going to let him come."

Svetlana clears her throat, then starts to walk away.

"Hang on," Saga says. "I can drive you to the station if you want."

39

PENELOPE'S AND BJÖRN'S feet and knees ache. They've been walking for what feels like forever and have just emerged onto a gravel path. Björn looks around, whispers to her to follow him, then starts heading south, toward the more populated area around Skinnardal. It can't be far. She limps a few steps, then follows him. When they get to the road, they see two people: a woman in her twenties in a short tennis dress and a man with a red motorcycle. Penelope zips up her hooded jacket and tries to breathe more calmly.

"Hi," she says.

They stare at her, and she can understand the looks on their faces. She and Björn are both filthy and streaked with blood.

"We've been in an accident," she says quickly between breaths. "Can we borrow your phone?"

"Okay," the young man says, pulling his phone out and handing it to Penelope.

"Thanks," Björn says, looking along the road and into the forest.

"What happened?" the young man asks.

Penelope doesn't know what to say and swallows as tears start to run down her dirty cheeks.

"An accident," Björn replies.

"I recognize her," the girl in the tennis dress says to her boyfriend. "She's that crazy lefty we saw on TV."

"Which one?"

"The one talking shit about Swedish arms exports, who wants to shut down factories. The one who doesn't care if hardworking people lose their jobs."

Penelope doesn't understand why the young woman is angry. Her mind is racing as she glances back at the trees and hears the phone ring, a distant, crackling ringtone.

"Don't you think jobs are important?" the woman says in an agitated voice.

Penelope looks at Björn, hoping he can come to her rescue, say something to the young woman to keep her happy. She sighs when she hears her mother's voice mail.

You've reached Claudia—I can't answer right now, but if you leave a message I'll get back to you as soon as I can.

The phone crackles. The reception is bad, and she moves, but that only makes it worse: the line goes silent, and she doesn't know if the connection has been broken when she says, "Mom, I need help, I'm being hunted by—"

Suddenly the girl snatches the phone from her and gives it back to the young man.

"Why don't you get a job!" he says.

Penelope staggers and looks at the young couple in surprise as the young woman gets on the motorcycle behind her boyfriend and wraps her arms around his waist.

The motorcycle's back wheel spins and kicks up gravel before they drive off. Björn calls out to them to stop, and they start to run after them, but the motorcycle disappears.

"Björn," Penelope says, stopping.

She's out of breath and looks back along the road, thinking that they're making a mistake. He stops, leans his hands on his thighs for a while, then starts walking.

"He knows what we're thinking," she says seriously. "We need to do something different."

Björn slows down, turns around, and looks at her, though he is still backing away.

"We have to find help," Björn says.

"Not now."

He walks back to her and grabs her shoulders.

"Penny, it's probably no more than ten minutes to the nearest house. You can manage that. I'll help—"

"We have to get back into the forest again," she says, cutting him off. "Trust me on this."

"When we were in the house," he says, "why did you call out to him to come in?"

"Because otherwise he would have opened the door and come straight in—it was the only thing he wasn't expecting."

"But . . ."

"He's been one step ahead of us the whole time," she goes on. "We've been scared, and he knows how scared people behave."

"They don't tell him to come in," Björn says.

"That's why we can't stay on the road to Skinnardal. We need to keep changing direction, running deeper into the forest, not heading toward anything. We need to think differently. Instead of trying to get from this island to the mainland, we should make our way farther out into the archipelago, away from the mainland."

"It would be crazy to do that," Bjorn says, and a weary smile spreads across his face.

40

AXEL RIESSEN slowly removes his cuff links and puts them in the bronze bowl on his dresser. He inherited the cuff links, two crossed palm leaves, from his grandfather, Admiral Riessen.

Axel looks at himself in the mirror. He loosens his tie, then walks to the other end of the room and sits down on the edge of the bed. The radiator is making a rushing sound, and through the walls he can hear fragments of music.

The sound is coming from his younger brother's rooms next door. A lone violin, he thinks, and immediately pieces together the fragments in his imagination: Bach's Violin Sonata No. 1, in G minor, the opening movement, the adagio, but much slower than most interpretations. Axel not only hears the intended notes but also enjoys each squeak and accidental knock of the frame.

His fingers tingle as the music changes tempo, and his hands long to pick up a violin. It's been a long time since he let his fingers merge with the music, running across the strings and up the neck.

The music in Axel's head goes quiet when his phone rings. He gets off the bed and rubs his eyes. He's very tired. He's hardly slept in the past week.

According to his caller ID, the call is coming from a

government office. Axel clears his throat before answering calmly: "Axel Riessen."

"My name is Jörgen Grünlicht. I'm chair of the government's Committee for Foreign Affairs."

"Good evening."

"Sorry to call so late."

"I was awake."

"I was told that you would be," Grünlicht says. "We've just had a committee meeting at which we agreed that we would like to recruit you as director general of the Inspectorate for Strategic Products."

"I see."

Neither of them speaks for a moment.

"I assume you know what happened to Carl Palmcrona."

"Only what I've read in the paper."

Grünlicht clears his throat weakly and says something Axel can't hear before raising his voice again.

"You're familiar with our work and—if you accept our proposal—would be able to start very quickly."

"I have to complete my duties with the UN," Axel replies.

"Do you anticipate that taking long?" Grünlicht asks, with a trace of anxiety in his voice.

"No."

"Take a look at the suggested terms. . . . There's nothing that isn't open to discussion," Grünlicht says. "We'd very much like to have you on board."

"Let me think about it."

"Do you have time to meet first thing tomorrow morning?"

"Is there any particular urgency?"

"We always take the time we need," Grünlicht replies. "But, obviously, bearing in mind what's happened . . . the trade minister is eager for us to reach a resolution on one specific issue that has already started to drag out."

"What's that?"

"Nothing unusual ... just an export license. We've been preapproved, and the Export Control Council has done its job. The report is ready, but Palmcrona didn't have time to sign it."

"And he needed to do that?" Axel asks.

"Only the director general can authorize the export of military equipment," Grünlicht explains.

"But surely the government authorizes some deals?"

"Only if the ISP's director general decides to refer the case to the government."

"I see."

Axel spent eleven years working as an arms inspector under the old system, for the Foreign Ministry, before he moved to the United Nations Office for Disarmament Affairs. He is now a senior adviser in the analysis-and-assessment division. Riessen is only fifty-one years old, and his graying hair is still thick. His features are regular and attractive.

Axel goes into his library and sits down in his reading chair. He closes his stinging eyelids and considers the fact that Carl Palmcrona is dead. He read the short report of his death in *Dagens Nyheter*. It was hard to figure out exactly what happened, but something about the article suggested that Palmcrona's death had come out of the blue. He evidently hadn't been ill, because they usually mention that. Axel thinks back to the many times they've met over the years.

And now Palmcrona is dead. In his mind's eye, Axel can see the tall, pale man with his cropped hair and air of loneliness.

He feels suddenly anxious. The apartment is too quiet. Axel stands up and looks into the other rooms, listening for noises.

"Beverly?" he calls quietly. "Beverly?"

She doesn't answer. He starts to feel scared. He walks quickly through the other rooms, then downstairs, to grab his coat and go out to look for her; but then he hears her humming to herself. She pads barefoot across the carpet from the kitchen. When she sees the worried look on his face, her eyes widen.

"Axel," she says in her high voice, "what is it?"

"I was just worried that you might have gone out," he mumbles.

"Into the big, bad world." She smiles.

"I just mean you can't always trust everyone."

"I don't. I look at them, at their auras," she explains. "If they have a bright aura, I know they're kind."

Axel doesn't know how to respond, so he just says that he's bought her some chips and a soda.

She doesn't even seem to hear him. He tries to read her face, so he can see if she's starting to become restless or depressed or withdrawn.

"Do you think we should still get married?" she asks.

"Yes," he lies.

"It's just that flowers make me think of Mom's funeral, and Dad's face when . . ."

"We don't have to have flowers," he says.

"But I like lilies of the valley."

"Me, too," he says weakly.

"I'm so sleepy," she says, and leaves the room. "Are you ready for bed?"

"No," Axel says to himself, but gets up and follows her.

He walks through the apartment with a strong sense that parts of his body are trying to stop him. He feels clumsy and slow as he follows her through the hallway, across the marble floor, and up the stairs into the suite of rooms he usually occupies in the evenings.

The girl is slender and short. She only reaches his chest. Her hair has started to grow again after she shaved it off last week. She gives him a quick hug, and he smells caramel.

41

AXEL FIRST MET Beverly Andersson ten months ago. It was all because of his acute insomnia. He's had trouble sleeping ever since a traumatic event occurred thirty-four years earlier. His life functioned as long as he took sleeping pills, which gave him a chemical sleep without dreams, and perhaps without real rest.

But he kept having to increase the dose. The tablets created a soporific buzz that drowned out his thoughts. He loved his medication and mixed it with expensive single-malt whisky. But after twenty years of high consumption of both, his brother found him in the hallway, unconscious, blood pouring from his nostrils.

At Karolinska Hospital, he was diagnosed with cirrhosis. The damage was so extreme that he was placed on the list for a liver transplant. But because he was blood group O and his tissue type was extremely unusual, the number of potential donors was minuscule. His younger brother could have donated part of his liver, but he suffers from severe arrhythmia, which meant his heart wouldn't be able to cope with such a serious operation.

So, though the chances of finding a donor were almost nonexistent, Axel wouldn't die as long as he kept away from alcohol and sleeping pills. With regular doses of Konakion,

Inderal, and spironolactone, his liver was able to function and he could lead a relatively normal life.

The problem was that sleep was as good as gone. He slept for no more than an hour each night. He was admitted to a sleep clinic in Gothenburg. Since medication was out of the question, he was given advice on different sleep strategies, such as meditation, hypnosis, and autosuggestion, but nothing helped.

Four months after his liver gave out, he spent nine days awake and suffered a breakdown. At his own request, he was admitted to a private psychiatric clinic.

That was where he met Beverly.

As usual, Axel was lying awake in his room. At around three o'clock in the morning, when it was completely dark, she opened his door.

He lay there, sleepless and confused, when she came in and stopped in front of him, her long nightgown dragging on the floor.

"I saw the light in here," she whispered. "You're glowing."

Then she just walked over to him and curled up on his bed. He was still ill from lack of sleep, didn't know what he was doing. He turned his back to her and felt the warmth from her body.

She just lay there in silence. He heard her calm breaths, and suddenly he fell asleep.

It was only a few minutes the first time, but after that she came to him every night. She climbed into his bed; he turned away and fell asleep.

He recovered from his breakdown, and Beverly stopped wandering the hallways.

Axel and Beverly left the clinic and entered into a desperate, silent agreement. They understood that the true nature of their relationship must remain secret, but outwardly Beverly got permission from her father to lodge in a self-contained set of rooms in Axel's apartment while she waited for a student apartment to become available.

Beverly is now seventeen years old and has been diagnosed with a borderline personality disorder. She has no sense of appropriate behavior and lacks the ability to assert herself. She has no self-preservation instinct.

Girls like Beverly used to be locked away in institutions and forcibly sterilized or lobotomized.

Girls like Beverly still go home with people they shouldn't, place all their trust in people who take advantage of them.

But Beverly has been lucky to find Axel. He has no intention of harming her. He just needs her so he can sleep, so he can stay afloat.

Axel lets her weave her fantasies about a wedding, because it seems to make her happy. He tells himself that it's a way of protecting her from the outside world, but he knows he's exploiting her. Even though he feels ashamed, he can't think of any way out; he's terrified of finding himself back in the horrors of perpetual insomnia.

Beverly comes out of the bathroom with her toothbrush in her mouth. She nods toward the three violins hanging on the wall.

"Why don't you ever play them?" she asks.

"I can't," he replies with a smile.

"So they're just going to hang there? Give them to someone who plays instead."

"I like the violins because Robert gave them to me."

"You hardly ever talk about your brother."

"It's complicated. . . ."

"He makes violins in his workshop," she says.

"Yes, and plays in a chamber orchestra."

"Can he play at our wedding?" she asks, wiping toothpaste from the corners of her mouth.

Axel looks at her and hopes she doesn't notice the stiffness in his face when he says, "That's a good idea."

He feels tiredness washing over him, through his body and brain. He walks past her, into the bedroom, and sinks down on the edge of the bed.

"I'm so sleepy, I . . ."

"Poor you," she says seriously.

Axel shakes his head.

"I just need to sleep," he says. He feels as if he's about to cry.

Beverly looks at the big oil painting on the wall. It's by Ernst Billgren and shows a fox dressed up and sitting in an armchair in a nice home. "Creepy picture," she says.

"Do you think?"

She nods.

He walks over to the painting of the fox, takes it down, and puts it on the floor, facing the wall.

AXEL SLEEPS STIFFLY and heavily, with his face scrunched up and his jaw clenched. In the middle of the night, he wakes up suddenly and gasps for breath, as if he were drowning. He's sweating, and his heart is thudding. He switches the bedside light on. Beverly is sleeping like a small child, with her mouth open.

Axel finds himself thinking about Carl Palmcrona again. The last time they met was in the House of Nobility. Palmcrona had been drunk and behaved rather aggressively, complaining about the UN's various arms embargoes. Axel still remembers his remarkable parting words: "If it all goes to hell, I suppose one can always pull an Algernon to avoid seeing his nightmare come true."

Axel turns the light out again and makes himself comfortable as he thinks about Palmcrona's phrase: "pulling an Algernon." What did he mean? And what was the nightmare he referred to? Was that really what he said?

Avoid seeing his nightmare come true.

Carl-Fredrik Algernon's fate was a national mystery. He was a weapons inspector for the Foreign Ministry up until his death. In January 1987, he had a meeting with the head of Nobel Industries, Anders Carlberg, during which he told him that their investigation indicated that one of the group's subsidiaries, the Bofors company, had been smuggling arms to countries in the Persian Gulf. Later that day, Algernon fell in front of a subway car at Central Station in Stockholm.

Axel's thoughts wander off, circling around the allegations of arms smuggling and bribery that had been directed at the Bofors company. In his mind's eye, he sees a man in a trench coat fall backward in front of a speeding train.

The man falls slowly, his coat fluttering behind him.

Beverly's gentle breathing calms Axel down. He turns to her and puts his arm around her slender frame. She sighs as he pulls her to him. Axel holds her tightly and feels his thoughts dissipate.

He sleeps fitfully for the rest of the night and wakes up at five o'clock to find himself holding Beverly's thin arms in a viselike grip. He feels her cropped hair tickle his lips and wishes desperately that he were still able to take his pills.

42

At seven o'clock in the morning, Axel goes out onto the deck that he shares with his brother. He's going to meet Jörgen Grünlicht in Palmcrona's office at the Inspectorate for Strategic Products in an hour.

The air outside is already warm but not yet humid. His younger brother, Robert, has opened the doors to his apartment and is sitting on a deck chair. He hasn't shaved yet and is wearing his old silk bathrobe. It's the same one their father used to wear on Saturday mornings.

"Good morning," Robert says.

Axel nods, without looking at his brother.

"I finished repairing a Fiorini for Charles Greendirk," Robert says, attempting to start a conversation.

"I'm sure he'll be pleased," Axel replies quietly.

Robert looks up at him. "Are you stressed?"

"A little, to be honest," Axel replies. "It looks like I'm going to be starting a new job."

"Really?" Robert says absentmindedly.

Axel looks at his brother's friendly face, his deep wrinkles, his bald head. He thinks how different things could have been between them.

"How's your heart these days?" he asks. "It hasn't stopped yet?"

Robert puts his hand to his chest before replying: "Not quite."

"Good."

"How about your poor liver?"

Axel shrugs and starts to head back into his apartment.

"We're playing Schubert tonight," Robert says.

"That's nice."

"I thought maybe you . . ."

Robert falls silent, looks at his brother, then changes the subject. "That girl who has the room up there . . ."

"Yes . . . Beverly," Axel says.

"How long is she going to be living here?" Robert asks, squinting at Axel.

"I don't know," he replies. "I've promised her she can stay here until she gets a student apartment."

"Yes, you always did like to look after strays."

"She's a human being," Axel interrupts.

He sees his face slide across the uneven glass door as it swings open. Hidden behind the curtain, he watches his brother walk down the stairs that lead from the deck to the little garden and studio. As soon as Robert is gone, Axel returns to his room and gently wakes Beverly, who is still lying asleep with her mouth open.

THE INSPECTORATE FOR STRATEGIC PRODUCTS is the official body responsible for all matters concerning the export of arms and other equipment that can have a military use.

When Axel gets out of the elevator, he sees Grünlicht waiting for him inside the big glass doors. Grünlicht nods impatiently, even though Axel is two minutes early, then lets him through the doors. Grünlicht is a tall man with uneven pigmentation on his face, large white patches that stand out against his otherwise ruddy complexion.

They walk to Palmcrona's office, a corner room with two huge windows and a view of the southbound roads behind Central Station and, beyond that, Klara Lake and the dark, regular outline of the City Hall.

Despite the upscale address, there's something spartan about the ISP's premises. The floors are lined with linoleum, and the furniture is simple and neutral, white pine.

It feels rather macabre to be in Palmcrona's office so soon after his death.

Axel notes that the ceiling light is making a buzzing sound, like the undertone from an untuned piano. He remembers hearing the same note in a recording of composer John Cage's Sonata 1.

Grünlicht closes the door, and when he invites Axel to sit down, he seems tense, despite his friendly smile.

"Good that you could come so quickly," he says, handing Axel a folder enclosing a draft of their contract.

"Don't mention it," Axel says with a smile.

"Look through it," Grünlicht says, gesturing toward the desk.

Axel sits down on the unfussy chair, puts the folder on the desk, then looks up.

"I'll take a look and be in touch next week."

"It's a very strong contract, but the offer won't remain open indefinitely," Grünlicht says.

"I appreciate that you'd like to move quickly on this."

"The committee is extremely eager to have you, given your career, your reputation—there's no better candidate. That said, we can't let the organization sit idle."

Axel opens the folder and tries to suppress his unease, his

suspicion that he's being lured into a trap. There's something forced about Grünlicht's manner, something impatient.

If he signs the contract, he'll be director general of the ISP and will have final approval over all Swedish arms exports. Axel has spent his years at the UN trying to disarm regions where there's been armed conflict and limit the flow of weapons. He'd like to think of this appointment as a continuation of that work.

He very carefully reads through the agreement. It really is very generous, almost too generous. He blushes several times as he reads it.

"Welcome on board." Grünlicht smiles, handing him a pen.

Axel thanks him, signs his name on the contract, then stands up and looks out of the window, turning his back on Grünlicht. He can just make out the three crowns at the top of City Hall through the hazy sunlight.

"Not a bad view from here," Grünlicht murmurs. "Better than from my office in the Foreign Ministry."

Axel turns toward him.

"You have three cases on your desk at the moment, of which the Kenyan contract is the most urgent. It's a big, important deal. I'd advise you to look at that one first, preferably immediately. Carl already did a lot of the preliminary work, so . . ."

He trails off, pushes the document toward Axel, and then looks at him with an odd twinkle in his eyes. Axel gets the feeling that Grünlicht would really just like to force a pen in his hand and make him sign.

"I'm sure you're going to be a very worthy successor to Carl."

Without waiting for a response, he pats Axel's arm, then strides quickly across the floor. At the door, he turns back and says curtly: "Meeting with the committee at three p.m. today."

Axel is left standing by himself in the office. A mute silence settles around him. He sits down at the desk again and looks through the document Palmcrona left unsigned. The preliminary work is careful and thorough. The case concerns the export of 1.25 million rounds of 5.56 × 45–millimeter ammunition to Kenya. The Export Control Council voted in favor, and the manufacturer, Silencia Defense Ltd., is an established and reputable company.

But the deal can't proceed without his signature.

Axel leans back and thinks about Palmcrona's words about "pulling an Algernon" and dying without having to see his nightmare come true.

43

Göran smiles at Joona, then pulls an envelope from his bag and tips a key into his cupped hand. Saga is still standing outside the closed elevator door, her eyes downcast. The three of them are on the landing outside Carl Palmcrona's apartment.

"Our forensics team will be here tomorrow," Göran says.

"Do you know what time?" Joona asks.

"What time, Saga?" Göran asks.

"I think we—"

"Think?" he interrupts. "You're supposed to know what time."

"Ten," she replies in a low voice.

"You told them that I personally want them to start with IT and telephones?"

"Yes, I said—"

Göran silences her with a gesture when his phone rings. He answers it and walks a little ways down the staircase, stopping in an alcove.

Joona turns to Saga and asks in a subdued voice, "Aren't you in charge of the investigation?"

Saga shakes her head.

"What happened?" he asks.

"I don't know," she replies wearily. "It's always the same.

This isn't even Göran's area of expertise. He's never worked in counterterrorism."

"What are you going to do about it?"

"There's nothing—"

She stops speaking when Göran comes back up to join them. Saga holds out her hand for the key to Palmcrona's door.

"The key," she says.

"What?"

"I'm in charge of this investigation."

"What do you think about that?" Göran says with a laugh, looking at Joona.

"I'm sure you'd be a great lead investigator, Göran," Joona says. "But I was just at a meeting with our bosses where I agreed to work with Saga Bauer. . . ."

"She's allowed to come along," he says quickly.

"As head of the investigation," Saga says.

"So you want to get rid of me? What the hell is going on here?" Göran asks with a surprised, affronted smile.

"You're allowed to come along, if you'd like," Joona says calmly.

Saga takes the key from Göran's hand.

"I'm calling Verner," he says, and starts to walk down the stairs.

They hear his footsteps in the stairwell, then his conversation with his boss. His voice gets more and more agitated until he finally exclaims, "Bunch of cunts!" so loudly that it echoes up the stairs.

Saga forces the smile from her face, then inserts the key into the lock and opens the heavy door.

The police cordon was taken down after Nils Åhlén submitted his postmortem and the investigation was dropped: all of Nils's findings supported what Joona said about the suicide. Palmcrona took his own life by hanging a clothes-line with a noose from the lamp hook in the ceiling of his home. There was never an analysis of the samples sent to the forensics lab.

But now they know that the day before Palmcrona was found hanging in his home, Björn sent him an e-mail.

Later that day, Viola was murdered.

Björn is the link, the connection between the two deaths— two deaths that would have been written off as a suicide and a drowning, respectively, if things had gone according to plan.

Saga and Joona walk into the apartment and note that there's no mail on the ground. It smells like disinfectant. Sunlight is flooding through the windows.

The forensics experts' protective mats are gone, and the floor in the large drawing room has been mopped clean.

They walk slowly through the apartment. Oddly enough, Palmcrona's suicide isn't lingering. The place doesn't feel abandoned at all. Joona and Saga both sense it. The large rooms are full of comfortable tranquillity.

"She hasn't stopped coming," Saga says.

"Exactly," Joona replies with a smile. The housekeeper has been cleaning, opening the windows, picking up the mail, changing the sheets, and so on. They're both thinking that this isn't particularly unusual in a case of sudden death. People are reluctant to admit that life has changed.

The doorbell rings. Saga looks slightly alarmed but follows Joona out into the entryway.

A man with a shaved head, wearing a baggy black tracksuit, is standing by the front door.

"Joona told me to throw my hamburger away and come right over," Johan says.

"This is Johan Jönson, from IT," Joona explains.

Johan makes a lame attempt to imitate Joona's Finnish accent.

"And Saga Bauer is with the Security Police," Joona says.

"So are we here to talk or to work?" Johan asks, still speaking in a Finnish accent.

"Stop that," Saga says.

"We need to look at Palmcrona's computer," Joona says. "How long will it take?"

They head for the study.

"Will it be used as evidence?" Johan asks.

"Yes," Joona replies.

"So you want me to clone it?" he asks.

"How long will it take?" Joona asks.

"You'll have time to tell her a few jokes," he replies, without moving.

"What's the matter with you?" Saga says irritably.

"Are you single?" Johan asks with an embarrassed smile.

She looks him in the eye and shakes her head. He looks down, mutters something, then disappears into Palmcrona's study.

Joona takes a pair of protective gloves from Saga, pulls them on, and checks the mail on the shelf, but he doesn't find anything special. There isn't much, just a few letters from the bank and an accountant, some information from the Cabinet Office, test results from the Sophia Clinic's orthopedic department, and the minutes from the spring meeting of the residents' committee.

They return to the music room. Joona sits down on one of the sofas and gently moves his hand in front of the thin beam of light coming from the stereo. Music starts to play from the loudspeakers, a solo violin. A virtuoso is conjuring forth a fragile melody in the highest part of the instrument's register.

Joona looks at his watch, leaves Saga by the stereo, and goes out to the study. Johan isn't there. He's sitting in the kitchen, with his laptop on the table in front of him.

"Did it go okay?" Joona asks.

"What?"

"Did you manage to copy Palmcrona's computer?"

"All done—this is an exact clone," he replies.

Joona goes around the table to look at the screen.

"Can you get into his e-mails?"

"Ta-da," he says.

"We'll look at his mail from the past week," Joona goes on.

"Starting with the inbox?"

"Yes, starting there."

"Do you think Saga likes me?" Johan asks out of the blue.

"No," Joona replies.

"Love often starts with arguments."

"Try tugging her braid," Joona says, pointing at the screen.

Johan opens the inbox and grins.

"*Jackpot-voitto*," he says in Finnish.

Joona sees three e-mails from the address skunk@hotmail .com.

"Open them," Joona whispers.

Johan clicks on the first one, and Björn's e-mail fills the screen.

"Jesus Christ, Superstar," Johan whispers, moving out of the way.

44

JOONA READS THE E-MAIL, then opens the rest, reads them all through twice, then goes to find Saga.

"Did you get anything?" she asks.

"Yes," Joona says. "On June 2, Palmcrona received an e-mail with a blackmail threat from Björn Almskog. It was sent from an anonymous address."

"So it's all about blackmail." She sighs.

"I'm not so sure about that," Joona replies.

He goes on to give an account of Palmcrona's final days. First, he paid a visit to Silencia Defense's arms factory in Trollhättan. In all likelihood, he didn't read Björn's e-mail until he got home, because his response was sent at 6:25 p.m. In his reply, Palmcrona warned the blackmailer of serious consequences. At lunchtime the following day, Palmcrona sent a second e-mail to the blackmailer, expressing complete capitulation. After that, he presumably fastened the cord to the ceiling and asked his housekeeper to leave him alone. Once she left, he turned on some music, went into the living room, climbed up on his briefcase, and put the noose around his neck. Immediately after his death, Björn Almskog's second e-mail to Palmcrona arrived, and the third came the following day.

Joona places printouts of the five e-mails in the right

order on the table, and Saga stands next to him and reads the entire exchange.

The first e-mail from Björn, on Wednesday, June 2, at 11:37 a.m.:

Dear Carl Palmcrona,

I am writing to inform you that I am in possession of an original photograph of a sensitive nature. The picture shows you sitting in a private box drinking champagne with Raphael Guidi. Seeing as I fully understand the troubling nature of this documentary evidence, I am prepared to sell the photograph to you for one million kronor. As soon as you have transferred the money to transit account 837-9 222701730, the picture will be sent to you and all evidence of this correspondence destroyed.

Sincerely,

A Skunk

Palmcrona's reply, on Wednesday, June 2, at 6:25 p.m.:

I don't know who you are, but one thing I do know is that you don't understand what you're getting yourself into. You have absolutely no idea.

So I am warning you: this is extremely serious, and I beg you, give me the photograph before it's too late.

Palmcrona's second reply, Thursday, June 3, at 2:02 p.m.:

It's too late now, you and I are both going to die.

Björn's second e-mail, Thursday, June 3, at 4:02 p.m.:

I give up, I'll do as you say.

Björn's third e-mail, Friday, June 4, at 7:47 a.m.:

Dear Carl Palmcrona,
I have sent the photograph. Forget I ever contacted you.
Sincerely,
A Skunk

After reading the e-mails through twice, Saga Bauer says: "Björn wanted to sell a compromising photograph to Palmcrona. It's clear that Palmcrona believed the photograph existed, and it's clear that the content of the photograph was far more serious than Björn imagined. Palmcrona warned Björn. There's no suggestion that he was going to pay anything for the picture; he seemed to think its very existence was dangerous for both of them."

"So what do you think happened?" Joona asks.

"Palmcrona waited for a reply, either by e-mail or by letter," Saga says. "When he didn't get an answer, he sent the second e-mail, in which he said Björn and he were both going to die."

"And then he hanged himself," Joona says.

"When Björn got to the Internet café and read Palmcrona's second e-mail, 'It's too late now, you and I are both going to die,' he got scared and replied that he was going to do what Palmcrona suggested."

"Without knowing that Palmcrona was already dead."

"Exactly," she says. "It was already too late. Everything he did after that was pretty much in vain. . . ."

"He seems to have panicked after Palmcrona's second e-mail," Joona says. "He dropped the blackmail idea. He just wanted to get out of the situation."

"But the photograph was still taped to the door in Penelope's apartment."

"He didn't have a chance to get the picture until she went to that debate," Joona goes on. "He waited outside and watched her leave, rushed in, met the little girl on the stairs, hurried into the apartment, grabbed the photograph, took the train to Central Station, mailed the photograph to Palmcrona, e-mailed him, went back to his apartment to get his bags, caught the bus to Södermalm, and hurried to his boat."

"So what makes you think this is anything more than ordinary extortion?"

"Björn's apartment was completely destroyed by fire about three hours after he left it," Joona says. "The fire department's experts are convinced it was caused by an iron left on in the apartment next door, but . . ."

"I've stopped believing in coincidences when it comes to this case," Saga says.

"Me, too." Joona smiles.

They look at the e-mail exchange again, and Joona points at Palmcrona's two messages. "Palmcrona must have been in contact with someone between his first and second e-mails," he says.

"The first is a warning," Saga says. "The second says it's too late and that they're both going to die."

"I think Palmcrona called someone when he got the e-mail. He was scared, but was hoping to get help," Joona says. "Then, when he realized there was no way out, he sent the second e-mail."

"We can have someone go through his phone records," Saga says.

"Erixon's already started."

"What else?"

"We need to check the person mentioned in Björn's first e-mail," Joona says.

"Raphael Guidi?" Saga wonders.

"Do you know him?"

"People call him the Archangel," Saga says. "He's an Italian businessman who puts together arms deals in the Middle East and Africa."

"The arms trade," Joona says.

"Guidi has been active for thirty years and has built up a private empire, but I doubt he's involved in anything illegal. Interpol has never been able to get anything on him. There have been suspicions, but nothing more."

"Is it strange for Palmcrona to meet Guidi?" Joona asks.

"On the contrary," she replies. "It's part of his job, even though Guidi is a despicable human being."

"So not the sort of thing you commit suicide over or kill anyone for," Joona says.

"No." She smiles.

"So the photograph must have revealed something else, something dangerous."

"If Björn sent the photograph to Palmcrona, it should be in his apartment," Saga says.

"I looked through the mail, and—"

He stops abruptly, and Saga stares at him.

"What is it? What are you thinking?" she asks.

"There were only letters addressed directly to him in the box—no ads, no flyers," he says. "The mail is already sorted by the time it gets here."

45

THE HOUSEKEEPER, Edith Schwartz, doesn't have a phone. She lives north of Stockholm, outside Knivsta. Joona is sitting quietly next to Saga as she drives toward the address.

"The Security Police have finished the investigation of Penelope's apartment," she says. "I've been through all the material, and it doesn't look like she had any connection to any extreme left-wing groups. Quite the contrary, in fact—she distances herself from them. She's an outspoken pacifist and campaigns against their methods. I've also looked at what little we've got on Björn Almskog. He works at the Debaser club and isn't politically active, but he was arrested once in connection with a street party that was organized by Reclaim the City. "I've been through everything we've got on extremist groups in Stockholm, both left and right—it took most of the night. Obviously, it's all classified, but you need to know that the Security Police made a mistake: Penelope and Björn aren't involved in any sabotage, nothing like that. They're innocent."

"So you've dropped that line of inquiry?"

"Just like you, I'm convinced we're investigating something in a different league, way beyond left- or right-wing extremists . . . probably outside the purview of the Security Police or National Crime," she says. "I mean, Palmcrona's death, the fire in Björn's apartment, Viola's murder, and so on—this is about something big."

They stop speaking, and Joona thinks back to his encounter with the housekeeper, the way she looked him in the eyes and asked if they had taken Palmcrona down yet:

"What do you mean, 'take him down'?"

"I'm sorry. I'm only the housekeeper. I thought . . ."

He had gone on to ask her if she had noticed anything unusual.

"A noose hanging from the lamp hook in the living room," she had replied.

"You saw the noose?"

"Of course."

Of course, Joona thinks, and looks out at the highway. The sharp way the housekeeper said the words "of course" linger in his mind. He thinks back to the look on her face when he explained that she might have to come to police headquarters and talk to a police officer. She didn't react anxiously, as he had expected, but merely nodded.

They pass Rotebro, the site of a grisly discovery Joona had made in the course of the Tumba investigation.

Joona calls Pollock and hears his slightly nasal voice after just two rings.

"Pollock."

"You and Kofoed looked at the prints beneath Palmcrona's body."

"The investigation was dropped," Pollock replies, and Joona hears him typing on a keyboard.

"Yes, but now—"

"I know," he interrupts. "I've spoken to Carlos. He told me about the latest."

"Can you take another look?"

"That's what I'm doing right now," Pollock replies.

"Sounds good," Joona says. "When do you think you'll be done?"

"Now," he says. "The shoeprints come from Palmcrona and his housekeeper, Edith Schwartz."

"No one else?"

"No."

Saga is maintaining a steady speed of 140 kilometers per hour as they head farther north.

Earlier, Joona and Saga had listened to the recording of the interview with Edith Schwartz, while simultaneously reading John Bengtsson's handwritten comments.

Now Joona goes through the interview again in his head: After the introductory formalities, John explains that no one suspects that a crime has been committed but that he hopes she might be able to shed some light on the circumstances surrounding Carl Palmcrona's death. Then there's silence. John's notes show that he chose to wait for Edith to speak, because she seemed so completely indifferent.

It took a little more than two minutes for her to say something. That's a long time to sit at a desk across from a police officer in silence.

"Had Mr. Palmcrona taken his coat off?" she eventually asks.

"Why do you wonder that?" John asks amiably.

She remains silent again, for another thirty seconds or so, before John speaks again: "Was he wearing his coat the last time you saw him?" he asks.

"Yes."

"Earlier, you told Detective Linna that you'd seen a noose hanging from the ceiling."

"Yes."

"What did you think it was going to be used for?"

She doesn't answer.

"How long had it been hanging there?" John asks.

"Since Wednesday," she replies calmly.

"So you saw the noose hanging from the ceiling on the evening of June 2, went home, returned the following morning, June 3, saw the noose again, met Palmcrona, left the apartment, then returned again at two-thirty p.m. on June 5 . . . and that was when you met Detective Linna."

The notes indicate that Edith shrugged.

"Can you tell me about those days, in your own words?" John asks.

"I arrived at Mr. Palmcrona's apartment at six o'clock on the morning of the Wednesday. I'm only allowed to use my key in the morning because Mr. Palmcrona sleeps until half past six. He's careful to stick to a regular schedule, so he never sleeps in, not even on Sundays. I grind coffee beans in the manual grinder, cut two slices of bread, spread them with extra-salty spreadable butter, put two slices of liver pâté with truffle on them, then add sliced pickled gherkin and a slice of cheddar cheese on the side. I set the table with starched linen and the summer china. The morning paper should be empty of loose ads and the sports section, and placed to the right of the chair, folded."

She goes on to relate in detail the preparation of Wednesday's evening meal, minced beef patties in cream sauce, then lunch on Thursday.

When she reaches the moment on Saturday when she returns with the groceries for the weekend and rings the doorbell, she stops speaking.

"I appreciate that this is difficult," John says after a brief silence. "But I sat here and listened to you describe what happened on Wednesday and Thursday, in great detail, but you haven't mentioned anything about Mr. Palmcrona's sudden demise, not once."

She remains silent and makes no attempt to offer an explanation.

"I have to ask you to search your memory again," John goes on patiently. "Did you know that Carl Palmcrona was dead when you rang the doorbell?"

"No," she replies.

"Didn't you ask Detective Linna if we had taken him down yet?" John asks, with a degree of impatience in his voice.

"Yes," she replies.

"Had you already seen that he was dead?"

"No."

"What the hell?" John says irritably. "Can you not just tell me what you know? What made you ask if we had taken him down? You asked, after all! Why did you do that if you didn't know he was dead?"

In his report, John wrote that he had made a mistake by allowing himself to be provoked by her evasive manner and that she had clammed up completely after his outburst.

"Am I under suspicion?" she asks coolly.

"No."

"Then we're done."

"It would be a great help if—"

"I don't remember anything else," she says, cutting him off, as she rises from her chair.

JOONA LOOKS AT SAGA. Her eyes are focused on the highway and the truck ahead of them.

"I've been thinking about the interview with the housekeeper," Joona says.

"Me, too," she replies.

"John got annoyed with her. He thought she was contradicting herself. He claimed she knew Palmcrona was dead when she rang the doorbell," Joona says.

"Yes," Saga replies, without looking at him.

"But she was telling the truth. She didn't know he was dead. She thought he probably was, but she didn't know," he goes on. "That's why she said no."

"Edith Schwartz seems to be an unusual woman."

"I think she's trying to hide something from us, but she doesn't actually want to lie," Joona says.

46

BOTH JOONA AND SAGA doubt that they're going to be able to get Edith to say anything conclusive, but she might be able to lead them to the photograph, and that could help bring the entire case to a close.

Saga leaves the highway and slows down, then turns onto a narrow gravel road.

They're driving through low pine forest interspersed with cropped fields.

"This should be it," Saga says, glancing at the GPS.

When Joona gets out of the car, he can hear the traffic on the nearby highway as a rolling, lifeless roar.

Twenty meters away is a single-story building made of dirty yellow brick, with shuttered windows and mossy cement tiles on the roof.

They hear a peculiar whirring sound as they approach the house.

Saga looks at Joona. They move cautiously toward the front door, very alert. There's a rustling sound behind the house, then the metallic whirring again.

The sound is rapidly coming closer, and then a large dog, a German shepherd with a matted coat, throws itself at them. It stops on its hind legs with its mouth open, inches from Saga. Then it's yanked backward, puts its front legs down, and starts to bark aggressively, tossing its head and running from side to side. Only now do they see that the dog is attached to a long wire leash that rattles and whirrs as the dog runs.

The dog turns and rushes at Joona, but the leash stops it and it gets yanked backward again. It's still barking uncontrollably but stops at the sound of a voice through the wall.

"Nils!" a woman shouts.

The dog whines and walks around in a circle, its tail between its legs. The floor creaks, and a few seconds later the door opens. The dog runs into the house, dragging the leash behind it. Edith comes out onto the steps, dressed in a pilled purple bathrobe.

"We need to talk to you," Joona says.

"I've already told you all I know," she replies.

"Can we come in?"

"No."

Joona looks past into the gloomy house. The hall is dark and full of junk.

"Out here is fine," Saga says cheerfully.

Joona looks at his notes and starts by checking the details of what she said in her previous interview. This is a routine method of uncovering lies or inconsistencies. It's often hard to remember details that aren't true, details you came up with on the spur of the moment.

"What did Palmcrona have to eat on Wednesday?"

"Minced beef patties in cream sauce," she replies.

"With rice?" Joona asks.

"Potatoes. Always boiled potatoes."

"What time did you arrive at Palmcrona's apartment on Thursday?"

"Six o'clock."

"What did you do when you left Palmcrona's apartment on Thursday?"

"He'd given me the evening off."

Joona looks into her eyes and concludes that there's no point skirting around the important questions.

"Had Palmcrona hung the noose from the ceiling on Wednesday?"

"No," Edith replies.

"That's what you told our colleague John Bengtsson," Saga says.

"No."

"We've got a recording of the entire interview," Saga says with suppressed irritation, then stops herself abruptly.

"Did you say anything to Palmcrona about the noose?" Joona asks.

"We didn't talk about personal matters with each other."

"But isn't it a little odd to leave a man alone with a noose hanging from the ceiling?" Saga asks.

"I could hardly stay and watch," Edith replies with the trace of a smile.

"I suppose not," Saga says calmly.

For the first time, Edith seems to take a proper look at Saga. She lets her gaze wander from Saga's blond hair decked with colorful ribbons, to her face without makeup, then down to her faded jeans and sneakers.

"I still can't quite make sense of it, though," Saga says wearily. "You told our colleague that you saw the noose on Wednesday, but when I asked just now, you said the opposite."

Joona looks in his notebook at what he wrote a minute or so before, when Saga asked if Palmcrona had hung the noose on Wednesday.

"Edith," Joona says, "I think I understand what you're saying."

"Good," she replies in a low voice.

"When you were asked if Palmcrona hung the noose up on Wednesday, you said no because he isn't the one who hung it up."

The old woman raises her head and gives him a hard stare, then says stiffly: "He tried, but he couldn't do it. His back was too bad after the operation last winter. . . . So he asked me to do it."

"So you were the person who tied the noose to the lamp hook on Wednesday?" Joona asks.

"He made the noose and held the stepladder while I went up it."

"Then you put the stepladder away, returned to your usual duties, and went home on Wednesday evening, after you washed the dishes from dinner," Joona says.

"Yes."

"You returned the following morning," he goes on. "You let yourself in as usual and made his breakfast."

"Did you know that he wasn't hanging from the noose then?" Saga asks.

"I'd checked in the living room," Edith replies.

Something approaching a smile flits quickly across her otherwise impassive face.

"You've already said that Palmcrona ate breakfast at exactly the same time as usual, but he didn't go to work that morning."

"He sat in the music room for at least an hour."

"Listening to music?"

"Yes," she replies.

"Just before lunchtime, he made a short phone call," Saga says.

"I don't know anything about that. He was in his study with the door closed, but before he sat down to have his poached salmon he asked me to book a taxi for two o'clock."

"He was going to Arlanda Airport," Joona says.

"Yes."

"And at ten minutes to two he received a phone call?"

"Yes, he'd already put his coat on when he answered."

"Did you hear what he said?" Saga asks.

Edith stands still, scratches the Band-Aid on her cheek, and then puts her hand on the door handle.

"Dying isn't such a nightmare," she says quietly.

"I asked if you heard what he said," Saga says.

"You'll have to excuse me," Edith says curtly, starting to close the door.

"Wait," Joona says.

The door stops abruptly, and she looks at him through the gap without opening it again.

"Have you had time to sort through Palmcrona's mail today?" Joona asks.

"Of course."

"Bring me everything that isn't an ad," Joona says.

She nods and goes into the house, closing the door behind her, then returns with a blue plastic tray full of mail.

"Thank you," Joona says, taking it.

She shuts and locks the door. After a few moments, the dog's leash starts to rattle again. They hear it barking aggressively behind them as they walk back to the car.

Saga turns the car around. Joona puts on a pair of protective gloves, looks through the mail in the tray, opens a white envelope with a handwritten address, and carefully pulls out the photograph that at least two people have died for.

47

SAGA PULLS OVER on the side of the road. Joona is staring at the photograph.

The top of the image is obscured by something, but it's extremely sharp otherwise. Presumably, the camera was hidden and the picture was taken without anyone's knowing.

The photograph shows four people, three men and a woman, in a spacious box at a concert. Their faces are all visible and very clear, even though one of them is partially turned away.

There's an ice bucket with champagne, and the table next to them is set so that they can eat, talk, and listen to the music at the same time.

Joona immediately recognizes Carl Palmcrona holding a tall champagne glass in his hand, and Saga identifies two of the others.

"That's Raphael Guidi, the arms dealer mentioned in the blackmail e-mail," she says, pointing at a man with thinning hair. "And that one who's half turned away is Pontus Salman, the head of Silencia Defense."

"Weapons," Joona says in a low voice.

Onstage behind the box is a string quartet: two violins, a viola, and a cello. The musicians are all men. They're sitting in a semicircle, facing one another, with looks of calm concentration on their faces. It's impossible to say whether they're looking at their scores or if they have their eyes closed and are listening to the other instruments.

"Who's the fourth person, the woman?" Joona asks.

"It's on the tip of my tongue," Saga says thoughtfully. "I recognize her, but . . . Damn . . ."

Saga stares at the woman's face.

"We have to find out who she is," Joona says.

"Yes."

Saga starts the car, and just as she pulls away she remembers: "Agathe al-Haji," she says quickly. "She's a military adviser to President Omar al-Bashir."

"Sudan," Joona says.

"Yes."

"How long has she been his adviser?" Joona asks.

"Fifteen years, maybe more, I don't remember."

"So what's so special about this picture?"

"I don't know. Nothing. I mean . . . it wouldn't be unusual for these four to meet and discuss the possibility of doing business," Saga says. "Quite the opposite. Meetings like this are part of the job. It could be a first point of contact. They meet, discuss their intentions, maybe request a preliminary evaluation from Carl Palmcrona."

"And preapproval means that the ISP will probably award an export license?"

"Exactly. It's a good sign."

"Does Sweden usually export military equipment to Sudan?" Joona asks.

"No, I don't think so," she replies. "We'll have to talk to someone who specializes in that part of the world. I have a feeling that China and Russia are the main suppliers, but that isn't necessarily still the case. Sudan's civil war ended in 2005, so I presume the market opened up after that."

"So what does this picture mean? Why did it cause Palm-crona to commit suicide? I mean, the only thing it proves is that he met these people in a box at a concert."

They drive south in silence while Joona looks at the photograph and thinks.

"So the picture itself isn't remotely dangerous?" he asks.

"No, not to my eyes."

"Did Palmcrona kill himself because he realized that who-ever took the picture was going to reveal a secret? Maybe the picture was just a warning. Maybe Penelope and Björn are more important than the photograph?"

"We don't know a damn thing."

"Yes, we do," Joona says. "The problem is that we haven't managed to put together the pieces. We can still only guess at the fixer's mission, but it looks like he was trying to find this photograph so he could destroy it, and that he killed Viola Fernandez because he thought she was Penelope."

"Penelope could be the photographer," Saga says. "That's a possibility. But he wasn't content with killing only her."

"That's just what I've been thinking. We don't know what came first. . . . Is the picture a link to the photographer? Or is the photographer a link to the photograph?"

"The fixer's first target was Björn's apartment."

They drive in silence for half an hour and have almost reached police headquarters when Joona looks at the photo-graph again: the four people in the box, the four musicians onstage behind them, the champagne bottle.

"I'm looking at this picture," Joona says. "I see four faces . . . and I'm sure that one of them is behind Viola Fernandez's murder."

"Yes," Saga says. "Palmcrona is dead, so we can pretty much rule him out. Which leaves three ... and we aren't going to be able to talk to two of them. They're outside our reach."

"We need to get Pontus Salman to talk," Joona says tersely.

48

It's hard to track down anyone at Silencia Defense Ltd. All the phone numbers they find lead to the same labyrinth of automated options and prerecorded messages. Eventually, Saga manages to get through to the sales department. She ignores the salesperson's questions and explains why she's calling. At first the voice goes quiet; then she explains that Saga has the wrong number and that their time is already over.

"I'll have to ask you to call back tomorrow, between nine and eleven, and—"

"Just make sure Pontus Salman is expecting a visit from the Security Police at two p.m. today," Saga interrupts loudly.

She hears cautious tapping at a keyboard.

"I'm sorry," the woman says after a pause. "He's in meetings all day."

"Not at two o'clock," Saga says softly.

"Yes, it says here that—"

"That's when he's going to be talking to me," she interrupts again.

"I'll pass on your message."

"Thanks very much," Saga says, ending the call. She meets Joona's gaze across the table.

"Two o'clock?" he asks.

"Yes."

"Kofoed wants to look at the photograph," Joona says. "I'll meet you in his room after lunch, before we head out."

While Joona has lunch with Disa, the National Crime Unit's forensics experts ruin the photograph.

By the time they're done, the face of one of the four people in the box is blurred to the point where it is unrecognizable.

DISA SMILES TO HERSELF as she removes the container from the rice cooker. She passes it to Joona and watches as he wets his hands to see if the rice is cool enough for him to work with.

"Did you know that Södermalm had its own Calvary?" she asks.

"Calvary? Isn't that . . ."

"Golgotha." Disa nods. She opens Joona's fridge, finds two glasses, and pours wine in one, water in the other.

Disa's face looks relaxed. Her freckles are darker, and her unruly hair is tied back in a loose braid. Joona rinses his hands and takes out a clean dish towel. Disa stands in front of him and wraps her arms around his neck. Joona returns the embrace. He leans his face against her head and breathes in her scent as he feels her hands caress his neck and back.

"Can't we try?" she whispers. "We can, can't we?"

"Yes," he replies quietly.

She holds him tight, then pulls free from his embrace.

"Sometimes I get so angry with you," she mumbles, and turns her back on him.

"Disa, I am who I am. I mean—"

"It's a good thing we don't live together," she interrupts, walking out of the kitchen.

He hears her lock herself in the bathroom. He wonders

if he should go after her but assumes that she just wants to be alone for a while. Instead, he keeps making the food. He places a piece of fish gently in the palm of his hand, then rubs some strong wasabi on it.

After a few minutes, the bathroom door opens, and Disa comes back into the kitchen and looks on as he prepares the sushi.

"Do you remember," Disa says, laughing, "that your mom always took the salmon off the sushi and fried it before putting it back on the rice again?"

"Yes."

"Shall I set the table?" Disa asks.

"If you like."

Disa takes plates and chopsticks into the living room, then looks out the window. A clump of trees stand out, their summer leaves bright green. She looks off toward Norra Bantorget, across the pleasant neighborhood where Joona Linna has lived for the past year.

She sets the glass dining room table, then returns to the kitchen and takes a sip of wine. It's lost the crispness that it only really has when it's chilled.

"You've been outbidden," she says.

"Outbidden?"

She nods. She wants to be a little bit mean.

"Tell me," Joona says calmly, carrying the sushi to the table.

Disa picks up her glass again and says brightly, "It's just that someone at the museum has been asking me out to dinner for the past six months."

"Is that what people do these days? Ask ladies out to dinner?"

Disa gives him a wry smile.

"Jealous?"

"I don't know. A little, maybe," Joona says, and walks over to her. "It's nice to be asked out to dinner."

"Yes." Disa tugs her fingers through his thick hair.

"Is he handsome?" Joona asks.

"Yes, actually."

"That's good."

"But I don't want to go out with him." Disa smiles.

He doesn't answer, just stands there with his face turned away.

"You know what I want," Disa says softly.

His face is pale, and she can see tiny beads of sweat on his forehead. Slowly, he looks at her, and there's something off about his eyes: they're black, hard, bottomless.

"Joona, forget it," she says hastily. "Sorry . . ."

Joona opens his mouth to say something. He takes a step toward her, but his legs suddenly give out.

"Joona!" Disa cries, knocking her glass off the table.

She sinks down onto the floor beside him, holds him, and whispers that it will be over soon.

After a while, the expression on Joona's face changes. The pain slowly eases, little by little.

Disa sweeps up the pieces of her glass, and then they sit down at the table in silence.

"You're not taking your medication," she says after a while.

"It makes me tired, and it's really important that I think clearly right now."

"You promised you'd take it."

"I will," he says.

"It's dangerous, you know that," she whispers.

"I'll start taking it again as soon as I've solved this case."

"And if you don't solve it?"

FROM A DISTANCE, the Nordic Museum looks like an ornament of ivory, but it's actually built of sandstone and limestone. An ornate Renaissance palace with lots of towers and turrets, the museum was intended to sing the praises of Nordic sovereignty, but by the time it was opened, on a rainy day in the summer of 1907, the union with Norway had been dissolved and the king was dying.

Joona walks quickly through the vast museum hall, stopping when he reaches the top of the stairs. He composes himself, then walks slowly past the illuminated display cases. Nothing catches his eye. He's absorbed in memories and loss.

The security guard has already placed a chair in front of the display case for him.

Joona sits down and looks at the Sami bridal crown with its eight points, like two interwoven hands. It's glowing gently behind the thin glass. Joona hears a voice inside him, sees a face smiling at him as he sits behind the wheel, driving, that day. It had been raining, and the sun was shining off the puddles on the road, lighting them up from below. He glances around at the back seat to make sure that Lumi has her seat belt on.

The bridal crown looks like it's made of thin branches, leather, or braided hair. He stares at its promise of love and happiness and thinks about the serious set of his wife's mouth, the sand-colored hair falling across her face.

"How are you doing?"

Joona looks up at the security guard in surprise. He's a middle-aged man with stubble and tired eyes worn from rubbing. He's worked here for many years.

"I honestly don't know," Joona mumbles, getting up from the chair.

49

Joona and Saga are on their way to Silencia Defense's head office to interview Pontus Salman. They're taking the photograph that the technicians doctored. They head south along Highway 73 in silence.

Two hours ago, Joona had been looking at a clear photograph of the four people in the box: Guidi, with his calm face and thin hair; Palmcrona's slack smile and steel-rimmed glasses; Pontus Salman, with his handsome, boyish looks; and Agathe al-Haji, with her wrinkled cheeks and heavy, intelligent eyes.

"I had a thought," Joona had said slowly, meeting Saga's gaze. "If we could make the quality of the photo worse, so that it's no longer possible to identify Pontus Salman . . ."

He fell silent, thinking to himself.

"What do we achieve by that?" Saga asked.

"He wouldn't know we have a high-resolution original, would he?"

"There's no way he'd know. He'd probably assume we'd done everything we could to improve the sharpness, not make it worse."

"Exactly. We've done all we could to identify the four people in the picture but have only succeeded with three of them, because the fourth is turned away and is too unclear."

"You mean we give him the chance to lie?" Saga said quickly. "To lie and say he wasn't there, that he didn't meet Palmcrona, Agathe al-Haji, and Guidi."

"Because if he denies being there, then maybe it's the meeting itself that is sensitive."

"And if he starts to lie, we've trapped him."

They turn off the main road and roll into an industrial area surrounded by peaceful forest.

Silencia Defense's office is in a nondescript dull-gray concrete building.

Joona looks at the huge building, slowly scanning the dark windows and tinted glass, thinking again about the four people in the concert box. One or more of them have unleashed a chain of violence, leaving a dead girl and a grieving mother in their wake. Maybe Penelope and Björn are also dead because of them. As he gets out of the car, his jaw tenses at the thought that Pontus Salman, one of the four, is inside this building right now.

The photograph has been copied and the original sent to the National Forensics Laboratory in Linköping. Kofoed has digitally manipulated one copy so that it looks old and battered. One corner is missing, and fragments of tape are visible on the others. Kofoed has blurred Salman's face and hand to make it look as if he was moving when the picture was taken.

Salman will believe that he—and he alone—had the good fortune to be blurred and unrecognizable, Joona thinks, meaning that there's nothing to link him to the meeting with Raphael Guidi, Carl Palmcrona, and Agathe al-Haji. All he has to do to distance himself from it is to deny ever being there. It isn't a criminal offense not to recognize yourself in a blurred picture or not to remember meeting certain people.

Joona starts to walk toward the entrance.

But if he does deny it, we'll know he's lying, and that he wants to keep something secret.

The air is oppressively hot and humid.

Saga nods at Joona as they walk through the heavy, shining doors.

And when Salman starts lying, Joona thinks, we'll make sure that he keeps on lying, digging himself deeper into a hole, until we've got him.

They find themselves in a spacious but chilly reception area.

Behind the desk in reception is the illuminated logo: the company's name and a snakelike design filled with runes.

"'He fought as long as he had a weapon,'" Joona says.

"Can you read runes?" Saga asks skeptically.

Joona points at the sign bearing the translation, then looks back at the desk. Behind it is a pale man with thin, dry lips.

"Pontus Salman," Joona says tersely.

"Do you have a meeting scheduled with him?"

"Two o'clock," Saga says.

The receptionist looks at his papers, leafs through them, and reads something.

"Ah, yes," he says quietly, then looks up. "Pontus Salman has to cancel."

"The message didn't reach us," Saga says. "We need his help to—"

"I'm very sorry."

"Call him and explain the misunderstanding," Saga says.

"I can try, but I don't think . . . Because he's in a meeting."

"On the fourth floor," Joona says.

"Fifth," the receptionist replies automatically.

Saga sits down in one of the armchairs. The sun is shining through the large windows. Joona remains standing by the desk as the receptionist calls. The phone rings for a long time before he shakes his head apologetically.

"Don't worry," Joona suddenly says. "We'll surprise him instead."

"Surprise him?" the receptionist says, looking unsettled.

Joona merely walks over to the glass door and opens it.

"No need to tell him we're on our way," he says with a smile.

The young receptionist's cheeks flush bright red. Saga gets up from the armchair and follows Joona.

"Wait," the man says. "I'll try . . ."

They walk along the hallway, into the waiting elevator, and press the button for the fifth floor. When the doors close, they are carried upward silently.

Salman is waiting for them when the doors open. He's in his forties, and there's something haggard about his features.

"Welcome," he says in a subdued voice.

"Thanks," Joona says.

Salman looks them up and down. "You look like a detective," he says to Joona, before turning to Saga. "You, not so much."

As they follow him down a long hallway, Joona feels a cold shiver run down his spine—as if Viola Fernandez were watching him expectantly.

The windows in the hallway are tinted and give a sense of timelessness. The office is very big, with an elm desk and a pale-gray suite of sofas and armchairs around a black glass table.

They sit down in the armchairs. Pontus Salman smiles at them mirthlessly, steeples his fingers, and asks, "What's this about?"

"Are you aware that Carl Palmcrona from the ISP is dead?" Saga asks.

Salman nods twice. "Suicide, I heard."

"The investigation is ongoing," Saga says amiably. "We're looking into a photograph that we've found. We're very eager to identify the people with Palmcrona."

"Three of them are clear enough, but the fourth is badly blurred," Joona says.

"We'd like you to let your staff look at the picture. Someone might recognize him. One of his hands is relatively sharp, for instance."

"I see," Salman says, pursing his lips.

"Someone might be able to tell us who it is from the context," Saga continues. "It's worth a try, anyway."

"We've been to see Patria and Saab Bofors Dynamics," Joona says. "But no one there recognized the man."

Salman's haggard face is giving absolutely nothing away. Joona wonders if he's on medication to keep himself calm. There's something lifeless about his eyes, perhaps a lack of connection between emotion and expression that gives an impression of complete indifference.

"You must think it's important," Salman says, crossing one leg over the other.

"Yes," Saga says.

"May I see this remarkable photograph?" he asks in an easy, impersonal tone of voice.

"Apart from Carl Palmcrona," Joona says, "we've been able to identify Raphael Guidi, the arms dealer, and Agathe al-Haji, a military adviser to President Bashir ... but no one has been able to identify the fourth person."

Joona picks up his folder and holds out the plastic sleeve containing the photograph. Saga points at the blurred figure at the edge of the concert-hall box. Joona can see the concentration in her face. She's ready to register every nervous twitch, every tiny movement when Salman starts lying.

Salman licks his lips again, and his cheeks turn pale; then he smiles, taps the photograph, and says, "But that's me!"

"You?"

"Yes," he says, laughing to reveal his childlike front teeth.

"But . . ."

"We met in Frankfurt," he goes on with a slight smile. "Listened to a wonderful performance of . . . I can't remember what they played now, Beethoven, I think it was. . . ."

Joona tries to understand this abrupt confession and clears his throat.

"You're quite sure?"

"Yes," Salman says.

"Then that's that mystery solved," Saga says. Her voice betrays nothing of their miscalculation.

"Maybe I should come and work for the Security Police," Salman jokes.

"What was the meeting about?" Joona asks. "If I may ask?"

"Of course." Salman laughs, looking at Joona. "This photograph was taken in the spring of 2008. We were discussing sending ammunition to Sudan. Agathe al-Haji was negotiating on behalf of their government. The region needed to be stabilized after 2005. The negotiations were fairly advanced, but it all went up in smoke after what happened in the spring of 2009. We were shaken, of course, as you can understand. Since then we haven't had any contact with Sudan."

Joona looks at Saga. He has no idea what happened in the spring of 2009. Her face is neutral, and he decides not to ask.

"How many times did you meet?" Joona asks.

"Just this once," he replies. "So you'd think it's a little surprising that Palmcrona accepted a glass of champagne."

"Is that what you think?" Saga asks.

"There was nothing to celebrate . . . but maybe he was just thirsty," Salman says with a smile.

50

PENELOPE AND BJÖRN have been hiding in a deep crevice in a rock for what feels like forever. Before this, they spent two nights curled up in the shadow of a broken pine.

They didn't have the energy to run anymore—their bodies were too tired—and they each took turns keeping watch while the other slept.

So far, their pursuer has predicted their every move, but now his immediate presence seems to have faded. He's been quiet for a long time. The chilling, lurching sensation that he was right behind them disappeared the moment they left the road and made the unpredictable choice to head into the forest again, away from the more populated mainland.

Penelope isn't sure if she managed to leave a message on her mom's voice mail. But someone will find Björn's boat soon, she thinks. And then the police will start looking.

All they have to do is stay hidden, so that their pursuer doesn't find them.

The rock face is covered with green moss, but inside the crevice the stone is bare, and in several places clear water seeps out.

They've lapped up the water and then gone back to hiding in the shadows. The day is hot, and they've sat completely still, panting, but toward evening, when the hot sun descends behind the trees, they fall asleep again.

Dreams and memories merge inside Penelope's mind. She hears Viola playing "Twinkle, Twinkle, Little Star" on her miniature violin, with colored stickers to mark where she should put her fingers, then sees her put pink eye shadow on and suck in her cheeks in front of the mirror.

Penelope gasps for breath as she wakes up.

Björn is sitting with his arms around his knees, shaking.

When night starts to fade, they can't bear it any longer: they're so hungry and weak that they leave their hiding place and start to walk.

It's almost morning by the time they reach the shore. The water is still and calm, and they see two swans gliding on the surface, side by side, moving gently, slowly paddling their feet.

Björn holds Penelope's hand as they wearily climb down to the water. His knees buckle with exhaustion, and he staggers, slips, and reaches out one hand to the rocks to keep himself from falling.

Penelope stares vacantly ahead of her as she takes off her shoes, ties them together, and hangs them around her neck.

"Come on," Björn whispers. "We're just swimming. Don't think about it, just do it."

Penelope wants to tell him to wait—she isn't sure she's going to be able to make it—but he's already wading out into the water. She shivers and looks over at the other island.

She follows him, feeling the chilly water caress her calves and thighs. The bottom is stony and slippery and drops off quickly beneath her. She doesn't have time to think about it and slips into the open water.

With her arms aching and her clothes weighing her down, she starts to swim toward the other island. Björn is already far ahead.

It takes all her effort. Every stroke feels unbearable, and her muscles are screaming for rest.

Kymmendö lies in front of them. She kicks with tired legs and struggles to stay afloat. But the first rays of sunlight above the treetops dazzle her. Temporarily blinded, she stops swimming. Her arms can't take any more; they just give out. It's only for a few seconds, but in that time, before her arms start to obey her again, her wet clothes drag her under the water. When she breaks the surface to breathe, she's terrified. Adrenaline is pumping through her body; she's breathing quickly and has lost her sense of direction. She sees nothing but sea around her. Treading water desperately, spinning around, she manages to stop herself from crying out. Then she catches sight of Björn's bobbing head, just above the surface of the water, fifty meters away. Though Penelope keeps swimming, she isn't sure if she's going to be able to make it to the other island.

The shoes around her neck are impeding her swimming; she tries to get rid of them, but they're tangled with her crucifix. Then the thin clasp breaks, and the crucifix and her shoes sink into the water.

She swims on, feeling her heart racing. Far ahead of her, she can just make out Björn crawling ashore.

She gets water in her eyes, then sees Björn stand up on land. He's looking back for her when he should be hiding—their pursuer could be standing somewhere behind them, searching the area with binoculars.

Penelope's movements are getting slower and weaker. She can feel how tired and sluggish her legs are as the lactic acid spreads through her thigh muscles. Swimming is hard, and the last stretch feels insurmountable. Björn looks worried, and he wades out into the water toward her as she gets closer to the shore. She's on the point of giving up again but takes a few more strokes, then a few more, and then she feels the bottom beneath her. Björn is in the water now; he takes her hand and pulls her to him and drags her onto the shore.

"We have to get under cover," she gasps.

He helps her in among the pine trees. She can't feel her legs and feet, and she's so cold she's shaking. They move deeper into the forest, only stopping when the sea is no longer in sight. Exhausted, they sink onto the moss and blueberry bushes and hold each other until their breathing calms down.

"We can't go on like this," she whimpers.

"We can help each other."

"I'm freezing. We have to get dry clothes," Penelope says with her teeth chattering, pressing her face against the goose bumps on Björn's chest.

They stand up, and Björn supports her as they walk on through the forest on stiff legs. Björn's wet sneakers squelch with every step, and Penelope's bare feet shine white against the ground. Her tracksuit is hanging from her body, wet and cold. They make their way east in silence, and after twenty minutes they reach the other side of the island. The sun is already high in the sky, sparkling on the calm sea, and the air is starting to heat up. Penelope stops when she sees a tennis ball lying in the tall meadow grass in front of her. Yellow-green, it looks alien to her. Almost completely hidden behind a dense lilac bush is a little red cottage with a veranda facing the water. The curtains in all the windows are drawn, and there are no cushions on the couch swing in the arbor. The lawn is overgrown, and a broken branch from an old apple tree is lying across the stone path.

"There's no one home," Penelope whispers.

They creep closer to the house, ready for the barking of dogs or angry voices. They peer through the gaps between the curtains, then walk around and try the front door. It's locked. Penelope starts to look around.

"We have to get inside. We need to rest," Björn says. "We'll have to break a window."

Beside the door is a small lavender bush in a terra-cotta pot. Penelope can smell it as she bends over and picks up one of the stones on top of the soil. It's made of plastic, and contains a small hidden compartment. She opens it, removes a key, and puts the stone back.

They unlock the door and walk into a pine-floored hallway. Penelope can feel her legs shaking, on the verge of giving out, and reaches out her hand to support her. She is so tired and hungry that the house feels unreal, like a gingerbread house. There are framed photographs everywhere, with signatures written in gold and black ink. They recognize the row of faces from Swedish television shows: Siewert Öholm, Bengt Bedrup, Kjell Lönnå, Arne Hegerfors, Magnus Härenstam, Malena Ivarsson, Jacob Dahlin.

They move farther into the house, through a living room and into the kitchen, looking around anxiously.

"We can't stay here," Penelope whispers.

Björn goes over to the fridge and opens the door. The shelves are full of fresh groceries—the house isn't deserted, as they thought. Björn looks around, then takes out some cheese, half a salami, and a carton of milk. Penelope finds a baguette in the pantry and a box of cornflakes. They eat the food greedily with their hands, passing the cheese between them and biting off chunks to chew with the bread. Björn drinks large swigs of milk from the carton, and it dribbles from the corners of his mouth down his neck. Penelope eats some salami with the cornflakes, takes the milk from Björn, chokes on her first mouthful, coughs, and drinks some more.

They smile giddily at each other, move away from the window, and eat more; finally, they calm down.

"We need to find some clothes before we move on," Penelope says.

As they look through the house, they experience a strange, tingling sensation: the food is warming them up, and their bodies are waking up. Their hearts beat faster, their stomachs ache, and their blood flows more quickly through their veins.

In the largest bedroom, the one with a glass door facing the lilac arbor, is a built-in closet with mirrored doors. Penelope hurries over and opens it.

The big closet is full of peculiar clothes. Gold jackets, sparkling black sequined girdles, a yellow tuxedo, and a fluffy waist-length fur coat. Taken aback, Penelope hunts through skimpy bikinis: transparent, leopard-print, camouflage-patterned, even some crocheted briefs.

When she opens the other door, she finds simpler clothes: tops, jackets, and pants. She searches through them quickly and picks out several garments, after pulling off her wet clothes unsteadily.

She catches a glimpse of herself in the mirror, with big bruises all over her body, scratches on her face, cuts and bruises on her shins; she's still bleeding from a small wound on her thigh, and her hip has been scraped from when she slid down the rock. Her hair is hanging in black clumps.

She pulls on a crumpled men's bathing suit, a T-shirt with the words "Eat More Porridge," and a sweater that almost reaches her knees. She is starting to get even warmer and more relaxed, and her body wants nothing more than to rest. Suddenly she starts to cry but forces herself to calm down, wipes the tears from her cheeks, and goes to look for shoes. She finds a pair of blue Wellington boots and returns to the bedroom. Björn is muddy and wet but is pulling a pair of purple velvet pants over his dirty legs. His feet look terrible: filthy and covered with cuts, and he leaves bloody footprints on the floor when he walks. He pulls on a blue T-shirt and a slim-fit bright-blue leather jacket with wide lapels.

Penelope starts to cry in great, heaving sobs that rack her whole body. She's too tired; she has nothing left to hold back the tears.

"What's going on?" she whimpers.

"I don't know," Björn whispers.

"We haven't even seen his face. What does he want? What the hell does he want? I don't understand. Why is he hunting us?"

She wipes her tears on the sleeve of the sweater. "I've been thinking," she says. "I mean . . . what if Viola did something, something really stupid? Because, you know, her guy, Sergey—she broke up with him, but he could be sketchy. I know he used to work as a bouncer."

"Penny . . ."

"I just mean—Viola—she's so . . . Maybe she did something you're not supposed to do."

"No," Björn whispers.

"What do you mean, no? We don't know anything. You don't have to try to comfort me."

"I have . . ."

"He . . . the man chasing us . . . maybe he just wants to talk. . . . I know that isn't really true, I just mean . . ."

"Penny," Björn says seriously, "everything is my fault."

He looks at her. His eyes are bloodshot, and his cheeks flush brightly against his pale skin.

"What are you saying? What the hell are you saying?" she asks in a low voice.

He swallows slowly, then tries to explain. "I did something really stupid."

"What did you do?"

"It's the photograph," he replies. "It's all because of the photograph."

"What photograph? The one of Palmcrona and Guidi?"

"Yes. I contacted Palmcrona," Björn replies bluntly. "I told him about the picture and said I wanted money, but—"

"No," Penny whispers abruptly. She stares at him and moves away, knocking over a bedside table with a glass of water and a clock radio on it.

"Penny . . ."

"Shut up," she says loudly. "I don't get it. What are you saying? What the fuck are you saying? You can't . . . you can't . . . Are you crazy, trying to blackmail Palmcrona? Did you really try to . . . ?"

"Just let me finish! I changed my mind. It was wrong. I know it was wrong. He has the picture; I sent it back to him."

They fall silent as Penelope tries to make sense of what he's said. Thoughts are swirling helplessly around in her head.

"It's my picture," she says slowly, trying to gather her thoughts. "It could be important. It was given to me in confidence. Someone might know something that . . ."

"I just didn't want to have to sell the boat," he whispers, looking as if he might cry.

"I don't get it. . . . You sent the picture to Palmcrona?"

"I had to, Penny. I realized I'd done the wrong thing. I had to give him the picture."

"But . . . I have to get it back," she says. "Don't you understand? What if the person who sent me the picture gets in touch and wants it back? This is about serious stuff—Swedish arms exports. This isn't about you and your money problems. It isn't about us. This is real, Björn."

Penelope looks at him in despair, and her voice becomes shrill: "This is about people's lives," she says. "I'm so fucking angry with you I could hit you."

"Penny, I didn't know," he says. "How was I supposed to know? You didn't tell me anything. You said the picture was embarrassing for Palmcrona, but you didn't say—"

"What difference does that make?" she says, cutting him off.

"I just thought—"

"Shut up!" she shouts. "I don't want to hear your excuses. You're an extortionist, a greedy little extortionist. I don't know you, and you don't know me."

They face each other in silence for a while. A seagull cries above the water, and others join in.

"We need to get moving," Björn says limply.

Penelope nods, but a moment later they hear the front door open. Without looking at each other, they move backward, farther into the bedroom. They hear someone come in, one step at a time. Björn tries to open the door to the deck, but it's locked. Penelope loosens the catch on the window with trembling hands, but it's too late to try to escape.

51

PENELOPE TAKES A DEEP BREATH. A man is standing in the bedroom doorway. Björn looks around for something to defend them with, some sort of weapon.

"What the hell are you doing here?" the man asks in a hoarse voice.

Penelope realizes that he isn't their pursuer, but presumably the owner of the house. He's a short man, broad, and a little overweight. His face looks familiar somehow, as if she used to know him many years ago.

"Junkies?" he asks with genuine interest.

Suddenly she figures out who he is. They've broken into Ossian Wallenberg's house. Ossian used to host glitzy quiz shows, with mystery prizes and celebrity guests. Every episode of *Golden Friday* ended the same way, with Ossian trying, smiling and red-faced, to pick up his guest. Penelope remembers watching as a child when he picked up Mother Teresa. The frail old woman had looked terrified. Ossian was famous for his golden hair, his extravagant clothes, and also for his barbed sense of humor.

"We've been in an accident," Björn says. "We really need to contact the police."

"Oh," Ossian says without interest. "I only have a cell phone."

"Can we borrow it? It's urgent."

Ossian takes out his phone, looks at it, then switches it off.

"What are you doing?" Penelope asks.

"Whatever the hell I want," he replies.

"We really need to use your phone," she says.

"Then you're going to need my PIN code," Ossian says, smiling.

"What are you talking about?"

He leans against the door and looks at them.

"Imagine that a couple of junkies have found their way here, to my humble abode."

"We're not . . ."

"Who cares?" Ossian replies.

"I've had enough of this," Penelope says to Björn.

She wants to leave, but Björn looks exhausted. His cheeks and lips are pale, and he's leaning against the wall with one hand.

"We're sorry we broke into your house," Björn says. "And we'll pay for what we've taken, but right now we really need to borrow your phone. We're in a desperate situation and—"

"And your name is?" Ossian interrupts.

"Björn."

"You look good in that jacket, but didn't you see the tie? There's a tie that goes with it."

Ossian goes over to the wardrobe and takes out a thin leather tie, the same shade of blue as the jacket, and slowly knots it around Björn's neck.

"Call the police yourself," Penelope says. "Tell them you've caught two burglars red-handed."

"Not as fun as what I had in mind," Ossian says sullenly.

"What do you want?" she asks through clenched teeth.

He takes a few steps back and looks at them.

"I don't like her so much," Ossian says to Björn. "But you're very stylish, and my jacket suits you. She can have that ugly sweater, don't you think? Like an old owl. She doesn't look Swedish, she looks like—"

"Stop it," Björn says.

Ossian walks up to Björn with an angry look on his face and raises his clenched fist.

"I know who you are," Penelope says.

"Good," Ossian says with a trace of a smile.

Björn looks at her curiously, then at the man. Penelope feels sick and sits down on the bed and tries to breathe normally.

"Hang on," Ossian says. "I've seen you on television. I recognize you."

"I've been in a few televised debates. . . ."

"And now you're dead," he says with a smile.

Her whole body grows tense. She tries to understand what he's planning to do, and her eyes dart around, searching for an escape route. Björn, who has been standing against the wall, slides down toward the floor. All the color has drained from his face, and he can't get a single word out.

"If you don't want to help us," Penelope says, "we'll go and ask someone else who—"

"I want to—of course I want to," he interrupts.

Ossian goes out into the hall and comes back with a plastic bag, out of which he pulls a carton of cigarettes and a newspaper. He tosses the newspaper on the bed, then takes the bag and cigarettes out to the kitchen. Penelope sees a photograph of herself on the front page, alongside one of Björn, and a larger one of Viola. Above Viola's picture is the word "Dead," and above the other two, "Missing."

The headline reads "Boat Drama—Three Feared Dead."

Penelope imagines what her mother must be thinking. She can see her in her mind's eye, distraught and exhausted from crying, sitting quietly with her arms wrapped tightly around herself, as if she were back in prison.

The floor creaks, and Ossian Wallenberg comes back into the bedroom.

"Let's have a contest," he says eagerly.

"What do you mean?"

"Hell, I feel like a contest!"

"A contest?" Björn says with an uncertain smile.

"You don't know what a contest is?"

"Yes, but . . ."

Penelope looks at Ossian and realizes how vulnerable they are as long as no one knows they're alive or what's happened. "He wants to show how much power he has over us," she says.

"Will you let us use your phone if we play?" Björn asks.

"If you win," Ossian replies, looking at them with a glint in his eyes.

"And if we lose?" Penelope asks.

52

AXEL WALKS to the window, and he looks at the rosebushes growing by the metal railings, then up the street to the stairs leading to Engelbrekt Church.

The moment he signed the contract, he assumed all of the late Carl Palmcrona's responsibilities.

He smiles to himself at the unexpected turn his life has taken, then remembers that he's forgotten about Beverly. Anxiety begins to flutter in his stomach. One time, she told him she was just going to the store but still hadn't returned four hours later. He went out to look for her. Two hours after that, he found her in a bicycle shed. She was extremely confused and smelled like alcohol, and her underwear was missing. Someone had stuck gum in her hair.

She said she'd met some boys in the park. "They were throwing stones at a wounded pigeon," Beverly explained. "So I thought that if I gave them my money they'd stop. But I only had twelve kronor. That wasn't enough. They wanted me to do something instead. They said they'd stomp on the pigeon if I didn't do it...."

She trailed off. Tears welled up in her eyes.

"I didn't want to," she had whispered. "But I felt so bad for the poor little bird."

Now he takes out his phone and calls her.

As the call goes through, he looks down the street, at the buildings in the neighborhood.

Axel and his brother, Robert, share one of the large townhouses on Brage Street. The building is at the heart of the area known as Lärkstaden, where the buildings bear an external resemblance to one another, as if they all belonged to the same family.

The Riessen family residence consists of two large, separate apartments, each spread over three floors.

The brothers' father, Erloff, who died twenty years ago, was Sweden's ambassador in Paris, and later London; their uncle Torleif was a renowned pianist who performed at the Boston Symphony Hall and Grosser Musikvereinssaal in Vienna, among other places. The noble Riessen family has always consisted largely of diplomats and musicians, professions that have a lot in common—both demand a sensitive ear and a lot of dedication.

As a couple, Alice and Erloff had an unusual agreement: they decided early on that their elder son, Axel, should become a musician, and their younger son, Robert, should follow his father into the diplomatic corps. But that arrangement was turned upside down when Axel made his fateful mistake; at the age of seventeen, he was forced to abandon music and sent to a military school. Robert was left to take over the musical career. Axel accepted his punishment and hasn't played the violin since.

After what happened on that dark day thirty-four years ago, Axel's mother cut off all contact with her son. She didn't even speak to him when she was on her deathbed.

After nine rings, Beverly finally answers, coughing.

"Hello?"

"Where are you?"

"I'm ..."

She turns away from the phone, and he can't hear the end of the sentence.

"I can't hear," he says, anxiety making his voice sharp and strained.

"Why are you angry?"

"Just tell me where you are," he pleads.

"What's the matter with you?" she says, laughing. "I'm here, in my apartment. Isn't that a good thing?"

"I was just worried."

"Don't be silly. I'm just going to watch that show about Princess Victoria."

She clicks to end the call. Feeling a lingering concern because of how vague she sounded, he looks at the phone and wonders if he should call her again. Suddenly it rings in his hand; he jumps, then answers: "Riessen."

"Jörgen Grünlicht here."

"Hello," Axel says.

"How was your meeting?"

"I thought it was very worthwhile," Axel replies.

"You made Kenya a priority, I hope?"

"And the end-user certificate from the Netherlands," Axel says. "There was a lot to get through, so I'm withholding my judgment until I've had time to familiarize—"

"But Kenya," he interrupts. "You haven't signed the export license yet? Pontus Salman is on my back, wondering why the hell you're dragging this out. It's an important deal, and it's already been delayed. The ISP gave them such strong assurances that they started production. The consignment is ready. It's being moved from Trollhättan to Gothenburg, and the shipping company is bringing in a container ship tomorrow. They'll spend the day unloading their cargo and then be ready to load the ammunition the day after."

"Jörgen, I realize that. I looked at the documentation

and ... obviously, I'm going to give authorization, but I just started at the ISP, and it's important for me to be thorough."

"I've looked through the deal myself," Jörgen says brusquely. "And I didn't notice a lack of clarity."

"No, but—"

"Where are you right now?"

"I'm at home," Axel says, slightly bemused.

"I'll get the paperwork couriered to you," Jörgen says curtly. "The courier can wait while you sign it so we don't lose any more time."

"No, I'll look at it tomorrow."

Twenty minutes later, Axel goes out to meet the courier. He finds the pushiness troubling but can see no reason to delay the deal.

53

AXEL OPENS THE DOOR. The mild evening air spills in, along with thunderous music from a graduation party at the KTH School of Architecture.

He takes the folder but for some reason feels awkward about signing the contract in front of the courier. It's as if he were the sort of man who bows under pressure.

"Give me a minute," Axel says, leaving the courier in the hall.

He walks to the kitchen and takes a small bottle of water out of the fridge. After drinking some, he loosens his tie, sits down on one of the high barstools, and opens the folder.

It's all very neat and seems to be in order: all the appendixes are there, the declaration of the Export Control Council, the classification, the preapproval, the copies for the Committee for Foreign Affairs, and the purchase order.

He looks at the documents relating to the export license, the final authorization, and leafs through to the signature page.

A shiver runs through his body.

This is a big deal, with consequences for the nation's balance of trade. It's a routine transaction that's been delayed because of Carl Palmcrona's suicide. He understands that Pontus Salman is in a difficult position; there's always a chance that the deal will fall through if the process drags out any longer.

But he also recognizes that he's being pressured into authorizing the export of ammunition to Kenya without being personally able to vouch for the decision.

Axel formulates a plan and immediately feels more comfortable. He'll devote all his time over a couple of days to this particular deal, and then he'll sign the license.

He'll eventually sign, he knows that, but not right now. He doesn't care if they get upset. He's the one who makes the final decision; he's the director general.

He picks up his pen and draws a smiling stick figure with a speech bubble coming out of his mouth on the signature line.

Axel returns to the courier with a serious expression on his face and hands him the folder, then goes upstairs. He wonders if Beverly really is in her room, or if she lied to him about sneaking out.

What if she disappears?

Axel picks up the remote from a sideboard and puts on a compilation of David Bowie's early work.

He goes over to a glass cabinet, opens its curved door, and looks at the array of bottles. After a brief hesitation, he pulls out a numbered bottle of Hazelburn, from the Springbank Distillers in Campbeltown, Scotland. Axel has been there and remembers the mash tub, more than a hundred years old, that was still in use. It was bright red and worn; it didn't even have a lid.

Axel pulls out the cork and inhales the smell of the whisky: peaty, and as dark as a stormy sky. He puts the cork back in, then slowly places the bottle back on the shelf.

"But her friend is nowhere to be seen," David Bowie sings.

The door to his brother's apartment slams shut. Axel

looks out through the picture window that overlooks the small garden. He wonders if Robert is going to stop in, and at that moment there's a knock at the door.

"Come in," he calls to his brother.

Robert opens the door and walks into the living room, a troubled expression on his face.

"I know you only listen to this garbage to annoy me, but . . ."

Axel smiles and sings along.

His brother dances over to the glass cabinet and looks at the bottles.

"Help yourself," Axel says dryly.

"Do you want to see my Strosser? Can I turn this off for a little while?"

Axel shrugs his shoulders, Robert presses "pause," and the music gently fades to silence.

"Did you finish it already?"

"I was up all night," Robert replies with a broad smile. "Put the strings on this morning."

They sit in silence. A long time ago, their mother had been certain that Axel was going to become a famous violinist. Alice played second violin in the Royal Stockholm Opera Orchestra for ten years and openly favored her elder son.

It all fell apart when Axel was studying at the Royal College of Music and was one of three finalists for the Johan Fredrik Berwald competition for young soloists.

When Axel transferred to the Military Academy, his brother, Robert, took up the mantle of family musician. He never became a virtuoso violinist, but he does play with a chamber orchestra and has built a good reputation as a violinmaker, with clients all over the world.

"Show me the violin," Axel says after a brief pause.

Robert nods and goes to get the instrument, a charming violin with fiery red varnish and a base made of tiger-striped maple.

Robert starts to play a tremulous passage from a piece by Béla Bartók. Axel has always liked Bartók, an outspoken critic of Nazism who was forced to leave his country. As a composer, he was a worrier who occasionally managed to convey a few short moments of happiness. A sort of melancholic folk music among the rubble after a catastrophe, Axel thinks as Robert reaches the end of the piece.

"That sounds pretty good," Axel says. "But you need to move the sound post. There's a slightly muffled . . ."

His brother's face closes up.

"Daniel Strosser said that he wants that sound," he explains tersely. "He wants the violin to sound like a young Birgit Nilsson."

"You really should move the sound post." Axel smiles.

"You're not an expert. I just wanted—"

"Otherwise, it's really great," Axel says hurriedly.

"You can hear the tone, though? Dry and sharp and . . ."

"I'm not saying anything bad about it," Axel goes on blithely. "I'm just saying there's a tiny fraction that doesn't sound alive, and which . . ."

"Alive? This instrument's for someone who really knows his Bartók—that's not the same thing as Bowie."

"Maybe I heard wrong," Axel says quietly.

Robert opens his mouth to reply but changes his mind when he hears his wife, Anette, knock on the door.

She comes in and smiles when she sees him sitting there with the violin.

"Have you tried the Strosser, then?" she asks expectantly.

"Yes," Robert says curtly. "But Axel doesn't like it."

"That's not true," Axel says. "I'm sure your customer is

going to be delighted. That thing I mentioned is probably just in my head, and—"

"Don't listen to him; he doesn't know anything," Anette interrupts irritably.

Robert wants to leave and take his wife with him, but she walks over to Axel.

"Admit that you just made it up," she says in a shrill voice.

"There's no fault. It's just the sound post...."

"And when did you last play? Thirty, forty years ago? You were only a child then. I think you should apologize."

"Let it go," Robert says.

"Say sorry," she demands.

"Okay, sorry," Axel says, and feels himself blush.

"For lying," she goes on. "For lying, because you couldn't bear to give Robert the praise his new violin deserves."

"Sorry for that."

Axel turns his music on again, fairly loud. At first it sounds like gentle strumming from two untuned guitars, and a singer trying to find the right note in a weak voice: "Goodbye, love . . ."

Anette mutters something about Axel's lack of talent, and Robert tells her to stop as he pulls her out of the room. Axel turns the volume up more, and the drums and bass bring the music to life.

Axel closes his eyes and feels them sting in the darkness. He's already very tired. Sometimes he sleeps for half an hour, and sometimes he doesn't get any sleep at all, even when Beverly is lying beside him. On nights like that, he usually wraps a blanket around himself and goes to sit on the porch, gazing out at the beautiful trees in the dawn light. Axel thinks he knows what's causing his problems. He keeps his eyes shut and remembers the day that changed his life.

54

PENELOPE AND BJÖRN look at each other. Through the closed door, they can hear Ossian singing as he rearranges the furniture.

"We can overpower him," Penelope whispers.

"Maybe."

"We have to try."

"And then what? What do we do then? Torture him until he tells us the code to his phone?"

"I think he'll let us have it if the balance of power shifts," Penelope says.

"And if he doesn't?"

She sways with exhaustion as she walks over to the window to try to open it. Her fingers are weak. She stops and looks at her hands in the daylight. Her fingers, gray with mud and clay, are covered in congealed blood from cuts.

"He won't help us. We have to go on," she says. "If we keep to the shore, we'll . . ."

She trails off and looks at Björn, who is sitting huddled up on the edge of the bed.

"Fine," he says quietly. "You go."

"I'm not leaving you."

"I can't do it, Penny," he says without looking at her. "My

feet—I won't be able to run. I might manage to walk for half an hour, but my feet are still bleeding."

"I'll help you."

"There may not be any other phones on the island; we don't know."

"I'm not going to take part in his disgusting—"

"Penny, we . . . we have to talk to the police. We have to borrow his phone."

Ossian throws the door open, a big smile on his face. He's wearing a leopard-print jacket and a sarong. He beckons them toward the huge sofa with extravagant gestures. The curtains are closed, and he's pushed the furniture against the walls so that he can move freely. He walks into the glare of the two standing lamps, stops, and turns around.

"Friday night, people! Time flies when you're having fun!" he says with a wink. "We've reached the contest stage already, so let's welcome tonight's celebrity guest, a shitty little columnist and her underage lover. A really odd couple, if you ask me. A scruffy hag and a young man with a finely chiseled torso."

Ossian laughs and flexes his muscles toward the imaginary camera.

"Come on, now!" Ossian cries, jogging on the spot. "Climbing the walls! Have you all got your buttons ready? I give you . . . *Truth or Dare*! Ossian Wallenberg challenges— the Hag and the Studmuffin!"

Ossian places an empty wine bottle on the floor and spins it. It rotates several times, then comes to a stop with the neck pointing at Björn.

"Studmuffin!" Ossian cries with a smile. "First off the block! Here comes your question. Are you ready to tell the truth, and nothing but the truth?"

Björn sighs. "Absolutely."

A drop of sweat falls from Ossian's nose as he opens an

envelope and reads: "What do you think about when you're having sex with the Hag?"

"Funny," Penelope mutters.

"Do I get the phone if I answer?" Björn asks as calmly as he can.

Ossian purses his lips and shakes his head. "No, but if the audience believes your answer, you get the first number of the code."

"And if I choose 'dare'?"

"Then you'll be competing against me, and the audience will choose," Ossian says. "But the clock's ticking: tick, tock, tick, tock. Five, four, three, two . . ."

Penelope looks at Björn in the harsh glare: his dirty face, the stubble, his matted hair. His nostrils are black with caked blood, and his eyes are tired and bloodshot.

"I think about Penelope when we're having sex," Björn replies quietly.

Ossian boos, pulls a disgusted face, and jogs into the spotlight.

"You were supposed to tell the truth!" he shouts. "And that was nowhere near it. No one in the audience believes you think about the Hag when you have sex with her. That's one, two, minus three points to Studmuffin!"

He spins the bottle again, and this time it stops almost at once, pointing at Penelope.

"What's this?" Ossian cries. "A forfeit! And what does that mean? That's right! Automatic dare! No pickle on your burger! Straight to 'go'! I'll open the hatch and see what the hippopotamus whispers."

Ossian picks up a small wooden hippopotamus from the table, holds it to his ear, and nods. "You mean the Hag?" he asks, and listens again. "I see, Mr. Hippopotamus. Yes, thank you very much."

Ossian carefully puts the hippopotamus down and turns to Penelope with a smile. "The Hag has to compete against Ossian! And the category is striptease! If you can turn the audience on better than Ossian, you get all the numbers to the code—otherwise, Studmuffin has to kick you in the ass as hard as he can."

Ossian bounces over to the stereo and presses a button, and "Teach Me, Tiger" starts to play.

"I lost this round to Ann-Margret once," Ossian says in a stage whisper as he sways his hips in time to the music.

Penelope gets up from the sofa in her Wellington boots, striped bathing suit, and big knitted sweater.

"You want me to take my clothes off?" she asks. "Is that what this is all about? Getting to see me naked?"

Ossian stops singing and comes to a halt, a look of disappointment on his face. He looks at her coolly before replying: "If I was interested in seeing a refugee whore's cunt, I'd use the Internet."

"So what the hell do you want, then?"

Ossian slaps her, hard. She staggers and almost falls, but manages to stay on her feet.

"You need to be nice to me," he says seriously.

"Okay," she mutters.

A trace of a smile crosses his face before he goes on: "I'm someone who competes against television celebrities—and I've seen you on TV before I had time to change the channel."

She looks at his flushed, excited face.

"You're not going to give us your phone, are you?"

"I promise, rules are rules. You'll get it, as long as I get what I want," he replies quickly.

"You know we're in a desperate situation, and you're exploiting that to—"

"Yes! I am!" he screams.

"Okay, what the fuck, why not? We'll do some stripping, and then I get the phone."

She turns her back on Ossian and pulls off the sweater and T-shirt. In the harsh light, the scratches on her shoulder blades and hip stand out vividly, as do the bruises and dirt. She turns around, covering her breasts with both hands.

Björn claps his hands and whistles, with a sad look in his eyes. Ossian's face is sweating; he glances at Penelope and then, standing in the glare of the lights in front of Björn, he rolls his hips and suddenly pulls off the sarong, twirls it around, passes it between his legs, and tosses it at Björn.

Ossian blows him a kiss and makes a "call me" gesture.

Björn claps his hands again, whistling louder, as he sees Penelope pick up the wrought-iron poker from the fireplace.

The little shovel sways and tinkles against the tongs.

Ossian is skipping and dancing in his gold-sequined underwear.

Holding the poker in both hands, Penelope approaches Ossian from behind. He's rolling his hips in front of Björn now.

"Down on your knees," he whispers to Björn. "Go on, get down, Studmuffin!"

Penelope swings the heavy poker and hits him across the thigh as hard as she can. Ossian lets out a scream and collapses to the floor, clutching his thigh and rolling around in agony. Penelope marches over to the stereo and smashes it with four heavy blows.

Ossian is lying still now, breathing very fast, and whimpering. She walks over to him, and he looks up at her with frightened eyes. She stands there for a moment, the heavy poker swinging slowly in her right hand.

"Mr. Hippopotamus told me that he wants you to give me your phone and code," she says calmly.

55

IT'S WARM and oppressively stuffy inside Ossian's cottage. Time and time again, Björn gets up and goes over to the window to look down toward the pier. Penelope is lying on the sofa with the phone in her hand. When Emergency Services took her call, they promised to get back to her when the marine police were approaching. Ossian is sitting in an armchair with a large glass of whisky in front of him, watching them. He's taken some painkillers and told them in a subdued voice that he'll survive.

Penelope looks at the phone. The signal is weaker now but still good enough. The police will call back any minute. She leans back on the sofa. It's horribly humid, and her T-shirt is wet with sweat. She closes her eyes and thinks about Darfur, remembering the heat in the bus she took to Kubbum to meet up with Jane Oduya and Action Contre la Faim.

She had been on her way to the barracks that served as the organization's admin building when something stopped her. She saw some children playing a strange game. They seemed to be placing little clay figures in the road, hoping that they'd be squished by the vehicles. Cautiously, she went closer to see what they were doing. They laughed whenever one of their clay figures was run over:

"I killed another one! It was an old man!"

"I killed a Fur!"

One of the children ran out into the road again and put down two more clay figures, one big, one small. When a wheelbarrow squished the smaller one, the children were delighted: "The kid died! The whore's kid died!"

Penelope went over to the children and asked what they were doing, but they didn't answer, just ran off. She stood there, staring at the pieces of clay on the baked red road.

Because the Fur are traditionally farmers, there has been conflict between them and the nomadic Arab population in the region since time immemorial. But the real cause of the recent genocide is oil.

Even though the civil war is officially over, the Janjaweed have continued their systematic raids. They rape women, kill men and boys, then burn homes.

Penelope watched the Arab children rush off and was picking one of the last intact clay figures off the road when she heard someone call out: "Penny! Penny!"

She startled in fear and saw Jane Oduya waving at her. Jane was a short, rotund woman, dressed in faded jeans and a yellow jacket. Jane's face had become wrinkled and aged in just a few years, and Penelope hardly recognized her.

"Jane!"

They hugged each other hard.

"Don't talk to those children," Jane muttered. "They're just like the rest of them. They hate us because we're black. I can't understand it. They hate black skin."

Jane and Penelope started to walk toward the refugee camp. Here and there, people had begun to gather to eat and drink. The smell of burned milk mingled with the stench of the latrines. The UN's blue plastic sheeting was everywhere, used for all manner of things: curtains, tarps, sheets. Hundreds of the Red Cross's white tents jerked in the wind that swept across the plains.

Penelope followed Jane into the main hospital tent. The white fabric turned the sunlight gray. Jane looked through the plastic window to the surgical section.

"My nurses have become talented surgeons," she said softly. "They carry out amputations and simple operations all on their own."

Two young boys, no more than thirteen years old, were carrying a large box of bandages into the tent. They carefully put it down beside some other boxes, then came over to Jane, who thanked them and told them to help the women who had just arrived and needed water to wash their wounds.

"They used to belong to the Arab militia," Jane explained, nodding toward the boys. "But things are quiet now. Because of the shortage of ammunition, we've reached a sort of equilibrium. People don't really know what to do, and a lot of them have started to help out here instead. We've got a boys' school, with several young men from the militia in the class."

A woman let out a moan from a bunk, and Jane hurried over and stroked her forehead and cheeks. Though she looked no more than fifteen, she was heavily pregnant, and one of her feet had been amputated.

Penelope spent all day working at Jane's side, asking no questions, just doing anything she could to help, so that as many people as possible could get treatment.

In the afternoon, an African man in his thirties with a beautiful face and muscular arms hurried up to Jane with a little white box.

"Thirty new doses of antibiotics," he said, beaming.

"Really?"

He nodded, still smiling.

"Good work."

"I'll go and put some more pressure on Ross; he said we might be able to get a box of blood-pressure monitors this week."

"This is Gray," Jane said. "He's really a teacher, but I couldn't manage without him."

Penelope held out her hand and met the man's playful gaze.

"Penelope Fernandez," she said.

"Tarzan," he said, shaking her hand.

"He wanted to be called Tarzan when he arrived." Jane laughed.

"Tarzan and Jane." He smiled. "I'm her Tarzan."

"In the end, I agreed to call him Graystoke," Jane said. "But that's too much of a mouthful for everyone here, so he has to settle for 'Gray.'"

Suddenly a truck honked its horn outside the tent, and the three of them ran outside. Red dust was swirling around the rusty vehicle. Seven men with gunshot wounds were lying on the truck's open bed. They came from a village in the west where an argument about a well had developed into a firefight.

The rest of the day was spent performing emergency operations. One of the men died. At one point, Gray stopped Penelope and held a bottle of water out to her. Stressed, Penelope just shook her head, but he smiled back calmly and said, "You have time to drink."

She thanked him, drank the water, then helped him lift one of the injured men onto a bunk.

That evening, Penelope and Jane were exhausted. They sat on the veranda of one of the barracks and ate a late meal. It was still very warm. They chatted and looked out at the people finishing their evening chores.

As soon as darkness fell, an ominous silence spread. At first Penelope heard people hurrying back home, then noises from the bathrooms. But soon everything was quiet. There weren't even any children crying.

"Everyone's still scared the Janjaweed troops will come through," Jane said, gathering their plates.

They went inside, locked and barred the door, then washed the dishes together. They said good night, and Penelope went to the guest room at the end of the hallway.

She woke up two hours later with a start. She had fallen asleep in her clothes and now lay there listening to the heavy Darfur night. She couldn't say what woke her. Her heartbeat was starting to slow down again when she heard a cry outside. She got up and looked out through the small barred window. The road was lit up in the moonlight, and she could hear an agitated conversation somewhere. Three teenage boys were walking down the middle of the road. There was no doubt that they belonged to the Janjaweed. One of them was holding a revolver in his hand. Penelope heard them shouting something about killing slaves. An old African man who usually sold grilled sweet potatoes was sitting on his blanket outside one of the UN stores. The boys went over and spat at him. One raised the revolver and shot the old man right in the face. The shot echoed eerily between the buildings. The boys shrieked and took the sweet potatoes, eating some and trampling the rest into the dust on the road beside the dead man.

They looked around, pointed, then walked straight toward the barracks where Penelope and Jane were staying. Penelope remembers how she held her breath as she heard them on the porch, talking excitedly to one another and banging on the door.

Penelope gasps for breath and opens her eyes. She must have dozed off on Ossian's sofa.

A rumble of thunder fades away, dull and threatening. The sky has gotten darker.

Björn is standing at the window, and Ossian is sipping his whisky.

Penelope looks at the phone; no one has called.

The marine police should be here soon.

The thunder is quickly getting closer. The lamp in the ceiling goes out, and the fan in the kitchen goes quiet—power outage. The first drops of rain hit the roof and windowsills; then, suddenly, it's pouring.

The cell phone signal disappears completely.

A flash of lightning lights up the room, followed by a heavy rumble of thunder.

Penelope leans back and listens to the rain, feeling the cooler air stream in through the windows. She falls asleep again but wakes up when Björn says something.

"What?" she asks.

"A boat," he repeats. "A police boat."

She quickly gets to her feet and stares out. The water looks as if it's boiling in the heavy downpour. The big boat is already close, heading toward the pier. Penelope looks at the phone, but there's still no service.

"Hurry up!" Björn says.

He tries to insert the key into the porch door, but his hands are trembling. The police boat glides in beside the pier and sounds its siren.

"It won't fit," Björn says loudly. "It's the wrong key!"

"Oh dear." Ossian laughs, taking out his key ring. "It must be this one, then."

Björn takes the key and manages to turn it in the lock. He hears a metallic click inside the mechanism.

It's hard to see the police boat through the rain. It's already started to slip away from the pier when Björn gets the door open.

"Björn!" Penelope shouts.

The engine is roaring, and white foam is kicking up behind the boat. Björn waves and runs through the rain as fast as he can on the gravel path leading down the slope.

"Up here!" he cries. "We're over here!"

Björn's shoulders and thighs are drenched. He gets down to the jetty and sees the boat's engines shift into reverse. There's a first-aid box on the aft deck. Through the windshield, he can see a policeman. Another flash of lightning lights up the sky. The noise is deafening. The policeman behind the wheel looks as if he's talking into a radio. Rain is bouncing off the roof of the boat. Björn is shouting and waving his arms. The boat glides back, and its port side bumps against the jetty.

Björn grabs hold of the wet railing and clambers aboard. The boat is rolling on its own swell. He sways, opens a metal door, and goes in.

The cabin has a cloying metallic smell, like oil mixed with sweat.

Björn sees a suntanned police officer lying on the floor with his head smashed in. His eyes are wide open, and an almost black pool of blood is spreading out beneath him. Björn is breathing hard, looking among the police equipment, raincoats, and surfing magazines. He hears a voice over the noise of the engine. It's Ossian, calling from the path; he's limping toward the jetty with a yellow umbrella above his head. Björn feels his pulse thudding in his temples and realizes his mistake. He's walked straight into the trap. He sees the blood splattered across the inside of the windshield and fumbles for the door handle, then steps down to the cabin and sees his pursuer emerge from the gloom, wearing a police uniform. His face is alert, almost curious. Björn realizes that it's too late to run. He grabs a screwdriver from the shelf above the instrument panel to defend himself.

His pursuer holds on to the railing and reaches the top of the stairs, blinking in the bright light, then glances at the windshield and the shore. Rain is beating against the glass. Björn moves quickly. He aims for the man's heart with the screwdriver. He thrusts but then doesn't really understand what happens next. He feels his shoulder shake, then loses the feeling in his arm when the man parries his attack with a heavy sideswipe. It's as if his arm isn't there anymore. The screwdriver falls to the deck and rolls behind an aluminum toolbox. The man is still holding Björn by his numb arm. He yanks him forward, angles his body, and sweeps his legs out from underneath him with a kick. He directs the angle of Björn's fall and pushes him harder as his face crashes down onto the footrest below the wheel. His neck breaks on impact. Björn's face twitches slightly; then, moments later, he's dead.

56

PENELOPE IS STANDING at the window. The sky lights up with a flash of lightning, and thunder rolls across the sea. Rain is pouring down. Björn is on board the police boat and has disappeared into the cabin. The sea's surface is foaming in the heavy downpour. She watches Ossian limp down to the pier. The metal door to the cabin opens, and a uniformed policeman emerges, jumps onto the pier, and ties the boat up.

Only when the policeman starts to walk up the gravel path does Penelope see who it is.

Their pursuer doesn't bother to return Ossian's greeting; he just reaches out his left hand and grips Ossian's chin firmly.

Penelope doesn't notice that she's dropped the phone.

With businesslike brusqueness, the uniformed man turns Ossian's face to one side. The yellow umbrella falls to the ground and rolls partway down the slope. The whole thing is over in a matter of seconds. The man has barely stopped walking when he draws a short dagger with his free hand. He turns Ossian's face a little more, then, so swiftly, stabs him in the neck. Ossian's lifeless body hits the ground.

The man walks up the path toward the cottage with long strides. The glare from a flash of lightning illuminates his face, and Penelope meets his gaze through the rain. Before it fades, she has time to see the troubled look on his face. He has tired, sad eyes and a deep scar on his mouth. The thunder rumbles. The man keeps walking, but Penelope just stands at the window. Though she's breathing fast, she feels paralyzed, unable to run.

The rain beats against the window. The world outside seems strangely distant to her, but then a different, bright-yellow light flares up behind the man and illuminates the pier, the water, and the sky. A great plume of flame rises from the police boat. Fragments of metal are thrown into the air. The cloud of fire grows and pulsates in shades of fiery yellow as the heat sets the reeds and pier alight. The pressure and roar of the explosion reach the house.

Penelope doesn't react until the windowpane starts to shake, then cracks. The rain is still falling torrentially, meeting the black smoke billowing from the remains of the boat behind the man. He's marching toward the house. Penelope turns and rushes through the rooms, climbing over the armchair into the entryway. She opens the front door and runs across the wet, overgrown lawn. Though she slips, she keeps going, out into the rain, away from the house, along the path, around a clump of birches, and out onto a meadow.

There she meets a family with young children in raincoats. They're all clutching fishing rods and bright-orange life jackets. She runs straight through the little group, down toward a sandy beach. Out of breath, panting uncontrollably, she feels as if she's about to pass out. She has to stop. She has no idea what to do and crawls behind a small shed, where she throws up and then whispers the Lord's Prayer. Thunder echoes in the distance. Her whole body is shaking, but she gets to her feet again and wipes the rain from her face with the sleeve of her sweater. She leans forward cautiously and looks around the corner, back across the meadow. Her pursuer is just coming around the clump of birch trees. He stops next to the family, who immediately point in the direction she ran off in. She pulls back, slides down the rocks, and starts to run along the shore until she reaches the sandy beach. Her footsteps stand out white behind her on the wet sand. She's running out onto a long pier when she hears the heavy clatter of a helicopter's rotor blades.

Penelope sees her pursuer running between the trees, down toward the beach. A man in bright-yellow clothing has been winched down from the rescue helicopter and lands at the far end of the pier. The water around him is being churned up in choppy circles. Penelope runs straight for him. He shouts instructions, then attaches the harness to her and signals the helicopter pilot. Together they rise, flying close above the water, then get winched upward. The last thing Penelope sees before the beach disappears behind the trees is her pursuer crouching down with one knee on the ground, his black backpack lying in front of him. With practiced gestures, he is putting together a rifle.

Then she can't see him anymore. Just dense green trees. The surface of the water rushes away beneath her. Suddenly she hears a sharp crack and a crunching sound from up above. The wire jerks hard and her stomach clenches. The man behind her shouts something to the pilot. They lurch the other way as the helicopter banks steeply, and Penelope realizes what has happened: her pursuer has shot the pilot from the beach.

Without any conscious thought, Penelope loosens the safety catch on her harness, pulls free of the straps, and drops straight down. She rushes through the air as the helicopter loses altitude and tips sideways, starting to spin. The cable holding her rescuer gets caught in the main rotor, and there's a deafening roar, and then two distinct cracking sounds as the huge rotor blades are torn off. Penelope falls twenty meters before she hits the water; she sinks deep into the cold and slowly starts to rise again.

She kicks her legs, breaks the surface, and gasps for air, then looks around and starts to swim away from the island, straight out to sea.

57

Joona and Saga leave Silencia Defense after their short meeting with Pontus Salman.

"Do you know what he was talking about?" Joona asks. "What happened in the spring of 2009 that would make it impossible to negotiate an arms shipment to Sudan?"

Before they pull out onto Nynäs Road, Saga takes out her phone and calls Simon Lawrence, a Security Police agent.

"I presume you're calling to ask me out on a date," Simon says.

"Africa north of the Sahara is your area, isn't it? What happened in Sudan in the spring of 2009?"

"What are you referring to?"

"For some reason, Sweden wasn't able to export arms to Sudan after then."

"Don't you read the papers?"

"Yes," she says quietly.

"In March 2009, the International Criminal Court in The Hague issued a warrant for the arrest of the Sudanese president, Omar al-Bashir. The warrant indicted the president on five counts of crimes against humanity—murder, extermination, forcible transfer, torture, and rape—and two counts of war crimes—pillaging and targeting civilians."

"I see," Saga says.

Before they end the call, Lawrence gives her a short summary of the conflict in Sudan.

"What was it?" Joona asks.

"The International Criminal Court issued a warrant for the arrest of President Bashir," she says, fixing her gaze on Joona.

"I didn't know that," Joona says.

"The UN imposed an arms embargo against the Janjaweed and other armed groups in Darfur in 2004."

The summer sky is getting darker.

"Go on," Joona says.

"President Bashir has always denied any link to the militia," she says. "So, after the UN embargo, arms could only be exported directly to the Sudanese government."

"Because they weren't connected to the militia in Darfur."

"Exactly," Saga says. "And in 2005 a comprehensive peace agreement was reached, bringing the longest-running civil war in Africa to an end. After that, there were no fundamental obstacles to Sweden's exporting arms to the Sudanese military. Carl Palmcrona's role was therefore to determine whether it was suitable in terms of security policy."

"But the ICC evidently came to a different conclusion," Joona says bluntly.

"Yes ... they saw a direct connection between the president and the armed militia and issued a warrant for his arrest on the grounds of rape, torture, and genocide."

"So what's happened since then?"

"There was an election in April, and Bashir is still president, and of course Sudan has no intention of complying with the arrest warrant. But today it's out of the question to export arms to Sudan or make a deal with Omar al-Bashir and Agathe al-Haji."

"Just as Salman said," Joona says.

"That's why they stopped the deal."

"We have to find Penelope Fernandez," Joona says as the first drops of rain hit the windshield.

They drive into a heavy rainstorm, and visibility becomes very poor. The rain thunders on the roof of the car, and the windshield wipers sweep rapidly back and forth. It's very dark, but the sky lights up with flashes of lightning.

Joona's phone rings. It's Petter, who explains in a stressed voice that Penelope Fernandez called the emergency hotline twenty minutes ago.

"Why wasn't I told before now?"

"The marine police are already on their way. But I've also requisitioned a helicopter from the coast guard to bring them home quickly."

"Good work, Petter," Joona says, and sees Saga shoot him a quizzical glance.

"I know you'll want to talk to Penelope and Björn as soon as possible."

"Yes," Joona says.

"I'll call you when I know what condition they're in."

"Thanks."

"Our colleagues from the marine police should reach Kymmendö in a matter of . . . Hang on, something happened—can you wait a second?"

Joona hears Petter talking to someone, getting more and more agitated, until he eventually yells, "Just keep trying!"

Petter picks up the phone again. "I've got to go," he says tersely.

"What's happening?" Joona asks.

A rumble of thunder crashes overhead and slowly echoes away.

"We can't contact our colleagues on the boat. They're not

answering. It's that damn Lance—he's probably spotted a wave he needs to try out."

"Petter," Joona says loudly, in a serious voice, "listen to me. You need to act very quickly now. I think the boat has been hijacked and that—"

"Oh, come on—"

"Shut up and listen," Joona interrupts. "In all likelihood, our colleagues from the marine police are already dead. You only have a few minutes to put together a team and take control of the operation. Call the National Communications Center on one phone and Bengt Olofsson on the other; try to get two patrols from the National Response Unit, and ask for helicopter backup from the nearest naval base."

58

A STORM sweeps in across Stockholm. Thunder rumbles, lightning flashes across the sky, and the rain pours down. It patters against the windows of Carl Palmcrona's large apartment, where Tommy Kofoed and Nathan Pollock have resumed the abandoned forensics examination.

Even though it's the middle of the day, it's so dark that they have had to switch on the lights.

In one of the tall closets, beneath a row of gray, blue, and black suits, Pollock finds a blue leather folder.

"Tommy," he calls.

Kofoed comes in, hunched and morose.

Pollock taps the leather folder with a gloved finger. "I think I've found something," he says simply.

Pollock carefully opens the leather folder.

"Go on," Kofoed whispers.

Pollock gently removes the cover page, which bears the words "Carl Palmcrona's Last Will and Testament."

They read in silence. The document is dated March 1, three years ago. Palmcrona left all his assets to one single person: Stefan Bergkvist.

"Who the hell is Stefan Bergkvist?" Kofoed asks once they've finished reading. "Palmcrona had no family or friends, as far as I can see. He didn't have anyone."

"Stefan Bergkvist lives in Västerås ... or did at the time this was signed, anyway," Pollock says. "Number eleven Rekyl Street in Västerås, and—"

Pollock breaks off and looks up.

"He's a child. According to his ID number, he's only sixteen years old."

The will was drawn up by Palmcrona's lawyer at the firm Wieselgreen & Sons. Pollock leafs through the appendix, which lists all of Palmcrona's assets. There are four retirement funds, some forest land, a farm in Södermanland that's on a long-term lease, and the mortgaged apartment on Grev Street. His biggest asset appears to be an account at the Standard Chartered Bank in Jersey, whose balance Palmcrona estimated at nine million euros.

"It looks like Stefan's just inherited a fortune," Pollock says.

"Yes."

"But why?"

Kofoed shrugs his shoulder.

"Some people leave all they have to their dog or their personal trainer."

"I'll call him."

"The boy?"

"What else are we going to do?"

Pollock takes out his phone and dials a number, then asks to be put through to Stefan Bergkvist of 11 Rekyl Street in Västerås and is told that there's a Siv Bergkvist at that address. She's probably the boy's mother. Pollock looks out at the heavy rain and the overflowing gutters.

"Siv Bergkvist," a woman answers in a shaky voice.

"My name is Nathan Pollock. I'm a detective. . . . Are you Stefan Bergkvist's mother?"

"Yes," she whispers.

"Can I talk to him?"

"What?"

"There's no cause for alarm. I just need to ask—"

"Go to hell!" she screams, and ends the call.

Pollock calls the same number again but gets no answer. He looks down at the wet street and calls the number again.

"Micke," a male voice answers warily.

"My name is Nathan Pollock, and I—"

"What the hell do you want?"

Pollock can hear the woman crying in the background; she says something to the man, and he tells her he can take care of this.

"No," she says. "I'll do it. . . ."

The phone gets passed over, and Nathan hears footsteps walking away.

"Hello," the woman says quietly.

"I really do need—"

"Stefan's dead," she interrupts in a shrill voice. "Why are you doing this, why are you calling and telling me you need to talk to him? I can't bear it. . . ."

She sobs into the phone, and something falls to the floor with a clatter.

"I'm sorry," Pollock says. "I didn't know. I . . ."

"I can't bear it," she weeps. "I can't bear it anymore. . . ."

He hears footsteps again; then the man's voice comes back.

"That's more than enough," he says.

"Wait," Pollock says quickly. "Can you tell me what happened? It's important. . . ."

Kofoed has been following the conversation and watches as Pollock turns pale and strokes his silver ponytail.

59

A LARGE NUMBER OF OFFICERS have gathered in the hallways of police headquarters, waiting impatiently for fresh reports. There's a nervous atmosphere. First the Coordination Center lost contact with the police boat, then with the rescue helicopter.

Joona is sitting in his office, reading the postcard Disa sent him from a conference on Gotland. "I'm forwarding a love letter from your secret admirer. Hugs, Disa." He assumes she spent a lot of time looking for a card that was bound to make him shudder. He steels himself, then turns it over. On the front, the words "Sex on the Beach" are printed across a picture of a white poodle in sunglasses and white bikini. The dog is sitting on a lounge chair with a red drink in a tall glass beside it.

There's a knock on the door, and Joona's smile vanishes when he sees the somber expression on Pollock's face.

"Palmcrona left all he had to his son," Pollock says.

"I didn't think he had any family."

"The son's dead, only sixteen. Died in an accident yesterday."

"Yesterday?" Joona repeats.

"Stefan Bergkvist survived Carl Palmcrona by three days," Pollock says slowly.

"What happened?"

"I didn't quite understand.... Something about his motorcycle," Pollock says. "I've asked for the preliminary report...."

"What do you know?"

Pollock sits down on the office chair.

"I've spoken to his mother, Siv Bergkvist, and her partner, Micke Johansson.... It appears that Siv worked as Palmcrona's secretary at Number Four Naval Squadron. They had a brief relationship. She got pregnant. When she told him, he said he assumed she would be getting an abortion. Siv returned to Västerås, gave birth to the child, and has claimed ever since that she didn't know who the father was."

"Did Stefan know that Carl Palmcrona was his father?"

Nathan shakes his head. "The boy's mother said: 'I told him his dad was dead, that he died before he was born.'"

There's a knock on the door; Anja comes in and puts a report, still warm from the printer, on the desk.

"An accident," she says without further elaboration, and leaves the room again.

Joona picks up the plastic sleeve and starts to read the report from the preliminary forensics investigation. Because the fire spread rapidly, the cause of death wasn't carbon-dioxide poisoning. The boy burned to death. The pathologist had diagnosed fire-related hematoma, blood clots between the skull and the brain tissue caused when the blood starts to boil.

"Nasty," Joona mutters.

The investigation of the fire had been hindered by the fact that there was almost nothing left of the shack where Stefan's remains were found. It was just a smoldering heap of ash, twisted metal, and the scarred remains of a body in a contorted position behind where the door had been. The police's working theory is based upon the testimony of a single witness, the train engineer who called the fire department. He had seen the burning motorcycle lying like a wedge against the door. Everything suggests that sixteen-year-old Stefan Bergkvist had been inside the shack when his motorcycle toppled over in such a way that it blocked the door. The lid of the gas tank wasn't properly secured, and the gas poured out. It was still unclear what had set the gas on fire, but it was probably a cigarette.

"Palmcrona dies," Pollock says slowly. "He leaves his entire fortune to his son, and three days later his son is dead."

"So the fortune passes to his mother?" Joona says.

"Yes."

They hear slow, shuffling steps in the hallway before Kofoed appears in Joona's office.

"I've opened Palmcrona's safe," Kofoed says. "There was nothing in there other than this."

He holds up a beautifully bound leather book.

"What's that?" Pollock asks.

"Life story," Kofoed says. "Fairly common with people of his class."

"A diary, you mean?"

Kofoed shrugs. "More an unassuming sort of memoir, not intended for publication. It's supposed to add to the accumulated shared history of the family. Handwritten. It starts with a family tree, his father's career, and then there's a tedious account of his own schooling, exams, military service, and professional career. . . . He makes a number of unsuccessful investments, and his personal finances get rapidly worse, so he sells land and property. It's all described very dryly. . . ."

"What about his son?"

"His relationship with Siv Bergkvist is mentioned only

briefly, as a mistake," Tommy Kofoed replies, taking a deep breath. "But before long he starts to mention Stefan by name, and his entries for the past eight years are all about his son. He follows the boy's life from a distance. He knows what school Stefan goes to, what his interests are, who he social-izes with. He mentions a number of times that his inheri-tance is going to be restored. It sounds like he was saving all his money for his son. In the end, he simply writes that he's thinking of paying his son a visit when he turns eighteen. He writes that he hopes Stefan will forgive him and that they will be able to get to know each other after all these years. And now, all of a sudden, they're both dead."

"What a nightmare," Pollock mutters.

"What did you say?" Joona asks, looking up.

"I was just thinking that this is a nightmare," Pollock says. "He does all he can for his son's future, and then it turns out that the son only outlives him by three days, without ever finding out who his father was."

60

BEVERLY IS ALREADY LYING IN BED when Axel walks in. He only slept two hours last night and feels dizzy with fatigue.

"How long would it take for Evert to drive here?" she asks in a clear voice.

"Your dad, you mean? Six hours, maybe."

She gets out of bed and starts to walk toward the door.

"What are you doing?" Axel asks.

She turns around. "I thought he might be sitting in the car waiting for me."

"You know he's not coming to Stockholm," Axel says.

"I'll take a look out the window, just in case."

"We can call him—would you like to do that?"

"I've already tried."

He reaches out and pats her cheek gently, and she sits back down on the bed.

"Are you tired?" she asks.

"I feel almost sick, I'm so tired."

"I think Dad will want to talk to me tomorrow," she says in a low voice.

Axel nods: "I'm sure it'll be fine tomorrow."

Her big, shining eyes make her look younger than ever.

"Lie down, then," she says. "Lie down so you can get some sleep, Axel."

He blinks at her wearily and watches her lie down carefully on her side of the bed. Her nightgown smells like freshly laundered cotton. When he lies down next to her, he feels like crying. He feels like telling her that he's thinking of finding her a psychologist, to help her get through this phase, and that it will get better. It always gets better.

THE NEXT MORNING, Axel gets up early. He's slept for four hours, and his muscles ache. He stands at the window and looks at the dark flowers on the lilac bushes.

When he reaches his new office, he still feels tired and listless. Yesterday he had been moments away from signing his name on a contract drawn up by a dead man. He would have placed his own reputation in Palmcrona's hands, trusting his judgment and ignoring his own.

He feels a great sense of relief at his decision to wait but can't help thinking that it was a little bit stupid to draw a stick figure on the contract.

He knows that at some point in the next few days he's going to have to authorize the export of ammunition to Kenya. He opens the file and starts to read about Sweden's arms trade in the region.

An hour later, the door of Axel's office opens and Jörgen Grünlicht comes in. He pulls a chair up to the desk and sits down, takes out the contract, leafs through to the signature page, and then looks Axel in the eye.

"Hello," Axel says.

Jörgen can't help smiling. The stick figure with messy hair actually looks like Axel, and the word "Hello!" is written in the speech bubble.

"Hello," Jörgen says.

"It was too soon," Axel explains.

"I appreciate your response. I didn't mean to put you under pressure, even though it is rather urgent," Jörgen says. "The trade minister was on my back again, and Silencia Defense is calling several times a day. But I do understand, you know. You're completely new and . . . you want to be thorough."

"Yes."

"And that's good, of course," he goes on. "But, you know, if you're not sure, you can always leave the decision to the government."

"I don't feel unsure," Axel replies. "I'm just not ready. There's nothing more to it."

"It's just that . . . from their perspective, it's taking an unreasonable amount of time."

"I'm putting everything aside, and I can say that so far everything looks very good," he replies. "I'm not saying don't load the ship, but I'm not ready to sign off on this."

"I'll let the parties know that you're positively disposed toward the deal."

"By all means . . . as long as I don't find anything unusual."

"You won't. I've been through all the documents myself."

"Well, then," Axel says gently.

"I won't disturb you any longer," Jörgen says, getting up from his chair. "When do you think you'll have finished your evaluation?"

Axel glances at the material again. "I'd say a couple of days. I might have to request some information of my own from Kenya."

"Of course," Jörgen says with a smile, and leaves the room.

61

AT TEN O'CLOCK, Axel leaves the ISP to finish his work at home. He takes all the documentation regarding the export license with him. Fatigue is making him feel cold and hungry, and he drives to the Grand Hôtel and picks up brunch for two. He carries the food with him into the kitchen, where Beverly is sitting at the table, looking through a magazine, *Amelia: Brides and Weddings.*

"Are you hungry?" he asks.

"I don't know if I want to wear white when I get married," Beverly says. "Maybe pale pink . . ."

"I like white," he murmurs.

Axel fixes a tray of food, and they go upstairs, where they sit near the window. Between them is an octagonal eighteenth-century table with a garden motif.

Axel lays out the family porcelain with the silver coat of arms. He pours Coke into Beverly's glass and sparkling water with a slice of lime into his.

Beverly's neck is narrow, her chin fine and beautiful. Because her hair is so short, the whole of the gentle curve of the back of her skull is visible. She drains her glass and looks at him.

"Tell me about music again," she says.

"Where were we?" Axel asks, pointing the remote at the stereo.

Alexander Malter's superlative interpretation of Arvo Pärt's *Alina* starts to play from the speakers. Axel looks down into his glass, where bubbles in the water are popping, and wishes intensely that he could drink again. He wishes he had champagne to go with the asparagus, and then some Propovan and Stesolid before he goes to bed.

Axel pours Beverly some more Coke. She looks up and thanks him silently. He looks straight into her big, dark eyes and doesn't notice her glass overflowing until the Coke is spreading across the table.

He stands up and sees Beverly's reflection in the window glass. He suddenly realizes how much she looks like Greta.

Strange that he's never noticed that before.

Axel feels like running away, but he forces himself to get a towel, and his heartbeat calms down again.

He stops and rubs his mouth with a trembling hand.

He thinks about Greta every day, even though every day he tries not to think about her.

The week of the music competition's finals haunts him.

Though it was thirty-four years ago, it made everything in his life go dark. He was so young, only seventeen, but so much died that day.

62

THE JOHAN FREDRIK BERWALD competition was without a doubt the most prestigious contest for young violinists in Northern Europe. It helped several world-famous virtuosi come to prominence, putting them directly in the spotlight. There were just three soloists left in the final round. During the previous six rounds, fewer and fewer musicians had performed in front of a closed jury, but the final would be taking place the next day in front of a large audience in the Stockholm Concert Hall, in conjunction with a live television broadcast.

In musical circles, it was considered sensational that two of the finalists, Axel Riessen and Greta Stiernlood, were students at the Royal College of Music in Stockholm. The third finalist was Shiro Sasaki from Japan.

For Alice Riessen, a professional musician who had never quite broken out, her son Axel's success was a great triumph, particularly given that she had received a number of warnings from the school principal that Axel had been missing lectures and was unfocused and careless.

After getting through to the third round, Axel and Greta were excused from classes so that they could devote all their time to the competition. The contest had given them an opportunity to get to know each other. They took pleasure in each other's success, and before the final they started meeting at Axel's home to give each other support.

In the last part of the contest, each violinist would play a piece chosen in consultation with his or her tutor.

Axel and his younger brother, Robert, shared the seven rooms at the top of the large house in Lärkstaden. Axel spent practically no time practicing, but he loved playing—finding his way through new pieces, trying sounds he'd never heard before—and sometimes he would sit up late into the night, playing his violin until the tips of his fingers stung.

There was only one day left. Tomorrow Axel and Greta would be competing in the concert hall for the final. Axel was looking at the album covers spread across the floor in front of his record player, including three records by David Bowie: *Space Oddity*, *Aladdin Sane*, and *Hunky Dory*.

His mom knocked on the door and came in, carrying a bottle of Coke and two glasses with ice cubes and slices of lemon. Axel thanked her, surprised, and put the tray down on the coffee table.

"I thought the two of you were practicing," Alice said, looking around.

"Greta had to go home to eat."

"You can keep going in the meantime, though, surely?"

"I'm waiting for her."

"You know it's the final tomorrow," Alice said, sitting down next to her son. "I practice at least eight hours a day now, and sometimes I used to work ten."

"I'm not even awake ten hours a day," Axel joked.

"Axel, you have a gift."

"How do you know that?"

"I just know. But that's not enough. That's not enough for anyone," she said.

"Mom, I practice like an idiot," he lied.

"Play for me," she asked.

"No," he said abruptly.

"I appreciate that you don't want to have your mother as a tutor, but you could let me help, especially for something so important," Alice went on patiently. "The last time I heard you was two years ago, at a Christmas concert, and no one could figure out what you were playing. . . ."

"Bowie's 'Cracked Actor.'"

"It was immature of you . . . but quite impressive, for a fifteen-year-old," she admitted, reaching out her hand to pat him. "But tomorrow . . ."

Axel shrank away from his mother's hand. "Stop nagging."

"Can I at least know what piece you've chosen to play?"

"Classical," he replied with a broad smile.

"Thank God for that."

He shrugged his shoulders and wouldn't meet her gaze. When the doorbell rang, he rushed out of the room and down the stairs.

Dusk had started to fall, but the snow was creating an indirect light, so the darkness outside the house never grew thicker. Greta was standing on the steps in her beret and puffy coat, with her striped scarf wound around her neck. Her cheeks were glowing from the cold, and the hair draped across her shoulders was covered in snowflakes. She put her violin on the dresser in the entryway, carefully hung up her outdoor clothes, unlaced her boots, and took out her indoor shoes from her bag.

Alice came downstairs and said hello. She was very excited; her cheeks were flushed with happiness.

"It's good that you're helping each other practice," she said. "You must be stern with Axel—otherwise, he won't bother."

"I've noticed." Greta laughed.

Greta Stiernlood was the daughter of an industrialist. She had grown up alone with her father; her parents had divorced when she was very young, and she hadn't seen her mother since. But early on—maybe even before she was born—her father had decided that she was going be a violinist.

When they got up to Axel's music room, Greta went over to the grand piano. Her glossy, curly hair spread across her shoulders. She was wearing a white blouse, a checked skirt, a dark-blue sweater, and striped tights.

She took out her violin and attached the chin rest, then brushed some resin that had caught on the strings with a cotton cloth, adjusted her bow, and put her score on the stand. She checked that her violin was still in tune.

Then she began to practice. She played the way she always did, with her eyes half closed, focused in on herself. Her long eyelashes cast trembling shadows across her flushed cheeks. Axel knew the piece very well: the first part of Beethoven's String Quartet in A Minor. A serious, searching theme.

He listened, smiling, thinking that Greta had a feeling for music. The honesty in her interpretations filled him with respect.

"Lovely," he said when she finished.

She changed her score and blew on her sore fingers.

"I can't make my mind up. Dad says I should play Tartini, the Violin Sonata in G Minor."

She fell silent, scanning the notes with her eyes, counting the sixteenths, memorizing complex legatos.

"But I'm not sure, I . . ."

"Can I hear it?" Axel asked.

"It sounds terrible," she said, and blushed.

She played the piece with a tense face. It was beautiful and tragic, but toward the end she lost her tempo, while the violin's top notes were supposed to lick upward like flames.

"Damn," she whispered, and rested the violin under her arm. "I was going too slowly. I've been working like a dog, but I need to get right into the sixteenths. . . ."

"But I liked the vibrato. It was as if you were curving a big mirror up toward—"

"I played it wrong," she interrupted, blushing even more. "Sorry, I know you're trying to be nice, but I have to get this right. It's ridiculous, sitting here the night before, not even knowing what I'm going to play."

"But you know both of them so—"

"No, I don't. Tartini would be a risk," she said. "But give me two or three hours and I might risk taking a chance on it tomorrow."

"You can't do something just because your dad thinks . . ."

"But he's right."

"No, he's not," Axel said, slowly rolling a joint.

"I know the easy piece," she went on. "But that might not be enough. It depends on what you and Shiro choose."

"You can't think like that."

"How am I supposed to think, then? I haven't seen you practice once. What are you going to play—have you even decided?"

"Ravel," he replied.

"Ravel? Without practicing?" She laughed. "Seriously?" she asked.

"Ravel's *Tzigane*."

"Axel, sorry, but that's an insane choice. You know that. It's too complicated, too fast, too much of a challenge, and . . ."

"I want to play it like Perlman, but without the haste . . . because it doesn't actually go fast."

"Axel, it's ridiculously fast," she said, smiling.

"Yes, for the hare being chased . . . but for the wolf it goes slowly."

She gave him a weary look. "Where did you read that?"

"Paganini's supposed to have said it."

"Okay, so I only have Shiro to worry about," she said, putting the violin to her shoulder. "You haven't been practicing, Axel. You can't play Ravel's *Tzigane*."

"It's not as hard as everyone says," he replied, lighting the joint.

"No." She smiled and started to play again.

She stopped a short while later and looked at him sternly. "Are you going to play Ravel?"

"Yes."

She turned serious.

"Have you been lying to me? Have you spent four years practicing this piece, or what?"

"I just decided—when you asked."

"How can you be so stupid?" she said, laughing.

"I don't care if I come in last," he said, and lay back on the sofa.

"I care," she said simply.

"I know, but there'll be other chances."

"Not for me."

She started to play the difficult piece by Tartini again. It went better this time, but she still broke off, played the complicated section again, and then one more time.

Axel clapped his hands, put David Bowie's *The Rise and Fall of Ziggy Stardust and the Spiders from Mars* on the record player, and lifted the needle onto the record. He lay back, closed his eyes, and sang along. Greta hesitated, put her violin down, then went over to him and took the joint from his hand. She took a few puffs, coughed, and handed it back.

"How can anyone be as stupid as you are?" she asked, suddenly stroking his lips.

She leaned over and tried to kiss him but slipped and

ended up kissing his cheek. She whispered an apology and kissed him again. They carried on kissing, tentatively, searchingly. He pulled her sweater off, and her hair crackled with static electricity. When he touched her cheek, he got a small shock and quickly snatched his hand back. They smiled nervously at each other and kissed again. He unbuttoned her neatly ironed white blouse and felt her small breasts. Her long, curly hair smelled like snow and winter, but her body was as warm as freshly baked bread.

They went into the bedroom and sank onto his bed. With trembling hands, she unbuttoned her skirt, then held on to her underwear as he pulled her tights off.

"What is it?" he whispered. "Do you want to stop?"

"I don't know. Do you want to stop?"

"No." He smiled.

"I'm just nervous," she said honestly.

"But you're older than me."

"True—you're only seventeen, it's almost inappropriate." She smiled.

Axel's heart beat hard as he pulled her underwear down. She lay perfectly still as he kissed her stomach, her small breasts, her neck, chin, lips. She parted her legs cautiously, and he lay down on top of her and felt her slowly pressing her thighs against his hips. Her cheeks flushed bright red when he slid inside her. She pulled him to her, caressed his neck and back, and sighed quietly every time he sank into her.

When they slowed and stopped, gasping for breath, a thin layer of warm sweat had formed between their naked bodies. They lay intertwined on his bed with their eyes closed and soon fell asleep.

63

IT WAS ALREADY LIGHT OUTSIDE when Axel woke up. He and Greta had fallen asleep together on the bed and slept the entire night in each other's arms, exhausted and happy.

Axel got out of bed and looked at Greta, who was sleeping peacefully, with the thick comforter wrapped around her. He walked to the door, stopped in front of the mirror, and looked at his naked seventeen-year-old body for a while before going into the music room. Carefully, he closed the door to the bedroom and took the violin from its case. He put it to his shoulder, then stood by the window, looking out at the winter morning. The snow was blowing down from the rooftops, swept into long veils. He started to play Ravel's *Tzigane* from memory.

The piece began with a mournful Roma melody, slow and measured, but then the tempo increased. The melody conjured up increasingly rapid echoes of itself, like fleeting memories of a summer's night.

It went incredibly fast.

He played because he was happy. He didn't think, just let his fingers dance with the bubbling, trickling stream.

Axel started to smile to himself when he remembered the painting in his grandfather's drawing room. He claimed it was Ernst Josephson's most radiant version of his *Water*

Sprite. As a child, Axel had been very fond of stories about the magical creature who lured people into the water by playing his fiddle so beautifully.

Axel thought he resembled the water sprite at that moment, the naked youth sitting in the water, playing his violin.

His bow moved over the strings, changing notes with dizzying speed. He didn't care that some of the horsehair came loose and was hanging from the frog.

This is how Ravel should be played, he thought. He should be played as happy music, not exotic. Ravel is a happy composer, a young composer.

He let the echo of the last notes resonate through the violin, swirling like the snow on the roofs outside. He lowered the bow and was about to take a bow to the wintery view when he detected movement behind him.

When he turned around, he saw Greta standing in the doorway. She was holding the comforter around herself and looking at him with strangely dark eyes.

He grew worried when he saw the serious expression on her face. "What is it?"

She didn't answer, just swallowed hard. Two large tears trickled down her cheeks.

"Greta, what is it?" he repeated.

"You said you hadn't practiced," she said in a monotone.

"No, I . . . I . . . ," he stammered. "I told you before. I find it easy to learn new pieces."

"Congratulations."

"It's not what you think."

She shook her head. "I don't understand how I could be so stupid," she said.

He put the violin and bow down, but she went back into the bedroom and closed the door behind her. He pulled on a pair of jeans that were hanging over the back of a chair, went over to the door, and knocked.

"Greta? Can I come in?"

She didn't answer. He felt a lump of anxiety growing inside him. After a little while, she came out, fully dressed. Without looking at him, she walked over to the piano, packed her violin away, and left him.

THE CONCERT HALL was completely full. Greta was the first competitor to perform. She hadn't looked at him, hadn't said hello when she arrived. She was wearing a dark-blue velvet dress and a simple necklace with a heart-shaped pendant.

Axel sat in his dressing room waiting, his eyes half closed. It was completely quiet apart from a faint hum coming from behind a dusty air vent. His younger brother, Robert, came into the room.

"Aren't you going to sit with Mom?" Axel asked.

"I'm too nervous. I can't watch when you play. I'll sit here and wait instead."

"Has Greta started?"

"Yes, it sounds good."

"What piece did she choose? Was it Tartini's violin sonata or . . ."

"No, something by Beethoven."

"Good," Axel muttered.

They sat there in silence, saying nothing more. After a while, there was a knock at the door. Axel stood up and opened it, and a woman told him it would be his turn very soon.

"Good luck," Robert said.

"Thanks," Axel replied, then picked up his violin and bow and walked down the hallway with the woman.

Loud applause could be heard from the stage, and Axel caught a glimpse of Greta and her father as they hurried into her dressing room.

Axel waited backstage while the master of ceremonies introduced him. After he heard his name, he walked straight out into the blinding spotlight and smiled at the audience. A buzz ran through the whole hall when he said he was going to play Maurice Ravel's *Tzigane*.

He put the violin to his shoulder, raised the bow, and he began to play the melancholic opening. Then he increased the tempo toward the seemingly impossible. The audience held its breath. He could hear that it sounded astonishingly good, but this time the melody wasn't dancing like water in a stream. He wasn't playing happily. He was playing with a hot, feverish sorrow. When he was three minutes into the piece and the notes were falling like raindrops, he intentionally started to skip the odd note, slowed his pace, made a couple of mistakes, and then stopped altogether.

The concert hall was silent.

"I'm very sorry," he whispered, and stepped down from the stage.

The audience clapped politely. His mother stood up from her seat and walked after him; she stopped him in the aisle.

"Come here, my boy," she said, putting her hands on his shoulders.

She stroked his cheek, and her voice was warm and noticeably affected when she said, "That was incredible, the best interpretation I've ever heard."

"Sorry, Mom."

"No," she said. She turned away from Axel and walked out of the concert hall.

Axel went to his dressing room to get his clothes but was stopped by the great conductor Herbert Blomstedt.

"That sounded very good until you pretended to get it wrong," he said in a subdued voice.

THE HOUSE WAS SILENT when Axel got home late in the evening. He went up to his attic rooms, through the music room and into the bedroom, and closed the door. Inside his head, he could still hear the music. He could hear himself omitting notes, then unexpectedly slowing the tempo and stopping.

He lay down on his bed and fell asleep beside his violin case.

The next morning, he woke up to hear a phone ringing somewhere in the house.

Someone was walking across the floor in the dining room, making the floor creak.

After a while, he heard footsteps on the stairs. Without knocking, his mother walked straight into his bedroom.

"Sit up," Alice said sternly.

He got worried when he looked at her. She had been crying, and her cheeks were still wet.

"Mom, I don't understand. . . ."

"Be quiet," she interrupted in a low voice. "The school principal called, and he . . ."

"He hates me because—"

"Be quiet!" Alice screamed.

Silence fell, and she put a trembling hand to her mouth and held it there as tears ran down her face.

"It's about Greta," she eventually said. "She committed suicide."

Axel looked at her and tried to comprehend what she was saying. "No, because I—"

"She was ashamed," Alice interrupted. "She should have been practicing. You promised, and I should have known. I did know. . . . She shouldn't have been here, she . . . I'm not saying it's your fault, Axel, it isn't. She let herself down when it really mattered, and she couldn't bear . . ."

"Mom, I—"

"Quiet!" she snapped again. "It's over."

Alice left the room, and Axel got up from the bed in a roaring fog. He stumbled, then opened the violin case, took out the beautiful instrument, and smashed it on the floor as hard as he could. The neck broke, and the body flapped around on loose strings. He stomped on it, scattering splinters of wood around the room.

"Axel! What are you doing?"

Robert rushed in and tried to stop him, but Axel pushed him away. Even though Robert's back hit the large wardrobe, he walked over to Axel again.

"Axel, you got some notes wrong, but what does that matter?" Robert said tentatively. "I met Greta; she got some notes wrong, too, everyone—"

"Shut up!" Axel shouted. "Never mention her name to me again."

Robert looked at him, then turned and left the room. Axel went on stomping on the remains of the instrument until it was impossible to tell that it had once been a violin.

Shiro Sasaki from Japan won the Johan Fredrik Berwald competition. Greta had chosen the easy piece by Beethoven but had still made mistakes. When she got home, she overdosed on sleeping pills and locked herself in her room. She wasn't found until the next morning, when she failed to come down to breakfast.

AXEL'S MEMORIES SINK like Atlantis, down into the mud and weeds. He glances at Beverly, who is looking at him with

Greta's big eyes. He looks at the towel in his hand and the liquid on the table.

The light from outside falls across the back of Beverly's head when she turns and looks at the violins hanging on the wall.

"I wish I could play the violin," she says.

"We could do a course together." He smiles.

"I'd like that," she replies seriously.

He puts the towel down on the table, feeling an immense weariness roaring inside him. The piano music echoes through the room, and the notes blur dreamily into one another.

"Poor Axel, you want to sleep," she says.

"I have to work," he mutters, almost to himself.

"Tonight, then," she replies, standing up.

64

JOONA IS SITTING at his desk, reading Palmcrona's account of his life. In one note from five years ago, Palmcrona describes how he traveled to Västerås to attend the year-end festivities at his son's school. It was raining, and he had stood at a distance while everyone gathered in the schoolyard under umbrellas and sang the traditional school songs. Palmcrona described his son's white jeans and white denim jacket, his long blond hair, and said there was "something about his nose and eyes that made me start to cry." As he drove back to Stockholm, he was thinking that his son was worth everything he had done thus far and would go on to do for him.

The phone rings, and Joona answers at once. It's Petter, who's sitting in the mobile command unit out on Dalarö.

"I've just been in contact with the navy's helicopter unit," he says excitedly. "They're flying back across Ersta fjord right now, and they've got Penelope with them."

"She's alive?" Joona asks, feeling a surge of relief.

"She was swimming straight out to sea when they found her," Petter explains.

"How is she? Is she okay?"

"Sounds like it—they're on their way to Södermalm Hospital."

"'That's too dangerous," Joona says abruptly. "Fly her here to police headquarters instead—we can bring in a team of medics from Karolinska."

He hears Petter tell someone to contact the helicopter.

"What do you know about the others?" Joona asks.

"It's complete chaos, Joona. We've lost people. This is crazy."

"Björn Almskog?" Joona asks.

"He hasn't been found yet, but . . . it's impossible to get any information. We don't know anything."

"What about the fixer? Has he vanished?"

"We'll have him soon. It's a small island. We've got guys from the Response Unit on the ground and in the air, and boats from the coast guard and marine police are on their way."

"Good," Joona says.

"You don't think we're going to get him?"

"If you didn't get him right away, he's probably already gone."

"Is that my fault?"

"Petter," Joona says calmly and gently, "if you hadn't acted as quickly as you did, Penelope Fernandez would be dead. And without her we wouldn't have a thing—no connection to the photograph, no witness."

AN HOUR LATER, two doctors from Karolinska Hospital examine Penelope in a protected room directly below the National Police Authority headquarters. They tend to her wounds and give her a tranquilizer, as well as nutritional supplements and hydration.

Petter informs Carlos that the remains of their colleagues Lennart Johansson and Göran Sjödin have been identified, along with the body of Björn Almskog. Ossian Wallenberg has been found dead outside his house, and divers are on their way to the scene where the rescue helicopter crashed. Petter says that they're assuming that all three crew members on board are dead.

The police haven't managed to catch the fixer, but Penelope Fernandez is alive.

The flags in front of police headquarters are lowered to half-mast, and Carlos and Regional Police Chief Margareta Widding hold a subdued press conference.

Joona doesn't take part. Instead, he and Saga take the elevator down to the basement to see Penelope.

65

FIVE FLOORS BELOW the most modern part of police head-quarters is a section containing two apartments, eight guest rooms, and two dormitories. It was set up to provide secure accommodations for senior police officers during emergencies. For the past ten years, the guest rooms have also been used to provide protection for witnesses who are believed to be under exceptional threat.

Penelope, lying on a hospital bed, feels cool liquid enter her arm as the speed of the drip is adjusted.

"We're just rehydrating you and giving you nutritional supplements," Dr. Daniella Richards says.

In a soft voice, she explains what she's doing as she tapes the cannula to the inside of Penelope's elbow.

Penelope's wounds have been cleaned and dressed. Her injured left foot has been stitched and bandaged, the scratches on her back have been cleaned and taped, and the deep cut on her hip has been sewn together.

"I'd like to give you some morphine for the pain."

"My mom," Penelope whispers, moistening her lips. "I want to talk to my mom."

"Of course," Daniella replies. "I'll pass that on."

Hot tears trickle down Penelope's cheeks. She hears the

doctor ask the nurse to prepare half a milliliter of morphine and scopolamine.

The room looks like an ordinary hospital room, though it's maybe a little cozier. There's a simple vase of flowers on the bedside table and bright pictures on the yellow walls. A pale wooden bookcase is full of dog-eared books, so people have clearly had time to read in here. Though the room has no windows, a light set behind a curtain helps alleviate the feeling of being in an underground bunker.

Daniella gently tells Penelope that they're going to leave her alone but that she can press the illuminated alarm button if she wants help with anything.

"There'll be someone right outside in case you have any questions, or in case you would like some company," she says.

Penelope closes her eyes as the calm warmth of the morphine spreads through her body, pulling her toward sleep.

She hears a crunch as a woman in a black niqab stomps on two small sunbaked clay figurines. A girl and her little brother are reduced to dust beneath her sandal. The veiled woman, who is carrying a heavy pack of grain on her back, doesn't even notice what she's done. Two boys whistle and laugh, crying that the slave children are dead, that there are only a few infants left now, and that all the Furs will die.

Penelope forces the memories from Kubbum out of her head, but before she falls asleep, she experiences a short moment of panic, in which she feels as if tons of stone and concrete are lying on top of her. It's as if she's falling to the center of the Earth, falling and falling and falling.

WHEN PENELOPE WAKES UP, she doesn't have the strength to open her eyes. The morphine is still making her body heavy. She remembers that she's lying in a hospital bed in a secure room deep beneath police headquarters. She doesn't have to run anymore. The relief is followed by a great wave of pain and grief. She doesn't know how long she's been asleep and feels she could easily drift off again, but she opens her eyes.

When she does, the underground room is completely black.

She blinks but can't see anything. Not even the alarm button beside the bed is lit up. There must be a power outage. She's about to cry out but forces herself to keep quiet when the door to the hallway suddenly clicks. She stares out into the darkness, hearing her pounding heartbeat. Her body is tingling. Every muscle is tense. Someone is touching her hair, almost imperceptibly. She lies completely still and feels someone standing beside the bed, then fingers weaving slowly into her locks. She is about to start praying when the person beside her grabs her hair and pulls her out of bed. She screams, and he throws her against the wall, shattering the framed picture and toppling the IV drip. She collapses on the floor, surrounded by broken glass. Still holding her hair, he drags her back, rolls her over, and smashes her face against the locked wheel of the bed, then pulls out a dagger with a black blade.

Penelope wakes up when she falls to the floor. The door opens, and a nurse rushes in. All the lights are on, and Penelope realizes that she had a nightmare. The nurse helps her back onto the bed, speaking softly to her, then attaches guardrails to both sides of the bed to keep her from falling again.

The sweat on her body goes cold after a while. She can't summon up the energy to move, and goose bumps rise up on her arms. She lies on her back with the alarm button in her hand and is staring up at the ceiling when there's a knock on the door. A young woman with colorful ribbons woven into her blond hair comes in and looks at her. Behind her stands a tall man with messy blond hair and a friendly, attractive face.

"My name is Saga Bauer," the woman says. "I'm with the Security Police. This is my colleague Joona Linna, from the National Crime Unit."

Penelope looks at them blankly, then lowers her gaze and looks at her bandaged arms and the cannula in the crook of her elbow.

"We're very sorry for everything you've been through in the past few days," the woman says. "And we understand that you probably just want to be left alone, but I'm afraid we're going to have to talk to you, and we need to get started as soon as possible."

Saga pulls out the chair from the little desk in the corner of the room and sits down beside the bed.

"He's still hunting me—isn't he?" Penelope asks after a short pause.

"You're safe here," Saga replies.

"Tell me he's dead."

"Penelope, we need—"

"You couldn't stop him," she says weakly.

"We're going to get him, I promise," Saga says. "But you have to help us."

Penelope sighs deeply, then closes her eyes.

"This is going to be tough, but we need answers to some questions," Saga continues. "Do you know why all of this happened?"

"Ask Björn," she mutters. "He might know."

"What did you say?" Saga asks.

"I said you should ask Björn," Penelope whispers, and slowly opens her eyes. "Ask Björn—maybe he knows."

Penelope feels as if she brought a ton of spiders and insects with her from the forest and they're crawling all over her skin. She starts to scratch her forehead, but Saga gently stops her hands.

"You've been hunted by someone," Saga says. "I can't imagine how terrible it must have been, but we need to know if you recognized the man pursuing you. Have you ever seen him before?"

Penelope shakes her head almost imperceptibly.

"We didn't think so," Saga says. "But can you give us a description? A tattoo, maybe, or any unusual features?"

"No," Penelope whispers.

"Maybe you could help us put together a composite picture; it doesn't take much for us to be able to put out an alert on him via Interpol."

The man from the National Crime Unit comes closer, and his unusually pale-gray eyes look like stones polished by a stream.

"It looked like you were shaking your head a moment ago," he says calmly, "when Saga asked if you'd met your pursuer before—is that right?"

Penelope nods.

"So you must have seen him," Joona goes on amiably. "Because otherwise you wouldn't know that you hadn't seen him before."

Penelope stares into space and remembers how the man always moved as if he had all the time in the world, yet everything happened so quickly. In her mind's eye, she sees him kneel down and take aim as she was hanging from the helicopter. She sees him raise the gun and shoot. No haste, no nervousness. Then she sees his face again, lit up by the flash of lightning, when they looked right at each other.

"We understand that you're scared," Joona goes on. "But we ..."

He falls silent when a nurse comes into the room and says that they haven't been able to reach Penelope's mother yet.

"She isn't at home, and she's not answering her—"

Penelope lets out a moan and turns away, hiding her face in the pillow. The nurse puts a comforting hand on her shoulder.

"I don't want to," Penelope sobs. "I don't want to. . . ."

Another nurse hurries in and explains that she needs to add more tranquilizer to the drip.

"I'm going to have to ask you to leave," the nurse says quickly to Saga and Joona.

"We'll come back later," Joona says. "I think I know where your mother is. I'll sort it out."

Penelope has stopped crying but is still breathing fast. As she hears the nurse preparing the medication, she thinks about how the room reminds her of a prison cell. Her mom is never going to want to come here. She clenches her teeth and tries to hold back her tears.

There are moments when Penelope thinks she can remember her earliest years. The smell of sweating, dirty bodies can send her right back to the cell she was born in. She can almost see the beam of a flashlight sweeping across the prisoners' faces, and her mother passing her to someone else. The woman immediately starts singing gently in her ear as her mom is taken away by the guards.

66

CLAUDIA GETS OFF THE BUS at the Dalarö Strand Hotel.
As she walks by the harbor, she can hear helicopters and
sirens vanishing into the distance. The search can't be over;
they have to keep on looking. A few police boats are floating
some distance from the shore. She looks around. There's no
ferry in the harbor; no cars onshore, either.

"Penelope!" she shouts. "Penelope!"

She realizes how she must look, how strangely she's
behaving, but without Penelope she has nothing left.

She starts to walk along the water's edge. The grass is
brown and dry, and there's trash everywhere. She reaches
a sign with the word "Private" written on it in white paint.
She walks past the sign, out onto a concrete pier, then looks
back at the big rocks. *There's no one here*, she thinks, and
turns back toward the harbor again. A man is walking along
the road, waving to her, a dark figure with his jacket flapping behind him. She squints against the sunlight. The man
shouts something, but Claudia can't hear and looks at him in
confusion. He starts to walk faster, striding toward her, and
now she can see his friendly face.

"Claudia Fernandez?" he calls.

"That's me," she says.

"My name is John Bengtsson," he says when he reaches

her. "Joona Linna sent me. He said you'd probably come out here."

"Why?" she asks in a weak voice.

"Your daughter's alive."

Claudia looks at the man, who repeats himself.

"Penelope's alive," he says, and smiles at her.

67

THE ATMOSPHERE in police headquarters is almost fevered in its agitation. People are comparing recent events with the police murders in Malexander in 1999 and the case of Josef Ek the year before last. The papers are writing about the drama in the archipelago, calling the fixer "the police butcher." Journalists are speculating wildly and putting pressure on their sources in the force.

Joona and Saga are due to present a summary of the current state of the investigation to Carlos, Verner, Petter, and Benny Rubin, the head of operations, as well as Pollock and Kofoed from the National Homicide Commission.

They're walking along the hallway, discussing whether Penelope will be able to help them make any progress.

"I think she'll talk soon," Joona says.

"That's not a given; she could just as easily clam up," Saga replies.

They close the door, sit down, and say hello to the men already sitting around the table.

"I want to start by saying that we no longer suspect that any left-wing extremists were involved in these events," Saga says.

Verner whispers something to Pollock.

"Right?" Saga says, raising her voice.

Verner looks up and nods. "Yes, that's correct," he says, clearing his throat.

"Start at the beginning," Carlos says to Saga.

"Okay . . . Penelope Fernandez is a peace campaigner, the chair of the Swedish Peace and Arbitration Society," Saga goes on. "She's in a long-term relationship with Björn Almskog, who's a bartender at the Debaser club at Medborgar Square. She lives at 3 Sankt Pauls Street, and he lives at 47 Pontonjär Street. Penelope was in possession of a photograph that was taped to the glass door between her living room and entryway."

From her computer, Saga Bauer projects a copy of the photograph onto the screen.

"This picture was taken in Frankfurt in the spring of 2008," she explains.

"We recognize Palmcrona," Carlos says.

"Exactly," Saga says. She points out the other people in the box. "This is Pontus Salman, managing director of arms manufacturer Silencia Defense. And this is none other than Raphael Guidi. He's a well-known arms dealer. He's known in the trade as the Archangel, and he does most of his business in Africa and the Middle East."

"And the woman who's been allowed to join them for their little meeting?" Benny asks.

"Her name is Agathe al-Haji," Saga says without smiling. "She's a military adviser to the Sudanese government and closely connected to President Omar al-Bashir."

Benny slams his hand down hard on the table and bares his teeth when Pollock shoots him a disapproving look.

"Is this normal?" Carlos asks. "For them to meet like this?"

"Yes, I'd say so," Saga replies. "The meeting in this picture was convened to discuss a large shipment of ammunition to the Sudanese army. The deal was deemed to be politically acceptable and would have gone through if the International Criminal Court in The Hague hadn't issued a warrant for the arrest of President Bashir."

"That was in 2009, wasn't it?" Pollock asks.

"Passed me by," Carlos says.

"It didn't attract much attention here," Saga says. "But the warrant was issued because the president was suspected of being directly involved in torture, rape, and genocide in Darfur."

"So no deal?" Carlos concludes.

"No deal," she replies.

"And the photograph? What's so special about it? Nothing?" Verner asks.

"Penelope didn't seem to think it was dangerous, seeing as she had it taped to her door," Saga says.

"But she also must have thought it was important, because she had it on display," Carlos points out.

"We really don't know—maybe it was just a reminder of the way the world works," Saga speculates. "That there are a few people at the bottom fighting for peace, while the rich and powerful trade weapons and toast each other with champagne at the top."

"We're hoping to be able to question Penelope soon, but we're fairly sure that Björn acted on his own here," Joona goes on. "He may know more about the photograph than Penelope, unless he was just trying his luck, because, on June 2, Björn went to an Internet café and sent an e-mail from an anonymous account trying to blackmail Carl Palmcrona. The e-mail sparked a brief correspondence: Björn wrote that he knew the photograph would cause problems for Palmcrona and that he was prepared to sell it for a million kronor."

"Classic extortion," Pollock mutters.

"Björn used the word 'troubling' to describe the photograph," Saga goes on, "which makes us think he didn't understand how severely Palmcrona was going to react."

"Björn thought he was in control of the situation," Joona says. "So he was taken aback when Palmcrona replied with a serious warning. Palmcrona wrote that Björn didn't know what he was getting involved in and begged him to send him the photograph before it was too late."

Joona drinks some water.

"What's the tone of the e-mails?" Pollock asks. "Aggressive?"

Joona shakes his head and hands out printouts of the e-mails.

"I don't read them as aggressive, just serious."

Kofoed reads the exchange, then nods and writes something down.

"Then what happened?" he asks.

"Before Palmcrona's housekeeper went home on Wednesday, she helped him hang a noose from the ceiling."

Petter lets out a laugh. "Why?"

"Because he'd had a back operation and couldn't do it himself," Saga says.

"Okay," Carlos says.

"The following day, at lunchtime, after the mail had been delivered, we assume," Joona continues, "Palmcrona called a number in Bordeaux and . . ."

"It hasn't been possible to trace the number any more accurately than that," Saga points out.

"The number may have belonged to an exchange, so the call could have been forwarded to a different country, another continent, or even back to Sweden," Joona says. "Either way, it was a very short call, forty-three seconds. Maybe he just left a message. We believe he was calling about the photograph and the blackmail message and that he said he was expecting help."

"Because after that, just a few minutes later, Palmcrona's housekeeper called and booked a taxi to Arlanda Airport in Palmcrona's name for two o'clock. Exactly one hour and fifteen minutes after that brief call, Palmcrona's phone rang. He had already put his coat on, but he answered anyway. The call was from Bordeaux, the same number that he'd called. This second call lasted two minutes. Then Palmcrona sent a final e-mail to his blackmailer, with the following message: 'It's too late now, you and I are both going to die.' He sent his housekeeper home, paid the taxi driver for the lost fare, then went back upstairs. Without taking his coat off, Palmcrona went into the living room, stood his briefcase on its side, climbed on top of it, and hanged himself," Saga says.

There's silence around the table.

"But that isn't the end of the story," Joona says slowly, "because Palmcrona's telephone conversations set things in motion. . . . Whoever took that call sent an international fixer to get rid of all the evidence and take care of the photograph."

"How often—in Sweden, I mean—do we actually come across a professional hit man?" Carlos asks in a skeptical voice. "There must be a hell of a lot of money at stake to warrant this sort of action."

Joona looks at him blankly. "Yes."

"We believe that Palmcrona read the contents of the e-mail to whoever he called, including the bank account number Björn gave him," Saga says.

"It's not hard to trace someone if you have their bank account number," Verner mutters.

"At approximately the same time that Palmcrona hanged himself, Björn was in the Dream Bow Internet Café," Joona goes on. "He logged into his anonymous e-mail account and saw that he'd received two messages from Palmcrona."

"Obviously, he was hoping that Palmcrona had agreed to pay a million kronor for the photograph," Saga says.

"Instead, he found Palmcrona's warning and then the short message telling him it was already too late, and they were both going to die."

"And they're dead," Pollock says.

"You can imagine how frightened Björn must have been," Saga says. "He wasn't exactly an accomplished blackmailer; he just took a chance when he spotted it."

"What did he do?"

Petter is looking at them with his mouth open. Carlos pours him some water.

"Björn changed his mind and decided to send Palmcrona the photograph, to put an end to it all."

"But Palmcrona was already dead by the time Björn wrote to him explaining that he was backing down," Joona says.

"The problem was that the photograph was taped to the door in Penelope's apartment," Saga says. "And she didn't know anything about the attempted blackmail."

"He needed to get the photograph without having to explain the extortion," Kofoed says with a nod.

"We don't know how he was planning to explain the missing photograph to Penelope," Saga says with a smile. "He probably panicked. He wanted to put it all behind him and hoped it would all blow over while they were out on his boat in the archipelago."

Joona goes over to the window and looks out.

"Early the following morning, Penelope took a taxi to the television studio where she was set to appear in a debate," Saga goes on. "As soon as she left, Björn went into her apartment and grabbed the photograph. He took the subway to Central Station, where he bought stamps and an envelope and sent the photograph to Palmcrona. Then he ran to the

Internet café and sent Palmcrona a final e-mail, telling him that the photograph was on its way. Björn went home, collected his and Penelope's bags, and went to his boat, which was moored at the Långholmen marina. Penelope left the television studio to join him."

"By that point, the fixer had already searched Björn's apartment and started the fire that destroyed that entire floor of the building."

"But I've read the report. . . . The fire investigators concluded that the fire was caused by an electric iron that had been left on in the neighboring apartment," Petter says.

"And that's probably correct," Joona says.

"Just like a gas explosion would have caused the fire in Penelope's apartment," Saga says.

"The fixer's aim was presumably to get rid of any evidence," Joona goes on. "When he didn't find the photograph in Björn's apartment, he set it on fire, then followed Björn to his boat."

"To look for the photograph," Saga adds. "And to murder Björn and Penelope and make it look like a boating accident."

"What the fixer didn't know was that their plans had changed at the last minute and Penelope's sister was with them."

Joona falls silent and thinks about the dead woman lying in the mortuary: her young, vulnerable face, the red mark across her chest.

"My guess is that they dropped anchor at some island in Jungfrufjärden Bay, off Dalarö," Joona goes on. "And before the fixer arrived, Penelope and Björn went ashore for some reason. When the fixer got onto the boat, he found Viola. Believing her to be Penelope, he drowned her in a tub and then put her on the bed in the front cabin. While he waited for Björn, he probably looked for the photograph, and when he didn't find it, he prepared an explosion on the boat. You have Erixon's report in front of you. We don't quite know what happened, but somehow Penelope and Björn managed to get away."

"And the boat with Viola Fernandez's body on board was abandoned."

"We don't know how they got there, but on Monday they were on Kymmendö."

The corners of Benny's mouth twitch.

"In Ossian Wallenberg's house? He was great, but he was obviously too much for this dull country."

Carlos clears his throat as he pours more coffee.

"When the fixer realized he'd lost them, he went to Penelope's apartment to look for the photograph," Joona goes on, without acknowledging Benny's comment. "Erixon and I showed up and interrupted him. It wasn't until then, when I was actually confronted with him, that I understood that we were dealing with an expert international fixer."

"He can probably get into our systems, listen to our communications, and so on," Saga says.

"Was that how he managed to find Björn and Penelope out on Kymmendö?" Petter asks.

"We don't know," Joona replies.

"But he acts fast," Saga says. "He probably returned to Dalarö to look for Penelope right after the confrontation with Joona and Erixon."

"So he was already there when I spoke to the marine police," Petter says, leaning forward on the table and adjusting the sheet of paper with the agenda written on it.

"What happened?" Carlos asks.

"We just started work on the reconstruction," Petter says. "But somehow he managed to hijack the police speedboat and kill Lennart Johansson and Göran Sjödin. Then he got out to Kymmendö, where he murdered Björn Almskog and Ossian Wallenberg, blew up the police boat, set off after Penelope, and shot down the rescue helicopter."

"And vanished." Carlos sighs.

"But because of Petter's skillful leadership, we were able to rescue Penelope," Joona says, and sees Pollock turn to look at Petter with interest.

"The exact sequence of events obviously needs to be investigated," Petter says with a sternness that does nothing to hide his delight at the praise.

"That's going to take a hell of a long time." Kofoed smiles mirthlessly.

"What about the photograph?" Petter sighs.

"Ten people have died because of it," Joona says seriously. "And more will probably follow if we can't . . ."

Joona looks out the window. "The photograph could be a lock—a lock that requires a key," he says.

"What sort of key?" Petter asks.

"The photographer," Saga says.

"Penelope Fernandez—is she the photographer?" Pollock wonders.

"That would explain why she was being hunted," Carlos declares, rather loudly.

"It would," Saga says hesitantly.

"But?" Carlos says.

"What's the evidence to suggest otherwise?" Benny asks.

"That Joona doesn't think Penelope is the photographer," Saga says.

"Oh, for God's sake!" Petter exclaims.

Carlos clamps his mouth shut, stares at the table, and has the sense to stay silent.

"Penelope is understandably in a state of shock, so we don't know what her role in all this is yet," Saga says.

Pollock clears his throat and hands around copies of Palmcrona's will. "Palmcrona had an account with a bank in Jersey," he tells them.

"The tax-free paradise." Petter nods, removing the chewing tobacco from under his lip. He wipes his thumb on the table without noticing the exasperated look on Carlos's face.

"Can we find out how much he had in the account?" Verner asks.

"There's no way of getting access to his transactions," Joona says. "But, according to his will, it should be around nine million euros."

"His personal finances weren't great, so we don't understand how he could have earned money like that legally," Pollock says.

"We've been in touch with Transparency International— they're a global organization fighting corruption—but they don't have anything on Carl Palmcrona, or anyone else at the ISP. Not even a hint of anything."

"Palmcrona's assets were bequeathed to a sixteen-year-old boy by the name of Stefan Bergkvist, who, it turns out, was his son. A son he never met. But the boy died in a fire in Västerås just three days after Palmcrona committed suicide."

"The boy never found out who his father was," Saga adds.

"According to the preliminary police report, it was an accident," Carlos says.

"Yes, but does anyone believe that the fire that killed Palmcrona's son three days after his suicide is a coincidence?" Joona asks.

"How could it be?" Carlos says.

"This is completely sick," Petter says. "Why would anyone murder the son Palmcrona never even met?"

"What the hell is this all about?" Verner asks.

"Palmcrona keeps cropping up," Joona says, tapping his

finger on the man smiling in the photograph. "He's in the photograph, he's the subject of a blackmail attempt, he's found dead, his son dies, and he has nine million euros in an offshore bank account."

"The money's interesting," Saga says.

"We've taken a close look at his life," Pollock says. "He had no other family, no hobbies, didn't deal in stocks or shares, or . . ."

"If this money really is in that account, then it must somehow be connected to his position as director general of the ISP," Joona says.

"He could have engaged in insider trading, using fake accounts or intermediaries," Verner says.

"Or he could have been taking bribes after all," Saga says.

"Follow the money," Pollock whispers.

"We need to talk to Palmcrona's successor, Axel Riessen," Joona says, getting to his feet. "If there's anything fishy about the decisions Palmcrona was making, he might have found out about it by now."

68

FROM A DISTANCE, Joona can hear the sound of trumpets, whistles, and drums. A procession is heading along Oden Street. It looks like about seventy young people, carrying antifascist symbols and banners protesting the Security Police's treatment of the members of the Brigade. Joona sees one colorful flag with the rainbow symbol and a hammer and sickle fluttering in the breeze, and hears them chanting.

The angry sounds disappear as Joona and Saga walk up Brage Street. They've contacted the ISP and have been told that the director general is working from home this morning.

On the left side of the street is the attractive townhouse where the Riessen brothers live. The façade is striking, with dark bricks, leaded windows, elegant woodwork, and copper around the bay windows and chimneys.

They walk up to the wooden door bearing a brass sign with Axel Riessen's name on it, and Saga rings the doorbell. After a while, the heavy door is opened by a tall, suntanned man with a friendly face.

Saga introduces herself as a detective with the Security Police and explains why they've come.

Axel looks at her ID carefully, then looks up. "I'm not sure I'm going to be of any use to you, but . . ."

"It'll still be a pleasure to have a chat," Joona Linna says.

Axel looks at him in surprise but smiles appreciatively at the pleasantry as he shows them into the tall, bright apartment. He's wearing dark-blue suit pants, a pale-blue shirt unbuttoned at the neck, and a pair of slippers on his feet. He takes two more pairs of slippers from a low, polished cabinet and offers them to Saga and Joona.

"I suggest that we go and sit in the orangery. It tends to be a bit cooler there."

They follow Axel through the large apartment, past the wide mahogany staircase with its dark paneling, and two large reception rooms.

The orangery is a glazed conservatory facing the garden, where a tall hedge is casting green shadows, forming a wall of leaves. Pots of herbs and scentless orchids are arranged neatly on copper tabletops and tiled surfaces.

"Please, sit down," Axel says, gesturing toward the chairs. "I was just thinking of having some tea and crumpets, and it would be a pleasure if you'd join me."

"I haven't eaten crumpets since I went to Edinburgh." Saga smiles.

"Well, then," Axel says happily, leaving the room.

He comes back a few minutes later with a metal tray and puts the teapot, the sugar bowl, and a small saucer of lemon slices in the middle of the table. The warm crumpets are wrapped in a linen napkin beside a butter dish. Axel carefully sets the table for the three of them, laying out cups and saucers, plates and napkins, before he pours the tea.

Through the doors and walls, they can hear faint violin music.

"So, tell me, how can I help you?" Axel asks.

Saga gently puts her cup down and clears her throat. "We need to ask a few questions about the ISP, and we're hoping you can help us."

"Of course, but I should probably just make a quick call to make sure it's okay," he explains amiably, taking out his cell phone.

"By all means," Saga says.

"I'm so sorry, I've forgotten your name. . . ."

"Saga Bauer."

"Could I possibly see your ID again?"

She hands it over, and he stands up and leaves the room. They hear him talking briefly; then he comes back in, thanks her, and returns her ID.

"Last year, the ISP authorized export licenses for South Africa, Namibia, Tanzania, Algeria, and Tunisia," Saga says, as if the pause hadn't happened. "Ammunition for heavy machine guns, portable antitank guns, grenade launchers . . ."

"Sweden has long-standing relationships with a number of those countries," Axel adds.

"But never with Sudan?"

He looks her in the eyes, and a trace of a smile crosses his face.

"I can't imagine so."

"I meant before the warrant for President Bashir's arrest was issued," she explains.

"I realize that," he replies, amused. "Otherwise, it would be completely unthinkable, what we would call an insurmountable obstacle."

"Presumably, you've had a chance to look through a fair number of Palmcrona's old decisions?" Saga says.

"Of course," Axel replies.

"Have you noticed anything unusual?"

"What do you mean by 'unusual'?"

"Decisions that seem strange," Saga says, sipping her tea.

"Are there grounds to believe that there would be any?" he asks.

"That's what we're asking you." She smiles.

"In that case, my answer is no."

"How far back have you looked?"

Joona listens to Saga's introductory questions about classification, advance notification, and export licenses as he watches Axel Riessen's calm, attentive face. Suddenly he hears the violin music again. It's coming from outside, from the open window facing the garden. The high, mournful notes of a mazurka. Then the violin stops, and starts from the beginning again, stops once more, and then begins again.

As Joona listens to the music, he thinks about the photograph of four people in a private box at the concert and absentmindedly touches the bag containing a copy of the picture.

He thinks about Palmcrona, hanging from the ceiling with a clothesline tied around his neck, and his will, and his son's death.

Joona sees Saga nod at something Axel is saying. A hint of green crosses Axel's face, a reflection from the copper tray on the table.

Palmcrona realized instantly how serious it was, Joona reasons. All Björn had to say in his e-mail was that Palmcrona had been photographed in the company of the arms dealer Guidi. Palmcrona didn't doubt the veracity of the photograph for a moment.

Maybe he was already aware of its existence.

Axel pours more tea for Saga, who brushes a crumb from the corner of her mouth.

This doesn't make sense, Joona thinks.

Pontus Salman had been able to date the meeting. He didn't seem to find the picture's existence awkward. So why was it so problematic in Palmcrona's eyes?

He hears Axel and Saga discuss the way political and security conditions change whenever embargoes are imposed or removed on countries.

Joona murmurs slightly so that they think he's following the conversation, but he keeps thinking about the photograph.

The table in the box had been set for four people, and four people were visible in the photograph. That meant that the fifth person, the person holding the camera, wasn't one of the guests. That person wasn't going to be offered a place at the table, wasn't going to be offered a glass of champagne.

The fifth person could still hold the answer to the whole mystery.

We have to get Penelope to talk, and soon, Joona thinks. Because, even if she isn't the photographer, she could very well be the key that unlocks the riddle.

He returns in his mind to the people in the photograph: Carl Palmcrona, Raphael Guidi, Agathe al-Haji, and Pontus Salman.

Joona thinks about their meeting with Pontus Salman. According to him, the only remarkable thing about it was that Palmcrona hadn't declined the offer of champagne, seeing as there was nothing to celebrate and this was a first meeting.

But what if there was something to celebrate?

Joona's pulse quickens.

What if all four of them raised their glasses a moment later and drank a toast?

Pontus Salman had identified himself and told them the reason for the meeting, its location, and when it took place.

When it took place, Joona muses. The photograph could have been taken on a different occasion.

We only have Salman's word that the meeting took place in Frankfurt in the spring of 2008.

We need Penelope's help.

Joona looks at his hands, resting on his bag. He's thinking that it should be possible to identify the four musicians in the background of the photograph, because their faces are visible. Someone must be able to recognize them.

And if we can identify the musicians, it might be possible to confirm the date of the meeting. Four people playing—a string quartet. Perhaps the four of them only played together on that one occasion. That would set the date beyond all doubt.

Of course, he tells himself. They should have done this already. He considers leaving Saga with Axel and going back to police headquarters, to talk to Petter and ask if it's occurred to them that identifying this group of musicians might be able to give a precise date for the photograph.

He looks at Saga, sees her smile at Axel and then ask him about the consolidation of the U.S. defense industry.

Once again he can hear music through the open window, a faster piece this time. It stops; then it sounds as if two strings are being tuned against each other.

"Who's that playing?" Joona asks, sitting up.

"My brother, Robert," Axel replies in a rather surprised voice.

"I see—is he a violinist?"

"The pride of the family ... But first and foremost he's a violinmaker. He has his studio here, at the back of the house."

"Do you think I could ask him something?"

69

JOONA FOLLOWS AXEL along the marble path. They walk to the studio and knock on the door. The violin stops, and the door is opened by a middle-aged man with thinning hair, a handsome, intelligent face, and a body that had clearly once been skinny but had gradually filled out over the years.

"The police want to talk to you," Axel says seriously. "You're suspected of disorderly conduct."

"I confess," Robert says.

"Great," Joona says.

"Was there anything else?"

"We've actually got quite a few cases that haven't been solved," Joona says.

"I'm sure I'm guilty."

"Thanks very much," Joona says, and shakes Robert's hand. "Joona Linna, National Crime."

"How can I help?" Robert asks with a smile.

"We're looking into a sudden death, the former director general of the ISP, which is why I've been talking to your brother."

"I don't know anything about Palmcrona other than what's been printed in the papers."

"Can I come in for a few minutes?"

"Of course."

"I'll get back to your colleague," Axel says, shutting the door behind Joona.

A beautiful, polished wooden staircase leads down into the workshop. The studio ceiling is low and sloping, like an attic roof; it looks as if it was made from an existing cellar. The air is full of strong smells: fresh-sawed wood, resin, and turpentine. There are violin parts everywhere: specially selected wood, carved scrolls, special tools, planes the size of corkscrews, curved knives.

"I heard you playing through the window," Joona says.

Robert nods and gestures toward a beautiful violin.

"It needed to be adjusted slightly."

"You made it yourself?" Joona asks.

"Yes."

"It looks incredible."

"Thanks."

Robert picks the violin up and hands it to Joona. The polished instrument is almost weightless. Joona turns it over, then smells it.

"The varnish is the secret," Robert says, taking the violin and putting it in a case lined with wine-red padding.

Joona opens his bag, takes out the plastic sleeve, and hands over the photograph.

"Palmcrona," Robert says.

"Yes. But do you recognize any of the people in the background, the musicians?"

Robert looks at the picture again, then nods.

"That's Martin Beaver," he says, pointing. "Kikuei Ikeda . . . Kazuhide Isomura, and Clive Greensmith on the cello."

"They're famous musicians?"

Robert can't help smiling at the question.

"They're practically legendary . . . the Tokyo String Quartet."

"The Tokyo String Quartet—the same four people every time?"

"Yes."

"Always?"

"For a very long time; things have been going very well for them."

"Can you see anything unusual about this photograph?"

Robert looks at it intently.

"No," he says after a while.

"They don't just play in Tokyo, then?" Joona asks.

"No, they play all around the world, but their instruments are owned by a Japanese trust."

"Is that common?"

"Yes, when we're talking about really special instruments," Robert replies. "And the ones in this picture are undoubtedly among the finest in the world."

"I see."

"The Paganini Quartet," Robert says.

"The Paganini Quartet," Joona repeats, looking at the musicians again.

The dark wood is shimmering, and the musicians' black outfits are reflected in the varnish.

"They were made by Stradivarius," Robert says. "The oldest of them is Desaint, a violin dating back to 1680. . . . Kikuei Ikeda is playing that one. Martin Beaver is playing the violin that Count Cozio di Salabue gave Paganini."

Robert falls silent and gives Joona a questioning glance, but Joona nods to indicate that he'd like him to go on.

"All four instruments were owned by Niccolò Paganini. I don't know how much you know about Paganini, but he was a virtuoso, as both a violinist and a composer. He wrote pieces that people found ridiculous, because they were impossible to play—until Paganini himself picked up the violin. After his death, it's supposed to have been a hundred years before anyone could play his pieces again . . . and some of his techniques are still considered impossible. There are plenty of stories about Paganini and his violin duels."

Joona looks at the photograph again, at the four men sitting on the stage in the background. He looks at their instruments.

"So the Tokyo String Quartet often plays together using these instruments?"

"Yes, they probably perform eight or nine concerts a month."

"When would you estimate that this photograph was taken?"

"It can't be more than ten years old, based on Martin Beaver's appearance. I've met him a couple of times."

"Would it be possible to identify the date if we could specify the location?"

"That's the Alte Oper in Frankfurt."

"You're sure?"

"I know they play there every year," Robert says. "Sometimes several times a year."

"*Perkele*," Joona swears.

There has to be some way of identifying when the photograph was taken, either to confirm or to disprove Salman's version of events.

Joona opens the plastic sleeve in order to put the photograph away. Penelope is probably the only person who can cast any light on the circumstances.

He looks at the picture again, at one of the violinists, the movement of the bow, the right elbow, and then he looks up at Robert with his pale-gray eyes.

"Do they always play the same pieces when they tour?" Joona asks.

"'The same pieces? No, goodness . . . They've been through all of Beethoven's quartets, and that alone means there's lots of variety. But of course they also play plenty of other pieces, sometimes Schubert and Bartók. And Brahms, of course. It's a long list . . . Debussy, Dvořák, Haydn, lots of Mozart and Ravel, et cetera, et cetera."

Joona is staring ahead of him; then he walks a few paces, stops, and looks back at Robert.

"I have an idea," Joona says with sudden intensity. "From this picture, just by looking at the musicians' hands, would it be possible . . . would it be possible to identify what piece they're playing just by looking at the picture?"

Robert opens and closes his mouth and shakes his head, but he looks at the photograph again with a smile. In the spotlights on the stage of the Alte Oper, the Tokyo String Quartet is performing: Clive Greensmith's thin face looks oddly vulnerable. His high forehead is shining. And Kikuei Ikeda is playing a high note, with the little finger of his left hand on the fingerboard.

"I'm sorry. It's impossible. They could be playing . . . Well, I was going to say any notes, but . . ."

"But with a magnifying glass . . . you can see their fingers on the strings, the necks of the instruments. . . ."

"Of course, theoretically . . ." He sighs and shakes his head.

"Do you know anyone who might be able to help me?" Joona goes on, with a hard edge of stubbornness in his voice. "Some musician or teacher at the Royal College of Music, someone who might be able to analyze this photograph for us?"

"I wish I . . ."

"It's not going to be possible, is it?" Joona asks.

"In all seriousness, no," Robert replies, shrugging his

shoulders. "If not even Axel could do it, then I doubt it can be done."

"Axel? Your brother?"

"Hasn't he looked at the photograph?" Robert asks.

"No," Joona replies.

"But you've been speaking to him."

"Not about music—you're the musician, after all." Joona smiles.

"Talk to him anyway," Robert says by way of conclusion.

"Why would—"

Joona stops when there's a knock on the door of the studio. A moment later, Saga comes in, the sunlight shining through her blond hair.

"Is Axel here?" she asks.

"No," Joona replies.

"More detectives?" Robert asks with a smile.

"Security Police," Saga says curtly.

The silence that follows is slightly too long. Robert doesn't seem to be able to take his eyes off her.

"I didn't know the Security Police had a department for elves," he says with a broad smile, then tries to be serious: "Sorry, I don't mean to be rude. But you really do look like an elf in one of Bauer's paintings."

"Appearances can be deceptive," she says dryly.

"Robert Riessen," he says, introducing himself and holding his hand out.

"Saga," she says.

70

JOONA AND SAGA leave the Riessen residence and get into the car. Saga's phone buzzes, and she looks at the message and smiles to herself. "I'm having lunch at home," Saga says, blushing quickly.

"What time is it?"

"Eleven-thirty," she says. "Are you going to keep working?"

"No, I'm going to a lunch concert at the Södra food court with a friend."

"Could you drop me off on Södermalm, then? I live on Bastu Street."

"I can drive you home if you like," he says.

Axel had just started to describe his career at the United Nations to Saga when his phone rang. He looked at the screen, excused himself, and left the room. Saga sat and waited, but after fifteen minutes, she got up and started to look for him. When she couldn't find him, she went down to Robert's studio. Then Robert and Joona helped look for Axel, before concluding that he had left the house.

"What did you want with Axel's brother?"

"Just a feeling," Joona says.

"Hurray," Saga mutters. "A feeling."

"You know . . . when we showed the photograph to Salman," Joona goes on, "he identified himself, talked openly about the meeting, then said all negotiations had stopped when the ICC in The Hague issued that arrest warrant for—"

His phone rings; he breaks off, digs it out, and answers without taking his eyes off the traffic.

"That was quick."

"The timing fits," Anja says. "The Tokyo String Quartet played at the Alte Oper, and Salman was in Frankfurt."

"I see," Joona says.

Saga watches him nod and say thank you before ending the call.

"So Salman was telling the truth?" Saga says.

"I don't know."

"But the timing has been confirmed?"

"All we know is that Salman traveled to Frankfurt and that the Tokyo String Quartet was performing at the Alte Oper . . . but Salman has been to Frankfurt plenty of times, and the Tokyo String Quartet plays at the Alte Oper at least once a year."

"Are you trying to say that you think he lied about the timing, even though you've just had it confirmed?"

"No, but . . . I don't know. Like I said, it's just a feeling," Joona says. "He has a pretty good reason to lie if he and Palmcrona were negotiating with Agathe al-Haji after the arrest warrant was issued."

"That would be a criminal offense. Christ, that would look like they were exporting arms directly to the militia in Darfur, which would be a breach of international law."

"We believed Salman because he identified himself," Joona replies. "But the fact that he told the truth about one thing doesn't mean he was telling the truth about everything."

"Is that your feeling?"

"No. There was something about Salman's voice . . . when

he said that the only remarkable thing about the picture was that Palmcrona hadn't turned down the offer of champagne."

"Seeing as there was nothing to celebrate," Saga says.

"Yes, that was how he put it, but my instinct tells me that, on the contrary, there *was* something to celebrate and that they were drinking a toast because they'd come to an agreement."

"All the facts contradict what you're suggesting."

"But think about the photograph," Joona says stubbornly. "There's an atmosphere in that box . . . their faces. . . . They're happy, as if a contract's been signed."

"Even if that's true, we can't confirm the date of the picture without Penelope."

"What are her doctors saying?" Joona asks.

"That we'll be able to talk to her soon but that she's still too exhausted."

"We have no idea how much she knows," Joona says.

"No, but what the hell else do we have to go on?"

"The photograph," Joona replies quickly. "Because the four musicians are clearly visible in the background, and we might be able to tell what piece they're playing from the position of their hands and identify the date that way."

"Joona." She sighs.

"Yep." He smiles.

"That's completely insane—as I hope you realize."

"Robert said that it should be possible, theoretically."

"We'll have to wait until Penelope's feeling better."

"I'll call," Joona says. He takes out his phone, dials the National Police Authority and asks to be put through to Room U12.

Saga looks at his calm face.

"My name is Joona Linna, I'm . . ."

He falls silent and a wide smile spreads across his face.

"Of course I remember you, and your red coat," he says,

then listens. "Yes, but . . . I thought you might suggest hypnosis?"

Saga can hear the doctor laughing at his joke.

"No," he says. "But seriously—we really, really need to talk to her."

His face grows solemn.

"I see, but . . . it would be best if you could persuade her. Okay, we'll figure it out. Bye."

He ends the call and turns onto Bellmans Street.

"That was Daniella Richards," Joona tells Saga.

"What did she say?"

"She thinks we'll be able to talk to Penelope in a couple of days, but that she needs somewhere else to live first. She's refusing to stay in that underground room, and says—"

"There's nowhere safer."

"Not if she refuses to stay," Joona says.

"We'll have to explain how dangerous the situation is."

"She already knows that better than we do," he says.

71

Disa and Joona are sitting across from each other at a table in the dining room at the Södra Theatre on Mosebacke Square. Sunlight fills the huge windows looking out across Old Town, Skeppsholmen, and the sparkling water. They've eaten pan-fried herring with mashed potatoes and lingonberry sauce and are just pouring the last of their beer. Ronald Brautigam is sitting at a black grand piano on the little stage, and Isabelle van Keulen's right elbow is raised as she follows through with her bow.

The music stops, and the last violin note quivers in the air, outlasting the piano, ending on a high, tremulous tone.

Joona and Disa leave the restaurant after the concert and emerge onto the square, where they stop to look at each other.

"What was that about Paganini?" she says, adjusting his shirt collar. "You were talking about Paganini?"

He gently catches her hand. "I just wanted to see you. . . ."

"So that I can yell at you for not taking your medication?"

"No," he says seriously.

"Are you taking it, then?"

"I will soon," he replies with a hint of impatience in his voice.

She says nothing, just lets her pale-green eyes meet his gaze for a moment. Then she takes a deep breath and suggests they start walking.

"Well, that was a great concert," Disa says. "The music somehow matches the light outside, so soft. I always thought Paganini was ... you know, too balanced, too fast. I actually heard Yngwie Malmsteen play Caprice Number Five at Gröna Lund once."

"When you were going out with Benjamin Gantenbein."

"We're friends on Facebook now."

They walk hand in hand across Slussen, down toward Skeppsbron.

"It should be possible to tell what notes someone is playing on a violin just from their fingers, don't you think?"

"Without hearing anything, you mean?"

"From a photograph."

"More or less, I'd imagine. It probably depends on how well you know the instrument," she says.

"But how exact could it be?"

"I can ask Kaj if it's important," she says.

"Kaj?"

"Kaj Samuelsson, from the musicology department at the university. He was a friend of my dad's."

"Can you give him a call now?"

"Okay," Disa says, raising one eyebrow slightly. "You want me to call him right now?"

"Yes," Joona replies.

She lets go of his hand, takes out her phone, and calls the professor.

"Hello, it's Disa," she says with a smile. "Am I calling in the middle of lunch?"

Joona hears a cheerful male voice through the phone. After chatting for a while, Disa asks, "I've actually got a friend with me who wants me to ask you a question."

She laughs at something he says, then asks, "Is it possible to tell what notes a violinist is playing . . . no, not . . . I mean, from their fingers?"

Joona looks at Disa as she listens with a furrowed brow. They can hear the sound of a marching band from somewhere among the alleyways of Old Town.

"Okay," Disa says after a while. "You know what, Kaj? Maybe it would be best if you talk to him yourself."

She hands the phone to Joona without a word.

"Joona Linna."

"Whom Disa talks so much about," Kaj says breezily.

"A violin only has four strings," Joona says. "So there aren't that many different notes to play. . . ."

"What do you mean by 'play'?" the professor wonders.

"The lowest note has to be an open G string," Joona says calmly. "And somewhere there must be a highest note—"

"Nice idea," the professor interrupts. "The French scientist Mersenne published *Harmonie universelle* in 1636, in which he claimed that the best violinists can play up to an octave above every open string. That means the range stretches from G below middle C to E3 . . . which gives a total of thirty-four notes on the chromatic scale."

"Thirty-four notes," Joona repeats.

"But if we move forward to more modern musicians," Kaj goes on brightly, "the range has been expanded with the new fingerboard . . . so we can count on reaching A3, giving a chromatic scale of thirty-nine notes."

"Go on," Joona says, as Disa stops in front of a gallery with some odd, blurred paintings in the window.

"By the time Richard Strauss revised Berlioz's treatise on instrumentation in 1904, G4 was identified as the highest possible note for a professional violinist, giving forty-nine notes."

Kaj chuckles to himself in response to Joona's wary silence.

"The upper limit has by no means been reached," the professor explains. "And then there are all the harmonics and quarter-tones."

They pass a recently built Viking longboat docked down by Slottskajen and slowly head toward Kungsträd Park.

"How about a cello?" Joona asks impatiently.

"Fifty-eight," he replies.

Disa looks at him restlessly and points at an outdoor café.

"What I'm really wondering is if you could take a look at a photograph of four musicians: two violinists, a viola player, and a cellist," Joona says. "From a sharp photograph, would it be possible to tell, just by looking at the musicians' fingers, and the strings and necks of the instruments, what piece they were playing?"

Joona hears Kaj muttering to himself. "There'd be an awful lot of alternatives, thousands. . . ."

Disa shrugs and walks off without looking at him.

"Seven million combinations," Kaj says after a pause.

"Seven million," Joona repeats.

The line gets quiet again.

"But on my photograph," Joona goes on stubbornly, "you can clearly see the fingers and strings, so it would be easy enough to rule out a lot of possibilities."

"I'd be happy to look at the photograph," the professor says. "But I won't be able to guess the notes. That's simply not possible, and . . ."

"But . . ."

"And just imagine, Joona," he goes on cheerily, "imagine that you actually managed to identify the notes, more or less . . . how would you work out where that combination of notes appeared in all the thousands of string quartets . . . ? Beethoven, Schubert, Mozart. . . ."

"I get it. It's impossible," Joona says.

"Seriously, yes," Kaj replies.

Joona thanks him for his time, then goes and sits down next to Disa, who is waiting on a wall next to a fountain. She leans her cheek against his shoulder. Just as he puts his arm around her, he remembers what Robert said about his brother: "If not even Axel could do it, then I doubt it can be done."

72

As Joona strides quickly along the sidewalk up Brage Street, he can hear children's laughter and cries from the German School.

He rings Axel's doorbell and hears the melodic tone inside the house. After waiting awhile, he decides to go around the back. Suddenly he hears a jarringly shrill note from a stringed instrument. Someone is standing in the shadows under a tree. Joona stops at a distance. On the marble terrace, he sees a girl holding a violin. She looks about seventeen years old. Her hair is extremely short, and she's been drawing on her arms. Beside her stands Axel Riessen, nodding and listening intently as she draws the bow across the strings. It looks as if she's holding the instrument for the first time. Axel is looking at her with an affectionate, curious gaze.

The bow glances across the strings, making a shrieking, grating sound.

"It's probably out of tune," she suggests as an explanation for the terrible noise.

She smiles and carefully hands the instrument back.

"Playing the violin is all about listening," Axel says warmly. "You listen, hear the music inside you, then just convey that in reality."

He puts the violin to his shoulder and plays the introduction to "La seguidilla" from Bizet's opera *Carmen*, then stops to show her the violin.

"Now I'm going to retune the strings, a bit randomly, like this," he says, turning the pegs in different directions.

"But why . . . ?"

"Now the violin is completely out of tune," he goes on. "And if I'd merely learned the piece mechanically, with the precise finger positions, the same as I played it just now, it would sound like this."

He plays "La seguidilla" again, and it sounds terrible, almost unrecognizable.

"Beautiful," she jokes.

"But if you listen to the strings instead," he says, plucking the E string, "do you hear? It's far too low, but that doesn't matter, you just have to compensate by playing the note higher up on the neck."

Joona watches Axel Riessen put the violin to his shoulder and play the piece again on a violin that's completely out of tune, with very odd finger placings, but exactly the right notes. "La seguidilla" sounds perfect again.

"You're a magician." The girl laughs, clapping her hands.

"Hello," Joona says, walking over and shaking Axel's hand, then the girl's.

He looks at Axel, who's still holding the untuned violin. "Impressive."

Axel looks down at the violin and shakes his head. "I haven't played for thirty-four years," he says in an odd tone of voice.

"Do you believe that?" Joona asks the girl.

She nods, then answers enigmatically, "Don't you see the glow?"

"Beverly," Axel says quietly.

She looks at him with a smile, then walks off under the trees.

Joona nods to Axel. "I need to talk to you."

"I'm sorry I just vanished like that," Axel says as he starts to retune the violin. "But I was called away urgently."

"No problem—I'm back."

Joona looks at Axel, who is watching the girl pick some weeds that grow on the shady lawn.

"Is there a vase indoors?" she asks.

"In the kitchen," he replies.

She carries the little bunch of dandelion seed-heads in through the door.

"Her favorite flowers," Axel says, then listens to the G string, fine-tunes the peg, and puts the violin down on the mosaic tabletop.

"I'd like you to take a look at this," Joona says, removing the photograph from its plastic sleeve.

They sit down at the table. Axel takes a pair of reading glasses from his breast pocket and looks at the picture carefully.

"When was this taken?" he asks quickly.

"We don't know, but possibly the spring of 2008," Joona replies.

"Yes," Axel says, looking instantly more relaxed.

"Do you recognize these people?" Joona asks calmly.

"Of course," Axel says. "Palmcrona, Pontus Salman, Raphael Guidi, and ... Agathe al-Haji."

"I'm actually here because I'd like you to look at the musicians in the background."

Axel gives Joona a curious glance, then looks down at the photograph again.

"The Tokyo String Quartet. They're good," he says coolly.

"Yes, but I was wondering. I've been trying to work out if

it's possible for a knowledgeable person to identify, from the picture alone, what piece the string quartet is playing."

"Interesting question."

"Would it be possible to make a qualified guess, even? Kaj Samuelsson doesn't seem to think so, and when your brother, Robert, looked at the picture, he said it was completely impossible."

Joona leans forward, and his eyes look soft and warm in the leafy shade. "Your brother was certain that no one could do it—if you couldn't."

A smile plays at the corners of Axel's mouth. "He said that, did he?"

"Yes," Joona says. "But I wasn't sure what he meant. . . ."

"Nor am I," Axel says.

"I'd still like you to take a look at the photograph."

"You think that knowing what piece was being played could help you confirm when the photograph was taken?" Axel asks with new seriousness in his voice.

Joona nods, takes a magnifying glass from his bag, and hands it to Axel.

"You should be able to see their fingers now," Joona says.

He sits in silence as Axel studies the photograph, thinking once again that if the picture was taken before the warrant was issued, in March 2009, his gut feeling has led him in the wrong direction. But if it was taken after that, he'll be proved right, because then it is a record of criminal activity.

"I can certainly see their fingers," Axel says slowly.

"Can you hazard a guess as to what notes they're playing?" Joona asks in a subdued voice.

Axel sighs, hands the photograph and magnifying glass back to Joona, then sings four notes. He sings fairly quietly, but the notes are perfectly clear. After thinking for a while, he picks up the violin from the mosaic table and plays two higher, trembling notes.

Joona gets to his feet. "Are you kidding?"

Axel looks him in the eye.

"Martin Beaver is playing a C3, Kikuei is playing a C2. Kazuhide Isomura isn't playing, and Clive is playing a four-note pizzicato. That was what I was singing: major E, major A, A3, and C4 sharp."

Joona writes that down, then asks, "How precise a guess is that?"

"It's not a guess," Axel replies.

"Do you think this combination of notes is found in many pieces? I mean . . . from these notes alone, would it be possible to identify which piece the Tokyo String Quartet might have been performing in this picture?"

"This combination of notes only occurs once," Axel replies.

"How do you know that?"

Axel looks up at the window. The big, trembling leaves are reflected in the glass.

"Please, go on," Joona says.

"I'm sure I haven't heard all the music they've ever played. . . ." Axel shrugs his shoulders apologetically.

"But you still think these notes are only found in one particular piece?" Joona says.

"This combination of notes is only found in one place, as far as I'm aware," Axel goes on. "In bar 156 of the first movement of Béla Bartók's second string quartet."

He picks up the violin again and puts it to his shoulder. "*Tranquillo* . . . The music becomes wonderfully peaceful, like a lullaby. Listen to the first part," he says, and starts to play.

His fingers move tenderly; the notes tremble, swaying gently; they are light and perfectly soft. After four bars, he stops.

"'The two violins shadow each other, the same notes but different octaves," he explains. "It's almost too beautiful, but against the cello's major A the violins provide a degree of dissonance that . . ."

He breaks off and puts the violin down.

Joona looks at him.

"You're sure that the musicians are playing Bartók's second string quartet in this photograph?" he asks quietly.

"Yes."

Joona takes a few steps across the deck, then stops beside the blossoming lilac bushes. He has probably just heard all he needs to confirm the date of the meeting.

He hides his smile with his hand, then turns around, takes a red apple from the fruit bowl on the mosaic table, and meets Axel's wondering gaze.

"You're sure?" he asks again. "Really sure?"

Axel nods, and Joona hands him the apple, excuses himself, and calls Anja.

"Anja, this is urgent—"

"We were supposed to have a sauna together this weekend," Anja interrupts.

"I need help."

"I know." Anja giggles.

Joona tries to conceal the stress in his voice.

"Can you check the Tokyo String Quartet's repertoire for the past ten years?"

"I've already checked their repertoire."

"Can you see what they played at the Alte Oper in Frankfurt during that time?"

"Yes, they've played there every year, sometimes more than once."

"Have they ever played Béla Bartók's second string quartet?"

She checks, then replies:

"Yes, once. Opus 17."

"Opus 17," Joona repeats, looking at Axel, who nods in response.

"What?" Anja asks.

"When was it?" Joona asks in a serious voice. "When did they play Bartók's second string quartet?"

"November 13, 2009."

"You're sure?" Joona asks.

The people in the photograph met eight months after the warrant was issued for the Sudanese president's arrest, he thinks. Salman lied to us about the date. They met in November 2009. That's why all this happened. People are already dead, and more may end up dying. And someone in the photograph is killing them.

Joona reaches out his hand and touches the clusters of violet-colored lilac blossoms. He needs to get hold of Saga to tell her about the breakthrough.

"Was that everything?" Anja says over the phone.

"Yes."

"And what do we say?"

"Yes, sorry ... *Kiitokseksi saat pusun*," Joona says in Finnish. "You can have a kiss as thanks." He ends the call.

Salman lied to us, he thinks again. There was a complete arms embargo in place when he met Palmcrona, Guidi, and Agathe al-Haji.

But Agathe al-Haji wanted to buy ammunition, and the others wanted to earn money. They didn't care about human rights or international law.

Salman lied about the date, clinically and coolly. He assumed that a few unexpected truths in what he said would conceal the lie. By admitting unreservedly that he was in the picture, he thought we'd take his word for everything and accept the lie about the date.

In his mind's eye, Joona can see Salman's impassive face as he spoke, pale and gray and lined with deep wrinkles. Then his feigned frankness when he identified himself and told them the date of the meeting.

Arms smuggling, a voice in his head whispers. Arms smuggling is what this is all about: the photograph, the attempted blackmail, all the deaths.

"What did you find out?" Axel asks.

"What?" Joona says.

"Were you able to fix the date?"

"Yes," Joona replies curtly.

Axel tries to look him in the eye. "What's wrong?" he asks.

"I have to go," Joona mutters.

"Did they meet after the warrant for Bashir's arrest was issued? I have to know if that's the case!"

Joona looks him in the eye with a perfectly calm, radiant gaze.

73

SAGA IS LYING ON HER STOMACH on the shabby pale rug. She has her eyes closed while Stefan slowly kisses her back. Her fair hair is spread out across the floor. Stefan's warm face moves across her skin.

Keep going, she thinks.

The gentle touch of his lips tickles between her shoulder blades. She forces herself to lie still and shivers with pleasure.

The stereo is playing Carl Unander-Scharin's duet for cello and mezzo-soprano. The two melodies cross rhythmically and repetitively, and it has an erotic effect.

Lying perfectly still, Saga feels her body getting aroused. She is breathing through half-open lips and moistens them with her tongue.

His hands slide over her waist, around her hips, and lift her backside as lightly as a feather.

No other man she has ever met has moved so gently, Saga thinks, smiling to herself.

He looks at her, and she parts her thighs. She feels she's starting to glow inside.

She hears herself moan as she feels his tongue.

Very gently, he turns her body over. The rug has left stripes across her stomach.

"Keep going," she whispers.

"Or you'll shoot me," he says.

She nods and smiles, her face open and happy. Stefan's black hair has fallen over his face, and his thin ponytail is hanging across his chest.

"Come here," Saga says.

She pulls his face toward hers and kisses him, meeting his warm, wet tongue.

He quickly pushes his pants down and lies naked on top of her. She lets out a protracted moan, then breathes quickly when they pause for a moment, enjoying their dizzying closeness. Stefan thrusts very gently, his narrow hips moving slowly. Saga runs her fingers over his shoulder blades, back, butt.

Then her phone rings. Typical, she thinks. The sound of ZZ Top's "Blue Jean Blues" comes from the pile of clothes on the sofa.

"Let it ring," she whispers.

"It's your work phone," he says.

"I don't care. It's not important," she murmurs, trying to hold on to him.

But he pulls out of her, sits up on his knees, and feels around in the pockets of her pants for her phone. He can't find it, and the muffled ringtone keeps playing. In the end, he turns her jeans upside down and shakes the phone onto the floor, but it's stopped ringing. A little buzzing sound announces that she has a new voice mail.

TWENTY MINUTES LATER, Saga is half running through the hallway of the National Crime Unit. Her hair is still damp from her hasty shower, and she can feel the tingle of unsatisfied lust lingering in her body. Her underwear and jeans feel uncomfortable.

She glimpses Anja's face above her computer as she hurries toward Joona's office. He's standing in the middle of the floor with the photograph in his hand, waiting for her. When she meets his sharp gray gaze, a shiver of unease runs down her spine.

"Close the door," he says.

She does, then turns to face him. She's breathing fast but quietly.

"Axel Riessen remembers all the music he's ever heard, every note from every instrument in an orchestra. . . ."

"I don't understand what you're trying to say."

"He could see what piece the string quartet was playing in the photograph. Béla Bartók's second string quartet."

"Okay, you were right," she says. "It was possible to identify the piece, but we—"

"The photograph was taken on November 13, 2009," Joona interrupts with unusual sharpness in his voice.

"So those bastards were selling arms to Sudan after the warrant for Bashir's arrest was issued," she says coldly.

"Yes."

"They knew that the ammunition was going to be pumped into Darfur," she whispers.

Joona nods, and his jaw muscles move beneath his skin. "Palmcrona shouldn't have been in that box," he says. "Salman shouldn't have been there; none of them should have been. . . ."

"But now we've got them in a photograph," she says with restrained excitement. "And it seems like Guidi's behind it all."

"Yes," Joona replies, looking into Saga's blue eyes.

"The really big fish are always the meanest," Saga states. "That's nothing new—most people know that—but the big ones always get away."

They stand in silence, examining the photograph again. They look at the four people in the box at the Alte Oper: the champagne, their faces, the musicians playing Paganini's old instruments.

"Okay, now we've solved the first mystery," Saga says, taking a deep breath. "We know the photograph is directly linked to Sudan's attempts to buy arms despite the embargo."

"Palmcrona was there, so the money in his bank account is probably from bribes," Joona says hesitantly. "But . . . Palmcrona never authorized any arms exports to Sudan after the arrest warrant. That would have been unthinkable; he'd never have—"

He breaks off when his phone rings in his jacket pocket. Joona answers, listens for a moment in silence, then ends the call. He looks at Saga.

"That was Axel," Joona tells her. "He says he's figured out what the photograph is about."

74

IN THE BACKYARD of the Finnish Church in Old Town sits a solitary boy, fifteen centimeters tall and made of iron. Three meters away, Axel is leaning against the ocher wall, eating noodles from a carton. He waves his chopsticks when he sees Joona and Saga come through the gate.

"So—what have you figured out?" Joona asks.

Axel nods, wipes his mouth with a napkin, and then shakes hands with Saga and Joona.

"You said you'd figured out what the photograph was about," Joona presses.

Axel lowers his gaze, breathes out, then looks up again.

"Kenya," he says. "The four people in the concert box are drinking champagne because they've reached an agreement about a large shipment of ammunition to Kenya."

He falls silent for a moment.

"Go on," Joona says.

"Kenya's buying 1.25 million rounds of 5.56-by-45-millimeter ammunition manufactured under license."

"For assault rifles," Saga says.

"The shipment goes to Kenya," Axel says heavily. "But the ammunition isn't for Kenya. It's going to Sudan, to the militia in Darfur. I worked it all out."

"Where does Kenya fit into this?" Joona asks.

"The four people in that box met after Bashir's arrest warrant was issued, didn't they? Bartók's second string quartet was only played once. It's illegal to export arms to Sudan, but not to its southern neighbor; there are still no sanctions against Kenya."

"How can you be so sure?" Saga says.

"Palmcrona left this for me to deal with by committing suicide. It was the last thing he was working on, but he didn't complete it. I've promised to sign off on the export license today," Axel replies bitterly.

"It's the same ammunition, the same deal. After the warrant was issued for the president's arrest, they just crossed out 'Sudan' and wrote 'Kenya,'" Saga says.

"The plan was rock-solid," Axel says.

"Or was, until someone took a photograph of the meeting," Joona points out.

"The evaluation had been concluded by the time Palmcrona killed himself. Everyone probably thought he'd already signed the license," Axel says.

"They probably got pretty freaked out when they realized he hadn't." Joona smiles.

"The whole deal was left hanging in the air," Saga says.

"I was recruited very quickly," Axel tells them. "And then they quite literally put the pen in my hand to get me to sign this contract."

"But?"

"I wanted to conduct my own evaluation."

"And you have."

"Yes."

"And it looked okay?" Saga asks.

"Yes . . . and I promised to sign, and I would have done so if I hadn't seen that photograph."

They all stand in silence, looking at the little iron statue, Stockholm's smallest public work of art. Joona leans forward and pats the boy's shiny head. The metal seems to radiate heat after a day in the sun, almost as if it were alive.

"They're busy loading the ship in Gothenburg Harbor," Axel says in a low voice.

"So I understand," Saga says. "But without an export license . . ."

"That ammunition isn't going to be leaving Sweden," Axel declares.

"You said they're expecting you to sign today," Joona says. "How can you delay the process? It's vitally important to our investigation that they don't realize anything is wrong."

"They won't just sit back and wait."

"Say you're not quite finished," Joona says.

"That could be tricky—I'm already responsible for delaying the deal—but I can try," Axel says.

"This doesn't just affect our investigation. I'm worried about your security, Axel," Joona explains.

Axel smiles and asks, with a degree of skepticism in his voice, "You think they'd threaten me?"

Joona smiles back. "As long as they're expecting you to approve the deal, there's no danger at all," he replies. "But if you say no, people are going to lose huge amounts of money. I can't even imagine how big the bribes must have been, and a number of people have already died because of this."

"I'm not going to be able to delay signing the license indefinitely. Salman has been trying to get hold of me all day. These people know the business; they can't be fooled," Axel says, just as his phone starts to ring.

He looks at the screen and stiffens.

"I think it's Salman again. . . ."

"Take the call," Joona says.

"Okay," Axel says, and answers.

"I've tried to call you several times," Salman says in his drawling voice. "You know . . . we've finished loading the ship. It costs money to have it lying in port. The shipping company has been trying to reach you; they don't seem to have received the export license."

"I'm sorry," Axel says, glancing at Joona and Saga. "I'm afraid I haven't had time to go through the last few—"

"I've already spoken to the Cabinet Office. You were supposed to sign it today."

Axel hesitates as his thoughts head off in several different directions. He wishes he could just hang up. He clears his throat instead and apologizes.

"Something's come up."

Axel can hear the fake tone in his voice and knows he took a little too long to answer. He had been on the verge of telling the truth.

"The impression I got was that the matter was going to be dealt with today at the latest," Salman says, unable to conceal his irritation.

"You took a gamble," Axel says.

"What do you mean?"

"Without an export license, there can't be any—"

"But we've already . . . Sorry."

"You were given authorization to manufacture the ammunition, you got preliminary approval, and I'm favorably inclined, but that's all for the time being."

"There's a lot at stake here," Salman says, more amenably. "Can I pass on any message to the shipping company? Could you give me an idea of how long you think it's going to take?

They need to know how long they're going to be in the harbor. It's all about logistics."

"I'm still favorably inclined to the export, but I'm going to look through everything one last time, and then you'll be notified," Axel says.

75

SAGA HAS BEEN JUMPING ROPE in the police gym for fifty minutes when an anxious colleague walks over and asks how she's feeling. Her face is sweaty and impassive, but her feet are still dancing, apparently unaffected by the quickly passing rope.

"You're too hard on yourself," he says.

"No," she replies, jumping with her jaw firmly clenched.

Twenty-five minutes later, Joona comes down to the gym, walks over to her, and sits down on a sloped bench in front of some weights.

"Fuck," she says, without stopping. "They're going to pump ammunition into Darfur, and there isn't a damn thing we can do about it."

"At least we know what this is all about now," Joona says calmly. "We know they're using Kenya as a conduit."

"But what the hell are we going to do?" she asks as she jumps. "Bring in that bastard Pontus Salman? Contact Europol about Raphael Guidi?"

"We still can't prove anything."

"This is big, bigger than anyone could have imagined. Even I wish it wasn't this complicated. Palmcrona was caught up in it, and Salman, a Swedish national. . . . Raphael Guidi, he's a huge figure. . . . But there must also be someone in the

Kenyan government," she reasons, as the rope whizzes past her face and hits against the floor. "Otherwise, it wouldn't work—and maybe someone in the Swedish government . . ."

"We won't be able to get all of them," Joona concludes.

"The smartest option would probably be to drop the case," she says.

"Let's do that, then."

She laughs, still jumping.

"Palmcrona was probably taking bribes for years," Joona says thoughtfully. "But then he received Björn's e-mail, and he got scared that the party was over . . . so he called some-one, probably Guidi. But during the course of that conversa-tion, he realized that he was replaceable . . . and that, because of the photograph, he had become a problem for the peo-ple who had invested in the deal. They weren't prepared to lose their money and risk their livelihoods for him."

"So he killed himself," Saga says, jumping faster.

"Which meant he was out of the way. Leaving just the photograph and the blackmailer."

"So they employed a professional fixer to kill Björn and clean everything up," she says breathlessly.

Joona nods as she starts to pick her knees up higher.

"If Viola hadn't been on that boat, he would have mur-dered Björn and Penelope and then sunk the boat," he says.

Saga speeds up even more and then, finally, stops.

"And we . . . we would have written it off as an accident," she pants. "He would have taken the photograph, wiped all the computers, and left the country without a trace."

"My impression of him is that he isn't really worried about being seen; he's just being practical," Joona says. "Yes, it's easier to solve his problems if the police aren't involved, but if it comes down to a choice between fixing the problem or avoiding detection, he'll fix the problem—otherwise, he wouldn't have tried to burn both apartments. That sort of thing attracts a lot of attention, but he wanted to be thorough, and he prioritizes thoroughness above all else."

Saga is leaning on her thighs as sweat drips from her face. "Obviously, we would have connected the fires with the sinking of the boat sooner or later," she says, straightening up.

"But by then it would already have been too late," he replies. "The fixer's task is to get rid of all the evidence and all the witnesses."

"But now we have both the photograph and Penelope," she says with a smile. "The fixer hasn't fixed the problem."

"Not yet . . ."

She throws a few tentative punches at a bag hanging from the ceiling, then looks at Joona thoughtfully.

"While I was in training, I had to watch a tape from a bank robbery where you took out a guy using just a faulty pistol."

"I was lucky," he replies.

"Yes."

He laughs, and she moves closer. She circles around him, doing a bit of footwork, then stops, holds out her arms, and meets his gaze. She beckons him toward her with her fingers. She wants him to try to land a punch. He smiles, understanding the Bruce Lee reference: the beckoning hand. He shakes his head but doesn't take his eyes off her.

"I've seen how you move," he says.

"So you know," she says curtly.

"You're quick, and you might land the first blow, but after that . . ."

"I'd be gone," she concludes.

"Nice idea, but . . ."

She repeats the gesture, luring him to her, slightly more impatiently.

"But," he goes on, amused, "you'll probably come in too hard."

"No," she replies.

"Try it and see," Joona says calmly.

She beckons him to her, but he ignores the invitation and turns his back on her and starts walking toward the door. She moves quickly after Joona and aims a right hook at him. He simply bends his neck so that the blow passes over his head. And, in a continuation of the same movement, he spins around, draws his pistol, and knocks her to the floor by kicking out her knee.

"I have to say one thing," Saga says quickly.

"That I was right, you mean?"

"Don't get any ideas," she says with a flash of anger, then gets up.

"If you go in too hard against—"

"I didn't go in hard," she interrupts. "I slowed down because I realized something important about the case. . . ."

"Of course you did." He laughs.

"Whatever," she goes on. "I realized that we have to use Penelope as bait."

"What are you talking about?"

"I started to think about the fact that she's moving to a safe house, and just as I was going to hit you, I had an idea. I pulled my punch because I didn't want to knock you out if we were going to talk."

"So talk," he says amiably.

"I realized that Penelope is going to act as bait for the fixer whether we like it or not. She's going to draw him to her."

Joona is no longer smiling. He nods thoughtfully. "Go on."

"We don't know if the fixer is listening to our radio communications, but it seems pretty likely, seeing as he managed to find Penelope out on Kymmendö," Saga says.

"I agree."

"So he'll find her again somehow; that's what I think. And he doesn't care that she has police protection. Obviously, we'll do all we can to keep her location secret, but, I mean, we can't keep her safe without using radio communication."

"He's going to find her," Joona agrees.

"The only question is whether we're going to be ready for him. She'll get full protection, just as planned, but if we get Surveillance to monitor the location at the same time, we might be able to catch the fixer."

"You're absolutely right," Joona says.

76

CARLOS, SAGA, AND JOONA are walking quickly down the hallway leading to Security Police headquarters. Verner is already waiting on the sofa when they arrive. He starts talking the moment they close the door.

"Klara Olofsdotter at the International Prosecution Authority has been brought in. . . . This is a major operation for National Crime and the Security Police, but who exactly are we trying to catch?"

"We know very little about him," Saga replies. "We don't even know if he's working alone. We could be dealing with professionals from Belgium or Brazil, or ex-KGB or fighters from anywhere else in the former Eastern Bloc."

"It's not that difficult to listen to our radio communications," Carlos says.

"Obviously, the fixer knows that Penelope is being guarded and that it's going to be difficult to get to her," Joona says. "But doors have to be opened sometimes; bodyguards change shifts. She has to have food, see her mother, a psychologist, and—"

He breaks off when his phone rings. He glances quickly at the screen, then rejects the call.

"Our priority is to protect Penelope," Saga says. "But this

gives us a chance to get the man who killed several of our colleagues."

"I assume I don't have to remind anyone about how dangerous he is," Joona says.

THE SECURE APARTMENT is at 1 Stor Street. It has windows facing Sibylle Street and a view of Östermalm Square. There are no apartments across from the windows; the closest building is more than a hundred meters away.

Saga holds the steel door open as Daniella carefully leads Penelope from the gray police van. They are surrounded by heavily armed officers.

"This is the most secure aboveground residence in Stockholm," Saga says.

Penelope shows no reaction. She merely follows Daniella to the elevator. There are security cameras all over the lobby and stairwell.

"We've installed motion detectors, an extremely advanced alarm system, and two encrypted lines that feed directly into the Communications Center," Saga explains as the elevator carries them upward.

On the third floor, Penelope is led through a heavy security door to an airlock with a uniformed guard. The guard opens another door and lets them into the apartment.

"You're safe here," Daniella says.

Penelope raises her eyes and looks blankly at the doctor.

"Thanks," she says in a whisper.

"I can stay, if you like?"

Penelope slowly shakes her head, and Daniella leaves with Saga.

Penelope locks the door, then stands by one of the bulletproof windows, looking out over Östermalm Square. Some sort of foil on the glass makes the windows impossible to see through from the outside. As she looks out, she is thinking that some of the people moving in the square are probably undercover officers.

She touches the window tentatively. She can't hear any sound from outside.

Suddenly the doorbell rings.

Penelope startles, and her heart begins to beat faster.

She goes over to the monitor and presses the intercom. The female police officer in the airlock is looking up at the camera and explains that her mother is here to see her.

"Penny? Penny!" her mother asks anxiously behind the officer.

Penelope opens the heavy steel door.

"Mom," she says. She's shocked that her voice penetrates the silence hanging over the apartment.

She lets her mother in, closes and locks the door again, then stands by the door. She purses her lips and starts to shake, but she forces all emotion away from her face.

Though she glances quickly at her mother, she doesn't dare to look her in the eye. She knows she'll be blamed for not protecting her sister.

Claudia takes a few cautious steps across the entryway and looks around warily.

"Are they taking care of you now, Penny?" she asks.

"I'll be fine here."

"They have to protect you."

"They are. I'm safe here."

"That's the only thing that matters," Claudia says, almost inaudibly.

Penelope tries to swallow her tears. Her neck is straining, and it aches.

"There's so much I have to figure out," her mom says, turning her face away. "I ... I can't ... I just can't believe that I have to arrange Viola's funeral."

Penelope nods slowly. Then her mother reaches out and gently touches her cheek. Penelope flinches involuntarily, and Claudia quickly pulls her hand away.

"They say this will all be over soon," Penelope says. "The police are going to catch the man ... the man who ... killed Viola and Björn."

Claudia nods, then turns to look at her daughter again. Her face is naked and unprotected, and, to her surprise, Penelope sees that her mom is smiling.

"Just think, you're alive," Claudia says. "I still have you. That's the only thing that matters, the only ..."

"Mom ..."

"My little girl."

Claudia reaches out her hand again, and this time Penelope doesn't pull away.

77

Operational commander Jenny Göransson is sitting in the bay window of an apartment on the third floor of 4A Nybro Street, waiting. Hours pass, but no one has anything to report. Everything is quiet. She looks down at the square, up at the rooftop above Penelope's apartment, over toward the roof of 27 Sibylle Street, where some pigeons take off.

Sonny Jansson is stationed there. He probably moved and frightened the birds off.

When Jenny contacts him, he confirms that he changed position so he could see into another apartment. "I thought I saw a fight, but they're just playing with a Wii, waving their arms in front of a television."

"Resume your previous position," Jenny says dryly.

She picks up her binoculars and scans the darker area between the kiosk and the elm tree, a possible insecure location.

Blomberg, who is wearing a brown tracksuit and is running up Sibylle Street, contacts her.

"I can see something in the churchyard," he says in a tense voice.

"What is it?"

"Someone's moving under the trees, maybe ten meters from the railings facing Stor Street."

"Check it out, Blomberg, but be careful," she says.

He runs past the steps at the end of the Army Museum, then slowly makes his way into the churchyard. The summer night is warm and green. He walks silently along the grass beside the path. He thinks that he should probably stop and pretend to do some stretches, but he moves on instead. The sky is shadowed by branches, and the ground between the graves is dark. Suddenly he sees a face, close to the ground. It's a woman in her twenties. Her red hair is cropped, and her khaki backpack is lying next to her head. She's smiling happily as another woman pulls her shirt up and starts kissing her breasts.

Blomberg moves back cautiously before he reports back to Jenny.

"False alarm, just a couple making out."

THREE HOURS HAVE PASSED. Blomberg shivers. It's starting to get cold; there's dew on the ground. He jogs around a corner and comes face-to-face with a haggard-looking middle-aged woman. She appears to be very drunk and is swaying noticeably as she holds two poodles on leashes. The dogs are sniffing around, eager to go, but she yanks them back angrily.

A woman in a flight attendant's uniform is walking past the edge of the churchyard, the wheel of her navy suitcase rattling on the pavement. She glances neutrally at Blomberg, and he pretends not to have noticed her, even though they've been colleagues for more than seven years.

Maria Ristonen drags her suitcase toward the entrance to the subway station, to check out the person who's standing hidden in the doorway. She keeps walking, the click of her heels echoing off the walls. The suitcase catches on the curb, and when she has to stop and pull it up, she glances at the individual. It's a man, fairly well dressed, with a peculiar expression on his face. Seeming to be looking for something, he peers at her anxiously. Maria's heart skips a beat, and she turns away as she hears Jenny in her earpiece:

"Blomberg has eyes on him, too; he's on his way," Jenny says. "Wait for Blomberg, Maria. Wait for Blomberg."

Maria adjusts her suitcase but can't delay any longer; she's going to have to go. She tries to walk more slowly as she approaches the man. She has to pass him and then turn her back to him. The man retreats farther into the doorway when she approaches. He's holding one hand inside his clothes. Maria feels adrenaline pumping through her veins as the man takes a step toward her and holds up something he had been hiding inside his coat. Behind his shoulder, Maria sees that Blomberg has drawn his pistol to shoot, but he stops when Jenny calls through his earpiece that it's a false alarm, the man is unarmed. It's just a can of beer.

"Cunt," the man snarls, spraying beer at Maria.

"Dear God." Jenny sighs through the earpiece. "Just keep heading for the subway station, Maria."

THE NIGHT PASSES without incident. After the last night-clubs close, there are only a few dog walkers and people collecting trash out on the streets, then people delivering newspapers, followed by different dog walkers and some joggers. Jenny starts to long for eight o'clock, when her shift ends. She looks across at Hedvig Eleonora Church, then at Penelope's opaque windows, before glancing down at Stor Street and the building where the director Ingmar Bergman grew up. She puts a piece of nicotine gum into her mouth and studies the square: park benches, trees, the sculpture of the reclining woman with her legs apart, and the one of a man with a side of meat on his shoulder.

Jenny detects movement in the doorway covered by the tall steel gate that leads to Östermalm Market. It's dark, but in the weak reflection in the glass she sees rapid movement. Jenny calls Carl Schwirt, who's sitting with two trash bags full of empty beer cans on a bench between the trees.

"No, I can't see a thing," he replies.

"Stay where you are."

Maybe, she thinks, she should get Blomberg to leave his position by the church and jog down toward Humle Park to check out the doorway.

Jenny looks again: there seems to be someone kneeling behind the black gate. An unlicensed taxi has driven the wrong way and is turning around on Nybro Street. Jenny quickly picks up her binoculars and waits as the car's headlights slide across the brick walls of the market. But even when the light passes the doorway, she can't see anything. The car stops, then reverses.

"Idiot," she mutters, as the driver ends up with one wheel on the sidewalk.

But now the headlights are shining into a shopwindow a short distance away, and the reflection is lighting up the doorway.

There's someone behind the tall gate.

It only takes Jenny a second to put together her fragmentary impressions: a man adjusting the sights on a weapon.

She puts the binoculars down and calls over the radio: "Live situation, I can see a weapon," she says, almost shouting. "A military weapon with sniper sights. A man in the doorway of the market hall . . . I repeat, a sniper at ground level at the corner of the block, at the crossing of Nybro Street and Humlegårds Street!"

THE MAN IN THE DOORWAY is behind the gate. He has been watching the empty square for a while, waiting for a man who had been collecting empty cans to get up from a bench and walk off, but he decided to ignore him when it looked as if he was going to be spending the rest of the night there. Under cover of darkness, he unfolds the Modular Sniper Rifle, a semiautomatic designed for distances of up to two kilometers. Calmly, he inserts the magazine.

He had gone into the market just before it closed, to hide in a storeroom and wait for the cleaners to finish and the security company to do their rounds. Then, as soon as the premises were silent and dark, he left his hiding place.

From the inside, he had disconnected the alarm on the main doors, then gone out into the archway, which was protected from the street by a sturdy gate.

Behind the gate, the deeply recessed doorway is like a small room. He is protected on all sides but has a completely open view in front of him. He can't be seen at all when he's still. If anyone did walk up to the gate, all he would have to do is turn away, into the darkness.

He aims the rifle at the building where Penelope is staying and checks the rooms through the sniper sight. He is slow and systematic. He's been waiting for a long time, morning is approaching, and soon he will have to abandon his position and wait for the next night. But he knows that at some point she will look out at the square in the belief that the laminated glass will protect her.

He has already adjusted the sights when he is caught by the light from a car and turns away for a while. Then he goes back to studying the apartment. He discovers a source of heat behind a dark window almost immediately. The signal is weak and grainy, obscured by distance and the reinforced glass. Worse than he had expected. He tries to identify the outer edges of the hazy thermal image, then find its center. A pale-pink shadow moves in the speckled purple, then thins out before solidifying again.

Suddenly he notices something happening in the square straight ahead of him. Two undercover police officers are running toward him with their pistols drawn.

78

PENELOPE WAKES UP EARLY and can't get back to sleep.
Eventually, she gets up and puts some water on to make tea.

She takes the boiling water off the stove, fills the teapot,
and adds two lemon tea bags. Then she takes the pot and a
cup into the dimly lit living room, puts them down in the
window alcove, turns on the lamp with the green shade, and
looks down into the deserted square.

Suddenly she sees two people running across the cobble-
stones; then they fall and stay down. It looks strange. She
turns the lamp off quickly. It starts to sway and scrapes against
the glass. She moves off to the side of the window, then glances
out again to see a SWAT team running along Nybro Street,
and then something flickering in a doorway over by the market; a fraction of a second later, there's a sound, as if someone
had thrown a wet rag at the window. A bullet goes straight
through the laminated glass and the lamp and into the wall
behind her. She throws herself on the floor and crawls away.
Splinters of glass from the lamp are lying on the floor, but she
doesn't even notice when she cuts her palms.

STEWE BILLGREN has just transferred from a quiet post-
ing to the Special Operations Group. Now he's sitting in the

passenger seat beside his immediate superior, Mira Carlsson, in Surveillance Vehicle Alpha, a civilian car that's slowly driving up Humlegårds Street. Stewe has never been in a live situation before, but he has often wondered how he would handle it. The thought of it has started to worry him, particularly after his partner came out of the bathroom last week with a big grin on her face and showed him the pregnancy test.

STEWE IS TIRED after yesterday's soccer match. His calves and thighs are starting to ache.

Dull thuds come from outside, and Mira has just enough time to look out the windshield and wonder aloud, "What the hell ... ?"

She hears a voice shouting over the radio that two officers have been hit in the middle of Östermalm Square, that Group 5 needs to go in from Humlegårds Street.

"We've got him," the Security Police's operations coordinator says in a raised voice. "There are only four entrances to the market, and—"

"Are you sure of that?" Mira cuts in.

"One door on Nybro Street, one on the corner, and two on Humlegårds Street."

"Move more people in, more people!" Ragnar Brolin, the head of Deployment, calls to someone.

"We're trying to get a map of the market."

"Move Groups 1 and 2 to the main door!" someone else shouts. "Group 2, go in; Group 1, secure the door."

"Go, go, go!"

"Group 3, move to the side entrances and provide backup to Group 4," Jenny says in a focused voice. "Group 5 already has orders to go into the market. We'll have to use Surveillance Vehicle Alpha—they're already in the vicinity."

Ragnar Brolin contacts Vehicle Alpha. Stewe glances nervously at Mira, then takes the call. Brolin sounds stressed as he tells them to drive up Majors Street and await further orders. He quickly explains that the operational area has been expanded and that they're probably going to have to provide backup for Group 5.

He repeats several times that the situation is live and that the suspect is inside the market.

"Shit," Stewe whispers. "I shouldn't be here. I'm so damn stupid. . . ."

"Calm down," Mira says.

"My girlfriend's pregnant. I just found out last week. I'm going to be a dad."

"Congratulations."

He's breathing fast and bites his thumbnail as he stares in front of him. Through the windshield, Mira watches three heavily armed police officers rush down Humlegårds Street from Östermalm Square.

Stewe stops biting his nail when Brolin calls their car again.

"Surveillance Vehicle Alpha, come in!"

"Answer," Mira tells Stewe.

"Alpha, Vehicle Alpha!" the head of Deployment says impatiently.

"Go on!"

"Vehicle Alpha here," Stewe answers reluctantly.

"We don't have time to move people," Brolin says, almost shouting. "We're going in immediately; you have to provide backup for Group 5. I repeat, we're going in, you're providing backup for Group 5. Is that understood?"

"Yes," Stewe replies.

"Check your weapon," Mira says in a tense voice.

As if in a slow dream, he takes out his service pistol, releases the magazine, and checks the ammunition.

"Why are—"

"We're going in," Mira says.

Stewe shakes his head and mumbles, "He's killing police officers like flies. . . ."

"Now!" she says harshly.

"I'm going to be a dad, so maybe . . . maybe I should . . ."

"I'm going in," Mira snaps. "Get behind the car, watch the door, maintain radio contact, and be prepared for him to make a run for it."

Mira leaves the car without looking at her colleague. She runs over to the nearest door, which is swinging loose, broken, and glances quickly inside, then pulls her head back. Her colleague from Group 5 is standing on the top step, waiting for her. Mira takes a deep breath, feeling the fear coursing through her body, then goes in.

79

Joona wakes up in his apartment on Wallin Street, opens his eyes, and looks out at the summer sky. He never draws the curtains, because he much prefers natural light.

It's early morning.

Just as he rolls over in bed to go back to sleep, his phone rings.

He knows what the call is about before he answers. He listens to the garbled account of the operation, then opens his gun cabinet and takes out his pistol, a silver Smith & Wesson. The suspect is inside Östermalm Market, and the police have just stormed the building without a firm strategy.

Only six minutes have passed since the alarm was sounded and the killer disappeared into the market. Leadership is now trying to coordinate their actions, cordon off an expanded area, and move their teams without compromising Penelope's safety.

The summer sky has started to appear behind the grimy glass skylights. Mira's heart is beating very fast. Two heavy shots went off a few moments ago, followed by four pistol shots, then two more heavy shots. One police officer is silent; the other is wounded, screaming that he's been hit in the stomach and needs help.

"Can anyone hear me?" he moans.

Mira looks at the reflection in the pane of glass, at the figure moving behind the display of hanging pheasants and smoked reindeer meat. She gestures to her colleague that there's someone off to one side ahead of them. He calls the management team and asks quietly if they're aware of any police officers in the central aisle. Mira wipes the sweat from her hand, then grips her pistol again as she follows the peculiar movements with her eyes. Her colleague gestures to her. He is coordinating a move with three others who have come in. He moves toward the killer along the game counter. Suddenly a high-velocity weapon fires toward the restaurant. Mira hears the wet, sucking sound as the bullet goes through one of her colleague's protective vests and into soft flesh. The empty case from the weapon clatters as it hits the stone floor, very close to her.

The fixer sees his first shot enter the policeman's chest. He's already dead before his knees start to buckle. The fixer doesn't look at him as he collapses sideways, taking one of the tables down as he falls.

The fixer doesn't stop. He quickly moves deeper into the market hall, instinctively taking care to limit possible lines of fire. Realizing that there are police officers everywhere, he turns and fires two quick shots before heading for the kitchen of the fish restaurant.

Mira hears two more shots and sees her young colleague's body jerk. His semiautomatic hits the floor. He stumbles backward and collapses, hitting the ground so hard that his helmet comes off and rolls away. The light from his weapon is pointing straight at Mira. She moves away and curls up on the floor beside the vegetable counter. In an instant, the market is stormed by twenty-four police officers, six through each entrance. She tries to report back but can't contact anyone. Then she sees the perpetrator, just ten meters away. He's on his way into the fish restaurant's kitchen as Mira raises her Glock, aims, and fires three shots toward him.

The fixer is hit by a bullet in his upper left arm just as he's going into the dark kitchen. He can feel warm blood running over the back of his hand. Without stopping to examine the wound, he opens the door to a freight elevator and walks through it to the other side. He kicks a metal door open, then goes out into the morning light and across an inner courtyard where eight cars are parked. He runs over to an older red Volvo and kicks in one of the rear side windows, reaches in, and opens the front door. He gets in the car and pulls off the molding around the ignition switch, breaks the steering lock, and starts the car with his knife.

80

STEWE BILLGREN has just watched twelve heavily armed police officers run into the market, six through each of the side doors. He has been standing with his pistol aimed at the nearest door since Mira went in with their Group 5 colleague, less than ten minutes ago. Now she has backup. He straightens up, relieved, and gets in the driver's seat. Blue lights are flashing on the walls down near Sture Street. Stewe looks at the police radio.

Suddenly he sees unexpected movement in the rearview mirror. The front of a red Volvo is edging out of an archway beneath the building next to the market. It pulls out slowly and turns right on Humlegårds Street. The car approaches him from behind and turns onto Majors Street in front of him. The pale sky is reflecting off the windows, and he can't get a clear view of the person behind the wheel.

He looks up toward the square again and sees the head of the operation talking on her radio. Stewe is considering approaching her and asking about Mira when a number of observations slot together inside his head. It happens entirely out of the blue. He realizes that the man driving the red Volvo let go of the steering wheel in order to change gears; he didn't use his left arm. His black jacket looked shiny. It was wet, Stewe thinks, as his heart starts to beat faster. His left arm was wet, and the sky wasn't reflected in the rear side window because there wasn't a window. The back seat sparkled with fragments of glass. The window was broken, and the driver's arm was bloody.

Stewe reacts quickly. He calls the head of the operation just as the red Volvo starts to drive up Majors Street. When he doesn't get any response, he decides to follow the suspicious vehicle. He doesn't really even think, he just reacts, no longer concerned about his own safety. As he turns onto Majors Street, the red Volvo accelerates away from him. The driver knows he's been spotted. The tires shriek as they spin before they get purchase.

The two cars gain speed rapidly, heading up the narrow street, past the neo-Gothic Holy Trinity Church and up toward the T junction at the end of the street. Stewe shifts into fourth gear, thinking that he needs to pull alongside the car and force the driver to stop. The building on the other side of the T junction is approaching with dizzying speed. The Volvo turns right onto Linné Street, but the corner is so sharp that the car is forced up onto the sidewalk beneath a red canopy. It crashes into some outdoor tables at a café. Splintered wood and metal fly through the air. The car's left fender is now hanging off, scraping along the road. Stewe follows, accelerating up the narrow street. When he reaches the junction, he brakes and corners, slides, and gains a few seconds. He changes gear again, catching the Volvo from behind. The two cars speed down Linné Street. The Volvo's front fender breaks off and flies up into Stewe's windshield with a crash. He loses speed momentarily but accelerates hard again. They both pull into the wrong lane to pass two slower cars. Stewe just has time to notice the badly positioned roadblocks ahead, where curious onlookers have already begun to gather. The street gets wider near the History Museum, and Stewe tries to contact operational command again on the radio.

"Surveillance Vehicle Alpha!" he shouts.

"Receiving you," a voice replies.

"I'm following him in the car down Linné Street, heading toward Djurgården!" Stewe shouts into the radio. "He's driving a red Volvo, which . . ."

Stewe drops the radio handset, which falls into the passenger-seat footwell as his car hits a wooden barrier in front of a pile of sand. The front right wheel lifts off the ground, and the car veers left, skirting around the hole in the road. He slams the clutch down, steers into the slide, and crosses into the other lane before regaining control of the car and hitting the accelerator again.

He chases the Volvo toward Narva Street. A bus is forced to brake hard by the Volvo and slides out across the intersection. Its back end crashes into a lamppost. Another driver swerves to miss it and drives straight through a bus-stop shelter, whose glass sides shatter.

Stewe follows the Volvo toward Berwald Hall, pulls up alongside it, and sees the driver aim a pistol at him. He brakes just as the shot goes off and passes through the side window, right in front of his face. The car fills with swirling splinters of glass. The Volvo hits a stationary bicycle advertising Linda's Café. There's a crash as the bicycle hits the hood of the Volvo, then flies over the roof to hit the ground in front of Stewe's car.

They take the sharp turn toward Strand Street very fast, head straight across the central avenue between the trees. Stewe accelerates out of the curve, and his tires spin on the road. They race on through the early-morning traffic, hearing the shriek of brakes and a dull thud as two cars collide, then turn left at Berwald Hall, across the grass, and onto Dag Hammarskjölds Street.

Stewe draws his pistol and puts it on the passenger seat, among the shards of glass. His plan is to catch up with the Volvo on Djurgårdsbrunns Street and try to spin the car out. Their speed is approaching 130 kilometers an hour. The Volvo leaves the road abruptly, making a sharp left just after the Norwegian Embassy. It goes over the sidewalk and onto the footpath between the trees. Stewe reacts a little too late and is forced to make a wider turn. He careens in front of a bus, across the sidewalk, and through some low bushes. His tires thud against the curb as he goes past the Italian Cultural Institute. He swerves left onto Gärdes Street and sees the Volvo immediately.

It's standing in the middle of the road, approximately a hundred meters away.

Stewe can see the driver inside the car through the rear window. He picks his pistol up from the seat, takes the safety off, and drives slowly closer. The blue lights from a number of police cars on Valhalla Boulevard are visible beyond the studios of Swedish Television. The black-clad man gets out of the red Volvo and starts to run down the road toward the German and Japanese Embassies. Stewe accelerates just as the Volvo explodes in a ball of flame and smoke. He feels the pressure wave on his face while the blast knocks out his hearing. The world is miraculously silent as he drives onto the sidewalk, into the billowing black smoke, and across the burning debris. He can't see the driver anywhere. There's nowhere he could have gone. He speeds up and drives to the end of the road, then gets out of the car and starts to run back up it with his pistol in his hand.

The man has vanished. The world is still quiet, but now

there's a strange rushing sound, as if a strong wind were blowing. Stewe has a good view of the road and the embassies. The man couldn't have gotten any farther in such a short time. He must have made his way into one of the embassy compounds.

People have started to come out to see what caused the explosion. Stewe turns and scans his surroundings. Suddenly he sees the man, inside the compound of the German Embassy, beside the main building. He's walking in an ordinary way—simply opens the door of the main entrance and walks in.

Stewe lowers his pistol and tries to calm down and breathe slowly. A loud ringing sound is filling his head now. He knows that the diplomatic missions enjoy territorial privileges, which prevent him from going after the man without express permission. He has to stop. There's nothing he can do.

81

A UNIFORMED POLICE OFFICER is standing ten meters in front of the roadblock on Sture Street as Joona drives up. The officer tries to direct him to turn back and take a different route, but Joona keeps driving, then pulls over to the curb and gets out of the car. He flashes his ID, ducks under the plastic tape marking the cordon, and starts to run up Humlegårds Street toward the market.

Even though it's only been eighteen minutes since he received the call, the shooting is already over, and ambulances are starting to arrive at the scene.

Jenny Göransson is receiving a report about the car chase through the diplomatic quarter. The killer is believed to have entered the German Embassy. Saga is standing outside, talking to a police officer who has a blanket around her shoulders. Saga catches Joona's eye and beckons him over. He comes over to the two women and nods at Saga.

"I thought I'd be the first here," he says.

"You're too slow, Joona."

"Clearly," he says with a smile.

The woman with the blanket around her shoulders looks up at Joona and says hello.

"This is Mira Carlsson from Surveillance," Saga says. "She

was one of the first to go into the market, and she thinks she shot the suspect in the arm."

"But you didn't see his face?" Joona asks.

"No," Mira replies.

Joona looks at the entrance to the market, then turns to Saga.

"They said all surrounding buildings were going to be secure," he mutters.

"They must have thought this was too far away—"

"They were wrong," Joona says, cutting her off.

"Yes," Saga says, gesturing toward the market. "He was behind this gate and fired one shot through her window."

"So I heard. She was lucky," he says in a low voice.

The area around the main entrance is cordoned off, and small numbered signs indicate early forensics results: a shoe-print and an empty cartridge. Inside the open doors, Joona can see some tomatoes that have rolled onto the floor, and the curved magazine from a Swedish AK-5 assault rifle.

"Stewe Billgren," Saga says. "Mira's partner—he's the officer who followed the suspect to the diplomatic quarter and says he saw him go through the main entrance of the German Embassy."

"Could he have been mistaken?"

"It's possible. We've contacted the embassy, and they claim that"—she consults her notebook—"they claim that there has been no unusual activity in the area."

"Have you spoken to Billgren?"

"Yes."

Saga gives Joona a serious look.

"There was an explosion. He can hardly hear anything, but he's sure he saw the suspect go inside the embassy."

"He could have sneaked out through the back."

"We have people surrounding the entire property now,

and we've got a helicopter in the air. We're waiting for permission to enter the precinct."

Joona glances irritably at the market stalls.

"That could take time."

He takes out his phone and says, almost to himself, "I'll
call Klara Olofsdotter."

Klara is a senior prosecutor. She answers on the second
ring.

"I know it's you, Joona," she says without saying hello.
"And I know what you're calling about."

"Then, presumably, you also know that we need to get in,"
Joona says, a trace of his incorrigible stubbornness creeping
into his voice.

"It's not that easy. This is fucking sensitive stuff, if you'll
pardon the expression. I've spoken to the ambassador's secretary over the phone," Klara says, "and she claims that everything is as it should be at the embassy."

"We believe he's in there," Joona says obstinately.

"But how could he have gotten in?"

"He could be a German citizen, claiming to need consular
assistance. They had just opened for the day. He could be
a Swedish employee with an ID card or have some sort of
diplomatic status, possibly immunity. Or he could be protected by someone. We don't know yet. Maybe he's a close
relative of the defense attaché."

"But we don't even know what he looks like," she says.
"There are no witnesses, so how can we go into the embassy
without knowing what—"

"I can get a witness," Joona interrupts.

The line goes quiet for a few moments. Joona can hear
Klara breathing.

"Then I'll see to it that you get in."

82

JOONA AND SAGA are standing in the secure apartment. None of the lights are on, but the morning sky shines outside the windows. Penelope is sitting on the floor, with her back against the innermost wall, pointing at the window.

"Yes, that's where the bullet came in," Saga confirms quietly.

"The lamp saved my life," Penelope mumbles, lowering her hand.

They look at the remains of the lamp: the dangling cord and a broken plastic base.

"I turned it off so I could get a better view of what was happening out in the square," Penelope says. "The lamp started to sway, and he thought it was me, didn't he? He thought it was me moving, that the heat was from my body."

Joona turns to Saga. "Did he have an electro-optical sight?"

Saga nods. "Yes, according to Jenny."

"What?" Penelope asks.

"You're right—the lamp saved your life," Joona replies.

"Oh God," she moans.

Joona looks at her calmly, and his gray eyes shimmer.

"Penelope," he says seriously, "you've seen his face, haven't you? Not this time, but before. You told us you didn't, but you did. I understand that you're frightened, but . . . I want you to nod your head if you think you can describe him."

She wipes her cheeks quickly and then looks up at the tall detective and shakes her head.

"Can you tell us anything about him?" Saga asks gently.

Penelope thinks about the detective's voice, his soft Finnish accent, and wonders how he knows that she saw the killer's face. She did see him, but she doesn't know if she could describe him. It happened so quickly. She only caught a glimpse of him, with the rain in his face, moments after he had killed Björn and Ossian.

She wishes she could suppress the memory.

But his weary, troubled face keeps lighting up in the white flash of the lightning.

Saga goes over to Joona, who is standing at the window, reading a long text message on his phone.

"Klara has spoken to the chief legal officer, who's spoken to the ambassador," Joona says. "An hour from now, three people will have access to the embassy for forty-five minutes."

"We should head out there now," Saga says.

"There's no rush," Joona says, his gaze lingering on the square.

Journalists are jostling outside the police cordon around the market hall.

"Did you tell the prosecutor that we need armed backup?" Saga asks.

"We'll have to discuss that with the German security guards."

"Who's going in? How do we decide?"

Joona turns to her. "I'm thinking . . . the officer who followed the fixer. . . ."

"Stewe Billgren," she says.

"Yes, Stewe Billgren," Joona says. "Would he be able to identify him?"

"He didn't see his face. No one's seen his face," Saga replies.

She sits on the floor next to Penelope for a while, leaning against the wall, breathing slowly, before she asks her first question. "Do you know why all this is happening?"

"No," Penelope says carefully.

"He wants a photograph that you had stuck to the door in your apartment," Joona says with his back to her.

She lowers her head and nods weakly.

"Do you know why he wants the photograph?" Saga asks.

"No," she replies, and starts crying.

Saga waits a few seconds, then says, "Björn tried to blackmail Carl Palmcrona for money, and—"

"I didn't know anything," Penelope interrupts with hard-won calmness in her voice. "I wasn't part of it."

"We know," Joona says.

Saga gently puts her hand on Penelope's. "Were you the photographer?" she asks.

"Me? No, I . . . The picture was just sent to the Swedish Peace and Arbitration Society, and I'm the chairperson, so . . ."

She stops speaking.

"Was it mailed to you?" Joona asks.

"Yes."

"Who from?"

"I don't know," she replies quickly.

"There was no letter with it?" he asks.

"No, I don't think so. I mean, not that I saw."

"Just an envelope containing a picture?"

She nods.

"Do you still have the envelope?"

"No."

"What did it say?"

"Just my name and 'Swedish Peace and Arbitration Society' . . . just the name, not our post-office box number, 2088."

"'Penelope Fernandez,'" Saga says, "'Swedish Peace and Arbitration Society.'"

"You opened the envelope and took out the photograph," Joona says. "What did you see at that moment? What did the photograph mean to you?"

"What did it mean?"

"What did you see when you looked at it? Did you recognize the people in it?"

"Yes . . . three of them, but . . ."

She falls silent.

"Tell us what you thought when you looked at the picture."

"That someone must have seen me on television," she says. She collects herself for a moment before going on. "I thought that it was so damn typical. . . . Palmcrona is supposed to be neutral, that's the whole point . . . and there he was at the opera, drinking champagne with the boss of Silencia Defense and an arms dealer active in Africa and the Middle East. . . . It's scandalous."

"What were you thinking of doing with the picture?"

"Nothing," she replies. "There was nothing we could do with it. That's just the way things are, but at the same time . . . I remember thinking that . . . at least now I knew where Palmcrona stood."

"Yes."

"It reminded me of those idiots at the Migration Agency, whenever it was, drinking champagne because they'd managed to deport a family. They were celebrating after turning down a desperate family's application for asylum in Sweden, a family with a sick child. . . ."

Penelope trails off again.

"Do you know who the fourth person in the picture is? The woman?"

Penelope shakes her head.

"Agathe al-Haji," Saga says.

"That's Agathe al-Haji?"

"Yes."

"But why was—" Penelope breaks off and stares at Saga.

"Do you know when the photograph was taken?" Saga asks.

"No, but the warrant for Bashir's arrest was issued in March 2009, and—"

Penelope breaks off abruptly again, and her face turns bright red.

"What is it?" Saga asks, almost whispering.

"The photograph was taken after that," Penelope says in a shaky voice. "Wasn't it? The photograph was taken after the president's arrest warrant was issued."

"What makes you say that?" Saga asks.

"I'm right, aren't I?" Penelope says again.

"Yes," Joona replies.

All the color drains from her cheeks. "The deal with Kenya," Penelope says, her mouth trembling. "That's what's going on in the picture. That's what this is all about, the Kenyan contract. That's what Palmcrona's doing. He's authorizing the sale of ammunition to Kenya. I knew there was something sketchy about that, I just knew it."

"Go on," Joona says.

"Kenya already has long-standing contracts in place with Britain. It's Sudan that wants the weapons. The shipment is going to be delivered to Sudan and Darfur via Kenya."

"Yes," Saga says. "We believe that's the plan."

"But that's illegal. It's worse than illegal—it's treachery. It's a breach of international law, a crime against humanity. . . ."

She stops speaking again.

"That's why all this has been happening," she eventually

says, very quietly. "Not because Björn was trying to blackmail Palmcrona."

"His attempted blackmail only alerted these people to the fact that there was a photograph that could expose them."

"I just thought the photograph was embarrassing," Penelope says. "Embarrassing, but no more than that."

"From their perspective, it all started when Palmcrona called to tell them about the attempted blackmail," Saga explains. "They didn't know that the photograph existed until then. Palmcrona's message alarmed them. They couldn't be sure how much or how little the picture exposed. But they realized that it wasn't good. We don't know exactly what they were thinking. Maybe they thought either you or Björn photographed them in that box."

"Although . . ."

"They couldn't be sure how much you knew. But they weren't prepared to take any risks."

"I get it," Penelope says. "And the same thing still applies, doesn't it?"

"Yes."

Penelope nods to herself. "In their eyes, I could be the only witness to the deal," she says.

"They've staked an awful lot of money on this Kenyan contract."

"It's not okay," she whispers.

"Sorry, what do you mean?"

Penelope raises her head, looks Saga in the eye, and says: "They can't be allowed to pump ammunition into Darfur. It's not okay. I've been there twice. . . ."

"They don't care. It's just about money," Saga says.

"But it's about . . . it's about so much more," Penelope says, and turns to look at the wall. "It's about . . ."

She remembers the crunching sound as a clay figure was crushed beneath a goat's hooves. A tiny woman made of sun-dried clay, crushed to dust. A child laughed and shouted that it was Nufi's ugly mother. All Furs must die, they must all be wiped out, the other children shouted, grinning.

"What are you trying to say?" Saga asks.

Penelope gazes at her for a few moments but doesn't reply. She sinks back into memories of her month in Kenya and southwestern Sudan.

She remembers that the boys came over to the barracks where Penelope and Jane lived. Penelope held her breath as she heard them on the deck, talking excitedly to one another.

Suddenly they kicked in the door and marched into the hallway. Penelope lay motionless underneath her bed, reciting the Lord's Prayer, as they overturned furniture and kicked it to pieces. Then she heard the boys out on the road again. One of them was laughing and shouting that the slaves would die. Penelope crept out and went over to the window again. The boys had taken Jane. They were dragging her by her hair and threw her down in the middle of the road. The door to the other barracks flew open, and Gray came out with a machete in his hand. The skinny boy walked toward him. Gray was a good head taller than the boy, and very broad-shouldered.

"What do you want?" Gray asked.

His face was somber and wet with sweat.

The skinny boy didn't answer him; he just raised the revolver and shot him in the stomach. The blast echoed between the buildings. Gray stumbled backward and fell. He tried to get back up but could only lie there, clutching one hand to his stomach.

"One dead Fur!" shouted one of the other boys holding Jane.

The other boy forced Jane's legs apart. She struggled and spoke to them constantly in a hard, calm voice. Gray shouted something to the boys. The skinny boy with the revolver walked over to him again, screamed at him, pressed the barrel of the revolver to his forehead, and pulled the trigger. It clicked, and he tried again and again, but the revolver was empty. It clicked uselessly six times. The atmosphere out on the road changed; then the doors of other barracks opened, and African women emerged. The teenagers let go of Jane and started to run. Penelope saw five women chase after them. She grabbed the blanket from her bed, unlocked the door, and rushed through the hallway and out into the road. She ran over to Jane, put the blanket around her, and helped her to her feet.

"Get back inside," Jane said. "They could come back with more ammunition; you can't be out here. . . ."

Jane spent the rest of that night and most of the following morning at the operating table. She didn't go back to bed until ten o'clock in the morning, when she was sure she'd done enough to save Gray's life. When evening came, she was back at work as usual; by the following day, the routine in the hospital tent was back to normal. The young boys helped her, but they were more wary and sometimes pretended not to hear what she said when they thought she was being too demanding.

"No," Penelope whispers.

"What are you trying to say?" Saga repeats.

"They can't," she says, then trails off.

"You were better protected in the underground room," Saga says.

"Protected? No one can protect me," Penelope replies.

"We know he's in the German Embassy, and we've sur-rounded the building—"

"But you don't have him," Penelope interrupts in a raised voice.

"We believe he's injured. He was shot, and we're going to go in and—"

"I want to come," Penelope says.

"Why would—"

"Because I've seen his face," she replies.

Both Joona and Saga startle at this.

Penelope looks at Joona. "You were right," she says. "I did see him."

"We don't have long, but there's time to put together a composite," Saga says anxiously.

"There's no point," Joona says. "We can't take someone into custody from another country's embassy based on a composite."

"What if he's identified by a witness?" Penelope says, standing up and looking him calmly in the eye.

83

PENELOPE IS STANDING between Saga and Joona behind an armored police van. They're only fifty meters from the entrance to the German Embassy. She can feel the weight of the bulletproof vest over her shoulder and pressing across her chest.

In five minutes, they will be allowed into the embassy compound to try to identify and arrest the suspect.

Penelope allows Joona to place an extra pistol into a holster behind her back. He adjusts the angle several times so that he can easily grab the reserve weapon from her.

"She doesn't want that," Saga says.

"It's okay," Penelope says.

"We don't know what we're going to find in there," Joona says. "I hope it's all going to go smoothly, but if it doesn't, this weapon could make all the difference."

The entire area is crawling with Swedish police officers, people from the Security Police, SWAT teams, and paramedics.

Joona looks at the remains of the burned-out Volvo. There's hardly anything left. Pieces of the vehicle lie scattered across the intersection. Erixon has already found a detonator and traces of explosives.

"Probably hexogen," he says, pushing his glasses up his nose.

"Plastic explosives," Joona says, looking at his watch.

A German shepherd moves restlessly in front of a police officer, then lies down on the road, panting.

Saga, Joona, and Penelope are escorted to the fence by a rapid-response team; four German military police officers are waiting there, their faces impassive.

"Don't worry," Saga says gently to Penelope. "You're just going to identify the fixer, and once you've done that we'll escort you out. The embassy's security personnel will wait until you're safe before they remove him."

A heavily built German military police officer with a freckled face opens the gate and lets them into the loading area. He welcomes them in a friendly voice and introduces himself as Karl Mann, the head of security.

They walk with him to the main entrance.

The morning air is still cool.

"We're dealing with an extremely dangerous individual," Joona says.

"So we understand. We've been briefed," Karl says. "But I've been here all morning, and there are only diplomatic staff and citizens here."

"Can you get a list?" Saga asks.

"I can tell you that we're looking at footage from our security cameras," Karl says. "I have a feeling your colleague must be mistaken. I think your man went past the gates, but instead of going inside, he went around the embassy and across the grass, toward the television studios."

"That's possible," Joona says calmly.

"How many people are in the embassy?" Saga asks.

"The consular section is open, and right now four cases are being dealt with."

"Four people?"

"Yes."

"And how many staff?" Saga asks.

"Eleven."

"And how many security personnel?"

"There are five of us right now," he replies.

"No one else?"

"No."

"No workmen or . . ."

"No."

"So—twenty people in total," Saga says.

"Do you want to start by taking a look around for yourselves?" Karl Mann asks mildly.

"We'd like you with us, if possible," Saga says.

"How many?" Karl Mann asks.

"As many as possible, and as heavily armed as possible," Joona replies.

"You really must think he's dangerous." He smiles. "I can let you have another two men."

"We don't know how he'll react if—"

"You believe he's been shot in the shoulder," Karl Mann interjects. "I can't say that I feel particularly scared."

"Maybe he never came in, and maybe he's already left the embassy," Joona says quietly. "But if he is here, we need to be prepared for casualties."

Joona, Saga, and Penelope walk through the hallway on the ground floor in silence, accompanied by three military police officers armed with assault rifles and shock grenades. The embassy has been undergoing renovations for several years, during which time the staff moved to premises on Artilleri Street. This spring, even though the work isn't finished, they moved back in. The hallway smells like paint and freshly cut wood, and some of the floors are still covered with protective paper.

"First we'd like to see the visitors, anyone who isn't a member of staff," Joona says.

"Yes, I anticipated that," Karl Mann says.

Penelope walks between Saga and Joona. She feels oddly calm. For some reason, she can't imagine she's going to encounter the killer here at the embassy. It feels like far too ordinary a location.

Then she notices Joona become more alert. His pattern of movement beside her changes, and she sees him eyeing the doors and ventilation grilles.

An alarm starts to sound through the walls, and the group stops. Karl takes out his radio and exchanges a few words in German with a colleague.

"The alarm on one of the doors is acting up," he explains in Swedish. "The door is locked, but the alarm is reacting as though it's been open for thirty seconds."

They keep walking. Penelope becomes more aware of the pistol rubbing against her back with each step she takes.

"Martin Schenkel, our business attaché, is in the office straight ahead," Karl says. "He has a visitor at the moment, Roland Lindkvist."

"We'd like to meet them," Joona says.

"He asked not to be disturbed before lunch."

Joona doesn't answer.

Saga takes Penelope's upper arm, and they stop while the others walk on toward the closed door.

"One moment," Karl says to Joona, then knocks.

A voice answers, and Karl goes inside, closing the door behind him.

Joona looks over toward a room with no door. The doorway is covered with industrial gray polythene, and he can make out a stack of plaster inside the room. The plastic bulges outward like a sail, making a faint rustling sound. He is taking a step toward the plastic when there's a noise behind the closed door of the business attaché's office: voices, followed by a heavy thud. Penelope moves backward. She just wants to get away.

"We'll wait here," Saga says, drawing her pistol.

Penelope watches Joona walk to the business attaché's office door. The two other military police officers are standing completely still. Joona draws his pistol, clicks off the safety, and then knocks on the door.

A strange smell is spreading through the hallway, as if someone left a pan on the stove.

Joona knocks again, listens, and hears a monotonous voice. It seems to be repeating the same phrase over and over again. He waits a few seconds, hides the pistol behind his back, and presses the handle down.

Karl is standing below the ceiling light with his assault rifle hanging by his hip. He looks at Joona, then turns to the other man, who is sitting in an armchair at the back of the room.

"Herr Schenkel, this is the Swedish detective," he says.

Books and files are scattered across the floor, as if they had been swept off the desk in anger. Martin Schenkel is sitting in an armchair, staring at a television, which is showing a live broadcast of a soccer match from Beijing, DFB-Elf against the Chinese national team.

"Weren't you supposed to be seeing a visitor?" Joona asks in a reserved tone of voice.

"He's gone," Schenkel replies without taking his eyes off the screen.

They continue along the hallway. Karl is in a worse mood now, snapping at the two military policemen. A woman in a pale-gray cardigan quickly crosses the brown protective paper covering the freshly polished floor in the next hallway.

"Who's that?" Joona asks.

"The ambassador's secretary," Karl Mann replies.

"We'd like to talk to her and—"

A howling alarm rings out throughout the whole building, and a prerecorded voice announces in German that everyone should leave the building immediately and stay out of the elevator: "This is not a drill."

84

KARL TALKS QUICKLY into his radio, then starts walking toward the stairs.

"There's a fire upstairs," he says tersely.

"How far has it spread?" Joona asks, matching his pace.

"They don't know yet, but we're evacuating the embassy. There are eleven people left upstairs."

Karl takes an extinguisher from a red cabinet and pulls out the pin.

"I'll take Penelope out," Saga calls.

"He's the one who started the fire," Penelope says. "He's going to disappear while they try to put it out."

Joona heads for the stairs with the three military policemen. Their steps echo between the bare concrete walls as they run up. They can smell and see gray trails of smoke creeping along beneath the ceiling.

"It looks like the fire's in the Schiller Room. There's a kitchen next to it," Karl says, pointing.

A steady stream of black smoke is seeping out from beneath the double doors at the end of the hallway. Somewhere a woman screams. There's a low rumble in the building, like thunder. Suddenly there's an explosion behind the double doors, as if a large pane of glass had shattered in the heat.

"We need to get everyone out," Joona says. "It's—"

Karl gestures at Joona to stop when he gets a call on his radio, exchanges a few words, and then turns to the group.

"Okay, listen up," he says in a firm voice. "Security has just seen a man dressed in black on their monitors. He's in the men's bathroom, and there's a pistol on one of the sinks."

"That's him," Joona says.

Karl calls the control room and lowers his voice as he asks about the man's location.

"Two meters to the right of the door," Karl Mann says. "He's bleeding heavily from his shoulder and is sitting on the floor. The window is open, and it's possible that he's going to try to escape that way."

They run across the brown paper covering the floor and come to halt. It's noticeably warmer here, and the smoke is billowing across the ceiling.

"What's he armed with?" Joona asks quietly.

"They could only see the pistol on the sink, not—"

"Ask if he's got a backpack with him," Joona says. "Because he carries—"

"I'm leading this operation," Karl hisses.

He gestures toward his men, who quickly check their assault rifles, then follow him into the next room. Joona feels like warning them again as he watches them go. He knows that their standard tactics won't work against the fixer. They're like flies approaching a spider. One by one, they're going to get caught in his web.

Joona takes the safety off his Smith & Wesson and cautiously follows them. They've taken up positions outside the door to the men's bathroom. One of them, his long blond hair tucked under his helmet, removes the pin from a shock grenade. He opens the door briefly to roll the grenade in across the tiled floor. After a muffled blast, the other officer opens the door again and aims his weapon into the darkness. Karl gestures impatiently. Without a moment's hesitation, the blond officer rushes in, his assault rifle raised. Then Joona hears him say something in a frightened voice. A moment later, there's a powerful explosion, and the military policeman is thrown out of the bathroom in a whirl of smoke and brick dust. The door is torn from its hinges. The second officer drops his gun, falls sideways, and hits one knee on the floor. The pressure wave makes Joona take a step back. The blond policeman is lying on his back in the hallway. His mouth is open; there's blood between his teeth. He's unconscious, and a large piece of shrapnel has penetrated his thigh. Bright-red blood is pumping rhythmically onto the floor. Joona rushes over and drags him farther away, feeling the warmth of the gushing blood on his hands as he fashions a makeshift tourniquet from the man's belt and a torn shirtsleeve.

With his pistol in his hand, Karl goes into the bathroom, across the shattered tiles and mirrors on the floor. He finds the fixer lying on the floor. The man is still alive. His legs are twitching, his arms fumbling helplessly. His chin and large parts of his face have been blown off. Karl looks around, sees the metal wire, and concludes that the fixer was probably planning to set a trap using a hand grenade, before the shock grenade caught him by surprise.

"We'll evacuate everyone else," Karl whispers to himself, leaving the bathroom.

Joona wipes the blood from his hands and calls the command center to request an ambulance. He sees Penelope emerge from the stairwell. Saga is following her. Penelope's eyes look black, as if she's been crying for hours. Saga is trying to calm her down and hold her back, but she pulls free.

"Where is he?" Penelope demands in an uneven voice. "I want to see him."

"We have to get out," Joona calls. "This hallway is going to be in flames any second now."

Penelope pushes past Joona toward the men's bathroom, and looks inside the shattered room. She sees the man on the floor, his body twitching, his face a bloody mess. She lets out a moan, stumbles backward, and reaches out to the wall for support.

Penelope is breathing quickly. Her stomach is churning. She swallows and feels Saga try to lead her back toward the stairs.

"It's not him," Penelope whispers, so quietly no one can hear.

"We have to get out," Saga says, leading her away.

Paramedics in protective masks are carrying the injured military policeman out. There's another explosion, like a deep exhalation of breath. Splinters of glass and wood fly through the hallway. A woman stumbles and falls over, but she manages to get to her feet again. Smoke is pouring through an open door. A heavyset man is standing still in the corridor as blood runs from his nose, down over his shirt and tie. The military police are shouting at everyone to make their way to the emergency exit. Flames are flickering from the doorway to one of the offices. A woman whose dress is on fire is screaming, and one of the military police officers sprays her with white foam.

The smoke is making Joona cough, but he still goes into the men's bathroom to survey the devastation. The fixer is lying completely still now. His face has been provisionally wrapped in compresses and a gauze bandage. Dark-red blood is pulsing from the gunshot hole in his black jacket.

In one of the sinks is his pistol. Behind the toilet in the remains of one of the cubicles is the man's empty black nylon backpack.

He can hear cries, frightened voices, and barked orders. Karl appears in the men's bathroom with two paramedics.

"I want someone to watch him," Joona says, gesturing toward the fixer as the paramedics lift the body onto a stretcher and strap him down.

"He's going to die before the ambulance reaches the hospital," Karl replies.

"I still want you to keep him under observation for as long as he's on embassy property."

Karl looks Joona in the eye, quickly orders one of his men to watch the prisoner and hand him over to the Swedish police, then takes a call on his radio.

"One person's still missing. He should be up here," he says, coughing again.

"Evacuate the building!" someone shouts behind them.

Joona turns around and sees four firemen in full gear hurrying along the hallway, systematically searching the rooms.

Before Joona has time to warn them, one of the firemen shines his bright flashlight into the room. Two eyes glow in the darkness, and a Labrador barks wearily.

"We'll take over," one of the men says. "Can you get out on your own?"

"One person's missing," Karl tells them.

"Be careful," Joona says emphatically to the young fireman.

"Come on!" Karl calls to him.

"I just want to look at something."

Joona coughs, goes back into the men's bathroom, sees the blood on the floor and walls, then hurries into the remains of one of the cubicles and grabs the fixer's black backpack.

85

PENELOPE'S LEGS ARE SHAKING, and she's leaning against the fence with one hand, staring down at the ground. She's fighting the urge to throw up. The image of the men's bathroom is shimmering in front of her eyes: the unrecognizable face, the teeth, and all the blood.

The weight of the bulletproof vest makes her want to sit down. The sound of her surroundings reaches her in waves. She can hear the wailing siren of the ambulance and the police officers shouting at one another, talking into radios. She sees paramedics run past with a stretcher. It's the man from the bathroom. He's lying on his back. His face is covered, but the blood has already soaked through the compresses.

Saga is walking toward Penelope with a nurse. She says she thinks that Penelope is going into shock.

"A doctor will come and take a look at you in a moment," the nurse says. "But I can give you something to help calm you down. Have you ever had any problems with your liver?"

When Penelope shakes her head, the nurse hands her a blue pill.

"It has to be swallowed whole. . . . It's half a milligram of Xanor," she explains.

"Xanor," Penelope repeats, looking at the pill in her hand.

"It'll help calm you down. It's not dangerous," the nurse explains before hurrying away.

"I'll get you some water," Saga says, heading for one of the police vans.

Penelope's fingers feel cold. She looks at her hand, then at the little blue pill.

Joona is still in the building. They're bringing more people out, soot-smeared and suffering from smoke inhalation. The shocked diplomats have gathered by the fence in front of the Japanese Embassy while they wait to be taken to Karolinska Hospital. A woman in a dark-blue skirt and cardigan sinks to the ground, weeping openly. A female police officer sits down beside her, puts her arm around the woman's shoulders, and tries to reassure her. One of the diplomats keeps licking his lips and wiping his hands on a towel over and over, as if he fears he can never get clean again. An older man in a rumpled suit is standing stiffly, talking on the phone. The military attaché, a middle-aged woman with dyed red hair, has dried her tears and is trying to help, even though she looks badly dazed. One man with bandages on his burned hands has spent a while sitting with a blanket around his shoulders, his face lowered, but now he's standing up and drops the blanket on the ground as he starts to walk slowly up the road, staring distantly at the fence.

A military police officer is standing with a hand on the flagpole, crying.

The man with the burned hands turns right onto Gärdes Street.

Penelope suddenly gasps for breath. Like an injection of ice, a horrifying realization spreads through her body. She didn't see his face, but she saw his back. The man with the injured hands. She knows it's him, her pursuer. He's walking toward Gärdes, ambling slowly away from the police and paramedics. She didn't need to see his face, because she's seen his back and neck before, on the boat beneath the Skurusund bridge, back when Viola and Björn were still alive.

Penelope opens her hand and lets the blue pill fall to the ground.

With her heart pounding she starts to walk toward him, letting her blanket fall to the ground, just as he did. She turns into Gärdes Street and speeds up. She starts to run when she sees him slip in among a clump of trees straight ahead of her. He looks weak, probably because of the blood he's lost after being shot in the shoulder, and she already knows he won't be able to outrun her. Some crows fly up from the treetops and flap away. Penelope heads into the trees. She feels powerful as she strides through the grass and catches sight of him fifty meters away. He stumbles and reaches out his hand to steady himself against a tree. The bandage comes loose and dangles limply from his fingers. She runs after him as he leaves the shelter of the trees and starts to limp across the large expanse of grass. Without stopping, she draws the pistol that Joona strapped to her back. She looks at it and removes the safety as she moves between the trees. Then she slows down and holds the gun out with her arms straight, aiming at his legs.

"Stop," she whispers, and squeezes the trigger.

The gun fires, the recoil jolts her arm and shoulder, and the powder scorches the back of her hand.

Penelope can't see where the bullet lands, but the man starts to run.

You shouldn't have touched my sister, she thinks.

The man crosses a footpath, stops to clutch his shoulder, then runs across the grass.

Penelope chases after him, emerging into the sunlight. She's getting closer, crossing the path that he's just passed. She raises the gun again.

"Stop!" she shouts.

The shot goes off, and she sees the bullet tear into the grass ten meters in front of him. Penelope feels adrenaline pumping through her body, and she feels perfectly clear and focused. She aims at his legs and fires. She hears the shot, feels the recoil in her arm, and sees the bullet go in through the back of his knee. He screams out in pain and falls to the grass. Though he tries to keep moving, she closes in on him, marching toward him as he tries to get back on his feet.

Stop, Penelope thinks, raising the pistol again. *You killed Viola. You drowned her in a bucket, and then you killed Björn.*

"You murdered my little sister," she says out loud, firing again.

The shot hits him in his left foot, and blood sprays across the grass.

When Penelope reaches him, he's leaning back against the tree. His head is hanging, and his chin is resting on his chest. He's bleeding heavily, gasping for breath like an animal, but is otherwise completely still.

She stops in front of him, stands with her feet wide apart on the grass, and aims the pistol at him again.

"Why?" she asks in a low voice. "Why is my sister dead? Why is . . ."

She breaks off, swallows, then kneels down so she can see his face.

"I want you to look at me when I shoot."

The man moistens his mouth and tries to raise his head. It's too heavy—he can't do it. He's clearly on the brink of passing out. She takes aim at him with the pistol but stops herself again, reaches out with her other hand, lifts his chin, and looks at him. She clenches her jaw hard when she sees his features again; it's the face she saw during the storm out on Kymmendö. Now she remembers the calm in those eyes and the deep scar across his mouth. He looks just as calm now. Penelope is thinking how odd it is that he isn't afraid of her when he suddenly lunges. He moves with unexpected speed, grabs her by the hair, and yanks her toward him. Even though there's not much strength in his arm, she falls forward and hits her head against his chest. She doesn't have time to pull away before he changes his grip, grabs her wrist, and twists the gun from her hand. With all the strength she can muster, she throws her arms out and kicks hard and falls backward onto the grass. When she looks up again, he is already pointing the pistol at her. He fires two shots in quick succession.

86

IT ISN'T UNTIL JOONA EMERGES from the stairwell in the embassy that he feels the strain in his lungs and notices how badly his eyes are stinging. He has to get outside, has to breathe fresh air. He coughs, leans against the wall, then keeps going. Another explosion comes from up above, and a ceiling lamp crashes to the floor in front of him. He can hear the sirens outside. Quickly, he walks the last few steps toward the main entrance. Six German military police officers are on the paved driveway in front of the door. Joona breathes clean air into his lungs, coughs, and looks around. Two fire trucks have their ladders aimed at the embassy. The street outside the gates is full of police officers and paramedics. Karl is lying on the grass, and a doctor is leaning over him, listening to his lungs. Penelope is walking slowly along the fence of the Japanese Embassy with a blanket around her shoulders.

Joona went back into the men's bathroom at the last minute to retrieve the backpack because he couldn't understand why the fixer would have wanted to hide an empty backpack when he had left his pistol and magazines fully visible in the sink.

He coughs again, opens the backpack, and looks inside. It isn't completely empty. It contains three passports and an attack knife with fresh blood on the blade.

Who have you hurt now? Joona thinks.

He looks at the knife again and sees that the blood has started to congeal, and then he looks around again, at the ambulances and people on the other side of the embassy gates. A woman in a burned dress is lying on a stretcher, holding another woman's hand. An older man with soot stains on his forehead is talking on his phone, a completely blank look on his face.

Joona realizes his mistake, drops the backpack and the bloody knife on the ground, and runs to the gate, yelling to the guard to let him through.

He rushes out of the embassy compound, past some of his colleagues, steps over the plastic police cordon, and pushes past the journalists into the middle of the road. He stops in front of a bright-yellow ambulance that's about to drive away.

"Have you taken a look at the injury to his arm?" he calls as he holds up his ID.

"What do you mean?"

"The patient who was injured in the explosion, he had an injury to his shoulder, and I . . ."

"That was hardly the priority, considering . . ."

"I need to look at that injury," Joona says, cutting him off.

The ambulance driver is about to protest again, but something in Joona's voice stops him.

Joona goes around to the back of the ambulance and opens the doors. The face of the man on the stretcher is completely covered with compresses; he has an oxygen mask over his nose and a suction tube leading to what's left of his mouth. One of the paramedics quickly cuts open the black jacket and shirt and uncovers the injury to his shoulder.

It isn't a gunshot wound. There's no doubt that it was inflicted with a knife—a deep stab wound.

Joona gets out of the ambulance and scans the area until his eyes meet Saga's through the crowd of people and vehicles. She's holding a plastic cup of water, but as soon as she sees the look on his face, she throws the cup down and runs toward him.

"He's getting away again," he says to himself. "We can't let him get away."

Joona looks around, thinking about how, when he rushed out from the embassy just now, he saw Penelope walking along the fence of the Japanese Embassy.

"Get a rifle!" Joona yells, starting to run.

He follows the line of the fence, turns right, and looks around, but he can't see Penelope or the fixer anywhere.

Joona draws his pistol. The fixer was rescued from the smoke-filled embassy along with everyone else.

Saga shouts something behind him, but he doesn't hear: his heart is beating too fast, and there's a roaring sound inside his head.

He quickens his pace even more and is running for a small patch of trees when he hears a pistol shot. He stumbles into a ditch, struggles up a slope, and rushes into the trees.

More pistol shots, short and sharp.

Joona pushes through the dense branches and emerges onto the sun-drenched grass. Three hundred meters away, he sees Penelope beneath a birch tree, moving slowly. A man is sitting against the trunk with his head bowed. Penelope crouches down in front of him; then everything changes. She jerks forward, and falls backward. The man is aiming a pistol straight at her. Joona starts to run, raises his pistol, and takes aim, but he's too far away. He stops and is holding his gun with both hands when the fixer shoots Penelope in the chest with two rapid shots. Her body is thrown backward and remains lying on the ground. Joona runs. The fixer is tired, but he raises the pistol toward her again. Joona fires but misses. When he runs closer, he sees Penelope kicking her legs to get away. The fixer looks at Joona, then back at Penelope. He looks her in the eye and aims the pistol at her face. A shot rings out. Joona hears the powerful blast behind him, and a fraction of a second later, a cascade of blood shoots out behind the fixer. The blood splatters the white bark of the birch tree. The bullet has passed right through the fixer's chest and heart. Joona keeps running, still aiming his pistol in front of him. A second shot rings out, and Joona sees the already dead man jerk as the bullet hits his chest just centimeters above the previous entry hole. Joona lowers his pistol, turns around, and sees Saga standing at the edge of the clump of trees with a sniper rifle held to her shoulder. Her fair hair is shimmering in the sunlight, and there's a look of intense concentration on her face.

Penelope gets to her feet and moves back into the sunshine, coughing hard. She stares at the fixer. Joona walks over to him, kicks the pistol away from his hand, and feels his neck to make sure he really is dead.

Penelope unfastens the bulletproof vest and lets it fall onto the grass. Joona walks over to her. As she takes a step toward him, she looks as if she's going to faint. He puts his arms around her and can feel how exhausted she is when she leans her cheek against his chest.

87

THE MAN WHO WAS FOUND in the men's bathroom died an hour after he reached the hospital. He was identified as Dieter Gramma, the cultural attaché's secretary. On closer inspection, The Needle found traces of tape on his clothes, and bruises and cuts on his wrists and neck that indicated he had been tied up at the time of the explosion. Once the crime-scene investigation was complete and the security camera footage was analyzed, the sequence of events could be mapped fairly precisely. After he arrived at his office, Dieter opened his computer and checked his e-mails. He didn't reply to any but flagged three of them. Then he went to the bathroom. Just as he was opening the door to one of the cubicles, he saw a man in black wearing a balaclava standing in front of the mirror by the sinks.

The man in black was the wounded fixer. His German passport allowed him to gain access to the embassy.

The fixer quickly evaluated Dieter's build before casually placing a piece of tape over the security camera lens. Dieter presumably didn't have time to say much before the fixer forced him down on his knees at gunpoint and taped his mouth, swapped his black jacket for Dieter's blazer, tied Dieter to the water pipes with his back to the camera, then drew his knife and drove the double-edged blade deep into Dieter's left shoulder.

Pain, fear, and a rush of endorphins probably made Dieter so confused that he didn't really understand what was going on. The fixer cut a piece of steel wire with a pair of pliers, put it around his neck, and twisted the ends together. Through this noose he pulled a longer piece of steel wire; he fastened one end to a hand grenade, then held the detonator. If he let go, the grenade would have been triggered and three seconds later would have exploded.

But the fixer taped the grenade, with its detonator pressed closed, against Dieter's chest, passed the wire that was already threaded through the noose around his neck around the pipe beneath the sink, and pulled it tightly in front of the door, so that it acted as a tripwire.

The idea was that someone would come in and detonate the grenade, and in the midst of the ensuing chaos, the police would assume that the man with the bullet hole in his jacket was the person they had been searching for.

The fixer removed the tape from the camera lens, stepped over the tripwire, and left the room.

He went along the hallway to the conference room, where he started a fire. After that, he walked out and knocked on the office door of the counselor Davida Meyer. He had just started to explain a fabricated consular problem when the fire alarm went off.

88

JOONA, SAGA, AND PENELOPE are being driven through Stockholm in an armored police van, away from the diplomatic quarter; on their left is the glittering water.

"I'd seen him," Penelope says in a monotone. "I knew he was never going to give up, he was just going to keep hunting me. . . ."

She trails off and stares in front of her.

"Until he killed me," she says.

"Yes," Saga says.

Penelope closes her eyes, sits still, and feels the gentle movement of the van.

"Who was he?" Penelope asks.

"A professional hit man," Joona replies. "They're called fixers, or *grobs*."

"I'm sure that neither Europol nor Interpol has anything on him," Saga says.

"A professional hit man," Penelope repeats slowly. "So someone sent him?"

"Yes," Saga replies. "Someone sent him, but we're not going to be able to find any connection between him and his employer."

"Raphael Guidi?" Penelope suggests in a low voice. "Is it him? Or Agathe al-Haji?"

"We believe it's Raphael Guidi," Saga says. "Because a trial wouldn't affect Agathe al-Haji."

"Because, of course, what she's doing is no secret," Joona says.

"So Guidi sent a murderer, but . . . what does he want? Do you know? Is it all about the photograph? Is that it?"

"He probably thinks you took the photograph yourself. He thinks you're a witness, that you've seen and heard things that could incriminate him."

"Does he still think that?"

"Probably."

"So he'll send another killer?"

"That's what we're afraid of," Saga replies.

"How long will I have police protection? Am I going to get a new identity?"

"We'll have to discuss that, but—"

"I'm going to be hunted until I don't have the strength to run anymore," Penelope says.

They pass the NK department store and see three young people protesting in front of the main entrance.

"He's not going to give up," Joona confirms in a somber voice. "That's why we have to expose the whole deal. If we do that . . . then there won't be any reason to come after you."

"We can't get at Guidi, we know that," Saga says. "But we can do a hell of a lot in Sweden, and he'll feel the effects."

"Like what?"

"We can start by blocking the deal," Saga says. "Because that container ship can't leave Gothenburg without an export license from Axel Riessen."

"And why would he refuse to sign it?"

"He'll never sign," Joona says. "Because he knows as much about this as we do."

"Good," Penelope whispers.

"We stop the deal, and then we take down Salman and everyone else who's involved," Saga says.

They sit in silence.

"I need to call my mom," Penelope says after a while.

"You can use my phone," Saga says.

Penelope takes it, appears to hesitate, then taps in a number and waits.

"Hi, Mom, it's me, Penny. That man who . . ."

"Penny, there's someone at the door, I have to—"

"Mom, wait!" Penelope says anxiously. "Who's at the door?"

"I don't know."

"But are you expecting anyone?"

"No, but—"

"Don't open it!" Penelope snaps.

Her mother says something and puts the phone down. Penelope hears footsteps across the floor, then the doorbell ringing again. The door opens, and she hears voices. Penelope doesn't know what to do. She looks at Saga and Joona, who are watching her intently. The line crackles, there's an odd echo, and then she hears her mom's voice again.

"Are you still there, Penny?"

"Yes."

"It's someone who's trying to get hold of you," her mom says.

"Get hold of me?"

Penelope licks her lips.

"Okay, Mom. Pass the phone over."

The line crackles again; then Penelope hears a woman's voice: "Penelope?"

"Yes," she replies.

"We need to meet."

"Who am I talking to?" Penelope asks.

"I'm the person who sent you the photograph."

"I haven't received any photograph," Penelope replies.

"Good answer," the woman says. "We don't know each other, but I did send you the picture."

Penelope doesn't reply.

"I have to see you today, as soon as possible," the woman says, sounding agitated. "I sent you a photograph of four people in a private box at a concert. I took the picture in secret on November 13, 2009. One of the four people is my husband, Pontus Salman."

89

Pontus Salman's house is a 1960s villa located on Roskull Street on Lidingö. It still exudes the spirit of the age, even though it's seen slightly better days. They park on the paved driveway and get out of the car. Someone has drawn a childish, stylized penis on the garage door.

They decide that Joona should stay in the car with Penelope while Saga goes over to the house. Though the door is open, Saga still rings the doorbell, which is shaped like a lion's head. She hears a pleasant three-note ring, but nothing happens. Saga draws her Glock, rings the bell again, and enters.

It's a split-level house, and a large kitchen opens off the entryway. Tall windows afford a stunning view of the water.

Saga walks through the kitchen, looks in the empty bedrooms, then goes down the stairs. She can hear music behind a door with the letters "R&R" on a brass sign. When she opens the door, the music gets louder: Verdi's *La Traviata*.

At the end of the tiled hallway, she can see the reflected blue shimmer of an illuminated swimming pool.

Saga creeps forward, trying to listen for anything other

than the music. She thinks she can hear footsteps, bare feet on a tiled floor.

Keeping her pistol hidden by her side, she moves forward. Now she can see cane furniture and palm leaves. The air is warm and humid, and it smells like chlorine and jasmine. The pool is large, with pale-blue tiles and large windows facing the garden. A slender woman in her fifties is standing at a bar in a gold bathing suit, holding a glass of white wine in her hand. She puts the glass down when she catches sight of Saga and walks toward her.

"Hello, my name is Saga Bauer."

"What agency?"

"Security Police."

The woman lets out a laugh, kisses Saga's cheeks, and introduces herself as Marie-Louise Salman.

"Do you have your suit with you?" she asks, returning to the bar.

Her feet leave long, thin prints on the terra-cotta-colored tiles. Her body looks as if she works out. There's something artful about the way she walks, as though she wants to give people a chance to look at her.

Marie-Louise picks up the glass, then turns and looks curiously at Saga, as if to make sure that she is actually watching her.

"A glass of Sancerre?" she asks in her cool, modulated voice.

"No, thanks," Saga replies.

"I swim to keep in shape, even though I've cut back on the modeling. It's easy to succumb to narcissism in this business. Well, of course you know that. It feels like a kick in the face when no one lights your cigarette for you anymore."

Marie-Louise leans forward and whispers theatrically: "I'm having an affair with the youngest guy in the Chippendales. Do you know who they are? Never mind, they're all gay."

"I'm here to talk about the photograph that you sent to . . ."

"I knew he couldn't keep his mouth shut," she exclaims with feigned outrage.

"Who?"

"Jean Paul Gaultier."

"The designer?" Saga asks.

"Yes, the designer, with his vicious little mouth. He still hates me. I knew it."

Saga smiles patiently at Marie-Louise and offers her a robe when she sees the goose bumps on her skin.

"I like being cold—it makes me look better. At least, that's what Depardieu told me last spring, unless it was—I can't quite remember—perhaps it was Renaud, the little sweetheart, who said that. Well, no matter!"

Suddenly they hear footsteps heading toward the pool. Marie-Louise looks nervous and glances around for an escape route.

"Hello?"

"Saga?" Joona calls.

Saga takes a step forward and sees Joona and Penelope walk into the pool area with a woman in her fifties, her dark hair cut in a neat, boyish style.

"Marie-Louise," the woman says with an anxious smile. "What are you doing here?"

"I thought I'd have a swim," she replies. "Need to cool down between my legs."

"You know I said I wanted you to call before you come."

"Of course, sorry. I forgot."

"Marie-Louise is Pontus's sister, my sister-in-law," the woman explains, then turns to Saga and introduces herself.

"Véronique Salman."

"Saga Bauer, Security Police."

"Let's go and sit in the library," Véronique says, and starts to walk back along the hallway.

"Can I have a swim, since I'm here?" Marie-Louise calls.

"Not naked," Véronique replies without looking back.

90

SAGA, JOONA, AND PENELOPE follow Véronique into the library. It's a fairly small room, with leaded windows of yellow, brown, and pink glass. The books are kept in glass bookcases, and there are brown leather armchairs, an open fire, and a brass samovar.

"You'll have to excuse me for not offering refreshments, but I'm in a bit of a hurry. I leave an hour from now. . . ."

Véronique looks around nervously and runs her hands across her skirt before she goes on.

"I just . . . I just want to say what I have to say," she says in a subdued voice. "I won't testify in public. If you try to force me, I'll deny everything, regardless of the consequences."

She adjusts a lampshade, but her hand is shaking so much that it ends up crooked again.

"I'm traveling without Pontus. He won't be joining me," she says, looking at the floor. Her mouth trembles, and she takes a few moments to compose herself before she continues. "Penelope," she says, looking her in the eye, "I want you to know that I understand that you think Pontus is scum, but he isn't, he really isn't."

"I never said—"

"Please, just wait," she says. "I love my husband, but I . . . I no longer know what I think about what he does. Up until now, I've told myself that people have always traded in weapons; the arms trade has existed as long as human beings have been around. I don't mean that as an excuse. I spent several years working on security policy at the Foreign Ministry. And if you're involved in that sort of work, you soon realize that we're a long way from the utopian dream of a world without armed conflict. In practice, every country needs to maintain defense forces, but ... I can't help thinking that there are different nuances. ..."

She walks over to the door, opens it, looks out, then closes it again.

"Exporting arms to countries that are at war, to unstable areas, fanning the flames of conflicts by injecting more weapons—that can't be allowed to happen."

"No," Penelope whispers.

"I understand Pontus as a businessman," Véronique Salman goes on. "Because Silencia really did need that deal. Sudan is a large country with an unreliable ammunition supply. They use almost nothing but Fabrique Nationale, and Belgium isn't exporting to them, given the current situation. People have their eyes on them, but Sweden has never been a colonial power, we have a good reputation in the region, and so on. Pontus saw the opportunity and acted quickly once the civil war was over. Raphael Guidi put the deal together. They were about to sign the contract—everything was ready—when the International Criminal Court suddenly issued a warrant for the arrest of President Bashir."

"Any shipment would be a breach of international law," Saga says.

"Everyone knew that, but Guidi didn't cancel the deal. He just said he had a new interested party. It took several months, but he eventually explained that the Kenyan army wanted to continue with the suspended deal. The same amount of ammunition, the same price, and so on. I tried to talk to Pontus—I said it was obvious that the ammunition was going to end up in Sudan—but Pontus just claimed that Kenya had seen an opportunity. It was a good deal, and they needed ammunition. I don't know if he actually believed that, I don't think he could have, but he shifted all the responsibility onto Carl Palmcrona and the ISP. If Palmcrona granted an export license, then it was obviously all aboveboard, he said, and . . ."

"A good way of not having to take responsibility for anything," Penelope says.

"That was why I took the photograph. I wanted to know who was at the meeting. I just went into the box and took a picture on my cell phone; I said I was trying to make a call and told Pontus I wasn't feeling well and that I was going to take a taxi back to the hotel."

"That was brave," Penelope says.

"But I didn't know how dangerous it was, or I wouldn't have done it," Véronique says. "I was angry with Pontus; I wanted to get him to change his mind. I left the Alte Oper in the middle of the concert and looked at the picture in the taxi. The whole thing was crazy. The buyers were represented by Agathe al-Haji, and she's a military adviser to the Sudanese president, so it was obvious that the ammunition was going to be pumped into the civil war."

"Genocide," Penelope whispers.

"When we got home, I told Pontus he had to pull out of it. . . . I'll never forget the look on his face when he told me that was impossible. 'I've entered into a Paganini contract,' he said, and when I saw the look in his eyes I was really scared. He was terrified. There's no way I could keep that picture on my phone, so I printed it out, deleted it, and then sent it to you."

Véronique stands in front of Penelope with her arms hanging limply by her sides, a look of utter exhaustion on her face.

"I had no idea what was going to happen," she says quietly. "How could I have known? I'm so, so sorry, I can't tell you...."

The room is quiet for a moment.

"What's a Paganini contract?" Joona asks.

"Guidi owns several incredibly valuable violins," Véronique says. "He collects instruments that Paganini himself played over a century ago. He keeps some of the violins in his home, but he loans others to talented musicians and ..."

She runs her hand nervously over her hair before she goes on.

"This business with Paganini ... I've never really understood it, but Pontus says that Guidi somehow sees a connection to Paganini in his contracts. Paganini sold his soul so his music would be immortal. ... Guidi says his contracts are eternal—that's what he means. There's never any documentation, but Pontus told me that Guidi had really done his homework. He had all the figures in his head, he was familiar with the logistics, knew exactly how and when the deal could be put into practice. He told each and every one of them what was required of them and how much they would earn from the deal. Once you've kissed his hand, there's no going back. It's like a Faustian bargain. You've made a deal with the devil. You can't run, you can't hide, you can't even die."

"Why not?" Joona asks.

"Guidi is so ... I don't know, he ... This is so terrible," she says, her mouth trembling. "He somehow gets everyone involved to ... to tell him what their worst nightmare is."

"What?" Saga asks.

"Pontus said that, he said Guidi had the ability to do that," she replies seriously.

"What did he mean by 'nightmare'?" Joona asks.

"Obviously, I asked Pontus if he had told him anything," she says with a pained expression on her face. "But he wouldn't tell me. I don't know what to think."

Silence settles on the small library. There are large damp patches of sweat under the arms of Véronique's white blouse.

"You can't stop Guidi," she says after a while, looking Joona in the eye. "But you have to make sure that ammunition never reaches Darfur."

"We will," Saga says.

Véronique looks at her watch and tells Joona that she has to leave for the airport soon, then goes to the window and gazes out blankly through the colored glass.

"My boyfriend is dead," Penelope says, wiping tears from her cheeks. "My sister is dead, and I don't know how many more people."

Véronique turns to her.

"Penelope, I didn't know what to do. I had that photograph, and I thought that you, if anyone, would be able to identify those people," she explains. "I thought you'd understand the significance of Agathe al-Haji buying ammunition, because you've been in Darfur, you have contacts there, you're a peace campaigner, and—"

"You were wrong," Penelope snaps. "You sent the picture to the wrong person. I was aware of Agathe al-Haji, but I had no idea what she looked like."

"I couldn't send the photograph to the police or the newspapers—they wouldn't have understood its significance, not without an explanation, and I couldn't explain the circumstances. How could I? It was impossible, because, if there was one thing I understood, it was that there had to be no way to link me to the person I sent it to. I wanted to get rid of it, and I never wanted to have to acknowledge my connection to the picture."

"But now you have," Joona says.

"Yes."

"Why?" he asks. "What made you change your mind?"

"Because I'm leaving the country, and I needed to . . ."

She falls silent and looks down at her hands.

"What happened?"

"Nothing," she sobs.

"You can tell us," Joona says.

"No, it . . ."

"It's okay," Saga whispers.

Véronique wipes the tears from her cheeks and looks up.

"Pontus called me from our summerhouse in tears. He said he was sorry, and I don't know exactly what he meant, but he said he was going to do all he could to escape the nightmare."

91

A ROWBOAT made of varnished mahogany is bobbing on the water in the shelter of a large peninsula. There's a very mild easterly breeze, and it carries with it a faint smell of manure from the farms on the far side of the lake. Pontus Salman has drawn up the oars, but the boat has drifted no more than ten meters in the past hour. He's thinking that he would have brought something to drink if he'd realized it was going to take this long to shoot himself.

A double-barreled shotgun is lying across his thighs.

The only sounds are the water lapping against the hull and the gentle rustling of the leaves in the trees.

He closes his eyes for a while and takes several deep breaths, then opens his eyes and rests the butt of the shotgun on the bottom of the boat, making sure it can't slip. He holds the sun-warmed barrel in his hand and tries pointing it at his forehead.

He feels sick at the thought of his head being blown off.

His hands are shaking so badly that he has to wait for a while. He pulls himself together and aims the barrel at his heart instead.

Swallows are flying low, hunting insects above the surface of the water.

There'll probably be rain tonight, he thinks.

A white streak appears across the sky as a plane passes, and Pontus starts to think about his nightmare again.

Suddenly it feels as if the whole lake were getting darker, as if the water were being turned black from below.

He looks back at the shotgun, puts the barrel into his mouth, and feels it scrape against his teeth, leaving a metallic taste.

He reaches for the trigger, but now he hears the sound of a car. His heart flutters in his chest. All manner of thoughts flash through his head in the space of a second, but he realizes it must be his wife. She's the only person who knows where he is.

He puts the shotgun down again and feels his pulse throbbing through his body. He's shaking as he tries to see through the trees.

A man is walking down the path toward the jetty.

It takes Pontus a few seconds to realize that it's the detective who came to the office and showed him Véronique's photograph.

But when he does recognize him, an entirely different type of anxiety swells up inside him. Don't say it's too late, he thinks over and over again as he starts to row toward the shore. Don't say it's too late. Don't say my nightmare's come true. Don't say it's too late.

PONTUS STOPS ROWING before he reaches the jetty. His face is white, and he shakes his head when Joona asks him to come closer. He takes care to maintain the distance between them as he turns the rowboat around so that the front is pointing away from the shore.

Joona sits down on the sun-bleached wooden bench at the end of the pier.

"What do you want?" Pontus asks. He sounds scared.

"I've just been talking to your wife," Joona says calmly.

"Talking?"

"Yes, and I—"

"You talked to Véronique?" Pontus asks anxiously.

"I have some more questions."

"There isn't time."

"There's no rush," Joona says, glancing at the shotgun in the boat.

"What would you know?" Pontus mutters.

The oars move gently in the water.

"What I know is that the ammunition being shipped to Kenya is bound for Sudan," Joona says.

Pontus Salman doesn't reply.

"And I know that your wife took that photograph we showed you."

Pontus sits there, his face down-turned, and lifts the oars, feeling the water run down to his hands.

"I can't stop the deal," he says tersely. "I was in too much of a hurry; I needed the order. . . ."

"So you signed the contract."

"It was watertight. Even if it got out, everyone could claim to have acted in good faith. No one was to blame."

"But it still went wrong," Joona says.

"Yes."

"I was planning to wait before arresting you. . . ."

"Because you can't prove anything," Pontus says.

"I haven't spoken to the prosecutor," Joona goes on. "But I'm sure we can offer a more lenient sentence if you testify against Raphael Guidi."

"I'm not going to testify!" Pontus says heatedly. "You really don't get it. I've signed a very specific type of contract, and if I weren't such a fucking coward I'd have done the same thing Palmcrona did by now."

"We can protect you if you testify," Joona says.

"Palmcrona got away with it," Pontus whispers. "He hanged himself, and now his successor is going to have to sign the export license. Guidi lost all interest in Palmcrona, so he didn't have to confront his nightmare. . . ."

Pontus's lifeless face breaks into a smile. Joona looks at him, thinking that Palmcrona didn't get away with it: his nightmare must have been the death of his son.

"There's a psychologist on her way," Joona says. "And she's going to try to convince you that suicide isn't a way out of . . ."

Pontus starts to row back out.

"Pontus, I need answers to some more questions," Joona says, raising his voice. "You say the new director of the ISP is going to have to sign the export license, but what happens if he refuses? Can't he just refuse to enter into one of these Paganini contracts?"

Pontus stops rowing, and the boat continues to glide away from shore, its oars trailing in the water.

"He could," he replies calmly. "But he won't want to do that. . . ."

92

AXEL WAKES UP when his phone starts to ring on the bed-side table. It was almost morning when he finally fell asleep.

Now he looks at Beverly's face, and he can see traces of Greta again in her mouth and eyelids. Beverly whispers something in her sleep, then rolls onto her stomach. Axel feels a surge of tenderness at the sight of her.

He sits up in bed and is reaching for his book, *A Danger-ous Game* by Friedrich Dürrenmatt, when there's a knock on the bedroom door.

"Just a second!" Axel calls, even as Robert comes into the room.

"I thought you'd be awake," his brother says. "I'd like your opinion on a new instrument that—"

Robert catches sight of Beverly and stops abruptly. "Axel," he stammers. "What's going on, Axel?"

His voice wakes Beverly. When she sees Robert, she hides under the covers. Axel gets up and puts his bathrobe on, but Robert is backing toward the door.

"Fuck you," he says quietly. "Fuck you. . . ."

"It's not what—"

"Have you been taking advantage of her?" Robert asks, almost yelling.

"Let me explain," Axel tries to say.

"You bastard," Robert whispers, and grabs him, dragging him sideways.

Axel loses his balance and throws his arm out, knocking a lamp to the floor. Robert backs out of the room.

"Wait," Axel says, following him. "I know how it looks, but it's not like that. You can ask . . ."

"I'm taking her to the police," Robert says angrily. "I never would have believed that you . . ."

He chokes up, and his eyes fill with tears.

"I'm not a pedophile," Axel tries to explain in a subdued voice. "You have to understand that. I just need—"

"You just need to abuse a vulnerable girl," Robert snaps, in a state of utter despair. "You're taking advantage of someone you promised to care for and protect."

Axel stops in front of him in the library. Robert sits down heavily on the sofa, looks at his brother, and tries to keep his voice steady: "Axel, you do realize that I have to take her to the police, don't you?" he says.

"Yes," Axel replies. "I realize."

Robert can't look at his brother and wipes his mouth and sighs. "It would be just as well to go right away," he says.

"I'll go and get her," Axel says, walking into the bedroom.

Beverly is sitting in bed, smiling and wiggling her toes.

"Get dressed," he says seriously. "You're going out with Robert."

When he returns to the library, Robert gets up at once from the sofa. The pair of them stand there in silence, staring at the floor as they wait.

"You're staying here," Robert says quietly.

"Yes," Axel whispers.

After a while, Beverly comes out. She's wearing a pair of jeans and a T-shirt. Without any makeup, she looks even younger than usual.

93

ROBERT DRIVES IN SILENCE. He pulls up gently to a traffic light and waits for it to turn green.

"I'm so sorry, Beverly," he says in a subdued voice. "My brother said he was giving you somewhere to stay while you waited for student housing. I don't understand—I would never have believed that . . ."

"Axel isn't a pedophile," she says quietly.

"I don't want you to defend him. He doesn't deserve that."

"He doesn't touch me, just so you know. He never has."

"What does he do, then?"

"He needs me to sleep," Beverly replies.

"Sleep?" Robert repeats. "But you said . . ."

"He needs me to sleep so he can sleep, too," she says, in her high, frank voice.

"What do you mean?"

"It's nothing dirty."

Robert sighs and says she'll be able to tell the police everything. A rumbling despair is swelling in his chest again.

"It's all about his sleep," Beverly explains slowly. "He can't sleep without pills, but I make him calm. He gets—"

"You're underage," Robert interrupts.

Beverly stares out through the windshield. The bright-green leaves on the trees are dancing in the early-summer breeze. A group of pregnant women is chatting as they walk down the sidewalk. An old lady is standing still with her face turned toward the sun.

"Why?" Robert suddenly asks. "Why can't he sleep at night?"

"He says it's been that way for a hundred years."

"Yes, he ruined his liver with all those pills."

"He talked all about that at the hospital," Beverly says. "Something happened, but . . ."

Robert stops at a pedestrian crossing.

"A girl died," Beverly says slowly.

"Who?"

"He never wants to talk about it. . . ."

She falls silent, knits her fingers together, and drums her legs.

"Tell me what he said," Robert says in a tense voice.

"They were together one night, and then she killed herself," Beverly says, glancing at Robert. "I look like her, don't I?"

"Yes," Robert says.

"In the hospital, he said he'd killed her," Beverly whispers.

Robert startles and looks at her again. "What do you mean?" he asks.

"He said he was responsible."

Robert stares at her open-mouthed.

"He says . . . he says it was his fault?"

Beverly nods.

"It was his fault," she goes on, "because they should have been practicing on their violins, but instead they had sex, and she thought he'd tricked her into doing it so he could win the violin competition."

"It wasn't his fault."

"Yes, it was," she retorts.

Robert sinks lower in the driver's seat. He rubs his face with his hands several times.

"Dear God," Robert whispers. "I have to . . ."

The car swerves, and someone behind him honks irritably. Beverly gives him a worried look.

"What is it?" she asks.

"I . . . I have to tell him something," Robert says, making a U-turn. "I was standing behind the stage when he went on—I know what happened. Greta was on before him, she was first, and . . ."

"You were there?"

"Hang on," Robert says. "I heard everything. Greta's death had nothing to do with Axel."

He's so upset he has to stop the car again. His face is as gray as ash, and he turns toward Beverly and whispers: "Sorry. But I just have to . . ."

"Are you sure?"

"What?" he asks, looking at her.

"Are you sure it wasn't Axel's fault?"

"Yes," he replies.

"So what happened, then?"

Robert wipes tears from his eyes and opens the car door.

"Just give me a second. I have to . . . I have to talk to him," he says quietly. He steps out onto the sidewalk.

The large lime trees on Svea Boulevard are dropping clouds of pollen, which dances in the sun before landing on the cars and pedestrians. Robert grins to himself, pulls out his phone, and calls Axel's number. After three rings, his smile vanishes, and he returns to the car with the phone pressed to his ear. Only when he ends the call so that he can try Axel's cell phone instead does he realize that the car is empty. Beverly is gone. He looks around but doesn't see her anywhere.

94

AXEL ISN'T SURE how long he's been looking out of the window or how long ago he watched Robert and Beverly disappear. His thoughts have wandered back to the past. He forces himself to stop thinking about Greta and goes over to the stereo instead; he puts on the A-side of David Bowie's *The Rise and Fall of Ziggy Stardust and the Spiders from Mars* and turns up the volume.

Axel walks over to the liquor cabinet and picks out one of the most expensive bottles in his whisky collection, a Macallan from the first year of the Second World War, 1939. He pours himself half a glass, then sits down on the sofa. As he listens to the music, with downcast eyes, he detects the scent of oak barrels and dark cellars, straw, and lemon. He drinks, and the strong liquor burns his lips and fills his mouth. The whisky's flavor has matured for generations, through changes of government, through war and peace.

Axel is thinking that maybe it's just as well that this is happening now; maybe Beverly will get the help she needs after this. He has an impulse to call his brother and tell him that he loves him, then smiles at what a pathetic idea that is. He's not going to kill himself. He's going to meet what's coming toward him the best he can and try to stay standing.

He takes the whisky with him into the bedroom and

looks at the unmade bed. He hears his cell phone buzzing in the jacket hanging over the back of a chair, but creaking footsteps make him turn around.

"Beverly," he says in surprise.

Her face is dusty, and she's holding a dandelion in her hand.

"I didn't want to talk to the police. . . ."

"Where's Robert?"

"I got a ride back," she says. "Don't worry, it was all fine. . . ."

"Why do you do things like this? You should have—"

"Don't be angry. I didn't do anything wrong. I just needed to tell you something really important."

His phone starts to ring in his pocket again. "Hang on, Beverly, I need to get this. . . ."

He hunts through his pockets, finds the phone, and answers: "Axel Riessen."

He hears a distant voice. "Hello?"

"Hello," Axel replies.

"This is Raphael Guidi," the voice says in heavily accented English. "I'm sorry about the poor connection, but I'm at sea at the moment."

"Not a problem," Axel replies politely as he watches Beverly sit down on the bed.

"I'll get straight to the point," Raphael says. "I'm calling to see if you've had time to sign the export license for the Kenya shipment yet. I was counting on having the ship leave the harbor by now."

Axel holds the phone to his ear and goes out into the living room, but he can't hear anything except his own breathing. He thinks about the photograph and how Palmcrona was holding his glass of champagne and laughing so that his gums showed.

"Are you still there?" Raphael Guidi says over the crackly line.

"I'm not going to sign the export license," Axel replies curtly, feeling a shiver run down his spine.

"Perhaps I can persuade you to change your mind," Raphael says. "You'll have to think about whether there's anything I could offer you that might . . ."

"You have nothing I want."

"I think you're mistaken there. When I enter into a contract . . ."

Axel ends the call, and everything goes silent. He puts the phone back in his jacket and is filled with unease, almost as if he's having a premonition. He starts to walk toward the hallway leading to the stairs. When he looks out the window, he can see movement in the park, like a transparent shadow between the bushes heading for the house. Axel moves to the other window but can't see anything. There's a noise from downstairs, like a small pane of glass cracking. Even though Axel can't help thinking that it's absurd, he understands what's going on. His heart is beating very fast. His body fills with adrenaline, and all his senses become extremely alert. Moving as fast as he can without running, he goes back into the bedroom. Gorgeous sunlight is streaming through the gap between the curtains onto Beverly's feet. She's lying down on the unmade bed, with the Dürrenmatt book on her stomach.

"Axel," she says, "I came back to tell you something good—"

"Don't be scared," he interrupts as calmly as he can, "but you need to hide under the bed. Do it now, and stay there, for at least an hour."

She responds at once. Without asking any questions, she just crawls under the bed. He can hear rapid footsteps on the stairs. At least two people, he thinks. His heart is beating hard. He looks around, unsure of what to do. His mind is racing. He takes his phone out of his jacket and hurries into the living room. Behind him, he hears steps heading toward the library. With trembling fingers he unlocks the phone and hears the floor creak as someone runs in on soft feet. There's no time to make the call. He is trying to reach the window overlooking the street to yell for help when someone grabs his right wrist and presses something cool against his neck. It's a Taser. Sixty-nine thousand volts shoot into his body. There's an electrical crackle, but Axel just registers it as a series of heavy blows, as if someone were hitting his neck with an iron pipe. He doesn't know that he's screaming, because his brain has shut down and the world disappears.

The men have already taped his mouth shut when he starts to regain consciousness, one fragment at a time. He's lying on the floor, and his body is twitching spasmodically. His arms and legs are shaking. He can't possibly defend himself. His muscles feel paralyzed, but what feels like a burning insect bite on his neck overwhelms everything else in terms of sheer pain.

With brusque familiarity, the men tie his arms, thighs, and ankles, then roll him up in white plastic. It rustles softly, and he thinks he's going to suffocate, but the air doesn't run out. Though he tries to twist his body, it's hopeless; he can't even control his own muscles. The two men calmly carry him down the stairs, out through the front door, and into a waiting van.

95

JOONA TRIES TO CALL Pontus Salman back, but the row-boat slips farther out on the lake. Joona runs up to meet the psychologist and two police officers from Södertälje. He leads them down to the pier and tells them that they should be careful but that he doesn't believe Pontus Salman is going to hurt either himself or anyone else.

"Just make sure you keep track of him, and I'll be in touch as soon as possible," he says, then hurries back to his car.

As Joona drives across the bridge over Fittja Bay, he thinks about how Pontus said he was sure Axel would sign a contract with Guidi. Joona had asked if he could just refuse, but Pontus had said that he wouldn't want to.

He dials Axel's number, seeing Véronique, Pontus's wife, in his mind's eye: the disappointed set of her mouth and the fear in her eyes as she told them that once you've kissed Guidi on the hand there's no way back.

The word "nightmare" keeps coming back, Joona thinks. Palmcrona's housekeeper had used it. Véronique had said that Guidi managed to get everyone to talk about their worst nightmare, and then Pontus had claimed that Palmcrona managed to escape his nightmare by committing suicide.

"He didn't have to confront his nightmare," he had said.

Joona thinks about the fact that Stefan Bergkvist never

found out that Palmcrona was his father. He thinks about the intense heat that burned the flesh from his skeleton.

You can't break a Paganini contract even with your own death.

Joona calls Axel's cell phone again, then tries the direct number for the Inspectorate for Strategic Products.

"Director General Axel Riessen's office," a female voice answers.

"I'm trying to reach Axel Riessen," Joona says quickly.

"I'm afraid he's not available at the moment," she replies.

"I'm a detective, and I need to talk to him at once."

"I understand, but—"

"Interrupt him if he's in a meeting."

"He isn't here," she says, raising her voice. "He didn't turn up this morning, and I haven't been able to reach him on his phone."

"I see," Joona says, ending the call.

Joona parks his Volvo outside the gate of Axel's house. Spotting someone closing the door to his brother's part of the building, Joona runs over and rings the doorbell. The lock rattles, and the door opens again.

"Oh," Robert says when he sees Joona. "Hello."

"Is Axel home?"

"He should be, but I just got in," he replies. "Has something happened?"

"I've been trying to reach him."

"Me, too," Robert says, letting Joona in.

They go up half a flight of stairs into a large lobby with a pink glass chandelier. Robert knocks on a door, then walks into Axel's part of the house. They hurry upstairs in silence.

"Axel!" Robert calls.

They look around, walking through the rooms. Everything is the same as usual. The stereo is lit up but quiet, and there's a volume of the *Encyclopædia Britannica* on the library cart.

"Do you know if he went somewhere?" Joona asks.

"No," Robert says in a remarkably weary voice. "But he does so many strange things."

"What do you mean?"

"You think you know him, but . . . Oh, I don't know."

Joona goes into the bedroom and looks around quickly. He sees a large oil painting resting on the floor, facing the wall, a dandelion in a whisky glass, the unmade bed, and a book.

96

JOONA PARKS THE CAR by Kronoberg Park and walks quickly across the grass toward police headquarters as he calls the Södertälje Police. He's starting to worry that he didn't have time to wait while they were dealing with Pontus Salman.

His unease only gets worse when the officer in Södertälje explains that he doesn't know where Pontus is. "I'll call you back," says the man in a Gotland accent. "Just give me a couple of minutes."

"But you have him?" Joona asks.

"We're supposed to have him," the man says hesitantly.

"I made it very clear that he was to be held."

"You don't have to start in on me," the officer says. "I'm sure my colleagues did their jobs."

He taps at a computer and mutters to himself, then speaks again.

"Yes, we've got him, and we've seized his shotgun, a Winchester 400."

"Good. Hold him and we'll send a car to get him," Joona says.

He takes the elevator up, walks quickly along the hallway, and has almost reached Carlos's office when his phone rings.

It's Disa. Though he doesn't really have time to take the call, he answers anyway.

"Hi," Disa says. "Are you coming tomorrow?"

"You said you didn't want to celebrate your birthday."

"I know, but I was thinking . . . just you and me."

"That sounds good," Joona says.

"I have something important to tell you," she says.

"Okay," Joona says as he reaches Carlos's door.

"I—"

"Sorry, Disa," he interrupts, "but I can't talk right now. I'm on my way into an important meeting."

"I've got a surprise," she says.

"Disa, I've got to go now," he says, opening the door.

"But . . . ," Disa says.

"I'm really sorry, but I don't have time."

He hangs up, walks into Carlos's office, closes the door behind him, and sits down on the sofa next to Saga.

"We can't reach Axel Riessen, and we're worried it's connected to the export license," Joona says. "We think Raphael Guidi is behind this, so we need an arrest warrant as soon as—"

"An arrest warrant?" Carlos interrupts in astonishment. "Axel Riessen hasn't been answering his phone for two hours, and he didn't arrive at work this morning, and now you think he's been kidnapped by Raphael Guidi, a successful businessman who has never been charged with a crime?"

Carlos raises his hand and starts counting on his fingers. "The Swedish Police have nothing on him, Europol has nothing on him, Interpol has nothing, and I've also spoken to the police in France, Italy, and Monaco."

"But I've spoken to Anja," Joona says with a smile.

"You've spoken to . . ."

Carlos stops speaking as the door opens and Anja comes in.

"In the past ten years, Raphael Guidi's name has cropped up in six investigations relating to arms offenses, financial offenses, and deaths," she says.

"But investigations," Carlos interjects, "they don't mean—"

"Can I just tell you what I found?" she interrupts.

"Yes, of course."

"The suspicions against Guidi were dismissed at an early stage in almost every case, and nothing has ever gone to trial."

"Nothing," Carlos says.

"His business earned a hundred and twenty-three million dollars on Operation Desert Storm by supplying the Nighthawk attack plane with AGM-65 Maverick missiles," Anja goes on after consulting her notes. "But one of his subsidiaries also supplied Serbian forces with the rocket munitions used to shoot down the same planes during the Kosovo War."

Anja shows them a photograph of Guidi in sunglasses with bright-yellow lenses. He's wearing casual clothes: cornflower-blue pants and an ironed but loose shirt of the same color. He's standing between two black-clad bodyguards in front of a smoke-colored Lamborghini.

"Guidi's wife, Fiorenza Colini, used to be a famous violinist," Anja says. "Only a year after the birth of their son, Peter, she got breast cancer. She underwent all available treatments, but died when the boy was seven."

A newspaper clipping from *La Repubblica* shows Fiorenza Colini holding a beautiful red violin to her shoulder, with the orchestra of La Scala behind her and the conductor Riccardo Muti beside her. She is wearing a slim-cut, shimmering platinum dress with silver embroidery and tiny glass prisms stitched into it. She is smiling to herself with her eyes closed. Her elbow is held low, the bow on its way down, her left hand arching over the body of the violin as she plays a high note.

Anja flips to a *Newsweek* cover that shows Guidi, standing next to Alice Cooper, showing off his newborn son, under the heading "Billion-Dollar Baby."

Another clipping shows him wearing a pale suit and talking to Silvio Berlusconi, with three blonde women in minuscule bikinis sitting around a heart-shaped pink marble swimming pool behind them.

"Guidi is a resident of Monaco, but it looks like you have to head out to sea if you want to meet him," Anja goes on. "Since his wife's death, he spends almost all his time on his mega-yacht, *Theresa*. It was built by Lürssen fifteen years ago and was the most expensive yacht in the world at the time."

A small picture in the French edition of *Vogue* shows the dart-shaped white vessel on the open sea. A double-page spread inside, with the headline "Lion en Cannes," contains a number of pictures from a party held on board during the Cannes Film Festival. All the men are wearing dinner jackets. Kevin Costner is shown talking to Salma Hayek, and Guidi is seen standing between his wife and the famous Swedish *Playboy* model Victoria Silvstedt. Behind him stand two blank-faced bodyguards. The harbor is visible through the many windows of the dining room. Toucans in cages hang from the ceiling, and in the middle of the dining room is a cage containing a large male lion.

They hand the clippings back to Anja, who goes on calmly: "Now, shall we all listen to this? The Belgian Security Service recorded a phone call between an Italian prosecutor and Salvatore Garibaldi, who used to be a brigadier in the Italian army."

She distributes a hasty translation, then inserts a USB

stick into Carlos's computer and clicks on the audio file. A voice begins to talk rapidly, explaining the circumstances of the call in French: location, date, and time. Then there's a metallic click as a call goes through.

When the file has crackled for a moment, a voice can clearly be heard:

"I'm listening, and I'm prepared to instigate an investigation," the prosecutor says.

"I'd never testify against Raphael, not even under torture, not . . ."

Salvatore Garibaldi's voice disappears in static, then becomes audible again, weaker, as if through a closed door.

". . . with recoil buffers and recoilless rocket launchers . . . and a hell of a lot of mines, landmines, antipersonnel mines, antitank mines . . . Raphael would never . . . Like Rwanda, he didn't care. That was all clubs and machetes—there was no money in that. But when it changed and spilled over into the Congo, he wanted to be part of it, because that's when it became dynamic, in his opinion. First he armed the Rwandan Patriotic Front to put Mobutu under serious pressure, then he started to pump heavy weaponry to the Hutus again, so that they could fight back against the RPF."

There's a weird whistling noise through the static, then a clicking sound, before his voice comes back. He's breathing quickly, muttering to himself, and then says, very clearly: "This business about the nightmare, I didn't believe it was real. I had to stand alongside, holding her sweating hand. . . . My daughter, she was fourteen. So beautiful, so perfect . . . Raphael . . . he did it himself, he wanted to wield the knife, kept yelling that he owned my nightmare. It's beyond belief."

The line crackles, and they can hear shouting and glass breaking; the recording stutters.

"Why would anyone want to do things like that . . . ? He got the knife from one of his bodyguards . . . my daughter's face, her beautiful, beautiful . . ."

Salvatore Garibaldi is sobbing loudly, moaning, shouting that he just wants to die.

The recording crackles again, then stops. Silence descends on Carlos's office.

"This recording," Carlos says after a while, "it doesn't prove anything. He said at the outset that he wasn't going to testify, so I presume the prosecutor dropped the investigation."

"Three weeks after this phone call, Salvatore Garibaldi's head was found by a dog walker," Anja says. "It was lying in a ditch."

"What was that about his daughter?" Joona asks in a low voice. "What happened?"

"Fourteen-year-old Maria Garibaldi is still missing," Anja says bluntly.

Carlos sighs, mutters something to himself, then goes over to the aquarium and looks at his paradise fish for a while before turning back to the others. "What am I supposed to do? You can't prove that the ammunition is going to Sudan, and you've got nothing to show that Axel Riessen's disappearance is in any way connected to Raphael Guidi," he says. "Give me just a shred of evidence and I'll talk to the prosecutor, but I need something definite, not just—"

"I know it's him," Joona interrupts.

"Not just Joona telling me that he knows," Carlos concludes.

"We need the authority and resources to arrest Guidi for crimes in violation of Swedish and international law," Joona persists stubbornly.

"Not without proof," Carlos says.

"We'll get proof," Joona says.

"You need to persuade Pontus Salman to testify."

"We're picking him up today, but I think it's going to be hard to get him to agree. He's still too scared—so scared that he was prepared to kill himself," Joona says.

"But if we arrest Guidi, Salman might talk. I mean, if things calm down," Saga says.

"We can't just arrest a man like Raphael Guidi without any evidence or witnesses," Carlos says emphatically.

"So what in the hell are we supposed to do?" Saga asks.

"We put pressure on Pontus Salman, that's all we can—"

"But I think Axel Riessen is in danger," Joona says. "There's no time to lose, because . . ."

The four of them stop talking and look at the door as Senior Prosecutor Jens Svanehjälm walks into the room.

97

THE AIR-CONDITIONING makes the car feel cold. Pontus's hands are shaking on the steering wheel. He's already half-way across the Lidingö Bridge. One of the Finland ferries is on its way out, and someone is burning leaves.

Only a couple of hours have passed since he was sitting in his rowboat trying to put the barrel of his shotgun in his mouth. He can still taste the metal and feel the way it scraped against his teeth. It's a terrifying memory.

A woman came down onto the pier with the detective and asked him to come closer. She looked as if she had something important to tell him. She was about forty, with a bluish, punk, spiky hairstyle and red lipstick. Later on, when he was sitting across from her in a small gray room, he found out that her name was Gunilla and that she was a psychologist.

She had spoken to him sternly and seriously about the shotgun and about what he was thinking of doing out on the lake.

"Why did you want to die, Pontus?" Gunilla had asked.

"I didn't," he had replied truthfully.

The silence filled the little room. Then they kept talking, and as he answered her questions, he became more and more convinced that he didn't want to die, that he'd much rather run away, and he had started thinking about going somewhere—just disappearing and starting a new life as a different person.

The car is across the bridge now. Pontus looks at his watch and feels the warmth of relief spread through his chest. By now, Véronique's plane must have left Swedish airspace.

He's talked to Véronique about French Polynesia and can see her in his imagination, walking out of the airport with a blue bag in her hand, wearing a wide-brimmed hat that she has to hold on to in the wind.

Why shouldn't he escape, too? All he has to do is hurry back to the house and get his passport from the desk drawer.

I don't want to die, Pontus thinks, watching the traffic rush past.

He rowed out onto the lake to escape his nightmare, but he was incapable of firing the gun.

I'll take any flight, he thinks. *I can go to Iceland, Japan, Brazil. If Guidi really wanted to kill me, I wouldn't be alive now.*

Pontus turns into the driveway in front of his house and gets out of the car. He breathes in the smell of sun-warmed asphalt, exhaust fumes, and greenery.

His street is deserted. Everyone is at work, and the children still have a few days of school left.

Pontus unlocks the door and walks in. The house is dark; the blinds are closed.

He keeps his passport in his office, so he starts to go downstairs. When he reaches the ground floor, he suddenly stops and listens, hearing an odd dragging sound, like a wet rag being pulled over a tiled floor.

"Véronique?" he says, in a voice that's almost inaudible.

Pontus sees the calm light of the pool reflected off the white stone wall. He walks forward slowly, his heart thudding.

98

Jens Svanehjälm says a muted hello to Saga, Joona, and Carlos, then sits down. The material that Anja has uncovered is lying on the low table in front of him. Svanehjälm drinks his soy latte, looks at the top picture, then turns to Carlos.

"I think you're going to have a hard time trying to convince me," he says.

"But we'll do it," Joona says with a smile.

"Make my day," the prosecutor says.

Svanehjälm's thin neck, with no visible Adam's apple, and his narrow, sloping shoulders only emphasize the impression that he's a boy dressed as a grown-up.

"It's pretty complicated," Saga says. "We believe that Axel Riessen from the ISP has been abducted and that his disappearance is connected to everything that's happened in the past few days."

She stops when Carlos's phone rings.

"Sorry, I thought I'd made it very clear that we weren't to be disturbed," he says, then picks up the phone. "Yes, Carlos Eliasson . . ."

He listens, his cheeks flush, he mumbles that he understands, says thanks for the call, and puts the phone down with a reserved gesture.

"I'm sorry," Carlos says.

"No problem," Jens Svanehjälm replies.

"I mean, I'm sorry to have dragged you to this meeting," Carlos explains. "That was Axel Riessen's secretary at the ISP. I contacted her earlier today. . . . She says she's just spoken to Axel."

"What did she say—had he been kidnapped?" Svanehjälm asks with a smile.

"He's on Raphael Guidi's boat, to discuss the outstanding issues relating to the export license."

Joona and Saga glance quickly at each other.

"Are you happy with that answer?" the prosecutor asks.

"Apparently, Axel requested a meeting with Guidi," Carlos says.

"He should have talked to us first," Saga says.

"His secretary says they've been in a meeting out on the boat all day to sort out the last details of a case that's been dragging on, and Axel is hoping to fax the signed export license to the ISP this evening."

"The export license?" Saga repeats, getting to her feet.

"Yes." Carlos smiles.

"What's he going to do after the meeting?" Joona asks.

"He . . ."

Carlos trails off and looks at Joona in surprise.

"How did you know he was going to do anything after the meeting?" he asks. "The secretary said Axel had booked some vacation time to sail along the coast, all the way to Kaliningrad."

"Sounds lovely," Svanehjälm says, standing up.

"Idiots," Saga snaps, kicking the garbage can over. "Surely you can see that he was forced to make that call?"

"Let's all try to behave like adults," Carlos mutters.

He picks the garbage can up and starts to gather the trash that fell out.

"We're done here, aren't we?" Svanehjälm says seriously.

"Axel is being held captive on Guidi's boat," Joona says. "Give us the resources to get him back."

"I might be an idiot, but I can't see a single reason to take any action at all," Svanehjälm says, walking out of the room.

They watch him close the door behind him without any hurry.

"Sorry I lost it," Saga says to Carlos. "But this doesn't make any sense. We don't believe Axel Riessen would ever sign the export license."

"Saga, I've had two lawyers look at this," Carlos explains calmly. "All they could see is that Silencia Defense's application is perfect. It's been thoroughly analyzed, and—"

"But we have that photograph where Palmcrona and Salman are meeting Guidi and Agathe al-Haji to—"

"I know that," Carlos interrupts. "That was the answer to the mystery, and now we have it, but there's nothing else we can do without evidence. We have to be able to prove what we know, and the photograph alone just isn't enough."

"So we're going to sit back and watch this ship leave Sweden even though we know the ammunition is on its way to fuel the genocide in Sudan?" Saga asks angrily.

"Just bring in Pontus Salman," Carlos replies. "Persuade him to testify against Guidi. Promise him anything, just get him to testify. . . ."

"And what if he won't do it?" Saga says.

"Then there's nothing we can do."

"We have another witness," Joona says.

"I'd be very interested in meeting this witness," Carlos says skeptically.

"We just need to get to him before he's found drowned off the coast of Kaliningrad."

"You're not going to get your way this time, Joona."

"Yes, I am."

"No."

"Yes," Joona says in a hard voice.

Carlos looks at Joona sadly. "We'll never be able to convince the prosecutor," he says after a short pause. "But because I don't want to spend the rest of my life sitting here saying no when you say yes . . ." He trails off, sighs, then goes on. "I'm giving you permission to look for Axel Riessen on your own, just to reassure yourself that he's okay."

"Joona needs backup," Saga says quickly.

"This isn't an official police operation; it's just a way to get Joona to shut up," Carlos says, throwing one arm out.

"But Joona will—"

"Right now," Carlos interrupts, "I want the two of you to get Pontus Salman from Södertälje, as I've already said. . . . Because, if you can get a witness statement that holds up, I'll see to it that we go full-force to bring Raphael Guidi in, once and for all."

"There isn't time," Joona says, heading for the door.

"I can talk to Salman on my own," Saga says.

"What about Joona? What are you—"

"I'm going to pay Guidi a visit," he says, leaving the room.

99

After lying in the trunk of a car for more than an hour, Axel is finally allowed out at a private airfield. The concrete runway is surrounded by a high fence. A helicopter is waiting in front of the control tower.

Axel can hear the plaintive cries of seagulls as he walks between the two men who abducted him. There's no point trying to talk. He climbs into the helicopter, sits down, and fastens the safety harness. The other men get into the cockpit; the one piloting the helicopter flicks a couple of switches and presses a pedal down.

The man beside the pilot takes out a map and puts it on his lap.

A strip of tape on the windshield has started to come loose.

The engine rumbles, and after a while the rotor slowly begins to turn. The narrow blades sweep sluggishly through the air as the engine heats up and the rotor spins faster and faster. The noise of the blades is deafening. The pilot grips the joystick in his right hand; then, suddenly, they take off.

At first the helicopter rises almost vertically, very gently. Then it tilts forward and starts to gain speed.

Axel's stomach lurches as they fly over the fence and up above the trees, then turn left so sharply that it feels as if the helicopter is going to roll onto its side.

They fly quickly across the green landscape below them, crossing the occasional road.

It's very loud, and Axel can see the rotor blades whirring in front of the windshield.

The mainland comes to an end, and the choppy lead-gray sea takes over.

Axel tries once more to understand what's happening to him. It began when he got the call from Guidi, who was on his boat in the Gulf of Finland, on his way out into the Baltic and down toward Latvia. It couldn't have been much more than a minute after Axel told Guidi that he wasn't going to sign the license that the two men broke into his home and zapped him in the neck with a Taser.

After half an hour in the first car, they stopped and carried him to a second car. An hour after that, they let him out onto the landing strip and led him to the helicopter.

The monotonous sea zips by beneath them. The sky above is overcast. They fly quickly at an altitude of fifty meters. The pilot is in radio contact with someone, but it's impossible to hear what he's saying.

Axel dozes off for a while, so he doesn't know how long he's been in the helicopter when he catches sight of a magnificent luxury yacht, a huge white boat with a pale-blue swimming pool and several sundecks.

They're getting closer.

Axel reminds himself that Guidi is an incredibly wealthy man and leans forward to get a better view of the yacht. It's the most astonishing boat he's ever seen. Slender and pointed like a flame, it's as white as icing. It must be a hundred meters long, with a grand two-story bridge above the aft deck.

With a thunderous roar, they sink down toward the helicopter pad on the foredeck. The rotor blades make the swell from the boat change direction and flatten as it gets pushed away.

The landing is so gentle that he almost doesn't feel it: the helicopter hovers, then descends very slowly until it's standing on the platform, rocking gently. They wait until the rotors have stopped moving. The pilot remains in the cockpit while the other man leads Axel across the landing pad. They crouch down until they get past a glass door. On the other side, the sound of the helicopter almost disappears. They're in an elegant waiting room, with a suite of armchairs, a coffee table, and a television. A man dressed in white welcomes them and invites Axel to sit down, gesturing toward the armchairs.

"Would you like anything to drink?" the man asks.

"Water, please," Axel replies.

"Still or carbonated?"

Before Axel has time to answer, another man comes in through a door.

He looks like the man who was sitting next to the helicopter pilot. Both of them are tall and broad-shouldered, with strangely similar bodies. But the new man has very fair hair and almost white eyebrows and a nose that has clearly been broken, whereas the first has gray hair and is wearing horn-rimmed glasses.

Moving silently and efficiently, they lead Axel to the rooms belowdecks.

The yacht feels peculiarly deserted. Axel notices that the pool is drained; it looks as if it hasn't been used for years. There's some broken furniture at the bottom: a cushionless sofa and some damaged office chairs.

The elegant wicker furniture on the small balcony has also seen better days. The weaving has cracked, and there are splinters sticking out from the armchairs and coffee table.

The farther in they go, the stronger Axel's impression that the boat is an empty, abandoned shell. His footsteps echo on the deserted hallway's scratched marble floor. They go in through a pair of double doors with the words "Sala da Pranzo" carved into the dark wood in elaborate lettering.

The dining room is vast. Through the panoramic windows, Axel can see nothing but open water. A wide staircase with a red carpet leads up to the next deck, where ornate crystal chandeliers hang from the ceiling. The room is made for grand dinners, but on the dining table stand a photocopier, a fax machine, two computers, and a large collection of folders.

At the far end of the dining room, a short man is sitting at a smaller table. His hair is flecked with gray, and he has a large bald spot in the middle of his scalp. Axel recognizes him immediately as Raphael Guidi. He is wearing a pair of baggy pale-blue sweatpants and a matching top with the number "7" on the chest and back. On his feet he has on a pair of white sneakers without socks.

"Welcome," the man says in heavily accented English.

His pocket rings; he pulls out his cell phone, checks the screen, but doesn't answer. Almost at once, he receives a second call, and he takes it, says a few brief words in Italian before hanging up, then looks at Axel Riessen. He gestures toward the picture windows looking out on the dark expanse of the sea.

"You kidnapped me," Axel says.

"I'm sorry about that; there wasn't time for—"

"So what do you want?"

"I want to earn your loyalty," Raphael says curtly.

The two bodyguards smile down at the floor before becoming very serious. Raphael takes a sip of the energy drink in front of him and belches quietly.

"Loyalty is all that counts," he says in a low voice, looking

Axel right in the eyes. "You said before that I have nothing you wanted, but . . ."

"It's true."

"But I think I have a very good proposal," Raphael goes on, his face contorting into a joyless grimace that's supposed to be a smile. "To win your loyalty, I know I have to offer you something you really want, maybe the thing that you wish for most of all."

Axel shakes his head. "I don't even know what I wish for most of all."

"I think you probably do," Raphael says. "You wish you could sleep again, sleep all the way through the night without—"

"How did you know—?"

He stops abruptly, and Raphael gives him a chilly, impatient glance.

"Then you presumably already know that I've tried everything," Axel says slowly.

Raphael waves his hand dismissively. "You can have a new liver."

"I'm already in line for a liver transplant," Axel says with an involuntary smile. "But there are almost no suitable donors. . . ."

"I've got a liver for you, Axel Riessen," Raphael says in his accented English.

Silence falls, and Axel can feel his face starting to flush. His ears feel warm.

"And in return?" Axel asks, swallowing hard. "You want me to sign the export license for Kenya."

"Yes. I want us to enter into a Paganini contract," Raphael replies.

"I'll never do it."

"No rush, you can think it over. It's a big decision. You need to see the exact details of the organ donor, and so on."

Thoughts are spinning through Axel's head. He tells himself he can sign the export license; then, if he gets a new liver, he can testify against Raphael afterward. He'd get police protection, he knows that. He might be forced to assume a new identity, but he'd be able to sleep again.

"Shall we eat? I'm hungry—are you hungry?" Raphael asks. "But before we eat, I want you to call your secretary at the ISP and let her know you're here."

100

SAGA HOLDS THE PHONE to her ear and stops in the hallway next to a large recycling bin.

"Don't you have anything better to do in Stockholm?" a
man with a strong Gotland accent says when she finally gets
through to the Södertälje Police.

"I'm calling about Pontus Salman," she says, trying to con-
tain the stress in her voice.

"Yes, well, he's gone now," the police officer says happily.

"What the hell do you mean?" she asks, raising her voice.

"Look, I just spoke to Gunilla Sommer, the psychologist who went with him to the emergency mental-health
unit."

"And?"

"She didn't think he was serious about committing suicide, so she let him go. Hospital beds aren't free, after all,
and—"

"Put out an alert for him," Saga says quickly.

"What for? A halfhearted suicide attempt?"

"Just make sure you find him," Saga says, and ends the call.

She starts toward the elevators, but Göran Stone steps in
front of her and stops her, holding his arms out.

"You wanted to question Pontus Salman, didn't you?" he
asks in a teasing tone.

"Yes," she replies tersely, and starts walking again, but he doesn't let her pass.

"All you have to do is wiggle your ass," he says, "and maybe flutter your eyelashes a little, and you'll get promoted or—"

"Move," Saga snaps as angry red dots flare up on her forehead.

"Okay, sorry for trying to help," Göran Stone says, pretending to be affronted. "I only wanted to tell you that we just sent four cars to Salman's home on Lidingö because—"

"What happened?" Saga asks quickly.

"His neighbors called." He smiles. "Apparently, they heard gunshots and screaming."

Saga shoves him out of the way and starts to run.

"'Thanks very much, Göran,'" he calls after her. "'You're the best, Göran!'"

.

As she drives out to Lidingö, Saga tries not to think about everything that's happened, but her mind keeps going back to the recording of the man sobbing as he talked about what Guidi did to his daughter.

Saga tells herself that she'll do a hard session in the gym that evening, then get an early night. She needs to do something to push this day out of her head.

She can't get through on Roskull Street. There are so many people out on the road that she has to park a couple of hundred meters away from Salman's house. Curious onlookers and journalists are pressed against the blue-and-white police tape, trying to get a glimpse of the house. Saga mutters apologies as she pushes her way through. Her colleague Magdalena Ronander is leaning against the dark-brown brick wall, throwing up. Pontus Salman's car is parked in front of the garage. The car's hood and the driveway are littered with tiny, bloody cubes of glass. A man's body is visible through the side window.

Pontus.

Magdalena looks up wearily, wipes her mouth with a handkerchief, and stops Saga as she's on her way into the house.

"No, don't," she says in a hoarse voice. "You definitely don't want to go in there."

Saga stops and turns toward Magdalena as if to ask something. She needs to call Joona to let him know that they no longer have a witness.

101

JOONA IS RUNNING through the arrivals hall of Helsinki-Vantaa Airport when his phone rings.

"Saga? What's happening?"

"Pontus Salman is dead. He's sitting in his car outside his house—looks like he shot himself."

Joona goes outside to the first taxi in the line and tells the driver he wants to go to the harbor.

"What did you say?" Saga asks.

"Nothing."

"We have no witnesses," Saga says, sounding agitated. "What the hell are we going to do?"

"I don't know," Joona says, closing his eyes for a few moments.

He can feel the car's movements. The taxi leaves the airport and speeds up as it pulls out onto the highway.

"You can't head out to Guidi's boat without backup...."

"The girl," Joona says suddenly.

"What?"

"Axel was playing the violin with a girl," Joona says, opening his gray eyes. "She might have seen something."

"What makes you think that?"

"There was a dandelion, a dandelion in a whisky glass...."

"What the hell are you talking about?" Saga asks.

"Just try to get hold of her."

Joona leans back in the seat before he continues to speak. He remembers how Axel was standing with his violin in his hand when the girl brought over a bunch of dandelions that had gone to seed. Then he thinks again about the dandelion with the bent stem leaning over the edge of a whisky glass in Axel's bedroom. She had been there, which means that she just might have seen something.

JOONA GOES ON BOARD the Finnish patrol vessel *Kirku*. When he shakes hands with the ship's commander, Pasi Rannikko, his mind goes automatically to Lennart Johansson, from the marine police on Dalarö—the guy who loved surfing and called himself Lance. Pasi looks a lot like Lance: a young, suntanned man with bright-blue eyes.

"Nothing about this makes me happy," Pasi Rannikko says dryly. "But my commanding officer is friends with your boss . . . and apparently that was enough."

"I'm counting on getting permission from the prosecutor while we're under way," Joona says, feeling the vibration of the boat as it heads out to sea.

"As soon as you get it, I'll contact the FNS *Hanko*. That's a fast attack craft with twenty officers and seven national-service cadets."

He points out the attack craft on the radar.

"She can get up to thirty-five knots. It'll take her less than twenty minutes to catch up with us."

"Good."

"Guidi's yacht has passed the island of Hiiumaa and is still off the coast of Estonia. . . . I hope you know that we can't board a vessel in Estonian waters unless it's an emergency or there's criminal activity openly taking place."

"Yes," Joona replies.

"Here comes the entire crew," Pasi says ironically.

A huge man with a blond beard climbs up onto the bridge. The boat's first and only mate, he introduces himself as "Niko Kapanen, like the ice-hockey player." He glances at Joona, scratches his beard, then asks tentatively: "So what's Guidi suspected of doing?"

"Kidnapping, murder of civilians, murdering police officers, arms smuggling," Joona says.

"And Sweden's sending just one police officer?"

"Yes." Joona smiles.

"And we're contributing an unarmed old barge."

"As soon as we hear from the prosecutor, we'll have almost a whole platoon," Pasi says in a monotone. "I'll call Urho Saarinen on the *Hanko*, and he'll be with us in twenty minutes."

"What about an inspection?" Niko says. "Surely we have the right to conduct a damn inspection?"

"Not in Estonian waters," Pasi says.

"Fucking hell," Niko mutters.

"It'll be okay," Joona says.

102

AXEL IS LYING FULLY DRESSED on the bed in the five-room suite he has been given. Beside him is a folder containing detailed notes about the liver donor, a man in a coma after an unsuccessful operation. All the test results are perfect—his tissue type is an exact match.

Axel stares up at the ceiling and feels his heart beating in his chest. He jumps when there's a sudden knock on the door. It's the man in white, the one who met him after the helicopter landed.

"Dinner," the man says curtly.

They walk together through the spa area. Like the rest of the yacht, it's in a state of disrepair that adds to Axel's uneasiness. He notes that the large green tubs set into the deck are full of empty bottles and beer cans. There are still plastic-wrapped towels on the elegant white marble shelves along the walls. He can see a gym behind frosted-glass walls. A double door made of matte metal slides open silently when they pass the spa area. The room is suffused with soft light that's casting slippery shadows across the walls and floor. Axel looks up and realizes that they are underneath the swimming pool. The bottom of the pool is made of glass, and the pale sky is just visible through the trash and broken furniture.

Raphael Guidi is sitting on a sofa dressed in the same sweat-pants as before, and a white T-shirt that's stretched across his stomach. He pats the seat beside him, and Axel walks over and sits down. The two bodyguards are standing behind Raphael like shadows. No one speaks. Raphael's phone rings; when he answers, he launches into a long conversation.

After a while, the white-clad man returns with a serving tray. He silently sets the table with plates and glasses, a large platter of fried hamburgers, bread, and fries, with a bottle of ketchup and a large plastic bottle of Pepsi.

Raphael doesn't look up, just continues with his phone call. He is discussing details of production rates and logistics in a neutral voice.

They all wait patiently in silence.

After fifteen minutes, Raphael ends the call and looks calmly at Axel. Then he starts to talk, softly and gently.

"Perhaps you'd like a glass of wine?" he says. "You can have a new liver in a couple of days."

"I read through the information about the donor several times," Axel says. "He's perfect. I'm impressed. It all matches. . . ."

"It's interesting, this business of wishes," Raphael says. "The things people wish for most of all. I wish my wife was still alive and that we could be together."

Axel nods.

"But, for me, wishes are closely connected to their opposites," Raphael says.

He helps himself to a hamburger and some fries, then passes the platter to Axel.

"Thank you."

"A wish on one side of the scales balances a nightmare on the other," Raphael goes on.

"Nightmare?"

"I just mean . . . as we live our lives, we get caught up in all sorts of trivialities. We carry wishes that never get fulfilled and nightmares that never come true."

"Maybe," Axel replies, taking a bite of his burger.

"Your wish—to be able to sleep again—can be fulfilled, but . . . I wonder what your nightmare looks like?"

"I don't actually know." Axel smiles.

"What are you afraid of?" Raphael asks, putting salt on his fries.

"Illness, death . . . pain."

"Of course, pain, I agree," Raphael says. "But, speaking for myself, I've started to realize that it's all about my son. He's almost an adult now, and I've started to worry that he's going to move on, leave me behind."

"Loneliness?"

"Yes, I think so," Raphael says. "Total loneliness is probably my nightmare."

"I'm already alone." Axel smiles again. "The worst has already happened."

"Don't say that," Raphael jokes.

"Well I am, but the idea of its happening again . . ."

"What do you mean?"

"Forget it. I don't want to talk about it."

"You mean, causing another girl to commit suicide?" Raphael says slowly, putting something down on the table.

"Yes."

"Who would kill herself?"

Axel sees that the object Raphael put on the table in front of him is a photograph.

It's facing the table.

Axel reaches out his hand without really wanting to. His fingers are shaking when he turns the picture over.

"Beverly," he whispers. He snatches his hand away and

gasps for breath. The photograph shows Beverly's puzzled expression caught by the flash of a camera. He stares at the picture and tries to understand what's going on. He realizes that it's meant as a warning, because the photograph was taken several days ago, inside his house, in the kitchen, when Beverly had been trying to play the violin.

103

AFTER TWO HOURS ON BOARD, Joona catches his first glimpse of Guidi's luxury yacht, gliding gracefully across the horizon. In the bright sunlight, it looks as if it's made of sparkling crystal.

Pasi comes over to join him, and nods toward the huge yacht. "How close do we get?" he asks tersely.

Joona gives him a look. "Close enough to see what's happening on board," he says calmly. "I need . . ."

He feels a stab of pain in his temples and reaches for the railing and tries to breathe slowly.

"What's the matter?" Pasi asks. "Seasick?"

"Nothing to worry about," Joona says.

The pain throbs again, and he only just manages to stay upright. He knows he can't possibly take his medication now, though, because it might make him lose focus.

Joona feels the chill wind cooling the beads of sweat on his forehead. The sun glints off the surface of the water, and in that moment he sees the bridal crown before him, shimmering in its display case in the Nordic Museum, its woven points glowing softly. He thinks about the scent of wildflowers, a church decked out for the summer wedding, and his heart is beating so fast that at first he doesn't realize that the captain is talking to him.

"What do you mean?"

Joona looks confusedly at Pasi, then over toward the big white yacht.

104

Axel can't eat any more. He feels sick. His eyes keep going to the photograph of Beverly.

Raphael is dipping fries into a little pool of ketchup on the side of his plate.

Now Axel sees a young man standing in the doorway, watching them, looking tired and anxious. He's holding a cell phone in his hand.

"Peter," Raphael calls. "Come here!"

"I don't want to," the young man says weakly.

"It wasn't a question," Raphael says irritably.

The youth walks over and shyly says hello to Axel.

"This is my son," Raphael explains, as if it were a perfectly ordinary dinner.

"Hello," Axel says.

The man who sat next to the helicopter pilot is standing by the bar, tossing peanuts to a large shaggy dog.

"Nuts aren't good for him," Peter says.

"After dinner can you bring us the violin?" Raphael asks with a sudden weariness in his voice. "Our guest is interested in music."

Peter nods. He's pale and sweating, and the rings under his eyes look almost purple.

Axel makes an effort to smile.

"What kind of violin do you have?"

Peter shrugs his shoulders. "It's much too good for me; it's an Amati. My mom was a musician. It's hers."

"An Amati?"

"Which instrument is best?" Raphael asks. "Amati or Stradivarius?"

"It depends on who's playing," Axel replies.

"You're from Sweden," Raphael says. "In Sweden, there are four Stradivarius violins, but none that Paganini played on."

"That sounds about right," Axel says.

"I collect string instruments that still remember— No," he says, interrupting himself. "Let me put it another way. If these instruments are handled correctly, you can hear the longing of a lost soul."

"Possibly," Axel says.

"I make it my business to provide a reminder of that longing when it's time to sign a contract," Raphael goes on, smiling mirthlessly. "I gather the interested parties, and we listen to music—to this unique, mournful tone—and then we sign a contract, with our wishes and nightmares as the stake. . . . That's a Paganini contract."

"I understand."

"Do you?" Raphael says. "It can't be broken, not even by death. Anyone who tries to breach the terms or take their own life will reap the fruits of their worst nightmare."

"What do you want me to say?" Axel says.

"I'm just saying that this isn't the sort of contract you can break, and I . . . How can I put it?" he asks hesitantly. "I can't see how it would benefit my enterprise if you were to mistake me for a kind person."

Raphael goes over to the large television mounted on the wall. He takes a disc from his inside pocket and inserts it in the DVD player. Peter sits down on the edge of one of the sofas. The boy looks awkwardly at the men in the room. He doesn't look anything like his father. His hair is fair, his features are sensitive, and his frame isn't broad-shouldered and compact, but long-limbed.

The screen flickers; then gray streaks appear. Axel feels a tangible, physical dread when he sees three people walk out through the door of a brick villa. He instantly recognizes two of them: Detective Joona Linna and Saga Bauer. The third person is a young woman with Latin American features.

Axel looks at the screen and watches as Joona takes out a phone and makes a call but doesn't appear to get an answer. The three of them, looking anxious and stressed, get into a car and drive away.

The camera moves slowly toward the door, which opens, and the screen goes momentarily dark from the light change until the focus adjusts. There are two large suitcases in the entryway. The camera moves into the kitchen, then down a flight of stairs, along a tiled hallway, and into a large room with a swimming pool. A woman in a bathing suit is sitting on a lounge chair, and a second woman, with a boyish haircut, is talking on her phone.

The camera moves back furtively, waits for the woman to finish her call, then moves forward again. Footsteps can be heard, and the woman with the phone turns her face toward the camera and stiffens. An expression of utter dread fills her face.

"I don't think I want to watch any more, Dad," Peter says in a thin voice.

"It just started," Raphael replies.

Suddenly the screen goes dark as the camera is switched off. When the picture comes back again, flickering as the light level stabilizes, the camera is now fixed to a stand, and the two women are sitting side by side on the floor with their backs to the tiled wall. On a chair in front of the women sits Pontus Salman. He looks as if he's breathing fast, and his body keeps shuffling nervously on the chair.

The clock in the corner of the screen indicates that the recording was made only an hour ago.

A black-clad man, his face covered by a balaclava, walks over to the woman with short hair, grabs her neck, and forces her face toward the camera.

"Sorry, sorry, sorry," Raphael says in a squeaky voice.

Axel looks at him quizzically, then hears the woman's voice: "Sorry, sorry, sorry."

Terror makes her sound clipped.

"I had no idea," Raphael squeaks, and points at the television.

"I had no idea," she pleads. "I took the photograph, but I didn't mean any harm. I didn't know how stupid it was. I just thought . . ."

"You have to choose," the man in the balaclava says to Pontus. "Who do I shoot in the knee? Your wife . . . or your sister?"

"Please," Pontus whispers, "don't do this."

"Who should I shoot?" the man asks.

"My wife," Pontus replies, almost inaudibly.

"Pontus," his wife begs. "Please, don't let him . . ."

Pontus starts to cry, his body racked with loud sobs.

"It's going to hurt if I shoot her," the man warns.

"Don't let him do it!" she screams in panic.

"Have you changed your mind? Should I shoot your sister instead?"

"No," Pontus replies.

"Ask me."

"What?" he asks, his face distraught.

"Ask me nicely to do it."

Silence. Then Axel hears Pontus Salman say, "Please ... shoot my wife in the knee."

"Seeing as you asked so nicely, I'll shoot her in both her knees," the man says, and holds his revolver to the wife's leg.

"Don't let him do it!" she screams. "Please, Pontus ..."

The man fires; there's a sharp bang, and her leg jerks. Blood sprays across the tiles. The woman screams so hard that her voice breaks. He fires again. The recoil makes the barrel of the pistol jump. Her other leg bends at an impossible angle.

Pontus's wife screams again, hoarse, almost inhuman. Her body jerks with pain, and blood spreads out across the tiled floor beneath her.

Pontus throws up, and the man in the balaclava watches him.

His wife leans sideways, breathing hard as she tries to reach her wounded legs with her hands. The other woman looks as if she's in shock. Her face is pale, and her eyes are just big black holes.

"Your sister's mentally ill, isn't she?" the man asks curiously. "Do you think she knows what's going on?"

He pats Pontus's head consolingly, then says: "Shall I rape your sister or shoot your wife?"

Pontus doesn't answer. He looks as if he's going to pass out—his eyes start to roll back in his head—but the man slaps him across the face. "Answer me: Shall I shoot your wife or rape your sister?"

Pontus Salman's sister shakes her head.

"Rape her," Pontus's wife whispers between gasped breaths. "Please, Pontus. Please! Tell him to rape her."

"Rape her," Pontus whispers.

"What?"

"Rape my sister."

"Okay, soon," the man says.

Axel looks down at the floor between his feet. He tries hard not to hear the moaning from the television, the pleading, the raw, terrified screams. He tries to fill his head with memories of music, to conjure up the spaces Bach creates, spaces full of radiant beams of light.

Finally, the television is silent. Axel looks up at the screen. The two women are lying dead against the wall. He sees the man in the balaclava breathing heavily, a knife in one hand and the pistol in the other.

"The nightmare has come true—now you can kill yourself," the man on the screen says, tossing the pistol to Pontus and then walking away, behind the camera.

105

Saga walks away from Magdalena and steps back over the cordon. The crowd is even bigger now, and a large truck from Swedish Television has arrived. A uniformed police officer is trying to get people to move so that the ambulance can get through.

Saga leaves it all behind her and takes a detour, up a paved path into someone's garden. She runs across a lawn toward the car.

"The girl," Joona had said out of the blue on the phone. "Just try to get ahold of her."

He was quiet for a short while before he started to speak again.

"There was a girl in Axel's house. He called her Beverly. Talk to his brother, Robert. She's about seventeen years old. We must be able to trace her."

"How long do I have to get the prosecutor on our side with this?"

"Not long," Joona had said. "But you'll do it."

As Saga drives into Stockholm, she tries calling Axel, but there's no answer. She calls the main number for the National Crime Unit and asks to be put through to Joona's assistant, Anja.

"Anja Larsson," a voice replies after just half a ring.

"Hi, this is Saga Bauer from the Security Police; we met earlier in . . ."

"I know," Anja replies coolly.

"I was wondering if you could track down a girl. Her name might be Beverly, and—"

"Shall I invoice the Security Police for that, then?"

"Do whatever the hell you like, as long as you get me a fucking phone number before . . ."

"Watch your language, young lady."

"Forget I asked."

Saga swears and honks loudly at a car that's stopped at a green light. She's about to end the call when Anja speaks.

"How old is she?"

"Around seventeen."

"There's a Beverly of that age, Beverly Andersson. She doesn't have a registered phone number . . . but she's listed at the same address as her father, Evert Andersson."

"Okay, I'll call him. Can you text me his number?"

"I already have."

"Thanks—thank you, Anja. Sorry I was impatient. I'm just worried Joona will do something stupid if he doesn't get backup."

"Have you spoken to him?"

"He's the one who asked me to look for the girl. I've never even met her. I don't know. . . . He's counting on me to sort this out, but . . ."

"Call Beverly's dad, and I'll keep on looking," Anja says, and hangs up.

Saga pulls over and dials the number Anja has sent her.

106

IN A KITCHEN in the middle of Skåne, a man startles when his phone rings. He's just spent over an hour trying to disentangle one of the heifers that got itself caught on the neighbor's barbed wire fence. Evert Andersson has blood on his fingers and on his blue overalls.

His dirty fingers aren't the only things stopping him from answering the phone—there isn't really anyone he feels like talking to right now. He leans over and looks at the screen and sees that it's a withheld number. Probably one of those marketing calls.

He waits until it stops ringing. But then it starts again. Evert Andersson takes another look at the screen and eventually answers: "Andersson."

"Hello, my name is Saga Bauer," a stressed-sounding female voice says. "I'm a police officer, a detective with the Security Police. I'm trying to contact your daughter, Beverly Andersson."

"What's happened?"

"She hasn't done anything, but we believe she may have important information that could help us."

"And now she's missing?" he asks weakly.

"I thought you might have a phone number I can reach her at," Saga says.

Evert thinks of how he once saw his daughter as his heir, someone to carry on the family business, take over running the house, barns, offices, and fields. She would walk the farm the way her mother had, in a sheepskin coat, with her hair in a braid over one shoulder.

But even as a small child there had been something different about Beverly, something that scared him.

As she grew up, she became more and more unusual. One time, when she was eight, maybe nine years old, he walked into one of the barns to find her sitting in an empty pen on an overturned bucket, singing to herself with her eyes closed. She was lost in the sound of her own voice. He had been about to yell at her to stop being so silly, but the joyous expression on her face bewildered him. From that moment, he knew there was something inside her that he would never understand. And he stopped talking to her. As soon as he tried to say anything, all his words would vanish.

When her mother died, the silence on the farm became absolute.

Beverly started to wander. She could be missing for hours at a time, even whole days. The police frequently had to bring her home. She would go anywhere with anyone who spoke to her kindly.

"There's nothing I want to say to her. So why would I have a phone number?" he says in his brusque, dismissive Skåne accent.

"Are you sure you—"

"It's not the sort of a thing a Stockholmer would understand," he snaps, putting the phone down.

He looks at his fingers, sees the blood on his knuckles, the dirt under and around his fingernails, in every crease and crack. He walks slowly to the green armchair, picks up the entertainment supplement of the evening paper, and starts to leaf through it. They're broadcasting a tribute to the television personality Ossian Wallenberg. The paper falls to the floor when Evert's tears catch him by surprise, as he suddenly remembers that Beverly used to sit on the sofa next to him and watch *Golden Friday*.

107

SAGA SWEARS LOUDLY TO HERSELF. She closes her eyes and slams her hand on the steering wheel several times. Slowly, she tells herself that she needs to focus, to find a way to make progress before it's too late. She's so immersed in thought that she startles when her phone rings.

"It's me again," Anja says. "I'm putting you through to Herbert Saxéus at the Sacred Heart Clinic."

"What . . . ?"

"Saxéus looked after Beverly the two years she lived at the clinic."

"Thanks, that's—"

But Anja has already connected Saga to another line.

Saga waits as the phone rings. Sacred Heart Clinic, she thinks, remembering that the hospital is in Torsby, east of Stockholm.

"Hello, Herbert here," a warm voice says in her ear.

"Hello, my name is Saga Bauer. I'm a police officer, a detective with the Security Police. I need to get in touch with a girl who used to be one of your patients, Beverly Andersson."

The line goes quiet.

"Is she okay?" the doctor asks after a pause.

"I don't know. I need to talk to her," Saga says quickly. "It really is urgent."

"She's still staying with Axel Riessen, who . . . Well, he's her informal guardian."

"So she lives there?" Saga asks, turning the key in the ignition.

"Axel is letting her stay there until she finds a place of her own," he replies. "She's only seventeen, but it would have been a mistake to try to force her to move back home."

The traffic is relatively light, and Saga is able to drive fast.

"Can you tell me what Beverly Andersson was being treated for?" she asks.

The doctor takes a deep breath, then says in his deep, friendly voice, "As her doctor, I'd say she was suffering from a serious personality disorder when she first came here, called Cluster B."

"What does that mean?"

"Nothing," Herbert Saxéus replies, clearing his throat. "If you were to ask me as a human being, I'd say that Beverly is healthy, probably healthier than most people. I know it sounds ridiculous, but she isn't the one who's sick."

"The world is."

"Yes," he says with a sigh.

Saga thanks him and ends the call as she turns onto Valhalla Boulevard. The back of the driver's seat is sticky with her sweat. Her phone rings, and she accelerates past the traffic light just as it's turning red before she answers.

"I thought I'd have a word with Beverly's dad as well," Anja says. "He's a very nice man, but he's had a rough day, looking after a wounded cow. His family's always lived there, and now he's the only one left on the farm. We talked about *The Wonderful Adventures of Nils*, and in the end he went and got some letters that Beverly had sent him. He hadn't even opened them. Can you imagine such a stubborn man? Beverly had written her phone number in every letter."

Saga thanks Anja several times, then calls the number. She pulls up outside Axel and Robert's house as her call to Beverly goes through.

Ring after ring disappears into the void. Saga can feel her body trembling from exertion. Time is running out. Joona is going to end up completely alone when he confronts Guidi.

With the phone clutched to her ear, she walks up to Robert's door and rings the bell. Suddenly there is a click on the phone, and she hears a faint rustling sound.

"Beverly?" Saga says. "Is that you?"

She can hear someone breathing.

"Answer me, Beverly," Saga says, in the gentlest voice she can muster. "Where are you?"

"I . . ."

The line goes quiet again.

"What did you say? What did you say, Beverly? I couldn't quite hear you."

"I can't come out yet," the girl whispers, and ends the call.

ROBERT IS SILENT and pale when he leaves Saga in Beverly's room and asks her to lock up behind herself when she's done. The room looks almost uninhabited. The only things in it are some basic items of clothing, a pair of boots, a down jacket, and a phone charger.

Saga locks the door behind her, then goes into Axel's apartment to try to figure out what Joona had meant about the girl's being able to testify. She passes through the silent rooms. The door to Axel's bedroom is ajar. Saga walks past the bed and into the adjoining bathroom, then returns to the bedroom. Something has put her on edge. There's an anxious atmosphere in the room, and Saga puts one hand on the Glock in her shoulder holster. On the table is a whisky glass with the wilted remains of a dandelion.

Dust is moving slowly in the sunlight. Her heart starts to beat faster as a branch outside scrapes the window.

She goes over to look at the unmade bed.

She imagines she can hear careful footsteps from the library and is about to creep in that direction when a hand grabs her ankle. There's someone lying under the bed. She pulls free, draws her pistol, and accidentally knocks over the table holding the glass.

Saga gets down on her knees, pointing the gun, but quickly lowers it again.

From the darkness under the bed, a girl is looking at her with big, frightened eyes. Saga puts her pistol back in its holster, then lets out a deep sigh.

"You're glowing," the girl whispers.

"Beverly?" Saga asks.

"Can I come out now?"

"I swear, you can come out now," Saga says calmly.

"Has an hour passed? Axel told me not to come out until an hour had passed."

"It's been much longer than an hour, Beverly."

Saga helps her out of the cramped space. The girl is stiff from having lain still for so long. Her hair is very short, and her arms are covered with drawings.

"What were you doing under Axel's bed?" Saga asks, trying to keep her voice steady.

"He's my best friend," Beverly replies quietly.

"I think he's in danger. You have to tell me what you know."

Beverly's face turns red, and her eyes fill with tears. "I haven't . . ." Beverly's mouth begins to quiver.

"Hey, don't get upset," Saga says, trying again to stifle the anxiety in her voice.

"I realized that something had happened as soon as I came in," Beverly says quietly, "because Axel's face was really pale."

She stops and turns her face away.

"Please, go on, Beverly. We're in a hurry."

Beverly whispers an apology, wipes her cheeks quickly, then looks at Saga with moist eyes. "Axel came into the room," she goes on, more composed now. "He told me to crawl under the bed and stay hidden for a whole hour.... Then he rushed out into the living room, and I don't know ... I only saw their legs, but two men went in behind him. They did something terrible to him. He screamed, and they threw him on the floor and wrapped him in white plastic and carried him out. It all happened really fast. I didn't see their faces.... I don't even know if they were people...."

"Hold on a second," Saga says, taking her phone out. "You need to come with me and tell this to a man named Jens Svanehjälm."

Saga calls Carlos, her hands shaking with stress. "We've got a witness who saw Axel Riessen being abducted against his will. We've got a witness," she repeats. "The witness saw Riessen being attacked and kidnapped. That has to be enough."

Saga looks into Beverly's eyes as she listens to the response.

"Good, we're coming in," she says. "Get Svanehjälm, and make sure he has Europol prepared."

108

GUIDI WALKS through the dining room, a black leather folder in his hand. He puts it down on the table and pushes it across to Axel.

"Pontus Salman's nightmare, as you may have guessed, was being forced to choose between his wife and his sister," he explains. "I don't know, I've never found it necessary to be so explicit before, but I have—how can I put it?—I have found that some people imagine that they can escape their nightmare by dying. Don't misunderstand me: Most of the time, everything is perfectly pleasant and civilized. I'm a very generous man toward people who are loyal."

"You're threatening to hurt Beverly."

"You can choose between her and your brother, if you'd prefer that?" Raphael says, and swallows some of his energy drink. After wiping one corner of his mouth, he asks Peter to fetch the violin.

"Have I told you I only own instruments that Paganini himself played?" he asks. "That's the only thing I care about. It's said that Paganini hated his face. Personally, I believe he sold his soul to the devil to be worshipped. He called himself an ape, but when he played, women threw themselves at him. It was worth the cost. He would play and play until he seemed to be on fire."

Axel looks out through the huge windows at the great expanse of water. He can make out the white helicopter he arrived on through the smaller windows facing the foredeck. His thoughts keep alternating between the hideous film and possible escape routes.

He feels incredibly tired as he sits and listens to Raphael talking about violins: Stradivarius's fixation on the higher notes, the hardness of the wood, the slow growth of maple and fir trees.

Raphael pauses, smiles lifelessly once again, and says: "As long as you are loyal, you can have it all—a healthy liver, deep, untroubled sleep, a good life. All that is required is that you don't forget your contract with me."

"And you want the export license signed."

"I would want that in either case, but I don't want to force you. I don't want to kill you. That would be a waste. I want . . ."

"My loyalty," Axel concludes.

"Is that foolish, do you think?" Raphael asks. "Think for a moment, then count the number of people in your life whom you know to be completely loyal."

Silence settles between them. Axel stares blankly in front of him.

"Exactly," Raphael says sadly.

109

AXEL OPENS THE FOLDER and sees that it contains all the documentation necessary for the MS *Icelus* to be granted permission to leave Gothenburg Harbor with its cargo of ammunition.

The only thing missing is his signature.

Raphael's son, Peter, comes back into the room, his face pale. He's holding an extremely beautiful violin, a reddish-brown instrument with a bowed top plate. Axel can see at once that it's an Amati, and an extremely well-preserved one at that.

"As I think I mentioned, I believe certain music is best suited to what we're about to do," Raphael says softly. "That violin belonged to his mother . . . and, long before that, Niccolò Paganini played it."

"It was made in 1657," Peter says. He takes his keys and cell phone out of his pockets and puts them on the table before raising the violin to his shoulder.

The boy places the bow on the strings and hesitantly starts to play. Axel immediately identifies the opening notes of Paganini's most famous work, 24 Caprices. It's reputed to be the most difficult violin piece in the world. The boy plays far too slowly, as if he were underwater.

"It's a generous contract," Raphael says quietly.

It's still bright outside, and light from the big picture windows spreads a shimmer over the room.

Axel thinks about Beverly, how she had crept up onto his bed at the clinic and whispered: "I saw the light in here. You're glowing."

"Have you had enough time to think it over?" Raphael asks.

Axel can't bring himself to look into Raphael's desolate eyes. He looks down as he picks up the pen. He can hear his own heart beating and tries to hide the fact that he's breathing very fast.

This time he isn't going to draw a stick figure; he's going to sign his name and pray to God that Raphael will be content with that and let him return to Sweden.

Axel feels the pen shake in his hand. He puts his other hand on top of it to hold it still, takes a deep breath, then puts the tip of the pen to the empty line on the page.

"Wait," Raphael says. "Before you sign anything, I want to know if you're going to be loyal."

Axel looks up and meets his gaze.

"If you really are prepared to confront your nightmare if you breach the contract, you need to prove it by kissing my hand."

"What?" Axel whispers.

"Do we have a contract?"

"Yes," Axel replies.

"Kiss my hand," Raphael says.

His son is playing more and more slowly; though he is trying to get his fingers to obey him, to change position, he keeps getting the difficult transitions wrong. He loses his place and gives up.

"Keep going," Raphael says without looking at him.

"It's too hard for me. It doesn't sound good."

"Peter, it's very immature to give up before you've even—"

"Play it yourself," his son says.

Raphael's face becomes completely rigid, like a rock.

"Do as I say," he says, forcing himself to remain calm.

The boy stands still, looking at the floor. Raphael's right hand goes to the zipper of his jacket. "Peter, I thought it sounded good," he says in a composed voice.

"The bridge is crooked," Axel says, almost in a whisper.

Peter looks at the violin, blushing. "Can it be repaired?" he asks.

"Adjusting it is easy. I can do it if you'd like," Axel says.

"Will it take long?" Raphael asks.

"No," Axel replies.

He puts the pen down, takes the violin, and turns it over, feeling how light it is. He's never held a genuine Amati before, and certainly never one that Paganini played.

Raphael's phone rings. He takes it out and looks at it, then moves away as he listens to someone on the other end.

"That can't be right," he says, an odd expression on his face.

A strange smile plays across his lips; then he says something in a tense voice to the bodyguards. They leave the dining room and hurry up the stairs after Raphael.

Peter watches Axel as he loosens the strings. The instrument creaks. Axel carefully moves the bridge, then stretches the strings across it.

"Is it okay?" Peter whispers.

"Yes," Axel replies as he tunes the violin. "Try it now and you'll see."

"Thanks," Peter says, taking the violin.

Axel notices that Peter's cell phone is still on the table, and says: "Keep playing. You'd just finished the first progression and were about to play the pizzicato."

"Now I'm even more embarrassed," Peter says, turning away.

Axel leans on the table, carefully reaching out his hand

behind him to touch the phone and manages to nudge it in a way that makes it spin around silently.

With his back to Axel, Peter puts the violin to his shoulder and raises his bow.

Axel gets the phone, holds it hidden in his hand, and moves to the side a little.

Peter lowers the bow to the strings, then stops, turns around, and tries to see past Axel.

"My phone," he says. "Is it behind you?"

Axel lets the phone slide out of his hand back onto the table before turning around and picking it up.

"Can you see if I have a text message?" Peter asks.

Axel looks at the phone and notes that it has full reception, even though they're in the middle of the sea. He realizes that the boat must have a satellite connection.

"No messages," he says, putting the phone back on the table.

"Thanks."

Axel stays by the table as Peter continues playing 24 Caprices, slowly and with increasing awkwardness.

Peter isn't talented, and even though he clearly practices a lot, there's no way he's going to be able to master this piece. Even so, the timbre of the violin is so wonderful that Axel would have enjoyed it even if a small child had been plucking at the strings. He leans back against the table and listens, trying to reach the phone again.

Though Peter keeps struggling to find the right settings for his fingers, he loses the tempo, stopping and starting again, while Axel continues to try to reach the phone. He moves sideways but doesn't have time to grab it. Peter plays a wrong note, stops, and turns to Axel again.

"It's hard," he says, making another attempt.

He quickly makes another mistake.

"It's impossible," he says, lowering the violin.

"If you keep your ring finger on the A string, it'll be easier to make—"

"Can you show me?"

Axel glances at the phone lying on the table. There's a glint of light from outside, and Axel turns to look through the picture windows. The sea is oddly still and empty. There's a rumble from the engine room, a persistent noise that he hasn't noticed until now.

Peter hands Axel the violin, and Axel puts it to his shoulder, tenses the bow slightly, then starts to play the piece from the beginning. The flowing, melancholic introduction spreads through the room. Axel plays it at a fast tempo. The tone of the instrument isn't powerful, but it's wonderfully soft and clean. Paganini's music coils around itself, increasingly faster and higher.

"God," Peter whispers.

The pace is dizzying, prestissimo. It's playful and beautiful and suffused with abrupt note changes and sharp jumps between octaves.

Axel has all the music in his head. He just has to let it out. Not every note is perfect, but his fingers can still find their way over the neck of the violin, darting across the wood and strings.

Raphael shouts something from the bridge, and something hits the ceiling, making the chandelier tinkle. Axel keeps playing; the twittering progressions sparkle like sunlight on water.

Suddenly there are footsteps on the stairs, and Axel sees Raphael walk in, sweating, with a bloody military knife in his hand. Axel stops playing abruptly. The gray-haired bodyguard is walking beside Raphael with an assault rifle raised.

110

JOONA IS STANDING with a pair of binoculars next to Pasi and the bearded first mate. They're watching the yacht sit motionless on the sea. The wind has dropped during the day, and the Italian flag hangs limply. There's no visible sign of activity on the boat; it's as if the passengers and crew have been lured into an enchanted sleep. The Baltic Sea is calm, the water reflecting the clear blue sky.

Joona's phone rings in his pocket. He hands the binoculars to Niko and answers.

"We've got a witness!" Saga yells. "The girl saw everything. Axel was kidnapped. The prosecutor has already acted—you can go on board to look for him!"

"Good work," Joona says tersely.

Pasi looks at him.

"We got the go-ahead from the prosecutor to arrest Raphael Guidi," Joona says. "He's wanted in connection with an abduction."

"I'll contact the FNS *Hanko*," Pasi says, hurrying over to the radio.

"They'll be here in twenty minutes," Niko tells Joona animatedly.

"This is a request for assistance," Pasi says into the microphone. "We have authorization from the Swedish prosecutor to go on board Raphael Guidi's boat immediately and arrest him. . . . Yes, that's correct. Yes. Get moving! Get fucking moving!"

Joona looks through the binoculars again, from the painted white stairs from the platform in the stern, across the lower decks, and up to the aft deck and its folded umbrellas. Though he looks for movement through the dark dining room windows, he sees nothing but black. He looks along the railing, then up to the next deck.

The air coming from the funnels above the bridge is vibrating. Joona points the binoculars at the dark windows. He thinks he can see movement through the glass. There's something white sliding across the inside of the pane. At first it reminds him of a huge wing, with its furled feathers pressed against the glass.

Then it looks like a piece of fabric or white plastic being folded up.

Squinting to see better, Joona now finds himself looking at a face staring back at him, through a pair of binoculars.

The steel door to the bridge of the yacht opens, and a fair-haired man in dark clothes comes out, climbs quickly down the stairs, and hurries across the foredeck.

It's the first time Joona has seen anyone on board.

The man walks over to the helicopter, loosens the straps over the runners, and opens the cockpit door.

"They're listening to our radio," Joona says.

"We can change the channel," Pasi calls out.

"Doesn't matter now," Joona says. "They're not staying on the boat. It looks like they're going to use the helicopter."

He passes the binoculars to Niko.

"We'll have reinforcements in fifteen minutes," Pasi says.

"That'll be too late," Joona declares quickly.

"There's someone in the helicopter," Niko says.

"Guidi knows we're authorized to board," Joona says. "He got the information the same time we did."

"Can the two of us go on board?" Niko asks.

"Looks like that's the only option," Joona says, glancing at him.

Niko inserts a magazine into his assault rifle.

Pasi pulls his pistol from his holster and passes it to Joona.

"Thanks," Joona says, checking the ammunition and then familiarizing himself with the gun. It's an M9A1, semiautomatic.

Without saying anything, Pasi steers the patrol vessel toward the platform at the aft of the yacht, which is just above the waterline. As they get closer, the yacht feels huge, like a high-rise building. The *Kirku*'s engine slips into reverse, and the boat brakes with a surge of foam. Niko slings the fenders over the railing, and the hull nudges the platform with a creak.

The minute Joona has climbed on board, the boats start to glide apart. Niko jumps, and Joona catches his hand. His assault rifle clatters against the railing. Their eyes meet briefly; then they head toward the stairs.

111

Raphael is standing on the bridge with his bodyguard. The captain stares at them anxiously and rubs his stomach with his hand.

"What's happening?" Raphael asks quickly.

"I gave the order to warm up the helicopter," the captain says. "I thought—"

"Where's the boat?"

"There," he says, pointing toward the stern.

The unarmed patrol vessel is clearly visible beyond the yacht's decks. Swell is lapping against the speckled gray hull.

"What did they say? What exactly did they say?" Raphael asks.

"They were in a hurry. They asked for backup, said they had an arrest warrant."

"None of it makes sense," Raphael says, looking around.

Through the helicopter window, they can see the pilot already sitting in the cockpit. The rotors have just started to move. The sound of Paganini's 24 Caprices comes from the dining room below.

"There's their backup," the captain says, pointing at the radar.

"I see it. How long do we have?" Raphael asks.

"They're maintaining a speed of just over thirty-three knots, so they'll be here in ten minutes."

"No problem," the bodyguard says, glancing at the helicopter. "We can get you and Peter away in time, at least three minutes before . . ."

The other, fair-haired bodyguard rushes in. He looks worried.

"There's someone here. There's someone on the boat," he cries.

"How many?" the gray-haired bodyguard asks.

"I only saw one, but I don't know. . . . He was carrying an assault rifle, but no special equipment."

"Stop him," the gray-haired man tells his colleague tersely.

"Give me a knife," Raphael snaps.

The bodyguard pulls out a knife with a narrow gray blade. Raphael takes it and walks closer to the captain, a tense look on his face.

"So they were going to wait for backup?" he yells. "You said they were going to wait for backup!"

"As I understood it, they—"

"What the hell are they doing here? They've got nothing on me," Raphael says. "Nothing!"

The captain shakes his head and takes a step back. Raphael moves closer.

"What the hell are they doing here if they don't have anything on me?" he screams. "There's nothing . . ."

"I don't know, I don't know," the captain replies with tears in his eyes. "I just repeated what I heard. . . ."

"What did you say?"

"Say? I don't understand. . . ."

"I don't have time for this," Raphael yells. "Just tell me what the fuck you said to them!"

"I didn't say anything to them."

"Weird. Fucking weird, isn't it? Isn't it?"

"I've been monitoring their channels, just like I'm supposed to. I haven't—"

"Is it really so hard to confess?" Raphael roars, then darts forward and drives the knife straight into the captain's stomach.

It glides through his shirt and into his guts with very little resistance. Blood sprays out like steam above a bath, splattering Raphael's hand and sleeve. The captain tries to take a step back to get away from the knife, an incredulous expression on his face, but Raphael follows him and stands there, staring at him.

Violin music is still coming from the dining room, its light notes dancing and bubbling.

"It could be Axel," the gray-haired bodyguard says. "He could be bugged. He might be in contact with the police via . . ."

Raphael pulls the knife out of the captain's stomach and rushes down the steep flight of stairs.

The captain stands there, clutching his stomach, as the blood drips onto his black shoes. He tries to take a step, but slips, and lies there staring up at the ceiling.

The bodyguard follows Raphael with his assault rifle raised, staring out through the picture windows of the dining room.

Axel stops playing when Raphael comes in and points the bloody knife at him.

"Traitor!" he roars. "How could you be so fucking . . ."

The gray-haired bodyguard fires his assault rifle. The bullets pass straight through the windows, and the shells clatter onto the stairs.

112

JOONA AND NIKO head carefully up the stairs, up to the expanse of the aft deck. The silent sea spreads out in all directions like a vast pane of glass. Now Joona hears violin music. He tries to see through the glass doors. Though he can make out dark shapes through the reflective surface, he can only see a small portion of the dining room. There's no one in sight. The music continues feverishly, muffled, as distant as a dream.

Joona and Niko wait a few seconds, then run quickly across an open area next to the drained swimming pool and in under the projecting roof to the next flight of metal stairs.

Hearing footsteps on the deck above, they press up against the wall beside the ladder.

The violin music is clearer now. It's rapid, playful. The violinist is obviously very talented. Joona glances cautiously into a huge dining room with office equipment on various tables, but he still can't see anyone. Whoever is playing the music must be hidden by the staircase.

Joona gestures for Niko to follow him and cover his back and points to the bridge above them.

Suddenly the violin stops playing, in the middle of a beautiful passage.

Very suddenly.

Joona throws himself behind the ladder just as he hears the muffled sound of automatic fire. Sharp, hard bangs. The bullets hit the ladder where he was standing a moment before.

Joona pulls back farther behind the stairs, feeling adrenaline course through his body. Niko has taken cover behind the lifeboat winch and is returning fire. Joona, crouching and moving around, sees the row of bullet holes across the dark window.

113

THE GRAY-HAIRED BODYGUARD goes down the stairs with his gun aimed at the picture windows. The barrel of the assault rifle is smoking, and the empty shells clatter down the stairs.

Peter has curled up and put his hands over his ears.

The bodyguard leaves the dining room through a side door.

Axel moves between the tables, with the violin and bow in his hand. Raphael points at him with the knife.

"How could you be so fucking stupid?" he screams, moving after Axel. "I'm going to cut your face, I'm going to . . ."

"Dad, what's happening?" Peter cries.

"Get my pistol and go to the helicopter—we're leaving the boat!"

The boy nods. His face is pale, and his chin is trembling. Raphael starts to walk past the tables toward Axel again. Axel moves backward, toppling chairs in front of him to block Raphael's path.

"Load it with Parabellum, hollow-tipped," Raphael says.

"One magazine?" the boy asks, sounding more focused.

"Yes, that'll be enough—but get moving!" Raphael replies, kicking a chair out of the way.

Axel tries to open the door on the other side of the room. He twists the lock, but the door won't budge.

"We're not finished, you and me," Raphael roars.

Axel yanks at the handle with his free hand, then notices the bolt at the top of the door. Raphael is only a few meters away now. As he gets closer with the knife, Axel acts instinctively. He turns around and throws the beautiful violin at Raphael. It spins through the air, red and shimmering. Raphael darts to the side and stumbles over a fallen chair in order to save the instrument. He almost catches it. It drops, but he manages to break its fall. The violin slides onto the floor with a dull clang.

Axel gets the door open and rushes into a cluttered passageway. There are so many things in it that it's hard to move. He climbs over a pile of lounge chairs and slips on a heap of goggles and wetsuits.

"You will sign!" Raphael says, coming after him with the violin in one hand and the knife in the other.

Axel falls over a rolled tennis net, catches his foot in the broken netting, and crawls away from Raphael, who's marching toward him. He kicks wildly to free himself.

The sound of automatic gunfire comes from outside—a series of short, hard shots.

Breathing heavily, Raphael lunges with the knife, but Axel pulls free. He scrambles to his feet, backs away, and pulls a large foosball table over in front of Raphael. He rushes to the next door. His hands fumble with the lock and handle. There's something blocking the door, but he manages to open it a little.

"There's no point," Raphael calls.

Axel tries to squeeze through the gap, but it's too tight; a large cupboard full of stacked clay pots stands in the way. He throws himself at the door again, and the cupboard shifts a few centimeters. Axel can feel Raphael behind him, getting closer. A chill runs down his spine as he shoves the door again. He forces his body through the gap and cuts himself on the lock, but he doesn't care, he just has to get away.

Raphael swipes at him with the knife, and the point of the blade cuts into Axel's shoulder. He feels a sudden flare of pain.

He tumbles into a room full of light, with a glass roof. It looks like an abandoned greenhouse. He feels his shoulder with his hand and looks at the blood on his fingers as he knocks into a withered lemon tree. He hurries on, crouching down between the potted plants with their shriveled leaves.

Raphael is kicking the door hard, grunting loudly with each kick. The pots rattle, and the cupboard slowly moves.

Knowing he has to hide, Axel quickly crawls under one of the benches and shuffles sideways, beneath a dirty plastic sheet. He moves on, in among buckets and tubs. He's hoping that Raphael is going to give up and leave the boat with his son.

There's a thunderous noise from the door, and several pots fall to the deck and shatter.

Raphael comes into the room, panting, and leans against a trellis covered with dead vines.

"Come out and kiss my hand!" Raphael calls.

Axel does his best to breathe silently. He tries to move farther back, but he can't. His path is blocked by a large metal cabinet.

"I promise to keep my promises," Raphael says with a smile, looking around at the stumps of dead plants. "Your brother's liver is waiting for you, and all you have to do to get it is kiss my hand."

Feeling sick, Axel sits there shaking with fear, his back against the metal cabinet. His heart is beating fast. He does his best to be completely silent. There's a roaring sound inside his head. He looks around him, trying to find a way out, and realizes that there's a sliding door leading to the yacht's foredeck just five meters away.

He can hear the sound of the helicopter as its engines warm up.

Axel thinks he could crawl under the table laden with soil-filled clay pots, and then run the last stretch. He starts to move sideways, very cautiously. The door seems to be held only by a clasp.

He raises his head to get a better view and is just thinking he'll be out on the foredeck in a few seconds when he suddenly feels as if his heart has stopped. The cold blade of a knife is being held to his throat. The touch of the metal stings slightly. Raphael has crept up behind his back. Only now does he hear Raphael's breathing and smell his sweat. The knife blade is resting against his throat, and it feels as if it's burning him.

114

THE GRAY-HAIRED BODYGUARD leaves the dining room silently, slipping out between the doors and running quickly along the deck with his assault rifle held to his shoulder. The light glints off his glasses. Joona sees that the bodyguard is heading toward Niko from behind and will reach him in just a few seconds.

Niko is completely unprotected.

The bodyguard raises the gun and moves his finger to the trigger.

Joona stands up quickly, takes a step forward to clear his line of sight, and shoots the bodyguard twice, directly in the chest. The gray-haired man staggers backward, reaches out his hand, and grabs the railing to keep himself from falling. He looks around, sees Joona rushing toward him, and raises the assault rifle.

Only now does Joona see that he's wearing a bulletproof vest under his black jacket.

Already upon him, Joona pushes the barrel of the rifle away with one hand and slams his pistol into the body-guard's face with the other. It hits his nose and glasses hard. His legs buckle, the back of his head hits the railing with a dull clang, and sweat and snot spray from his face as his body collapses.

Joona and Niko make their way toward the bow of the yacht on either side of the dining room. The helicopter's rotors are spinning faster and faster.

"Come on! Get in!" someone shouts.

Joona runs as close to the wall as he can, then slows down and cautiously walks the last stretch, looking out across the open foredeck. Guidi's son is already sitting in the helicopter.

Joona hears voices from the bridge above him and has taken a step forward when he realizes that Guidi's other bodyguard has spotted him. The fair-haired man is standing twenty-five meters away, his pistol aimed straight at Joona. There's no time to react before the shot goes off. Joona hears a blunt bang. It feels like the crack of a whip in his face, and then everything goes white. He crashes over some lounge chairs and lands hard on the metal deck, hitting the back of his head against the railing. The hand holding the pistol slams into the bars holding the railing. His wrist almost breaks, and the gun falls from his grasp. The pistol echoes as it falls through the bars.

Joona blinks, and his sight starts to come back. He crawls in behind the wall. His hands are shaking, and he can't really understand what has happened. Warm blood is running down his face as he tries to get to his feet—he needs to get Niko to help him, needs to figure out where the bodyguard went.

He quickly feels his cheek. A flash of pain when his fingers move farther up tells him that the bullet merely grazed his temple. It's a superficial wound.

He can hear a strange ringing sound in his left ear.

His heart is beating fast.

When he uses the metal wall to help himself up, the pain in his head gets even worse. The ringing tone is getting louder.

Joona presses one thumb against his forehead, between

his eyebrows, and closes his eyes, forcing the flaring pain from the migraine away.

He glances over at the helicopter, trying to see Niko.

The Finnish navy's vessel is approaching from behind like a black shadow across the calm sea.

Joona twists off a long strip of metal from the broken lounge chair so that he has some sort of weapon for when the bodyguard comes for him. He presses himself against the wall.

Then, suddenly, he sees Guidi and Axel on the foredeck. They're standing close together, backing slowly toward the helicopter. Guidi is holding a knife to Axel's throat with one hand. In his other hand he is clutching a violin. Their clothes and hair are blowing in the downdraft from the helicopter.

The bodyguard who shot Joona is slipping smoothly sideways to get a clear view of him behind the wall. He obviously isn't sure whether he hit the intruder in the head. It all happened too quickly.

Knowing the bodyguard is looking for him, Joona tries to pull back, but his headache is slowing his movements.

He has to stop.

Not now, he thinks, as he feels the sweat running down his back.

The bodyguard turns the corner and raises his weapon; gradually, Joona's shoulder comes into view, followed by his head and neck.

But in that instant the bearded figure of Niko Kapanen rushes out from the other side, with his assault rifle raised. The bodyguard is fast; he spins around and fires his pistol, a series of four shots. Niko doesn't even notice that the first bullet hit his shoulder, but he stops when the second hits him in the stomach, penetrating his small intestine. Though the third shot misses, the fourth hits him in the chest. Niko's legs buckle, and he falls sideways, behind the bulkhead at

the base of the helipad. He's seriously wounded and probably unaware that he's squeezing the assault rifle's trigger as
he falls. The bullets fly off aimlessly. He empties the entire
magazine in two seconds, straight out over the water, until
the rifle just clicks.

Niko gasps, and his eyes roll back into his head as he slides
onto his back, leaving a bloody stain across the bulkhead. He
drops the rifle. His chest hurts terribly. He closes his eyes for
a few seconds, then looks up groggily and sees the massive
bolts beneath the helipad. He notes that rust has penetrated
the white paint.

He coughs weakly and is on the brink of losing consciousness when he sees Joona, hidden against the dining room
wall with a length of metal in his hand. Their eyes meet.
Niko summons the last of his strength and kicks the assault
rifle over toward Joona.

AXEL IS TERRIFIED. His heart is racing, the sound of the
shots is ringing in his ears, and his body is trembling. Raphael
is dragging him along like a shield. They both stumble, and
the blade of the knife cuts into the skin on his neck. He feels
warm blood start to trickle down his chest. He sees the last
bodyguard approaching Joona's hiding place, but he can't do
anything about it.

JOONA REACHES FORWARD QUICKLY and grabs the hot
assault rifle. The bodyguard in front of the helicopter fires
two shots at him. They ricochet off the walls, floor, and railing. Joona removes the empty magazine, seeing Niko feel
in his pockets for more ammunition. Niko gasps. He's very

weak and has to pause for a moment with his hand pressed against his bloody stomach. The bodyguard shouts for Guidi to get in—the helicopter is ready to take off. Niko reaches into one of his pants pockets and pulls his hand out again. A candy wrapper flies off in the wind, but in his palm is one bullet. Niko coughs weakly, looks at the single bullet, and then rolls it across the deck toward Joona.

The jacketed bullet spins across the metal floor, its brass case and copper tip glinting in the light.

Joona grabs it and quickly pushes it into the magazine.

Niko's eyes are closed now, and a bubble of blood has appeared between his lips. He's still breathing, but very shallowly.

The bodyguard's heavy steps resound across the deck.

Joona slides the magazine into the assault rifle, feeds the only bullet into the chamber, raises the gun, waits a moment, then leaves his hiding place.

Guidi is still backing away, holding Axel in front of him. His son is shouting from the helicopter, and the pilot is beckoning at Guidi to get in.

"You should have kissed my hand when you had the chance," Raphael whispers into Axel's ear.

The strings of the violin ring out as Axel's arm brushes against them.

The bodyguard walks quickly to Niko, leans over the bulkhead, and points the pistol at his face.

"*Jonottakaa*," Joona says in Finnish.

He sees the bodyguard raise the gun to point it at him instead of at Niko, and darts sideways, trying to find the right line—he has to make his only shot count.

It all happens in a matter of seconds.

Guidi is standing immediately behind the bodyguard,

holding the knife to Axel's throat. Drops of blood fly through the air. Joona crouches down slightly, lowers the sights a few millimeters, then fires the assault rifle.

Jonottakaa, he thinks. Get in line.

There's a bang, and he feels the hard recoil against his shoulder. Without making a sound, the bullet goes in through the bodyguard's throat and out through the back of his neck, and continues straight through Raphael Guidi's shoulder and on across the sea.

Guidi's arm flails from the impact, and the knife clatters across the deck.

Axel sinks to the deck.

The bodyguard stares at Joona in surprise as blood streams down his chest. He tries to raise the pistol but doesn't have the strength. He makes a weird gurgling sound and coughs, and a surge of blood pours down his chin.

He sits down, fumbles for his throat, and blinks twice; then his eyes stay wide open.

Raphael's lips are pale. He's standing in the helicopter's powerful downdraft, pressing the hand holding the violin to his bleeding shoulder, staring at Joona.

"Dad!" his son cries from the helicopter, tossing a pistol toward him.

It lands on the deck with a clatter, bounces, and stops in front of Raphael's feet.

Axel is sitting against the railing, dazed, trying to stop the flow of blood from his neck with his hand.

"Raphael! Raphael Guidi!" Joona shouts loudly. "I'm here to arrest you."

Raphael is standing five meters away from his helicopter, with the pistol between his feet. His tracksuit is flapping around his body. With immense effort, he bends down and picks up the pistol.

"You're suspected of arms smuggling, kidnapping, and murder," Joona says.

Raphael's face is sweaty, and the pistol is shaking in his hand.

"Put the gun down," Joona calls.

Raphael holds the heavy pistol in his hand, but his heart starts to beat faster when he looks Joona in the eye.

Axel is staring at Joona and tries to tell him to run.

Joona stands still.

Everything happens at the same time.

Raphael raises the pistol toward Joona and squeezes the trigger, but the pistol just clicks. He tries again and takes a deep breath when he realizes that his son didn't fill the magazine. Raphael feels a terrible loneliness embrace him. Then the sound of the shots rings out across the sea. He realizes that it's too late to drop the gun and surrender just as his body is rocked by three gentle thuds, one after the other. To Raphael, it feels as if someone is punching him hard in the chest, followed by sharp pain as he staggers backward and loses all feeling in his legs.

The helicopter doesn't wait any longer. It takes off without Raphael, rising into the air with a roar.

The FNS *Hanko* is alongside the yacht. The three snipers fire again. All three bullets hit Raphael's torso, but the sounds of the shots merge into one. Raphael takes a few steps back and falls. He tries to sit up but can no longer move.

His back feels hot, but his feet are already ice-cold. He stares up at the helicopter, which is rising quickly into the hazy sky.

In the helicopter, Peter gazes down at the shrinking yacht. His father is lying in the center of the helipad's circles, at the middle of a target.

Raphael is still clutching Paganini's violin in his hand.

A pool of dark blood is spreading out rapidly around him, but the blank look in his eyes proves he's already dead.

Joona is the only person still standing on the foredeck of the boat.

He doesn't move as the helicopter disappears.

Three vessels lie still on the expanse of calm water, drifting side by side as if they've been abandoned.

Soon the Finnish rescue helicopters will arrive, but right now it's quiet, like the moment after the last note of a concert, while the audience is still enchanted by the music and the silence that follows it.

115

JOONA, AXEL, NIKO, and the gray-haired bodyguard were transported by emergency helicopter to the HUS surgical hospital in Helsinki. At the hospital, Axel couldn't help asking Joona why he didn't move when Guidi picked up the pistol from the deck.

"Didn't you hear me shouting?" Axel asked.

Joona just looked him in the eye and explained that he had already seen the snipers on the boat and expected them to fire their weapons before Guidi had time to fire his.

"But they didn't," Axel pointed out.

"You can't be right all the time," Joona replied with a smile.

Niko was awake when Joona and Axel went in to say goodbye.

"Say hello to Sweden," he told them. "But . . . tough little Finland came in a very respectable second!"

Though Niko's injuries were very serious, they were no longer life-threatening. He would have to undergo a number of operations over the next few days and would be allowed home in a wheelchair within a couple of weeks.

Guidi's bodyguard was arrested and taken to Vantaa Prison to wait until his extradition was processed, and Joona and Axel went home to Stockholm.

———

THE LARGE CONTAINER VESSEL, MS *Icelus*, never left Gothenburg Harbor. Its cargo of ammunition was unloaded and taken to the Swedish Customs Office warehouses.

Jens Svanehjälm was put in charge of the protracted legal proceedings, but, with the exception of Guidi's nameless bodyguard, all the guilty parties were already dead or couldn't be reached.

It was impossible to determine if anyone else at Silencia Defense Ltd. had been involved in criminal activity. The only person who had committed an offense at the Inspectorate for Strategic Products was its former director general, Carl Palmcrona.

A case was prepared against Jörgen Grünlicht, for suspected bribery and as an accessory to arms offenses, but none of the charges were deemed strong enough to take him to trial. The prosecution determined that the Export Control Council and any Swedish politicians involved in the deal had all been deceived and had been acting in good faith.

The material gathered during the investigations relating to two Kenyan politicians was handed over to Roland Lidonde, minister for governance and ethics, but it seemed that even the Kenyan politicians had been duped.

The staff of the freight company Intersafe Shipping was unaware that the cargo was to be taken from Mombasa Harbor to South Sudan, and no one at the Kenyan transport company Trans Continent knew that the goods they had been commissioned to carry to Sudan consisted of ammunition.

AXEL RIESSEN

AXEL FEELS THE STITCHES pull at his neck as he gets out of the taxi. The street looks pale, almost white, in the blazing sunlight. The moment he puts his hand on the gate, the front door swings open. Robert has been watching for him from the window.

"What on earth did you get mixed up in?" Robert says, shaking his head. "I've spoken to Joona Linna, and he told me some of it. It sounds insane. . . ."

"You should know by now that your big brother's pretty tough." Axel smiles.

They hug each other hard, then start to walk toward the house.

"We set the table in the garden," Robert says.

"How's your heart? Hasn't stopped yet, then?" Axel asks, following his brother through the front door.

"I was actually booked for an operation next week," Robert replies.

"I didn't know that," Axel says, feeling the hair on the back of his neck stand up.

"To have a pacemaker fitted. I don't think I mentioned it. . . ."

"An operation?"

"It got canceled."

As Axel looks at his brother, he feels as if his soul is going through contortions. He realizes that Guidi had booked Robert's operation, that it was predestined to go horribly wrong, and that Robert was supposed to die on the operating table and donate his liver to Axel.

He has to stop in the entryway and calm down before he goes any farther. His face feels hot, and a sob is welling up in his throat.

"Are you coming?" Robert asks breezily.

Axel stays where he is for a moment before following his brother through the house and into the back garden. The table under the large tree is laden with food.

He's on his way toward Anette when Robert takes his arm and stops him.

"We had fun when we were kids," Robert says, a serious look on his face. "Why did we stop talking? How did that happen?"

Axel looks at his brother in surprise, at the wrinkles at the corners of his eyes, the ring of hair around his bald scalp.

"Things happen in—"

"Wait a second. . . . I didn't want to say over the phone," Robert interrupts.

"What is it?"

"Beverly said that you think it was your fault that Greta took her own life, but I—"

"I don't want to talk about it," Axel says instantly.

"You have to," Robert says. "I was there on the day of the competition. I heard everything. I heard Greta and her father talking. She couldn't stop crying. She'd made a mistake, and her dad was horribly upset, and . . ."

Axel pulls free from his brother.

"I already know everything that—"

"Just let me say what I have to say," Robert interrupts.

"Go on."

"Axel . . . if only you'd said something, if only I'd known you thought it was your fault that Greta died. I heard her dad. It was his fault, and his fault alone. They had a terrible fight. I heard him say the most appalling things: that she'd made a fool of him in public, that she was no longer his daughter. He said he didn't want her in the house, that she'd have to leave school and move in with her junkie mother in Mora."

"He said that?"

"I'll never forget the way Greta's voice sounded," Robert goes on steadily. "She was so scared. She tried to tell her dad that everyone makes mistakes, that she'd tried her hardest, that it wasn't such a disaster, there'd be more competitions. . . ."

"But I've always . . ."

Axel looks around. He doesn't know what to do with himself. All the energy goes out of him, and he just sits down heavily on the marble floor and covers his face with both hands.

"She was crying, and she told her dad she'd kill herself if she wasn't allowed to stay and continue with her music."

"I don't know what to say," Axel whispers.

"Thank Beverly," Robert replies.

BEVERLY ANDERSSON

It starts to rain heavily while Beverly is standing on the platform of the Central Station in Stockholm. Her journey south takes her through a summer landscape shrouded in gray mist. The sun doesn't appear again until the train reaches Hässleholm. She changes trains in Lund, and then takes the bus from Landskrona to Svalöv.

It's been a long time since she was last home.

Dr. Saxéus has assured her that it's going to be okay. "I've talked to your dad," the doctor said. "He's serious about wanting you to come home."

Beverly walks across the dusty square and sees an image of herself lying in the middle of the square, getting sick, two years ago. Some boys had persuaded her to drink hooch. They took photographs of her, and then they left her in the square. That was the incident that made her dad decide he didn't want her in the house anymore.

Her stomach clenches when she sees the road open up outside the town. The farm is three kilometers away. It was along this stretch of road that drivers used to pick her up. Now she can't remember why she thought going with them was a good idea. She thought she could see something in their eyes. A glow, she used to think.

Beverly switches her heavy bag to her other hand.

In the distance, she sees a car approaching.

She recognizes it, doesn't she?

Beverly smiles and waves.

Her dad's coming. Dad's coming.

PENELOPE FERNANDEZ

ROSLAGS-KULLA CHURCH is a small, red wooden church with a big, beautiful bell tower. The church is in a tranquil location out in the countryside near Wira Bruk, away from the region's busiest roads. The sky is bright blue, and the air is clear, and the scent of wildflowers is being carried on the wind across the churchyard.

Yesterday Björn was buried in Stockholm's Northern Cemetery, and now four men in black suits are carrying Viola Maria Liselott Fernandez to her final resting place. Penelope and her mother, Claudia, are walking with the priest behind the pallbearers: two uncles and two cousins from El Salvador.

They stop at the open grave. One of the cousin's children, a nine-year-old girl, looks at her father. He nods, and she takes out her recorder and starts to play Psalm 97 as the coffin is lowered into the ground.

Penelope holds her mother's hand, and the priest reads from the book of Revelation: "'And God shall wipe away all tears from their eyes, and there shall be no more death.'"

Claudia adjusts Penelope's collar, then pats her cheek as if she were a small child.

As they are walking back toward the cars, Penelope's phone buzzes. It's Joona. Penelope gently drifts away from her mother and goes into the shade of one of the large trees before she answers.

"Hello, Penelope," Joona says in his unmistakable voice, singsong but somber.

"Hello, Joona," Penelope says.

"I thought you'd like to know that Raphael Guidi is dead."

"And the ammunition for Darfur?"

"We stopped it."

"Good."

Penelope looks over at her family and friends, and her mother, who's still standing where she left her, not taking her eyes off Penelope.

"Thank you," she says.

She returns to her mother, who's waiting with a sad look on her face. Penelope takes her hand again, and together they head for the people waiting by the cars.

Penelope.

She stops and turns around. She thought she heard her sister's voice, very close by. A shiver runs down her spine as a shadow crosses the fresh green grass. The little girl who played the recorder is standing among the gravestones, looking at her. She's lost her headband, and her hair is blowing in the summer breeze.

SAGA BAUER AND ANJA LARSSON

THE SUMMER DAYS never seem to end. The night shines like mother-of-pearl until dawn.

The Swedish Police Force is holding a staff party in the Baroque garden in front of Drottningholm Palace.

Joona is sitting with his colleagues at a long table under a tree.

On a stage beside the dance floor, a group of musicians is playing "Hårgalåten," a traditional Swedish folk song.

Petter Näslund is dancing with Fatima Zanjani from Iraq. He says something that makes her smile.

The song tells the story of how the devil played the violin so well that the young folk didn't want to stop dancing. They danced all night, and when they made the mistake of not respecting the church bells, they were physically unable to stop. They were crying from fatigue. Their shoes got worn down; then their feet got worn down. In the end, only their heads were bouncing around to the violin music.

Anja is sitting on a folding chair, wearing a flowery blue dress. She is glaring at the couples dancing; her round face is sullen, disappointed. But her cheeks flush when she sees Joona leave his seat at the table.

"Happy Midsummer, Anja," he says.

Saga is skipping across the grass between the trees. She's

chasing soap bubbles with Magdalena's twins. Her billowing blond hair with its colorful braids is shimmering in the sunlight. Two middle-aged women have stopped to watch her.

"Ladies and gentlemen," the singer says after the applause. "We've had a special request. . . ."

Carlos smiles and glances at someone backstage.

"My roots are in Oulu, in Finland," the singer says with a smile. "So I'm delighted to be asked to sing you a classic Finnish tango called 'Satumaa.'"

Magdalena, with a garland of flowers in her hair, walks over to Joona and tries to catch his eye. Anja is staring down at her new shoes.

The band starts to play the sad, melodic tango. Joona turns to Anja, bows slightly, and asks quietly, "May I have the pleasure?"

Anja's forehead, cheeks, and neck turn bright red. She looks up at his face and nods seriously. "Yes," she says. "Yes, you may."

She takes his arm, casting a proud glance at Magdalena, and walks onto the dance floor with her head held high.

At first Anja dances with great concentration, frowning slightly. But her round face soon relaxes into a smile. Her hair is arranged in a complicated knot at the back of her head. She lets Joona guide her around the dance floor.

As the sentimental song approaches its end, Joona suddenly feels Anja nip his shoulder with her teeth, but it doesn't really hurt.

When she bites again, a little harder, he feels obliged to ask, "What are you doing?"

Her eyes are sparkling.

"I don't know," she replies honestly. "I just thought I'd see what would happen. You never know unless you try. . . ."

At that moment, the music comes to an end. He lets go

of her and thanks her for the dance. Before he has time to escort her back to her chair, Carlos glides over and takes Anja's hand.

Joona steps back and looks on as his colleagues dance, eat, and drink; then he heads for his car.

People dressed in white are sitting on picnic blankets or strolling through the trees.

Joona opens the door of his Volvo. On the back seat is a huge bouquet of flowers. He gets into the car and calls Disa, but her voice mail clicks in on the fourth ring.

DISA HELENIUS

DISA IS SITTING in front of her computer. She's wearing her reading glasses and has a blanket wrapped around her shoulders. Her cell phone is lying on the desk, next to a mug of cold coffee and a cinnamon bun.

On the screen is a picture of an overgrown, eroded pile of stones: the remains of the cholera cemetery at Skanstull in Stockholm.

She types some notes into the document, then stretches and picks up the mug, but changes her mind. She gets up to make some fresh coffee as her phone buzzes on the desk.

Without checking to see who it is, she switches it off and then stands staring out the window. Motes of dust dance in the sunlight. Disa's heart beats faster and harder as she sits back down in front of the computer. She's not sure she ever wants to see Joona again.

JOONA LINNA

STOCKHOLM IS IN VACATION MODE, and the traffic is thin as Joona walks slowly down Tegnér Street. He's given up on reaching Disa. Her phone is switched off, and he assumes she wants to be left alone. Joona walks around the Blue Tower and down the stretch of Drottning Street that's lined with secondhand bookshops and boutiques. An old woman is standing in front of the New Age bookshop, Vattumannen, pretending to look in the window. When Joona passes her, she gestures toward the glass, then starts to follow him at a distance.

It takes him a while to realize he's being followed.

He turns around when he reaches the black railings outside Adolf Fredrik's Church. Just ten meters behind him is a woman in her eighties. She looks at him seriously, then holds out some cards. "This is you, isn't it?" she says, showing him one of the cards. "And here's the crown, the bridal crown."

Joona walks up to her and takes the cards. They're from a pack of cards for Cuckoo, one of the oldest card games in Europe.

"What do you want?" he asks calmly.

"I don't want anything," the woman says. "But I have a message from Rosa Bergman."

"There must be some mistake, because I don't know anyone named—"

"She's wondering why you're pretending that your daughter's dead."

EPILOGUE

IT'S EARLY AUTUMN in Copenhagen, and the air is clear and cold by the time a discreet group arrives at the Glyptotek in four separate limousines. The men go upstairs and walk through the Winter Garden and along hallways lined with ancient sculptures before they arrive in the ornate banquet hall.

The audience is already in place, and the Tokyo String Quartet is sitting on the low stage with their legendary Stradivarius instruments, the same instruments that were once played by Niccolò Paganini himself.

The guests take their places at a table in the pillared aisle, slightly separate from the rest of the audience. The youngest of them is a fair, long-limbed man by the name of Peter Guidi. He is little more than a boy, but the expressions on the other men's faces say otherwise. They will shortly be kissing his hand.

The musicians nod to one another and start to play Schubert's *Death and the Maiden*. The piece opens with great pathos, a sense of emotion and suppressed energy. One violin responds with excruciating beauty. The music pauses for breath one last time, and then pours forth. Though the tune is joyful, the instruments seem to convey a sense of grief at the loss of more souls.

EVERY DAY, thirty-nine million bullets are made for various projectile weapons. A conservative estimate of global military spending each year is $1.226 billion. Even though vast quantities of arms are being produced at all times, demand is still insatiable. The nine largest exporters of conventional weapons in the world are the United States, Russia, Germany, France, Great Britain, the Netherlands, Italy, Sweden, and China.